Praise for Ciara Geraghty:

'My favourite author does it again in this superbly written perceptive, poignant novel that makes you laugh and cry! Oh, I envy you the read of this. Treat yourself to a brilliant book!' Patricia Scanlan on *Now That I've Found You*

'Ciara Geraghty is a superb writer . . . Her books are meticulously researched, beautifully written, and infused with warmth, humour and human understanding.' *Irish Examiner*

'Heart-breaking and funny, poignant and life affirming.' www. novelicious.com on *Lifesaving for Beginners*

'A beautifully written, somewhat whimsical and very encouraging tale about grabbing hold of life's reins, breaking away from the monotony of a dull routine and following your dreams . . . emotional, joyous . . . I adored it.' *Daily Mail* on *Finding Mr Flood*

'Sad, funny and wise.' *Marie Claire* on *Finding Mr Flood*

'Certain to appeal to fans of chick-lit supreme Marian Keyes.' *Herald Sun*, Australia on *Becoming Scarlett*

'Move over Marian, it's Ciara . . . impressive and highly entertaining [with] one of the most authentic female characters I've read in women's fiction for a long time . . . lots of biting humour and a darker side beneath the laughs.' *Irish Independent* on *Saving Grace*

'So funny and so much fun, it's impossible to believe it's Geraghty's first . . . Warm, moving and hilarious.' *Evening Herald* on *Saving Grace*

'I loved this . . . it's warm, funny and made me cry (a couple of times). It is also really well written . . . you'll want to read it in one sitting.' *Daily Mail* on *Saving Grace*

Ciara Geraghty lives in Dublin with her husband, three children and their dog.

Also by Ciara Geraghty

Saving Grace
Becoming Scarlett
Finding Mr Flood
Lifesaving for Beginners
Now That I've Found You

CIARA GERAGHTY

This is Now

HACHETTE
BOOKS
IRELAND

First published in Ireland in 2016 by
Hachette Books Ireland
An Hachette UK company

1

Copyright © Ciara Geraghty 2016

A CIP catalogue record for this title is available from the British Library

Trade paperback ISBN 978 1 444 72587 2
Ebook ISBN 978 1 473 61911 1

Typeset in Goudy Old Style by Hewer Text UK Ltd, Edinburgh
Printed and bound by CPI Group (UK) Ltd, Croydon, CR0 4YY

Hachette Books Ireland policy is to use papers that are natural, renewable and recyclable
products and made from wood grown in sustainable forests. The logging and manufacturing
processes are expected to conform to the environmental regulations of the country of origin.

For Neil MacLochlainn; even if I had many sons, you'd still be my favourite one.

One

There was no way of knowing what would happen.

Swords was its usual self that Monday. A steady procession of traffic along the curves of the main street, groups of office workers arguing about where to go for lunch, reggae music floating from the barber's, the hiss of the number 33 as its doors opened at the bus stop.

As they approached the bank, Tara Bolton's normally swift gait slowed and slowed until she wasn't walking at all. She was standing still.

Martha Wilder was a full two strides ahead before she noticed. She turned.

'Will you hurry the fuck up,' she said to Tara.

'Cursing at me is not going to help.'

'What about whacking you with my bag?'

'Can't you be serious?'

'I am being serious.'

'This is not a good idea.'

'You thought it was a good idea yesterday.'

'But now it's today.'

'And the day after is tomorrow. What's your point?'

'I just . . .' Tara shrugged as passers-by altered their trajectory to pass her by. Martha strode towards her, a long stream of bright red hair tumbling down her back, tamed only by a single clip at the side in the shape of a treble clef, which brought scant order to the wildness of her hair. She folded her arms across her chest.

1

'What?' she said, looking down. She had always towered over Tara but had never considered her friend small. Today she looked small. And pale, despite the immaculate make-up that gave the – false – impression of hours of painstaking application.

Tara worried at a fingernail with her teeth, the polish coming away in long curls. She shook her head. 'I . . . I can't do it.'

'You can.'

'Do you really think so?' Even Tara's voice was small now. It was difficult to see her as the wildly successful entrepreneur who bought companies the way some women bought shoes, then sold them for exorbitant prices after she'd given them what the financial media dubbed the *Tara Touch*.

Martha nodded. 'I do,' she said. 'Think of it as a business meeting and you'll be grand.'

Tara nodded without conviction but began to move forward. Martha did her best to match Tara's reluctant pace.

The bank had seen better days. The white plaster of its facade was crumbling and, inside, the carpet was worn thin, bald in parts, from the march of so many feet across it over the years. A short line of people shuffled towards a counter, behind which two tellers worked. One of them waved at Tara. 'I'll tell your sister that you're here,' she said, reaching for the phone on her desk. Martha nodded towards a bench. They sat down.

The door of the bank opened again and an elderly man in a wheelchair appeared, pushed by a woman who seemed smaller than she was. Martha studied her without appearing to study her, as was her habit. The woman negotiated the chair through the door with little fuss and took her place at the end of the queue, making no sound. The skin of her face was taut, the colour a faded sallow, as if she didn't spend much time out of doors. Her hands, resting on the handles of the chair, were dry and reddened and there were dark smudges beneath her careful, grey eyes.

The man's nurse, perhaps? From behind the shade of her sunglasses, Martha's eyes travelled towards the woman's charge. He had close-cropped white hair, an impeccable navy suit, a little baggy across the shoulders, and blue eyes that some might consider cold and others arresting. Martha noticed the slackness around the left side of the old man's mouth, the way his left hand lay limp in his lap while the right one gripped the arm of the chair before snapping open the locks on each side of the black briefcase that lay across his knees, attending to some paperwork inside.

'Stop it,' Tara hissed.

'Stop what?' said Martha.

'You know what.'

Martha moved her line of vision from the old man. It was an occupational hazard, she supposed, even though it had been two years since she'd worked as a reporter for RTÉ. 'You certainly went out with a bang,' Tara had conceded when the dust – eventually – settled.

Martha shifted on the bench, glanced at the clock on the wall: 12.30 p.m. All going well, Tara would have told her news to her sister and, afterwards, her mother and be back on a plane to London by dinnertime. That was the plan and, because it was Tara's plan, Martha never doubted it.

The queue shuffled forward. The wheelchair creaked as the woman manoeuvred it forward, while the man pulled at a heavy gold chain draped across his navy waistcoat, inspecting the face of the watch dangling at the end.

Someone coughed. A mobile phone chirped briefly. The tap-tap-tap of the tellers' fingers on their keyboards. The click-click-click as Tara's fingers worried at the clasp of her handbag.

The front door burst open and two men dressed in black, wearing balaclavas over their faces, rushed inside, locked the door, pulled the blinds.

Both were carrying guns.

At first, everything seemed to happen in slow motion, Martha felt. The door crashing open, the dark blur of the men racing inside, the reach of their hands inside their jackets, the guns now, the way they smashed the CCTV cameras with the handles, the forming of words around their mouths. No sound penetrated Martha's head. Not at first. And then, when it did, it was a cacophony of sound, a solid wall of shouting and screaming and roaring. Beside her, Tara was stiff with stillness, her hands covering her face like a child counting to ten at the start of hide-and-seek.

'Shut the fuck up, or I swear I'll put a bullet in someone's skull.' The gunman was solidly built. The kind of solid that hinted at steroids. His breathing was laboured and he twitched from one leg to the other. Martha could almost see the furious flow of adrenalin around his body.

'Calm down,' the skinny one said and his low voice had an edge that was sharp as a razor blade and Martha knew at once that he was in charge. 'Go and get the manager and the other two in the back,' he said and his accomplice nodded and headed towards the offices behind the counters.

The other man advanced on the line of customers, who backed up until they were corralled into a corner. The two tellers stiffened behind the counter, their hands inching above their heads in a gesture of surrender. Martha knew they would have received training for this kind of scenario. Saw in their faces the inevitable clash of theory against reality. Was there an emergency button near their desks? Had they pressed it? If they had, how long would the guards take to get there? And what then? What would happen to them all then?

The man pointed his gun towards the semi-circle of customers in the corner and the two tellers moved, fluid as dancers, from behind the counter to join them.

This is what a gun achieves, Martha thought. People do what you want them to do without any recourse to language.

Now the man turned and trained his gun on Martha and Tara. Martha felt her throat constrict, a pounding in her chest that must be her heart. She had never been so aware of it. It felt much too big for her body, too frantic.

'Get the fuck over there with the others,' he said. Martha stood up but Tara did not. Martha had to grip her friend's arm, drag her to her feet, pull her across the floor. The gunman nudged the small of Martha's back with the hard butt of his gun, and she cried out, walked faster. Tara allowed herself to be pulled along. She never made a sound.

They dropped their mobiles and tablets into the plastic Centra bag proffered by the gunman.

Then three people walked in single file from the back offices, their hands on the backs of their heads. Behind them, the accomplice had wrapped his arm around the neck of a woman, perhaps in her mid-forties, with dark, greying hair cut in an easy-to-manage bob. He pushed the barrel of his gun against her temple as he dragged her along. A name badge pinned on the lapel of her navy jacket read *Katherine Bolton* and, underneath, *Manager*.

Tara's navy eyes – the same shape and colour as Katherine's – widened with anxiety and Martha placed a warning hand on her arm.

The man released his hold on Katherine's neck, pushed her towards his boss. 'There she is,' he said. 'The main woman herself.'

The gunman's eyes slid down the length of Katherine's body, lingering on the curve of her breasts through the cotton of her blouse. 'Nice work,' he said and now his voice was silky. From behind the balaclava, Martha saw the shape of his mouth lifting into a smile. Beside her, Tara swayed and Martha tightened her grip on Tara's arm, steadied her, steadied herself. Her mind was like some volcanic eruption, bubbling and boiling: too beside itself to make sense of anything. To come up with a plan.

The boss snapped his head away from Katherine then, cleared his throat, looked towards the door. 'All clear?' he asked. It was only then that Martha noticed the third gunman. He stood at the door, slighter than the other two; the gun in his hand seemed bigger than the others', perhaps because his hand was smaller. With his face hidden behind a balaclava, it was difficult to guess at his age, but his body had the loose-limbed build of a teenage boy.

He nodded.

The silence that descended then was thick and hot. There was an anticipatory edge to it. An expectancy. Everybody seemed to be waiting.

'Now,' the boss said, and his tone was conversational. 'You all know how this works. You've seen it on the telly, I'm sure.' He nodded towards his second-in-command, who tossed him a bag. 'And by the way, don't be worrying about the guards coming because they're not. The panic-button system was disabled before we arrived so there'll be no interference from our lovely boys in blue, OK?'

He looked at Katherine, held the bag out. 'I need to make a withdrawal,' he said. 'You can put it in there.' He threw the bag at her and she caught it and Martha nearly cheered. It seemed like some small display of courage, the deftness of her catch.

It was a Nike sports bag, its familiar *Just do it* message written along the side like an echo of his order.

For a moment, Katherine didn't move, as if there were a delay between the commands given by her brain and their execution by her body. The gunman nudged her shoulder with his gun. 'The sooner you fill the bag, the quicker we'll be on our way, yeah?'

Everybody watched as she slipped behind the counter, punched a series of buttons on a keyboard. The gunman in charge followed her, his gun trained at her head. 'Hurry the fuck up,' he shouted and there was his smile again as Katherine jumped and emitted a short, sharp grunt. She pushed her hair away from her face, squeezed her eyes closed, gathered herself, pressed one more button on the keyboard and waited.

A click and the drawers at each of the work stations slid open. Martha thought it was the most beautiful sound she had ever heard. The neatness of the click, the hiss of the slide.

The accomplice – the solid one – started at the sound, swinging his gun away from the group he was guarding and towards the manager, his breathing high and fast.

'Take it easy, will ya?' his boss told him. 'We're nearly there.'

The room was quiet again. A dense, layered kind of quiet. The air-conditioning droned and Martha could hear the breathing of her fellow hostages and it was something of a comfort to know that she wasn't alone.

Katherine stepped from one drawer to the next, filling the Nike bag with cash.

When she had emptied the last one, she carried the bag to the gunman in charge. He glanced inside, then looked at her. 'How much?' he said.

'I . . . I'm not sure.'

'Make a fucken educated guess.' His voice was strained now. High and thin.

'Maybe four thousand,' she said.

'You said there'd be more than that!' shouted his accomplice. He pulled at the balaclava, scratched his face through the material.

Martha jumped at the sound of a door handle being pulled down. Everybody looked towards the door. The handle moved down, then up, then down again before it was released, springing back into its original position. The sound of voices outside. A conversation. The words were inaudible but the tone was one of annoyance. A second voice, clipped and assured. The conversation continued as the sound of it dribbled away.

The third member of the gang – the one who might be a boy, standing at the door – pushed a slat downwards with his finger, made a narrow slit through which he peered onto the street. He turned back, nodded at the boss, who turned again to Katherine. He put his hand on her shoulder and she almost managed not to flinch.

'Now, sweetheart,' he said. 'I need you to open the safe, nice and quick, and don't give me any shit about time-delay locks, right?'

The shake of her head was slight, seemed involuntary. Martha took a breath and it felt like a collective breath, taken by all of them. Fear had a smell and she smelled it now. It was a sour smell. The air was heavy with it.

'I can't. It's locked and I—' The man lunged at her, one hand around her neck, the other pressing the gun against her hair.

'Kitty!' Tara's voice was shrill. Terror had twisted the features of her usually calm face.

'No, Tara,' Katherine screamed as the gunman twisted his head to look at her sister.

'How convenient,' he said, his tone jovial now. Martha felt every muscle in her body clench.

'You two know each other.' He grabbed a fistful of Katherine's collar, dragged her closer to Tara. Now the muzzle of his gun pressed against Katherine's temple. There was a click as he released the safety. He looked at Tara again. 'Well?' he said. Tara opened her mouth but said nothing. The man stepped closer.

'DO. YOU. KNOW. THIS. BITCH?' He punctuated each word by banging the muzzle of the gun against Katherine's head.

'She's my sister,' Katherine roared, straining away from the gun.

'Well, this is easy, isn't it?' the gunman said. 'You open the safe like a good little girl and—'

'I can't,' Katherine shouted at him. 'I can't override the system.'

'You fucking CAN,' he screeched, and he pushed Katherine away from him, reached for Tara, forcing her onto her knees, pressing the gun into her neck where a pulse was visible, pumping against her pale skin like it was trying to jump free.

'Or I'll rearrange your sister's pretty little face for her.'

'No,' screamed Katherine.

Martha launched herself at the gunman. It was not a conscious decision. The action seemed to happen outside of herself. Outside of her control. She reached for his neck, raking her nails along the bare skin where a line of blood now bloomed. The surprise of her attack made him stumble backwards. His gun flew out of his hand, slid across the floor. The second gunman ran towards it at the same time as Martha dived for it and, for a moment, she felt she could reach it, could maybe even shoot it. Briefly, her mind registered a boot – ankle boot, silver buckle on the side, pointed toe, block heel – as the gunman lifted his foot, drove it into Martha's ribs. She wasn't sure if she was screaming or if it was somebody else. The next kick was to her face, close to her eye. The sound was a wet crack. For a moment, light blared all around her like she was looking directly at the sun, then it dimmed and blurred. She didn't feel the pain of it. Not then. She thought she might throw up.

'You fucking bitch.' The gunman stood beside her now, leaned towards her. Martha felt something warm and sticky on her face. It hurt to breathe. She heard somebody crying and she closed her eyes against the hopelessness of the sound.

'I have cash. In my safe deposit box.' The words were low, precise. Martha opened her good eye. It was the old man. The one in the wheelchair.

'How much?'

'A large sum.'

'How large?'

'I'd rather not discuss my personal business in front of strangers.'

The gunman snorted. Then he pointed the gun at the old man's head. 'How about now? How about you tell me now?'

The old man shook his head with slow deliberation. 'I do not care about your gun, young man. But I will give you my money if you let these people go.'

Now there was a throbbing coming from deep inside Martha's head, like a drum in a marching band, moving closer.

The boss leaned towards the wheelchair. 'I fucken decide what's going to happen here, understand?' The old man lifted his right hand and wiped the gunman's spittle from where it had landed on the side of his face.

The gunman straightened, looked at Katherine. 'Where are the safe deposit boxes kept?'

She pointed to a room just off the foyer. 'It's locked,' she said. 'Unlock it.'

When Martha sat up, she felt blood drip down the side of her face.

'Stay out here and watch them,' the gunman told his accomplice. 'Especially that one.' He pointed at Martha.

'You!' he shouted at the lookout. 'Wheel the auld fella in here and keep the bead on him while I open the box.'

The three of them entered the room and the door closed. The others were ordered to lie face down on the floor with their hands behind their heads and their mouths shut. Steroid – as Martha had dubbed him – paced up and down the line they formed on the floor.

The position brought the pain in Martha's ribs into sharp focus and she pressed her face into the carpet to stop herself from crying out.

It was difficult to know how long they were there. Martha tried to count in seconds but she kept losing her place. She estimated that maybe as much as five minutes passed before it happened.

Before the shot was fired.

Afterwards, there was a brief moment of absolute silence. The silence was like a sound in itself. A white noise into which images bled. Martha saw the silhouette of her father, leaning against the door of her bedroom, the clink of ice cubes against the glass in his hand like a lullaby. *'Lights out, kiddo.'*

She saw Tara, her hair gathered in pigtails, her eyes glaring from behind thick-lensed glasses at a group of kids on a green. *'If you won't let Martha play, then I'm not playing either. And I'm taking my kite with me.'*

She saw the note Cillian had left for her. Before she tore it up. After he left her apartment for the last time.

I love you. We can sort this.

Now there was shouting. Now there was screaming. The tinny insistence of an alarm sounding somewhere. Fists pounding on the main door of the bank.

'Shut the fuck up,' Steroid roared, pointing the gun at each of them as he paced up and down. Martha heard the fidget of his finger against the trigger, the crack of his neck as he snapped his head towards the room containing the safe deposit boxes just as its door was thrown open. Martha glanced up. A boy stumbled out. The Lookout. Martha reckoned he was about fourteen. The skin of his face was flushed. In his hand, a gun.

'What the fuck did you do that for?' The gunman – the one in charge – ran out of the room, the boy's balaclava in one hand, the Nike bag – bulging now – in the other. From the corner of her eye, Martha saw the wheelchair inside the room. It was empty.

The gunman didn't wait for the boy's answer. Instead, he ran towards the front door, yanked it open and disappeared outside, his accomplice running after him.

'Roman.' The boy's head jerked at the word. The woman who said it was the one who'd wheeled the old man into the bank. She said his name again and again and the word was a cry now. A wail. Her small, reddened hands clenched against her face as she shook her head, repeating his name, louder each time, until it seemed as if the building itself was flooded with the word.

In the distance, Martha heard the sirens.

Two

Roman ran out of the bank, struggled through a crowd of people who had gathered outside. He heard the roar of an engine and glanced down the road, saw Tommy behind the wheel of the car Lenny had stolen driving towards him. Jimmy was in the front passenger seat, slumped low, a peaked cap casting his face in shadow. The car slowed, the back door opened. Roman hesitated.

'Get in,' Tommy hissed. 'Now!'

Lenny, in the back seat, pushed Roman down until he was lying on his stomach across the floor, his face scratching against the rough carpet. Lenny threw a blanket over him.

Roman closed his eyes, felt the hum of the engine vibrate through his body, tried not to think about where they might be going or what might happen. Tommy drove without speaking. He never said much. Jimmy and Lenny said little either. Roman was grateful for that. Maybe he could come up with a plan.

Instead, he thought about his mother. Saw her pale face, her grey eyes, her reddened hands. The way she had looked at him in the bank.

Everything was supposed to have been different in Ireland. Better.

'A new start,' Mama had said that day. She showed him how to fasten his seatbelt. It had been his first time on a plane. They had ordered chicken curry from the air hostess even though

Mama had made sandwiches wrapped in greaseproof paper. She said the curry smelled too good. She bought Roman a can of Coke. He remembered the crackle of the fizz when he pulled the tab. How it went up his nose when he bent to listen to the sound. Afterwards, Mama fell asleep but Roman did not. He looked out of the window and tried to guess which countries they were passing. Germany, Netherlands, England.

Uncle Lech's house had three bedrooms. One for Roman, one for Mama and one for himself. The master bedroom, Uncle Lech called it. Because of the en suite, he explained, when Roman asked why.

Roman remembered lowering himself onto the edge of the bed in his new room. His own room. Spreading his hands across the Harry Potter duvet cover. He bounced a little but the springs made no sound. It was a new bed. He closed the bedroom door to see how quiet the room could become. The sound of his mother laughing muted. He opened it again. She was talking now, her voice high and breathy, the way it got when she was happy. Excited. He left the door open.

It wasn't a house: it was a duplex. That's what his uncle called it. His uncle had Sky. And the television screen was nearly as wide as the cinema screen back in Puck, a village fifty kilometres north of Gdansk where Roman had lived until he was nearly twelve. There was a Blu-ray player and the cupboards were crammed with food. 'I asked your Mama what you liked,' Lech said when the light inside the fridge spilled across Roman's face. 'You can have whatever you want. This is your home now.'

Poland seemed a long way away: the top bunk in the room he'd shared with Mama in the apartment where she had grown up; his aunts in the next bedroom, sometimes squabbling, sometimes laughing, sometimes exchanging gossip through the thin walls; his grandmother – Babcia – crooked and swollen with arthritis, bent over a pot of *bigos* on the stove, stirring and tasting and stirring again, all the while talking about her father, Roman's great-grandfather, even when no one was listening.

A hero. That's the word his grandmother used.

His great-grandfather had been a war hero.

The duplex had seemed a million miles away from all of that.

Uncle Lech was born almost exactly nine months before Aunt Arianna, and no more than a year separated Arianna from Aunt Nadia. His mother came last, two years later. Nineteen years later, Roman arrived. Even when his grandfather died and his uncle left for Ireland, the house still seemed full of noise and people.

'I can't hear myself think,' Babcia sometimes shouted over the din.

You could definitely hear yourself think in the duplex.

Mama told him not to sit too close to the television screen. His uncle handed him a box and inside the box was a pepperoni pizza and he didn't even have to share it with anyone. He found a Harry Potter movie on Sky. It didn't matter that it was in English with no subtitles. He'd read the books that Uncle Lech had sent him. There were some passages he knew off by heart.

From the kitchen, the low hum of conversation between his mother and her brother. It had made Roman feel good. As good as warm pizza on an empty stomach. He knew how much Mama had missed Lech when he'd left for Ireland five years before.

His mother had always told Roman things. Confided in him. 'It's you and me against the world, my Roman,' she whispered into his hair before she hugged him or kissed him or tickled him or pushed him higher on the swing in the playground.

He knew about the names Babcia had called Mama when she'd told her about Roman. Except his name wasn't Roman then. He didn't have a name then. He was just a blob on a scan. Rosa had shown him the grainy black and white photograph they had taken of him at the big hospital in Gdansk.

When the film was over, he'd dropped the empty pizza box in the bin and put his glass and plate into the dishwasher. Uncle Lech showed him how to turn it on. It looked like it had never been used, it was so shiny inside.

In the hall, he listened to the clip of his shoes against the ceramic tiles. When he inhaled, he could smell the paint on the walls. Everything was brand new. Even their lives, Roman felt.

It had taken Roman less than ten minutes to unpack. He folded his jeans before he put them in a drawer and even put his two shirts on hangers in the wardrobe. He decided, in that moment, that he was going to be a different person here, in Ireland. Someone responsible, who tidied up after himself, put stuff where it was supposed to go. Mama would be working for Lech, who had his very own company. He said Ireland was a place where you could make a million euros if you worked hard enough.

A million euros!

Back in Poland, Lech had worked as a chef in a cafe. In Dublin, he supplied hospitals with catering staff. Mama didn't have any experience in hospitals or in catering. But she knew how to cook the best *pierogi* in the world and she was a hard worker. Maybe the hardest worker in the world, Roman thought.

Lech had promised her a job, a good salary, a place to stay. 'But I'll only go if you want to go,' Mama told Roman.

'Will there be a cinema in Ireland?' he'd asked.

'Of course.' She'd smiled. 'And I only have to work Monday to Friday so we can go at the weekends. Twice, if you like.'

There had been no toothpaste in the bathroom so Roman knocked on Lech's bedroom door and, when there was no answer, he went inside and opened the door into his uncle's en suite. Lech was sitting on the lid of the toilet, holding what looked like a small square mirror. On the mirror's surface was a line of white powder.

'What are you doing? Sneaking into my room?' Lech shot to his feet, careful not to drop any of the powder when he placed the mirror on top of the cistern.

'Sorry, Lech. I just . . . I was looking for toothpaste. That's all. I knocked first.'

'What's going on?' Mama climbed the stairs in a hurry.

'Nothing, Rosa. The kid walked in on me.' Lech hurried out of the en suite, closed the door behind him. 'No harm done, eh?' He put his hand on Roman's shoulder. Smiled. Roman nodded.

'You're not getting too big to kiss your mama goodnight, are you?' Rosa stood in front of his bedroom door with her arms spread, barricading it. Roman kissed her cheek. Mama still smelled like Babcia's house but her skin was soft, tickled his lips.

It had taken Roman a long time to fall asleep that first night. Everything was strange but in a way that made him feel excited. He thought about what had happened in Lech's en suite. He had a vague feeling that it hadn't been a good thing but he didn't know why. Still, he supposed Lech was right.

There was no harm done.

That's what he had thought back then. Back when he hadn't had a clue. Back when he'd been nothing but a stupid kid.

The car jerked to a stop. Tommy killed the engine. Roman's heart hammered against his chest, loud as a ticking bomb, waiting to explode. One of the front doors opened. The crunch of gravel now. Then a surge of cold air as the back passenger door was pulled open.

'Get out.' Jimmy's voice was dangerously conversational.

Roman crawled out. Glanced around. They were down a lane. Surrounded by fields. A body of water in one field. A lake, maybe. Or a reservoir. Roman thought about the kittens Babcia threw into the bucket every spring. She'd fill the bucket with water, throw the fluffy creatures inside, put a plank across the

17

top and sit on it till the job was done. 'Enough mouths to feed,' Babcia had said when Roman asked her once.

Lenny stood beside Jimmy. Without the benefit of his bala-clava and gun, Lenny looked harmless, with his wide-apart chocolate-brown eyes and hair that was losing both its grip and its colour. He had a sideline in window cleaning that was moder-ately successful, mostly because of his brown eyes and open smile that allowed housewives to believe their windows were in good hands as Lenny cased their homes, making a methodical inventory of valuable items he saw through their – now gleaming – windows.

The black jeep – Lenny called it the getaway car – was one of those valuable items. Lenny had assured Jimmy that the woman who owned it – with the recently cleaned windows in River Valley – wouldn't report it as stolen until she returned from holidays the following week.

Roman glanced at the jeep. Tommy had stayed behind the wheel while Jimmy, Lenny and Roman had gone into the bank. If things had gone to plan, they'd all be in the jeep. Watching Jimmy count the money maybe. Roman would have said no if Jimmy, in an unlikely fit of generosity, handed him a few notes. 'We're quits now, Jimmy, yeah?'

That's what he had planned to say at the end. That's what Jimmy had promised if Roman helped him with the bank job. 'You owe me, Romeo,' Jimmy had said. 'Two grand. That was the value of the package that you claim you lost, remember?'

'It fell out of my pocket, Jimmy, I swear.'

'So you keep saying. Don't look so worried, Romeo. I'll come up with a way that you can pay me back. You can bet your sweet little Mama's life on it.'

And Jimmy *had* come up with a way. And Roman had agreed. Nobody said *no* to Jimmy Carty.

If things had gone to plan at the bank, Roman and Rosa could have parted company with Jimmy and his colleagues, as Jimmy called them.

Wiped the slate clean.

Started again.

Tommy must have felt Roman looking at him as he stood there, wishing things were different. He turned in his seat so that he could see Roman, shook his head, smiled a small, knowing smile without opening his mouth.

'Jimmy, I—' Roman said. He didn't realise how afraid he was until he heard the sound of his own voice.

'Shut your fucken trap,' Jimmy said. Then he nodded at Tommy, who got out of the jeep, opened the boot, hauled a large plastic container out of it and emptied its contents over the bonnet, the roof, inside the boot, on the dashboard, all over the seats. The smell of petrol rammed up Roman's nose, made his eyes sting. He wondered how long it would take to be burnt to death.

Jimmy took a packet of cigarettes out of his pocket, slid one out, tapped the filter against the face of his watch as was his habit.

When he looked at Roman, he smiled his gold-crown smile, but his pale blue eyes, boring into Roman's, never blinked. He opened a book of matches, pulled a match out. When he finally spoke, his voice was quiet. Almost gentle. 'The problem is, Roman, the witnesses at the bank, they can identify you.'

'I'll go away. I'll go really far. The guards won't find me.'

'But if they do, my little Polak?'

'I won't say a word. I swear to God, Jimmy.'

Jimmy shook his head. 'I can't take that chance, I'm afraid.'

Roman clamped his mouth down on all the words he wanted to say. There'd be no point. Not with Jimmy. He'd seen him in action before. Tommy and Lenny called him a psycho, like it was a compliment. Still, they made sure they didn't get in his way. Roman knew they wouldn't help him. The feeling – that he was alone, that he had nowhere to run, no choices left to make – brought with it a strange sense of quietness inside Roman's head, almost like calm. He wondered if this was how his great-grandfather had felt before he had gotten shot by the Germans in the war. A calmness, just before. A resignation.

'You said nobody would get hurt.' Roman looked right into Jimmy's face. 'You're a liar.'

'What did you call me?' Jimmy stepped closer, close enough for Roman to feel the fetid heat of the man's breath against his face.

'You shot that old man. In the bank.' The fear Roman felt had been blunted by the resignation.

Jimmy shook his head. 'Roman, Roman, Roman,' he said, like he was humouring a child. 'I wasn't at the bank today. I was in my solicitor's office, wasn't I? That's what we call in the business an alibi, son. My brief is a very . . . accommodating young man.'

He looked at Lenny and Tommy. Grinned at them. 'All of us have watertight alibis, don't we, lads?'

Jimmy tossed the book of matches to Tommy, who struck one and threw it into the jeep. The fire got a grip on the seats first, sending great tongues of orange flame out through the windows and across the roof. The noise was furious, the heat like a wall of sound.

'We should get moving,' said Lenny, opening the door of a navy BMW with tinted windows parked behind the burning jeep. His voice was barely audible over the sound of the fire.

Jimmy glanced at Tommy. 'We'll wait in the car for you.'

Tommy nodded, drew his gun from the inside pocket of his jacket, moved towards Roman, jerked his head towards the body of water that might be a lake or might be a reservoir.

'No,' said Roman. Tommy, who spoke only when it was absolutely necessary, put his hand around the back of Roman's neck, pushed him forward.

Roman stumbled on, Tommy's gun boring into the small of his back. Behind him, the roar of the fire, the clunk of car doors, opening, closing. The engine starting up, like a crowd murmuring approval.

Despite all the ways that Roman had worried about this day, he had not imagined this. He supposed some things were too big to imagine. Too . . . unimaginable. If he *had* imagined a scene like this, he would have assumed that he would scream. Shake. Cry. Beg for his life.

Another twenty steps and they'd be at the water and his mother would never know what had happened to him. She would never know that he had done it for her. *It's you and me against the world, Roman.* She always whispered it. Like it was their secret.

Behind him, he could hear Tommy's laboured breath. He was a heavy-set man with a purple face and swollen fingers. Roman had never seen him walk so far before.

Ten steps to the water.

Roman looked at the sky. Although it was darkening around the edges, overhead it was still a bright blue, untroubled by cloud.

Roman walked faster.

'Slow down.' When Tommy spoke, Roman could hear the wheeze of his chest. The boy kept walking, faster now. Behind him, the crack of the joints in Tommy's legs as he tried to keep up. 'I said, slow the fuck *down.*' Tommy was panting now.

Roman spun around, his left arm connecting with Tommy's right hand, the way Adam had shown him when Adam had been practising for his red belt in tae kwan do. He heard Tommy grunt in surprise. The gun was still in the man's right hand but was pointing somewhere else now. Somewhere to the right of Roman's head. The boy brought his knee up, drove it into Tommy's groin, put every kilo he had into that action. Now Tommy was doubled over and the gun was still in his hand but it wasn't pointing at Roman and Roman knew he had only a moment.

A moment to do something.

Or do nothing.

Later, he told himself that he should have gone for the gun. Should have bitten into the fleshy skin of Tommy's hand holding the gun. Maybe got it off him that way. Instead, he left the gun where it was, in Tommy's hand, and ran.

He ran towards the lake. Or the reservoir. Across the field, zigzagging as he ran to make it as difficult as he could for Tommy to take aim, to hit him. Up ahead, maybe two hundred metres away, a line of trees signalled the boundary of the field that held Roman. He ran for the trees. In his ears, the wind, rushing past him. When he heard the shot, it sounded far away and he didn't think it had hit him.

He kept running.

He never stopped.

Three

The first thing Martha thought about when she got home was a drink.

A whiskey sour. Her father's favourite drink. And Martha's too, for a time. A long time. The amber liquid. Three ice cubes bobbing, clinking. In a cut-crystal glass. Heavy to lift. Heavy to hold. In her mind, Martha lifted it, held it, steered it towards her mouth.

She sat on the couch that was too big for the living room and worried at the corner of her mouth with her tongue. A metallic taste. Blood, she supposed.

The clearest image of the day was that of the old man's shoes. She'd glanced inside the room where he lay and looked at him. She never trusted second-hand information. She had to see things for herself. She looked inside and saw the man but when she closed her eyes now, bore down on the image, it was his shoes she saw.

Black patent shoes, tied with a double knot, polished to a sharp shine. Martha imagined him bent over the chore earlier in the day, dawn perhaps. He had the look of an early riser, she felt. She saw him working a brush along the toes, down the sides towards the heels, not stopping until he could make out his ancient face in the leather.

Martha swung her legs onto the couch, surprised by the quality of pain the action produced. She reached for a cushion, jammed it behind her head, closed her eyes. Her ankle was swollen but she couldn't remember why. She should probably prop it on something. Elevate it. The pain in her side was a dull ache now, not the sickening throb of earlier when the guards had arrived at the bank. Swarms of them. The static from their radios was deafening and useless.

When the ambulance staff had arrived, the bank was as thronged as the National Concert Hall during a Hilary Hahn recital. Tara sat on a chair that Katherine had dragged from behind one of the counters, shaking as if she were cold. Her teeth clattered together, her lips in narrow blue lines. She had to be helped into the ambulance. When it drove away in a blare of siren and flashing lights, Martha was overtaken by the urge to be where people were not. She wanted to go home.

She also wanted a drink, which sharpened her desire to be at home. In her flat. Where there were no drinks. She'd be safer in there.

Martha looked around, spotted a uniformed young garda on his own. He carried a notebook in which he was writing something in pencil with great concentration, the tip of his tongue sticking out of the side of his mouth.

Martha approached him. 'I want to make a statement,' she said.

'I'll bring you down to the station in a while, OK?' The guard glanced at her before returning to his notebook.

'No. I'm making a statement now and then I'm going home.'

The guard looked at her. Properly this time. 'You'll have to go to hospital. Your face looks nasty.'

'Yeah, well, you're no fucken oil painting yourself.'

'No, I didn't mean—'

'Look, I'm not sitting in A&E for eight hours to be told I have a fractured rib and a cut on my face. I'm either making a statement now or I'm going home. You choose.'

He took her statement, vaguely aware that the balance of power he usually enjoyed in these situations was not in evidence.

His pen was a blur as he tried to keep up with the details of Martha's recollections. Times. Actions. Descriptions. The guard could have drawn the boy's face afterwards, if he could draw. She had only seen the boy's face, not those of the two men, but she described their accents, their physiques, their clothes, the shapes of their faces beneath the balaclavas.

Afterwards, he insisted on driving her to her flat in Applewood.

'My car's parked in the Castle Shopping Centre.'

'I'll drop you home.'

'Why?'

'Well, it's just . . . I don't think you should be driving in your, eh, condition. You could be concussed.'

'I'm not.'

'It's not something you can be certain of.'

'I am certain.'

'But—'

'OK, fine.' Martha was as surprised as the guard when she folded. She put it down to the unexpected turn the day had taken. The pain in her ribs. Her ankle, for some reason. Her face. That, and a deep-seated tiredness that made her feel heavy and dim-witted.

'Do you want me to come up?' the guard asked, when he pulled up outside her apartment block.

'I'm not really in the mood, to be honest.'

He flushed furiously, making himself seem even younger than before. 'No, I didn't mean . . .' he said.

Martha closed the passenger door without hearing what it was he didn't mean. The lift wasn't working and she pulled herself to the third floor by gripping the handrail and naming every note on the score for Beethoven's Finale, which she was learning on her violin. By the time she got to her door, the pain was a drumbeat, loud and throbbing. The sharp sting at the side of her head. A burning sensation in her ribs, although it only hurt when she breathed so she concentrated on taking slow, shallow breaths and doing so as seldom as possible.

She thought about whisky. Neat, this time. No messing with ice and lemon. Scotch single malt. She had been a mostly discerning drinker. None of your Royal Dutch. Despite the time that had somehow passed since the last drink, she remembered with great clarity the peaty taste of it, the smooth track of it down her throat and the warmth of it; the way it spread itself around her body like a blanket tucked under the chin of a child. She tried to remember what her last drink had been and found that she could not. She could remember the anticipation of it, the sensation of her mouth against the glass. But not the drink itself. She supposed it was because, at the time, she hadn't known it would be her last drink. If she had, she might have afforded it more ceremony.

Her mouth watered like she was hungry. She wasn't hungry. She was thirsty. The kind of thirst water couldn't quench. She distracted herself by breathing deeply, focused on the scream of her ribs, pulled the pain around her like one of those bothy bags that Cillian used to bring with him when they went hiking. To shelter them in case a storm blew up. The weight of the pain might shelter her from her desire for a drink. She breathed, in and out, taking forever about it, in for five, hold for five, out for five. The pain was like something alive and furious.

When she closed her eyes, she saw the front door of the Pound pub, swinging open.

She forced herself to stay where she was, stay on the couch, not move her feet towards the floor, not fumble for her bag, not grab her keys, not reach for the handle of the door.

It was almost physical, the struggle.

In the morning, she would have to go to a meeting.

She never went *into* the meetings. She parked outside. She had been doing this for about a year now, although it had been longer than that since she'd had a drink.

Over a year.

One year, four months, two weeks and three days. Martha wondered if the accuracy of this calculation might dim in time.

'My name is Martha Wilder and I have an uneasy relationship with alcohol.' She never said alcoholic. She associated that word with fumbling, bloated men with wispy hair and bulbous noses and red faces and unfortunate wives.

She said the sentence – out loud – sitting in her car outside various parish halls and community centres. The often neglected appearance of these buildings from the outside – fading paintwork, cobwebbed windows, rusting door hinges, roofs with missing slates like rows of unfortunate teeth – reinforced her intention never to step inside.

She parked far enough away so no one could mistake her for a dithering, will-I-won't-I first-timer, but near enough so she could see them going in.

She parked the car, then she said what she had to say – My name is Martha Wilder and I have an uneasy relationship with alcohol – and she held her mobile against her ear when she said it, so that if anyone glanced into the car, they would presume she was having a normal conversation with a normal person on a normal mobile phone.

Just like a normal woman.

She imagined the people inside, sitting in a circle of hard plastic chairs, the soles of their shoes worrying at the floor, perhaps nodding after her little introduction, some of them mumbling, 'Hello, Martha,' the way they did in the movies.

'I haven't had a drink in one year, four months, two weeks and three days.' Would she get a round of applause for that? A shuffle of approval? Probably not.

People often peered into her car as she sat outside the meetings. She was not one of those women who blended into the background. It was her height, she supposed. When she reached five feet nine at the age of fifteen she had hoped that she might be overlooked for any further elongation but, in spite of the fervour of her hope, she had continued to stretch until she was finally spared, just below the six-foot mark. And she was big-boned. Sturdy, her father used to call her. That, coupled with her mane of long red hair – which ran riot if she didn't apply buckets of product – made it difficult for her to sit in her car outside an AA meeting unnoticed.

She opened her notebook where she had written her six reasons, at the end. Or perhaps it was better to think about it as a beginning. That's what Tara had said.

A new beginning, she'd called it. Martha had told her to cop onto herself and Tara apologised and said she was premenstrual and hungover and wasn't thinking straight. Then she apologised for saying *hungover* and Martha said, *Fuck sake*, and Tara said it was going to take her time to adjust to the changes and Martha said, *I feel for you, I really do*, and Tara said, *Let's eat mushroom risotto and watch* Countdown, and that's what they did – except Martha ate Pot Noodles instead of risotto and they watched *The Muppet Show* instead of *Countdown*, and the day passed and then another and another, and that's how Martha managed in the end. Or the beginning, she supposed.

Her routine outside the meetings never changed. Her brief introduction in the car, while pretending to be on the phone. The reading aloud of the six reasons. Although two of them were the same reason. Both one word. A name. The first reason and the last reason. She read them slowly and with intent, so that the part of her that scorned her attempts at sobriety would hear her and know that she meant it and back off.

Martha was not a woman given to superstition but that part of her – the part that scorned her attempts – made her feel nervous and she was not supposed to be a person who felt nervous, so she doused it with her six reasons that were really five reasons. Every time. And most times, the front door of the Pound pub stayed closed.

Except now it was wide open. She put this yearning down to the day. Not your usual put-out-the-bins-don't-drink-a-drink kind of day, with the situation at the bank and the fact that she hadn't filed the article that she'd undertaken to file by four o'clock that afternoon.

From the couch, she couldn't see the kitchen clock. Couldn't remember where her mobile was.

Not yet closing time, that was for sure. She could see right inside the pub now, the dark interior, the long legs of the bar stools, even the hooks under the counter where she had hung her coat, her bag and, once, the strap of a complicated camera belonging to a work colleague. She had left it behind, that camera, and when she eventually remembered, she went back but the camera was gone and she'd bought another one, hoping her colleague wouldn't notice but she did notice, of course she did, and Martha had felt the familiar sting of humiliation and dread and uselessness that she had felt on so many mornings when she managed to drag herself out of bed and wonder what she had done the day before, what she had said, what she had lost.

Martha opened her eyes, concentrated on what she could see: her violin stand with the sheet music in messy piles on the floor around its base; the arm of the couch, its velvet covering baggier now and not as deeply red as it had once been; one of her boots lying on its side near the door, a soft leather ankle boot, a dull olive green colour. She focused on the boot, thought about its comrade, where it might be; in her head, she retraced her steps and thought it might be in her bedroom. She remembered easing the boot off her foot with the toe of the other boot because she didn't think she could bend down. She didn't know why she had taken the other boot off in the living room. She must have gotten distracted. Now she looked at the bookshelf and tried to remember where she had bought each of the books. She began at the top shelf.

This was how she managed on days like this. This was how she closed the door of the pub. She knew it was pitiful. She felt like shouting *it's not fair* like some melodramatic teenager who has received a response from her parents that was not in keeping with her expectations.

She didn't shout. She waited. She knew this was the only way to douse the yearning that was all around her now. Maybe it had something to do with muscle memory. One traumatic experience and the brain reaches for the age-old solution, as if the last one year, four months, two weeks and three days meant nothing. As if they hadn't happened at all.

She must have lain on the couch for a long time because when darkness fell – suddenly, the way it did in winter, like a heavy curtain across the stage of the sky – she was still there. Still on the couch. Perhaps she had fallen asleep? Although she doubted it, with the pain and the trying not to breathe too much or too often and the memory of the black polished patent shoes, tied with a double knot, and the yearning and the open door of the pub and the worrying about Tara.

She checked her phone again. A missed call from Katherine. Had her phone even rung?

'They think she's in shock,' Katherine said when Martha rang back. Katherine sounded shocked herself. Martha understood. Tara didn't shock easily. Not even when she was ten and the chip pan went on fire in the kitchen when her mother was outside, flagging down the bread van and chatting with Mrs

O'Reilly from number fifty-two with whom she competed on a daily basis on matters of front-window cleaning, door-knocker polishing, net-curtain whiteness and the progress – social and intellectual – of their offspring. Tara had climbed out her bedroom window and sat on the roof of the extension, reading her book as she waited for the fire brigade to arrive following her brief call to the emergency services.

'She had a . . . it looked like a panic attack in the ambulance and then, since we arrived at the hospital and they got her a bed, she's been asleep.'

'It's probably the best thing for her,' said Martha.

'Maybe,' said Katherine with no conviction. Tara didn't believe in sleep. 'You'd be amazed at how much work you can get done when you don't waste time sleeping,' she sometimes said.

Last orders at the bar. She was nearly there. Martha concentrated on the second hand of the kitchen clock. The insistence of it. And the sound. Had it always made that sound? In the orange glow thrown by the streetlamp outside, she watched the hand inch around the face, saw the almost imperceptible shake of the smaller hand as each minute passed.

In the dark, the dense silence seemed to move around her, like a predator. Sounds leaked from the apartments above and below. A toilet flushing, a door closing, a stair creaking. She was glad she didn't have a lodger anymore. She'd needed one after she lost her job as a reporter in RTÉ, to help bail out the waters of negative equity with which the apartment was flooded.

When Kate had left six months ago, to move in with her Australian boyfriend, Martha hadn't had to replace her, as the freelance work began to pick up.

She braced herself, then reached her arm down her body to scratch an itch at the side of her knee and the pain rushed at her like a train and she told herself to stop being such a bloody baby and that did the trick for a while. She knew she should go to the freezer. Get a bag of frozen peas. Hold them against her face. She should wrap a bandage around her ribs. She didn't have a bandage and the freezer was in the kitchen and she didn't feel like moving. She should probably take a painkiller. Roll a cigarette. Eat something.

She did none of that. Instead, she lay on the couch in the dark and thought about the article she was supposed to have filed that afternoon. She hadn't been late with a piece since she'd begun freelancing nearly a year ago. It had taken a long time to regain even a fraction of the credibility she had squandered.

She found it difficult to attach any importance to this. Or to anything. The windows in the apartment were closed and the air in the room seemed heavy and stale and it made her think of a crypt or a grave and she felt alone.

Her phone rang. Martha's body jerked at the sudden noise, and she clamped her hand to her mouth to stop herself crying out. She picked up the phone, glanced at the screen. It was her mother. She let it go to voicemail.

It's your mother.

Her messages always began like that, as if she somehow doubted that Martha would recognise her voice.

I'm ringing to see how you are?

A pause there. Martha waited.

And to remind you about the memorial service in Sunshine House on Friday.

Martha had forgotten.

I'm sure you hadn't forgotten but . . .

She trailed off. Martha waited. Her mother hadn't mentioned Amelia by name yet which meant she hadn't finished the message.

I know your sister will appreciate having us all there so . . .

Her mother always spoke about Amelia as if she were still alive. As if she hadn't died thirty years ago.

So anyway, yes, I'll . . . I'm sure I'll see you on Saturday then? At the service. It's at eleven o'clock. Sharp. So . . . do try not to be late, won't you?

Martha deleted the message, closed her eyes. She couldn't blame her mother. She had missed many memorial services. The ones she had attended, she had arrived late. Or drunk. Or both.

She put a reminder into her phone. Just in case. Then set about persuading herself to do something. Get undressed. Brush her teeth. Go to bed.

In the end, she fell asleep on the couch and dreamed about a dog she once had long ago when she was a girl and the vet told her it was for the best and her mother said she had to be brave like her sister Amelia and the needle was long and pointed and her brothers were running round and round the surgery and the noise they made was sharp and vicious, like the screech of a train against tracks. When she woke, the noise was still there, as if it had leaked from her dream into the morning.

It was the doorbell ringing.

Four

Tobias knew he was in hospital. It was the smell. That hospital smell of disinfectant and dried-up dinners and withering flowers in stagnant water.

'Can Mr Hartmann hear me?' Rosa's use of the auxiliary verb, coupled with the correct positioning of the personal pronoun – which had proved a difficult lesson for her to learn – pleased Tobias. He wondered if he were smiling. He hardly thought so. According to the young man on his right – Tobias feared he had been fobbed off with one of those junior affairs, barely out of the trenches – he was in a coma.

'No,' the young man declared in that emphatic way that young men have. The fact that his declaration was incorrect made no impression whatever on his authoritative tone.

Tobias wondered if this was how it was going to end. In a hospital. In a coma. He presumed so. He was curious to know how long it would take.

Rosa's voice again. He strained towards it from wherever he was – he wasn't sure. Somewhere inside himself. Buried deep. Curiously, it was not unpleasant.

'Can I stay with him for the while?'

For *a* while.

A while.

Tobias had tried many times to impress upon her the difference between the direct and indirect article.

Some things were harder to learn than others, he supposed.

'Well, I suppose so, although there's not much point,' said the doctor. 'We've made him as comfortable as we can.'

'When will he awaken?'

Awaken. A lovely word, Tobias thought. Something quaint about it. Less abrasive than *wake up*. He felt the air in the room stir as the doctor sighed. A long, tired sigh. Perhaps he was nearing the end of his shift. There was no telling what time it was. The concept of time seemed quaint also. It had no place here, in the place where Tobias was now.

'He lost a lot of blood. We've given him a transfusion but, well, at his age . . . there's no way to know when he'll come to. Or if he will. You could ask one of the nurses to ring you, should there be any news. Are you his granddaughter?'

A rustling sound. Rosa, he presumed. Shaking her head. 'I need to speak to him. My son . . . I know he didn't shoot him. I *know*. Mr Hartmann can tell the police what happened when he wakes up. Can't he?'

Tobias remembered the first night he'd spoken to her. She had mentioned her son then too. He dipped his line into the bank of his memory, fished around for a name.

Roman.

Yes. Roman.

He remembered thinking how fierce a mother's love could be. His own mother had loved him and his brothers like that. And baby Greta. With that same brand of ferocity. Like a storm; his mother, the eye in the centre.

Something must have happened. Why else would he be here? But he wasn't here. Not really. He was someplace else.

At first, he had thought he was at the nursing home. Rosa was a cleaner there. When he'd arrived at the home, almost a year ago now, he hadn't spoken to her. Why would he?

All he knew about her was her nationality. She was Polish. A reminder of some of the things he struggled to forget.

But despite the strict structure of his days, Rosa had somehow breached his barrier. She was not someone who would barge in unannounced and uninvited. It was he who had issued the invitation in the end as he went about his business in his usual way, adapted to the slow monotony of the nursing home. She who had accepted his invitation in her quiet, careful way.

It must be eight months ago now.

Usually, after dinner, he repaired to his room, prepared for bed, read one of his history books. He liked ancient history – the Mycenaeans, for instance. Modern history didn't seem historical enough, Tobias felt.

That night, he had wheeled himself in the direction of the library instead. He hated the chair but it was true to say he was more adept at manoeuvring himself about than he had been. He could have gotten a battery-operated one but he'd refused, the last shred of independence being perhaps the most difficult one to relinquish.

Afterwards, when Tobias questioned the small but uncommon revision of his nightly routine, he arrived at no satisfactory answer.

The corridors were dimly lit. They smelled of gravy. Irish people poured gravy over everything, it seemed to Tobias. The purchase of the rubber against the linoleum produced a creaking sound that echoed in his wake.

A nurse nodded and smiled at him as she passed him on the corridor. 'Getting a book, Mr Hartmann?'

There was something ghostly about her. Perhaps it was her white uniform, her gliding, noiseless gait.

Tobias nodded. He didn't believe in ghosts. He was convinced that when he died – tonight or next week or next month or, God forbid, not till next year – that would be an end to it and he was glad about that.

The library was lit only by the moon, not quite full, glancing against the windows. Tobias didn't switch on any of the harsh fluorescent lights, didn't want to disturb the clarity of the silence the darkness afforded.

He thought the room empty and wheeled himself around the shelves, the wheels hissing now against the carpet tiles.

And then he heard another sound. A crackly, tinny noise, like somebody on the other end of a bad telephone line. It was coming from behind the shelf of audio books. He moved towards it even though it was none of his business. Perhaps it was just for something to do.

There was a bank of tables behind the shelf, each housing a computer. Tobias didn't have much truck with computers. He trusted the scratch of a pen across paper.

At one table, Rosa.

He knew her name was Rosa; perhaps he had heard the other staff addressing her thus.

She didn't see him. She wore headphones and her face was lit by the blue glare of the computer screen. She mouthed words, deepening a crease above her nose in her effort.

Her grace seemed effortless, something she was unaware of. It was in the length of her neck and the fineness of her collar bones, outlined against the navy bib the cleaners wore. For a brief moment, Tobias thought about drawing her. Sometimes that happened. He forgot about his hand. His useless hand.

His next instinct was to leave quietly, return to his room. To his routine.

'Do you want me to turn the lights on, Mr Hartmann?' When Tobias twisted his head around, the bones in his neck crackled like kindling. Freda, one of the care assistants, was a silhouette at the door. In his peripheral vision, he saw Rosa, her head snatched towards him, her hands on the earphones, lowering them. She looked startled, her grey eyes wide in her small face, and he was sorry then that he had disturbed her.

'No,' Tobias told Freda, straightening insofar as he could, given the limitations the chair imposed.

Freda took a step towards him, her movements slow and careful like he was a feral animal she'd discovered in her garden. 'Are you alright?'

'Yes. Of course.'

'If you like, I could—'

'I said I'm fine.' He knew the nursing staff thought him caustic. Perhaps he was. But they never stopped with their enquiries: what he ate, how he felt, what activity he might like to pursue, why he didn't want to take part in the activities they arranged, if he needed help shaving or showering or even moving his bowels, for goodness' sake.

When Freda finally took her leave, Tobias remained motionless for a moment before turning back towards Rosa.

'I sorry,' she began, 'I should not be here.' Her voice was a whisper, her body rigid.

Tobias held up his good hand, shook his head. 'It is none of my concern, where you should or should not be.'

'I finish at working and now I learn the English.' She nodded towards the computer screen.

'It doesn't appear that you are doing a good job, young lady. You are missing some key words.'

She nodded. 'Is true. I not do good job.'

Tobias said nothing. He had already said enough.

'Me and Roman here for two years and half. I need improve English and get more good job.'

'Who is Roman?' He didn't know why he'd asked the question. He didn't care who Roman was. Why would he?

'He is my boy. He has fourteen years.' Rosa's smile took him by surprise. It was wide and clear. When she smiled, he could see the youth in her face.

'Shouldn't you be getting home to your boy? Your son, I mean?' he asked.

'He staying with friend house tonight.' She stumbled along the sentence. Tobias shook his head.

'He *is* staying *at a* friend's house tonight,' he said, slowly and deliberately. 'It's the present participle so you need to conjugate the verb "to be". And be careful with your prepositions. You don't stay *with* an inanimate object, for example a house. You stay *at*. And then, you need the apostrophe "s" after friend to denote possession. The house *of a* friend. A friend's house. Do you understand?'

'Your English be good,' she said.

'Is good. My English is good,' Tobias said. He detected in his tone an irritation and he paused, took a breath. 'I have lived in Ireland for over sixty years. My English has no right to be anything other than excellent.'

'I understand,' she said. Tobias had his doubts.

'You have a lot of work to do,' he said, and that should have been an end to it. He was sure that his intention – after delivering the sage insight into her workload – was to place his working hand on the wheel of the chair, turn himself around, leave. Perhaps it was the way she nodded when he said that. Something stoic about the nod. Resolute. Or how she turned back to the screen, despite the fact that she was clearly learning nothing of value from the machine.

'Do you know how to conjugate verbs in the present tense?' he said.

Rosa looked at him and there was a question on her face and he answered it by telling her to switch off the computer, fetch him a notebook from the art supplies cupboard in the corner. He slid a fountain pen from the breast pocket of his shirt. When

Rosa moved, she made barely any sound. As if she were intent on negotiating the world without drawing attention to herself. A slip of a thing. When she smiled, he would have estimated that she was in her early twenties if it hadn't been for the boy. She must be closer to thirty. Perhaps even older than that. When one had lived this long, youth became an impossibility. Something difficult to fathom.

When she returned, he opened the notebook she had given him and wrote, in his neat, square handwriting, the words <u>To Be</u> at the top of the page, underlined once.

'We'll start with the present,' he said. Rosa nodded. He noted that her comprehension was competent. He felt this might help. Rosa sat beside him, studied the page as he wrote:

I am
You are
He/She is
We are
You (plural) are
They are

'You see?' he said, tapping his pen along the list.

'I see,' said Rosa. She smiled again and now he saw the gap between her front teeth and it reminded him of his brother, Bruno, and he remembered his mother insisting it was a sign of a good singing voice and the high sweetness of Bruno's voice when he sang 'Hänschen Klein'. His mother had clapped every time he sang it, said Bruno sounded like an angel.

He pointed to the first line of the conjugated verb. 'Put this in a sentence,' he said.

'I am,' Rosa began, her finger travelling below the words.

Tobias nodded. 'Finish the sentence. You are what?'

'I am Polish.'

'What else?'

'I am mother.'

'I am a mother,' Tobias corrected.

'I am a mother,' repeated Rosa, her face serious with concentration.

'Go on.'

'I am a cleaner.'

'Anything else?'

She shook her head. Tobias pointed to the second line. You are. Tapped it with his pen.

'You are teaching to me the English.' She seemed as surprised by the notion as he was.

'You are teaching me English, see? That's what's called a pronoun. We'll get to those in due course.'

'You are teaching me English,' Rosa repeated. There was a question in her voice as she studied Tobias's face. He answered by snapping the notebook shut, sliding it towards her. 'You need to learn this. It's one of the most important verbs in the English language. Tomorrow I shall leave a list of words on the bureau in my room. You must put them into sentences. If you don't know what they mean, look them up. I shall see you here next Thursday, same time.'

He left the library that first night without saying goodbye. He felt the weight of her stare as he moved towards the door. Probably wondering what his intentions were. If he had ulterior motives. A woman like Rosa must often come across people with ulterior motives, Tobias felt.

What was he up to? The whole thing happened so suddenly, without warning, he hadn't had time to come up with an explanation.

It was not in his plan, teaching English to a cleaner. An immigrant. Someone from Poland.

Not that he had a plan.

He had not had a plan in a long time.

You are teaching me English. That's what Rosa had said.

That was what he was doing.

And that's what he had done for the past eight months. Eight months of Thursday nights, teaching Rosa at the back of the library, where they couldn't be seen. It wasn't a secret as such. But Tobias understood that the management and staff would not look favourably on Rosa's lessons. They might consider it special treatment. Rosa getting singled out. There was a pecking order in the place, of course. The cleaners and kitchen assistants were at the bottom of the heap, and their meagre salaries reinforced that status. The managing director of the place drove this year's Lexus and Rosa – whose dry, red hands were a testament to hard work – walked to her job in the rain. That was the way of the world, Tobias knew, but the injustice of it niggled at him more and more as he became acquainted – despite himself – with Rosa.

'So,' said the doctor who sounded too young to be a doctor. 'You're not related to . . .' A brief pause, the shuffle of papers against a clipboard, 'Mr Hartmann, no?'

'No,' said Rosa.

'Oh. I see . . . well . . . I'm not sure if . . . there's hospital policy, you see, and . . .' Another sigh, and then, 'What is your relationship to this man?'

A pause then. Tobias imagined Rosa's small face, her careful grey eyes travelling across the doctor's face without seeming to. Trying to gauge him. See if she could trust him.

'Mr Hartmann is my friend.' That's what Rosa said in the end.

Present tense, correctly conjugated. Possessive article. Followed by a noun. A well put-together sentence.

Mr Hartmann is my friend.

Five

Cillian Larkin arrived into the station in Swords early the next day. He had been off duty when the bank robbery happened. He needed to get himself up to speed. He logged on to Pulse, opened the incident file and began to read. He stopped when he saw her name.

Martha Wilder.

The familiarity of it. He was stabbed by a feeling. A memory of a feeling that he had long ago put away. For a moment, he sat there, studied the letters of her name, collected himself.

Her father's funeral. That was the last time. She was with that drunken fool of a husband, masquerading as a spiritual pilgrim. Pillock more like.

Cillian had transferred to Donegal by then. After everything – their split and that case Cillian had been working on – it had seemed like a good move.

He had moved on. Put the familiarity of her face behind him.

And now there she was. Her name. On his computer screen, like a virus.

He sat at his desk and scanned her statement, unsurprised by her attention to detail.

He checked her mobile number. It was the same. He still knew it off by heart despite deleting it from his contacts two years ago. There had been nights, in the early days, when he'd been tempted to ring but, in the mornings that followed, he was relieved that he hadn't. Some things are best left alone.

He pushed his chair back.

'Going out, Cillian?' one of his colleagues asked.

'Yeah, a couple of calls to make.' Strictly speaking, he didn't have to talk to her. She'd made her statement and his six-month secondment from his permanent position in Donegal was nearly up. It would be better for one of his colleagues to handle it.

He put on his jacket.

'Any sign of the boy yet?' Cillian asked, nodding towards a photograph of Roman Matus on the corkboard. Most of the witness statements had included descriptions of the boy, after the shot was fired, suddenly appearing outside the room containing the safe deposit boxes with his balaclava off, the gun in his hand and the woman shouting 'Roman' at him like it was a question. 'My son is a good boy,' Rosa had insisted in her statement.

His colleague shook his head. 'Not yet.'

Cillian moved towards the door. He had hoped that Roman's name wouldn't end up on their system but he felt no surprise that it had. The boy and his mother lived in a house owned by Jimmy Carty, one of north Dublin's least charming drug dealers. It was entirely plausible that Carty had branched into armed robbery; he was arrogant enough to think he could pull it off. And Cillian suspected that Roman might have done a few jobs for Jimmy and his gang, despite Cillian's warnings about people like Jimmy, who would discard people like Roman once they'd served their purpose.

He was a quiet one, Roman. Quiet and clever. Cillian had met him a few times in the youth initiative in Swords where Cillian sometimes went to play chess with the kids. Roman took a while to learn the moves of the various pieces but once he had mastered them, he gave Cillian a run for his money.

He didn't say much, concentrated on the game. When he *did* speak, it was brief. But he had told Cillian snippets. Just little bits about Poland, his mother, his friends, Adam and Meadhbh, and – once – his uncle Lech.

And now this same boy was a number on a file that would be passed from one department to another, trudging through the system. Juvenile court, Trinity House, probably on to St Pat's – the charges were serious – and he'd be an adult when he got out then and the promising kid he'd been would be long gone.

There were loads of kids like that, of course, but there was something about Roman that reminded Cillian of another boy. Another case. A few years ago now.

Cillian picked up his car keys and headed down the corridor towards the front door of the station, and nearly made it before the superintendent flung open the door of his office, strode into the hall, pointed at Cillian. With his ferocious face, the solid muscle of his body and a pair of short, squat legs, he had the look of a bulldog.

'I've a favour to ask you, beanstalk.' The Super often began conversations like that. That was what he'd said to Cillian all that time ago. Three and a half years it must be. He used those exact words, Cillian was sure of it.

Cillian had just finished a case he'd been working for months which culminated with the interception of a consignment of drugs – worth over a million euros – at Dublin Port the day before. He was at his desk filling in the paperwork, which was the bit of the job that he could have done without.

The Super had flung open the door of the office, strode inside and said, 'I've a favour to ask you, beanstalk.'

Cillian had looked up.

'RTÉ are doing some report on drug crime in the city. I told them you'd talk to them.'

'Ah, boss, why'd you do that?'

'You can tell them all about your recent success. They'll lap that up.'

'Can't O'Grady do it?'

45

'With that stutter? You're f-f-fucken joking.'

'Or Murphy?

'That fella looks too pretty to be a guard.'

'Cheers, boss.'

'You know what I mean. You look like you haven't slept in a month and Murphy has a head on him like he just stepped out of a fucken – what d'ya call them? – a beauty salon or something. The hair. Jaysis.'

'I was going to go home after I've filed this report.'

'You're going nowhere. Now hose yourself down and shave that mush before you meet the reporter. You look like you've been dragged through a bush backwards.'

Cillian made a last-ditch effort. 'What about Clancy? Clancy could do it. He's in that amateur dramatic society. He loves an audience.'

The boss shook his head. 'She asked for you specifically. You're doing it.'

'Who?'

'Martha whatsherface. RTÉ journo.'

'Martha Wilder?'

'The one and only. And what Martha wants, Martha gets and she wants you, God help you.'

'Why did she ask for me?'

'Who the fuck knows. It's like throwing a lamb to a wolf.'

'Thanks.'

'You're welcome. And you know the drill. Talk to her but don't tell her anything, understood?'

He didn't know Martha Wilder, although he'd met her often in the course of his job. And she was on the telly most nights, of course. He felt a contradiction of things at the prospect of meeting her. Of being in a room alone with her. Not that he'd be alone with her. But still, the feeling persisted as he shaved his face and brushed his teeth. A sort of anxious anticipation.

Martha was one of those women you couldn't quite put your finger on. She wasn't pretty. Pretty had girlish connotations. She was too tall for pretty. There was a fierceness about her. Something untamed in the way she walked – more of a stride – and talked – fast, without reference to punctuation.

There was something sturdy about her. He could see the muscles in her thighs flex against her black skinny jeans when she moved around the room at the station where the Super had arranged the interview. The shoot, Clancy was calling it.

Martha looked up when he stepped inside the room, studied him like he was something she was cramming at the last minute for an exam. 'Detective Larkin,' she said, not quite a greeting. He extended his hand and she shook it briefly with a firm grip. Up close, he smelled mint from her chewing gum and something tart. Lemon, he thought. She had bright green eyes and very pale skin with a collection of freckles across her cheekbones and the bridge of her nose, which gave her a girlish impression. He was fairly sure she hated that.

Before they began filming, she gathered her long, red hair in her two hands – a tricky task, given the amount of it – and wound it around and around until it disappeared into a surprisingly tidy bun at the back of her head. She slipped her long, taut arms into the sleeves of a black jacket, buttoned it while someone clipped a small microphone onto the lapel. Someone else approached her – cautiously, Cillian felt – with one of those cosmetic brushes and dabbed at her face until the freckles disappeared.

Now she looked like the woman from the telly.

Martha's questioning style was quieter than he would have thought. Her voice was low-pitched, a little hoarse. He imagined her with a cigarette between her long fingers.

When the interview began, Cillian's palms were sweaty and he had to concentrate on not shifting in his seat. Martha, he realised later, must be good at her job because he forget about his sweaty palms and the hard plastic chair he was sitting on. He didn't dwell on Martha's reputation for chewing people up before spitting them out. He hardly ever watched the news. Didn't have the time. But he didn't find Martha *bolshie* as some people called her. He found her style of interviewing firm but fair enough. She wasn't afraid to ask the hard questions but she listened to his answers. Cillian felt those same people would describe her as *authoritative* had she been a man.

'What part of Donegal are you from?' Martha asked him when she'd finished the interview. He'd left years ago but the accent persisted. His boss said that crime never sounded as bad in Cillian's Donegal lilt.

'Killybegs.'

'How come you're not a fisherman?'

'I am. In my spare time.'

'Do you have much spare time?'

'The job keeps me fairly busy.'

'Are you seeing anyone?'

'Don't you ever stop asking questions?'

'Sorry. Occupational hazard. So are you?'

'Sorry?'

'Seeing anyone?'

'Eh, no.'

'Why not? What's wrong with you?'

Cillian laughed. 'My sister warned me about women like you.'

'Your mother should have done that. Has more of an impact when someone in authority makes those kinds of pronouncements.'

When Cillian didn't answer immediately, Martha's face clouded over. 'Oh, shit. Your mother's dead, isn't she? And I'm after putting my size sevens right in it. Fuck.'

'Size sevens?'

Martha shook her slip-on shoe off and held her foot up for inspection. 'Awful, isn't it? Like the foot of a farmer.'

'I've never seen the foot of a farmer.'

'Well, neither have I. But you'd imagine they'd be huge, wouldn't you?' The orange nail polish on her toes was chipped. Martha looked at him. 'Is your mother dead?' she said.

Cillian nodded. 'And so is my father. And I'm just telling you that so you don't put your size sevens into it later on, when we're having dinner.' This was well outside of Cillian's comfort zone. It was not that he was shy and retiring but he liked to be certain of things. With Martha, he did not feel certain of anything. He felt uncertain. He folded his arms across the breadth of his chest and looked at her, as if uncertainty was a language that he did not speak and would never learn.

'Dinner?' she said and her tone was one of mild surprise.

'Are you a vegetarian?' It was the first question he ever asked her.

'You don't get feet like these eating lentils.'

'I know a place that grills great steaks.'

'What about wine?'

'I'll throw in a bottle of wine.'

'Just the one?'

'As many as you like.'

'So long as you don't insist on paying. Men who pay think they're entitled to sex.'

'I won't insist on paying.'

'Cheapskate.'

That's how it began.

Three and a half years ago. They'd been happy, then they hadn't and then it had ended.

Simple as that.

It happened all the time.

*   *   *

49

He had wondered if he would bump into her while he was in Dublin but he hadn't. Until now. Her name on his screen.

'What's the favour, boss?' Cillian said.

'It's not really a favour, more of a demand,' the Super said, unnecessarily Cillian felt.

'Fine,' Cillian said, wrestling himself into his jacket.

'You don't even know what it is,' the Super said, a little put out by Cillian's lack of resistance. He loved a bit of verbal, the Super.

'OK, then, what is it?'

'Just . . . when the ex rings you . . .'

'Why would she ring me?' The Super and his wife were recently separated and neither were adapting well to the altered landscape of their lives. Despite their many differences, they shared a keen sense of melodrama and Cillian did not want to be in the middle of it; he was after a quiet life.

'I might have told her that I was seeing a French bird.'

'What does that have to do with me?' Cillian knew that the Super wasn't seeing anyone, French or otherwise.

'I said she was a friend of your sister Joan's. The French bird. I said she was a nurse. She's on sabbatical, at the same hospital where Joan works. We met in the Market Bar. We were having tapas, right? Are you writing this down?'

'This is the last time, boss.' Cillian pulled open the front door of the station.

'Where are you going?' said the Super.

'I've . . . got some business to attend to. I won't be long.'

'There's another case briefing in an hour.'

'I'll be back by then.'

He didn't have to go and see her. He probably shouldn't. He went anyway. He put it down to curiosity. That compulsion to turn to the last page of a book you were reading. To see how it ended.

The day, although dull and cold, was dry. The wind gathered around his head, blowing his hair into his eyes, and he remembered that he had promised Stella he would travel to Donegal at the weekend. Now that was out of the question. He probably wouldn't get back there until he'd reached the end of his six-month secondment in Dublin which, he was shocked to find, was only a couple of weeks away.

Stella had mentioned an occasion. Some family do. He couldn't remember exactly what. The Bennett family was huge and there was always some celebration or other. It was difficult to keep up.

'Will you get your hair cut?' she'd asked on the phone last night. He'd smiled at the request but acceded to it.

Martha used to cut his hair. She wouldn't say a word, just kick one of her kitchen chairs towards him, steer him onto it. *This shouldn't hurt*, she'd say before she came at him with the scissors.

He hadn't thought about her in ages. And now here she was, back in his head like she'd never left.

Cillian drove into the estate where Martha lived, negotiating the complicated series of lefts and rights that led to her apartment.

She mightn't even remember him.

She would remember him.

It had been something, back in the day.

And then it hadn't.

Martha had dispensed with him quicker than she could down a tumbler of Scotch and that had been that.

Water under the bridge.

The buzzer wasn't working and the main door of the apartment block was on the latch. He took the stairs to the third floor and stood outside her apartment door. It was not someplace he had expected to be again.

He wondered if she was looking at him through the peephole in the door. Wondered what she would see. If she'd think he had changed. Aged. It was two years since they'd split up. Two years was long enough for time to plant its fist on your face. Standing there, he felt every day of his forty-one years. He passed his hand along his jaw. He should have shaved.

The door opened and she stood there and his first feeling was one of relief. That she was unchanged. She was the same as he remembered. The long red hair. The pale face, cluttered with small circles of freckles. The green eyes. The lengthy, sturdy body, hidden beneath an oversized navy T-shirt and a baggy pair of track pants. The lump on her temple was impressive and a collection of bruises bloomed along one side of her face.

'What the fuck are you doing here?' she said.

'Lovely to see you too.'

'Aren't you supposed to be in the back of beyonds?'

'Do you mean Donegal?'

'That's what I said.'

'I've been seconded to Dublin these past few months. A task force. Short-term.'

'Is this about yesterday?' Martha asked. She'd always been like that. Keen to get to the point.

Cillian nodded. 'Can I come in?'

'Why?'

'Because I want to talk to you. About the robbery.'

'I gave a statement to one of your lot yesterday.'

'I know. I read it. It was great. Really detailed.'

'I know.'

'It's just . . . there's a kid involved . . . he's only fourteen years old. We haven't picked him up yet but we will and he'll face serious charges – attempted murder possibly – but . . . I'm not completely convinced that—'

'OK, OK, spare me the sob story, you can come in.' Martha

stepped back and widened the door so that Cillian could walk past her, into the sitting room that he remembered, where the couch still sat, the one that was too big for the room, the one she'd bought anyway. It was one of those squashy couches that made it difficult to get up once you'd sat down. The place was in darkness, the curtains shut tight across the patio door. He flicked the switch on the lamp beside the couch. He didn't sit on the couch. He pulled out a kitchen chair instead, sat down, glanced around. He couldn't see any sign of Dan. No meditation mats or empty bottles of . . . what was that fancy Champagne? Bollinger? On top of the sideboard lay her violin, intact now although the cracks along its body were still visible.

'Still playing?' he said, nodding towards the instrument. Martha looked at the violin and nodded, colouring slightly as if she, too, remembered the last time he had seen the violin.

He saw how she refused to wince as she settled herself on the couch.

'Have you been to A&E?'

'Don't be ridiculous.'

'Let me at least take a look at you,' he said.

'I'm fine. It looks worse than it is.'

He stood anyway, walked to the fridge. 'You need something to take the swelling down,' he said, opening the freezer door. It was better stocked than it used to be, not a single packet of Findus Crispy Pancakes to be seen. He rummaged through the frozen pastry and chicken fillets and found a bag of peas, which he handed to her. She hesitated but then held it against her face.

'I'll make tea,' he said, taking the milk out of the fridge. 'You look like you could do with a cup. Have you eaten?'

'No.'

'Do you want toast?'

'You don't have to bother yourself, I'm well able to—'

'Do you want toast?'

'Yes,' she said, adding a quiet, 'please,' after a pause.

He scanned the shelves quickly but could see no wine or whiskey bottles. He put the kettle on, dropped two slices of bread into the toaster.

'So . . .' began Cillian, leaning against the kitchen counter, waiting for the kettle to boil. 'How've you been?'

'Well, I've a lump growing out of my forehead and a bruise on my side the size of a football but apart from that, yeah, fine. I've been fine. You?'

'Well, I've a paper cut on my finger but other than that, yeah, fine. I've been fine.'

She smiled, then winced as the bruise on her face made itself felt. 'I've always said police work was dangerous,' she said.

It seemed almost normal, Cillian felt. Like their last conversation had never happened. Then Martha shifted on the couch and said, 'So, have you made any arrests?' and it wasn't normal anymore. Or it was. Just a different kind of normal. He was here on business.

Cillian shook his head. 'Not yet. The guy who I'm fairly sure organised the robbery has a credible alibi, as do his two cronies.'

'And the kid? The one you feel responsible for?'

'I don't feel responsible for him.'

'You always feel responsible for people.'

He knew what she was referring to. But it hadn't been an intervention. It had been concern. He shouldn't have. He had rocked their precarious boat until it capsized.

Cillian shrugged. 'He's a Polish lad. Roman Matus. Himself and his mother haven't had it easy since they moved to Ireland. I think Roman was doing a bit of running for the drug dealer who I suspect carried out yesterday's robbery but what happened at the bank . . . I don't know, it doesn't fit with what I know of the kid. You were there. I'd like to get your insight.'

54

'I see,' Martha said, and then she paused and looked at him. 'Why did you move back to Donegal?' She asked the question with her usual brand of curiosity and directness. It had taken him a while to get used to it in the beginning.

Cillian considered making something up or saying something glib, skirting the issue. Instead he said, 'Something happened on a job. A case I was working on. A kid got killed and . . . I needed a change of scene, I suppose.' It had happened a month after they'd split up but there was no need to mention that. They both knew about that.

'There was an enquiry, wasn't there?'

Cillian nodded. It had been reported in the papers.

The kettle whistled and he turned, glad of the diversion.

'Tea or coffee?' he called.

'Tea, please. Black, and will you leave the teabag in?'

He didn't tell her that he remembered.

He set the tea and toast on a coffee table, lifted the table and placed it beside the couch. He took out his phone, logged on to Pulse and located a photograph of Roman that had been taken when the boy had been cautioned a few months ago.

Roman looked younger than he was in the picture. Fear often had that effect on these kids' faces. He held the screen towards Martha and she nodded and said, 'That's him.'

'Did you see him shoot the old man?' Cillian resumed his seat on the kitchen chair.

Martha's eyes narrowed the way they had always done when she thought about things. She had never been a blurter, always considered questions before answering them, like she was checking the copy for accuracy.

She shook her head. 'No.'

'Tell me what happened.'

Martha leaned her head against the back of the couch. She seemed suddenly tired.

'I'm sorry,' said Cillian. 'It's just—'

'I know, I know, you feel responsible.' Her tone was dry but she told him anyway. Her recollection was almost word-for-word identical to the statement he had read that morning.

'So,' he said when she finished, 'you can't be a hundred per cent sure that it was Roman who fired the gun?'

Martha looked at him and her look was sceptical. She reached for her tea, wrapped her long hands around the mug, shook her head. 'No,' she said. 'Is that what you want to hear?'

'I'm just after the facts.'

'No,' she said again and there was a sigh in the word this time, a weariness, and he found himself wondering if she had slept and thinking that she probably hadn't and knowing that it was none of his business either way. He stood up to go.

'You didn't make yourself a coffee,' Martha said then.

'No.'

'You used to drink a lot of coffee.' Her voice was faraway, like she was remembering something about him. About them.

He looked at his notebook.

'You went into the bank with Tara, I see here. How's she doing?'

'She's met somebody, would you believe. She's even engaged, kind of,' Martha said.

'Kind of?'

'You know Tara. She's not your common-or-garden all-singing, all-dancing lesbian.'

Cillian nodded. 'I didn't have her down as the marrying kind.'

'Neither did she,' said Martha. 'But then she met Mathilde.' Martha shook her head. 'I suppose,' she said, 'people can change.' Her tone was flip, like it didn't mean anything, what she said. It was just a collection of words, a sentence, something to fill the gaps. He put his hand on the back of the kitchen chair he had vacated. He felt awkward now, standing.

'Anyway,' Martha went on as if he hadn't stood up, as if he wasn't feeling awkward, 'she had gone into the bank to tell her sister – you remember Katherine? She's the bank manager there – that she's gay and—'

'She still hasn't come out?'

'Not in any formal sense, no. And definitely not to her family, although nobody would blame her on that score. She dragged me along for a bit of support. She had to go to hospital afterwards. The doctor says she's in shock.'

'Understandable, in the circumstances,' said Cillian.

'Not for Tara.' Martha lifted the bag of peas from her temple, held it now against the bruising along her cheekbone. She chewed at a corner of her bottom lip and Cillian remembered that this was what she did when she was worried.

'Is she in Beaumont?'

'She is. I'm going to go in to see her this morning. Does your sister still work there?'

'Yeah. Joan's the sister-in-charge there now.'

'That's pretty impressive.'

'She loves it.'

In the silence that followed, Cillian could almost hear the two of them struggle to come up with something to say. The silence swelled, moved between them, like a complicated piece of music. 'I'll leave you to get some rest,' he finally came up with.

'It's funny seeing you after all this time,' Martha said and her voice was lower now, smaller somehow. He felt sort of relieved that he wasn't the only one feeling awkward.

'Yeah,' he said.

'How've you been?'

'Fine, yeah   .' He trailed off, then rallied with, 'And you? And your husband? Stan, isn't it?'

'Dan.' In spite of the bruising and swelling, Cillian could tell that there was a small smile on Martha's face and that it was probably related to his deliberate misremembering of Dan's name. He conceded that it was pretty childish. 'Oh, yeah, Dan. How is he?'

'Fine.'

'Good.'

Cillian looked at his notes, leafed through them.

'What about you?' Martha asked then, looking at him with her investigative journalist look. From Elona when she'd been an investigative journalist. Back when he'd first met her.

'Oh, you know, nothing major, just saving the world one case at a time.'

She smiled. She had always found his idealism both amusing and uplifting although she had never specified which finding held more weight.

'Are you seeing anyone?' Her directness was something he had learned to live with.

'Yes.'

'What's her name?'

'Stella.'

Martha nodded and he wondered if she already knew. About him and Stella. Although why would she? He couldn't read her. He could never read her, even back in the days when he'd thought he could.

'I should go.' He walked into the kitchen, picked his jacket off the handle of the fridge where he'd left it. Martha's eyes were on him as he turned.

'You'll be OK?' he said.

'I will.'

'I'll see myself out,' he said, struggling into his jacket.

'Thanks for making me tea and toast. I hadn't realised I was hungry.'

'You're welcome.' The awkwardness was there again, where it

had no business being. Cillian felt it as something physical. He didn't know how to say goodbye without it sounding graver than he intended. Final.

In the end, he didn't say goodbye. Instead, he said, 'We'll keep you posted. And if you think of anything else that might be relevant, you can . . . call me. Or the station.'

'OK,' said Martha, who looked exhausted now. Even the freckles on her face were pale.

'Get some sleep, Martha.' Her name, in his mouth, sounded strange. He hadn't said it out loud in a long time.

'I think I was asleep.' she said. 'I had a strange dream.'

He wanted to ask her about her dream. About the strangeness of it.

Instead, he let himself out as he said he would.

He had let himself out that last time too. Two years ago.

Six

Night had fallen. Roman stood in the middle of a field, looked around him. Up ahead, he could make out a dark line of trees. The only sound was the labour of his breath and the pounding of his blood through his veins. He gulped at the sharp night air. He could no longer smell the fumes of the burning car.

When his breath returned to him, he began to walk. He didn't know what time it was or where he was. Lech had shown him how to navigate using the moon and the stars. But the sky was black tonight, the stars hidden behind a thick blanket of low-lying cloud.

Roman kept walking. The wind whipped around his bare head, his body. His face was numb. So were his fingers, his feet. He supposed he must be hungry although he didn't feel it; he thought it was because of the cold, the insistence of it. He didn't mind the rain at first. It was just a drizzle.

In the absence of a plan, Roman decided a couple of things. He would not think about Jimmy. What he might be planning. What he might do. To Roman if he caught him. What he could do. To Mama. Roman knew what Jimmy was capable of.

One of his mother's newly learned expressions from her English classes at the nursing home was *caught between a rock and a hard place*. She had found it amusing, the expression, when she explained it to Roman. That was only last week and now, here he was, exactly as Rosa had explained. Caught between a rock and a hard place.

He thought trapped might be a better word.

He saw the building just as he thought he couldn't walk one more step. Mama would have called it a sign. Roman called it a barn. A rusting, listing barn but it was unlocked and a couple of hay bales inside gave off a dense, sweet smell. Roman pulled the door behind him and forced himself to stand still while his eyes adjusted to the dark. It was as thick as mud, the dark. It was like a living thing, moving around him.

He'd never been afraid of the dark before.

A scratching noise in the corner. Mice probably. Or rats. Adam had told Roman that only rats and cockroaches would survive a zombie apocalypse. He didn't know Roman was scared of rats. Not scared, exactly.

The noise was mice. Definitely mice. Roman wrapped his arms around himself and forced himself to stand there, wait.

Gradually, shapes grew out of the dark. Wooden stalls: empty. A three-legged milking stool. Frayed rope hanging off a long nail hammered into the wall. A shadow in the corner that looked like a man with his back to Roman which turned out to be an ancient overcoat that smelled of damp and moss.

He pulled handfuls of hay from a bale, arranged it on the ground in a stall. If Adam were here, he would call it an adventure. Find something to laugh about. Roman would laugh too because Adam was funny. Adam made him laugh.

He lay down and covered himself with the overcoat. He shut his eyes against the needle sharpness of the night air, the dampness of his clothes, the stink of the overcoat. Tried to will himself to sleep.

He was so tired. Even the act of falling asleep seemed like too much effort.

Mama would not be asleep. He knew that.

He pictured her lying in her bed in their rented room in Jimmy's house. The room that Rosa had divided in two by draping a sheet across a makeshift line between her single bed and his sofa bed. 'You need some privacy,' she'd told him the day she did that, 'now that you are becoming a man.' Roman was supposed to lift the duvet off the sofa bed every morning, store it on top of the wardrobe, fold the bed back inside the sofa. Make the room seem more like a living room than a bedroom. He rarely did.

He saw her, wide-eyed in the dark, staring at the sofa bed where Roman should be, worrying. Mouthing a prayer, maybe. She prayed every night. Asked God to bless everyone and mind everyone. Even Uncle Lech, who had left everything in such a mess.

'Don't speak ill of the dead,' Mama had told Roman.

Roman should have known, he often thought, afterwards. Everything had been going well. Too well. Something bad had to happen. That was the way things were.

Roman thought that bad things happened because of money. Not having enough of it. It was like a magnet, being poor. It attracted bad news. Like the way that he got that chest infection and Adam didn't. They both got soaked that day. Wandered around Swords in their rain-wet clothes all afternoon. But it was Roman who got the chest infection. And Adam – whose father had a boat in his front garden and whose mother went to the beauty salon every Friday and called it her 'me' time – didn't get a chest infection so his parents didn't have to spend fifty euro on a doctor, then another twenty-five euro on antibiotics and paracetamol. Instead, Adam got to go to his piano lesson and his scout meeting and his swimming class and his tae kwan do lesson.

He should have known that the bad thing – when it happened – would be really bad, seeing as there had been so many good things since they'd arrived in Ireland. A collection of good things. Great things, actually. Like Meadhbh, for example. It wasn't spelled the way it sounded. That happened a lot with Irish names. She was shorter than Roman, which didn't happen a lot. Blonde hair in a high ponytail. Clear blue eyes that fixed on Roman when he spoke, as if he were saying something interesting. Something she mightn't already know. Although she knew a lot. She was the cleverest girl in the class. The cleverest person. And still she looked at Roman when he spoke as if it might be interesting, whatever it was he was going to say. They walked home from school together: Meadhbh and Adam and Roman. They lived close enough to each other so it made sense but it was more than that, Roman felt. It was like he was part of something. Like the basketball team the three of them were on.

'Are you not too short for basketball?' Jimmy had asked him.

Roman flushed. He had thought the same thing. 'You are still growing, Roman,' Mama had said. She rooted out a photograph album, pointed to photographs of her father, her brother. 'Look,' she said. 'The Matus family produce tall men, see?'

He wanted to ask how tall his father had been, but he didn't. Nobody ever talked about Roman's father. Not Babcia, not Uncle Lech, not his aunts. Roman's father was the blank space on the forms his mother filled out.

Coach put Roman on the wing. She said that height wasn't the only thing that made you a good basketball player. Speed and stamina were important too.

That was another of the good things that had happened.

'It's football you should be at,' Jimmy told him. 'You'd make a ton of money and have the women crawlin' all over you.' Roman didn't want women crawling all over him. He wanted to shoot the winning basket in the final against St Michael's who almost always won the inter-schools league. To be named *man of the match* and have the team carry him off the court on their shoulders the way they'd done to Adam that time.

He practised shooting hoops for hours after school the week leading up to the final. On the day of the match, he walked home from school to get his gear that Mama had washed the night before and draped over the radiator in their room. She'd said it would be dry by the time he got home from school.

Jimmy's motorbike was parked outside that day. That meant Uncle Lech was home. Lech often came home in the middle of the afternoon when Mama was at work. Roman presumed it was because he was the boss and could do what he liked. He hoped his uncle wouldn't be in one of his moods.

Jimmy had already opened the front door by the time Roman reached for the lock with his key. He smiled when he saw Roman. 'Ah, Romeo, how's tricks?' he said.

Jimmy called him Romeo. It was because of Meadhbh. Jimmy thought Meadhbh was Roman's girlfriend. Adults always thought girls were your girlfriend. Jimmy looked like one of those adults who didn't realise they were an adult. He had long brown hair to his shoulders and a line of studs up his ear, one at the edge of his eyebrow and another on the side of his nose. He had a tattoo of a falcon coiled around his arm, the head of it huge against the swell of his upper arm muscle. Roman had only seen it once, ages ago. Jimmy didn't usually take off his leather jacket when he visited Uncle Lech. He didn't stay long enough.

'Hi, Jimmy.'

'Don't go disturbing your uncle, won't you not? He's having a bit of a lie-down.'

Roman shook his head. 'I won't.'

His gear smelled of washing powder. He folded it and unzipped his sports bag. Inside, Mama had packed a banana, a bottle of water, a chocolate bar and a piece of paper. Roman unfolded it. *Powodzenia!* it said. She signed the note as she always did: *ściskam mocno*. The English translation was even more embarrassing: *I'm hugging you tight*.

Still, he tucked the piece of paper into the zip pocket of his hoodie – a lucky charm – and checked his watch. Three o'clock. Plenty of time.

He stood at the kitchen counter, drank a pint of milk and ate half a packet of Hobnobs. Mama said he was like a leaky bucket: she could never fill him. He put the empty glass in the dishwasher, swept the crumbs up with his hands and threw them in the bin. Lech said he didn't expect Mama to clean the duplex. He said they could get a cleaner, but Mama said she didn't like the idea of a stranger in their home. Roman didn't have to do chores, she said. She wanted him to concentrate on his schoolwork. 'I have high hopes for you, my Roman.'

Later, he told the police that he didn't go looking for Lech because Lech was in his bedroom and he didn't like to be disturbed when he was in his bedroom. He didn't tell them about the sound he heard, just before he left. A bump. Or a bang, perhaps. Like Lech had dropped something, maybe. The dull thud of a book. Except that Lech didn't read books. Roman heard the sound, stopped for a moment, then continued on his way. He picked up his bag, wiped the milk off his top lip with the back of his hand and shouted, 'Seeya,' up the stairs. Perhaps Lech had said, 'Seeya,' back but the sound was lost in the crash of the front door closing behind him.

His mother always said he'd pull that door off its hinges some day.

The match was cancelled in the end. The minibus bringing the team from the school in Drogheda had been involved in a traffic accident and some of the players had to go to hospital for check-ups and observation. Nothing serious, their coach said. Just a precaution.

Roman walked home with Adam and Meadhbh. He kicked a stone all the way. 'The match is only postponed, Roman. We'll play it another day,' Meadhbh said.

'I know.' Roman liked things to happen when they were supposed to happen. Mama said that he had always been like that. Even as a baby, feeding every three hours, on the hour, two burps after a handful of gentle pats on the back.

'Let's get a bag of chips,' said Adam, who punctuated most of his activities – piano, scouts, swimming, tae kwan do – with food of one kind or another. It was a testament to these activities that he wasn't the size of a house. Or a duplex.

Roman was about to say yes to the chips, even though Mama had cooked an enormous curry last night and there was more than enough left for dinner. He could hear the two euros Jimmy had handed him before he left – *a bit of courtin' money for the young squire* – jingling in his pocket and he thought that hot, salty chips, crispy on the outside, soft on the inside, might dampen the disappointment of the cancelled – postponed – match. But then his phone rang and he answered it and it was Mama and she was crying.

Adam's mother drove him to the hospital. It took ages to get there, with the traffic and the rain that had begun a dreary, insistent onslaught on the day. Adam sat in the back with him but didn't say anything. It was never easy to get a word in when Adam's mother was around.

'I'm sure your uncle will be just fine,' she said, her eyebrows scarcer than usual after her Friday-morning trip to the beauty salon. 'Your poor mother. She must have gotten a terrible shock when she found him.

'And he's a young man still, isn't he, Roman? He couldn't be more than thirty-five, surely? I'm sure he'll be fine. He'll be right as rain.'

Roman did his best not to think about that day. He certainly never spoke about it. Not even to Mama. Especially not Mama. Her face was hard to look at, afterwards.

The police were involved because of the cocaine. They wanted to know where Lech got it. Roman thought about the small brown-paper packages he sometimes saw Jimmy slip to Lech before he opened the front door and left.

Roman said nothing.

He told Adam's mother, when she asked, that it had been a heart attack. Sudden and huge. He wouldn't have felt a thing. That's what Mama told Babcia when she rang her. She didn't mention the cocaine either. The overdose.

Everything was different when they got back from the funeral. It was in Puck, the funeral. Babcia said Mama had to bring her boy home. Said it was the least that she could do. She never called him Lech. She said, My boy. Mama said he was her mother's favourite and Roman thought that was true. It didn't seem to bother Mama. It was just one of those facts.

Mama nodded when Babcia talked about her boy's entrepreneurial spirit, his sense of adventure, his courage, his kindness and strength. She didn't tell Babcia about the lapsed health insurance policy and Lech leaving nothing behind him only debt. She nodded and made pots of coffee and poured careful measures of vodka into neighbours' glasses. She picked out a headstone and arranged to pay it off month by month. 'If it were you we were burying, my boy would write a cheque,' Babcia said.

Mama nodded again.

Everyone said Roman was like him. Like Lech. But Roman was never going to be like him.

A drug addict.

A loser.

Mama slapped Roman's face the day he said that. The day after they came back from Poland. They stood outside the duplex with their bags packed. Mama pushed the keys into the letterbox. Mortgage payments. There was another thing Uncle Lech had forgotten to do.

It was the only time she'd ever hit him. The noise was a sharp crack and, for a while afterwards, the outline of her fingers was red, across the side of his face.

'I'm sorry, I'm sorry, I'm sorry. Oh, my Roman, I'm so sorry.' She put her arms around him and cried into the side of his head.

Her tears dripped along the edge of his ear, made it itch. He wondered then why they had come back to Ireland after the funeral. They had nowhere to live, Mama had no job and the man with the sour face in the dole office told her that there would be no dole money coming her way because it turned out that Uncle Lech had forgotten to give the tax she had paid to whoever he was supposed to give tax to.

But Babcia didn't know any of that. Perhaps that was why they came back. Mama didn't want her to know any of that.

They stayed in a B&B for four nights while Mama looked for jobs and Roman went back to school and didn't tell Adam or Meadhbh about the duplex and the cocaine and the catering company that didn't seem to be a company anymore, just a lot of money owed to a collection of different people.

Then Jimmy came to visit. To pay his respects, he said.

The door of their bedroom in the B&B was ajar when Roman returned from school. Roman stopped at the door. Listened. He could hear Jimmy's voice. Not his usual voice. This one was low and sort of slithery, like the way Roman had imagined Voldemort's snake, Nagini, talked. Through the gap between the hinges, Roman saw them. Jimmy and his mother. Rosa's back was pressed against the door of the wardrobe and Jimmy stood in front of her, much too close, the tip of his forefinger tracing a line along her collar bone that jutted from the edge of the V-neck T-shirt she wore.

'. . . can come to some understanding, I'm sure,' Roman heard Jimmy say in his snake voice.

Roman shoved open the door and the handle banged against the wall, a loud thump, making Jimmy jump, swing around. Rosa sidled away, moved towards Roman.

'Are you alright, Mama?' said Roman. He felt the force of his pulse beating at the back of his throat. He clenched his fists.

Jimmy spread his hands. 'Of course she is, son. Your pretty Mama and I were talking about the future. Weren't we, darling?'

He looked at Rosa who nodded. Then he turned to Roman again. When Jimmy smiled, he looked like the front window of a jeweller's shop, with all the gold caps he had.

'And,' Jimmy went on, 'we've come up with a great idea. Haven't we, Rosa?' Another nod from Rosa. Jimmy stretched his arm out, clasped his hand around Rosa's slight shoulder. 'And don't you be worrying your pretty little head about paying a deposit, Rosa. As I said, I'm sure we can come to some arrangement, you and I.'

Mama said, 'No,' real quick and then, after a pause, she said, 'There's no need, I mean. We can pay,' in a voice that Roman could barely hear.

They moved into Jimmy's spare room the next day. Rosa got herself first one job, then another, and another and the first two things she paid every week were the rent and as much as she could off what Lech owed Jimmy. Four hundred euros a month for the room. The other bedrooms in the house were occupied by Jimmy himself and a couple that Jimmy said was hardly ever there. 'They work round the clock,' he told Rosa and Roman. 'Foreigners too. I'd say they're from Poland.'

They were Lithuanians.

At night, Mama dragged their suitcase against the door, jammed it under the handle. Jimmy said Rosa could store the case in the attic but she said, no. No, thank you. She told Roman they wouldn't be staying long; just long enough for them to get square with Jimmy. To get back on their feet.

Four hundred euros. Jimmy said it was bargain basement. Roman saw Mama count it out on the floor in their room. The last tenner came from the jar of coins she kept in the wardrobe. Roman organised the coins into groups of five, ten, twenty and fifty cents, then built towers out of them until he made it to ten euro.

Jimmy was often in the kitchen when Roman arrived home

from school. The air was blue with smoke. Sometimes, he offered Roman a cigarette.

'Ah, Romeo, Romeo, wherefore fart thou, Romeo?' Jimmy thought this was funny. Roman smiled when he said it because, well, it was Jimmy's house and, even though it wasn't nearly as nice as the duplex, Rosa told him to be nice to Jimmy. To be polite.

'But don't talk to him more than you have to. Make sure you do your homework. And you're to eat your dinner in our room,' Mama told him. 'OK?'

Roman didn't like eating upstairs in their room. The smell of food lingered for ages. At least in the kitchen there was somewhere to sit other than a bed. In the kitchen, you felt like you were eating a meal. In the room, it was just trying not to get crumbs on the sheets.

And sometimes Jimmy was nice. Like that time he took Roman to see the new Avengers film. Roman had seen the ads for it but he didn't mention the cinema anymore. Not since the coin towers.

He told Adam and Meadhbh that he'd already seen whatever film they asked him to go to now. 'You must spend your entire *life* in the cinema,' Adam had said, a look of naked admiration on his face. Meadhbh didn't say anything.

He went to the cinema with Jimmy in the end. He knew he shouldn't have. Mama would have been angry if she'd found out.

Still. He went. He somehow knew Jimmy wouldn't mention it to Rosa.

Mama managed to get a kitchen porter job in the Moon & Stars pub at lunchtimes. Early mornings, cleaning in Penneys. A few evening shifts at a nursing home. And in between, a handful of cleaning jobs in some houses in the area.

Roman told Adam and Meadhbh that he'd moved house. Like it was no big deal. And he said that he hated the food in the school canteen and that was why he brought a packed lunch every day now. Everything was different now. Still, life went on. Mama said that no matter what happened, life went on.

It just kept going on and on.

Roman must have fallen asleep eventually because he was awoken by a knocking sound, outside the barn. At first, he thought he was in his room in Jimmy's house. There was someone knocking on the front door which was weird because there was a bell so why weren't they ringing it?

Roman sat up, pulled a piece of straw out of his hair, rubbed his eyes. Through the gaps between the roof of the barn and the walls, he could see the light of day struggling to make an impact on the sky. His first feeling was one of relief. That the night was behind him.

The knocking noise wasn't a knocking noise at all. It was more like a hammering sound. The strike of a hammer against wood. It sounded close.

All of a sudden, it stopped and the silence that came in its stead was like a ringing in Roman's ears. He strained towards it. Now he could hear someone breathing.

Roman lifted the overcoat off him and stood up, careful not to make a sound. He steadied himself with a hand on the edge of one of the wooden stalls. His clothes felt stiff with damp, his jacket and jeans heavy on his body. He thought, if he wasn't so cold he'd feel hungry. The last thing he'd eaten was the porridge that Mama had left for him in the kitchen yesterday morning. That seemed like a long time ago now.

There was a small hole in the wall of the barn, big enough to accommodate Roman's eye. He peered through it and saw the rump of a horse. He blinked and looked again. Yes, it was a horse. A white one, saddled, with mud-spattered legs and a long, untidy mane. Beside the animal, a man crouched low to the ground with a hammer in his hand, which he was using to drive a wooden post into the ground beside a gate that Roman had not noticed last night. The man stood and turned, his face lined with concentration. He stayed in that position, the man, looking towards the barn, as if he could see something there. As if he could see Roman. The boy took a step back and there was a clatter as his foot connected with a bucket – something else he had not noticed the night before – and the thing tipped onto its side, spilling a small mound of dusty oats onto the concrete floor.

The noise was huge. Or so it seemed to Roman.

'Who's in there?' The man's voice was loud. Almost a shout. The horse whinnied.

The door was yanked open. The man, framed in the doorway, looked bigger now. In one hand, the hammer.

'What the hell are you doing in my barn, you pup?'

There was a gap between the man's leg and the edge of the barn. Roman dived through it and felt a tug as the man grabbed the end of his jacket. Now there was shouting and it was hard to tell if it was coming from Roman or the man or maybe both of them. Roman slithered out of his jacket and ran, leaving the man standing there, his jacket in one hand. The horse snorted, stamped his hoof against the ice-hard ground. 'I'm ringing the police,' the man roared after him. 'Trespassing and damaging property. Get back here.'

Roman cleared the gate, ran down a lane that turned into a muddy track. He knew if he stopped he would freeze without the jacket. He knew if he stopped he mightn't be able to start again. He kept running, didn't look back to see if the man was behind him.

Oddly, he thought about Meadhbh. The way they used to pick the dandelions that had gone to seed, blow on their white, fluffy heads and scatter the dried seeds to the wind. He felt like that now. Like one of those seeds he had watched, borne away on the wind.

As a kid, he had wondered where they would end up.

What might happen to them.

He ran.

Seven

When Cillian left, Martha hobbled into the kitchen, turned on the tap, scooped water in the cup of her hand and washed down two ibuprofen. She needed to move, keep busy, distract herself. Get dressed for starters. Go to the hospital, sit outside a meeting, ring the editor to whom she had promised the article yesterday at 4 p.m. She would explain that she had been indisposed and that the indisposition had been outside of her control and that she could send the article by four o'clock this afternoon instead. If the editor thought she'd been drinking, there was nothing Martha could do about that. She hadn't been drinking. But it had been a close call. Too close. In her head, she could still hear the creak of the door into the Pound pub, swinging open, telling her everything would be alright if only she'd step inside.

She spread her hands on the draining board, closed her eyes, tried to gather herself. Things had been OK. Better than OK. She had spent a long time – much longer than she'd antici- pated – carefully rebuilding. For a long time, there had been a scaffolding around her life as she had gone about the business of putting herself back together. And for a while there – a good while – she had been fine. A stand-alone structure. Fortified. And now, all of a sudden, the ground beneath her felt unstable. Tara in hospital. And Cillian. Reappearing all of a sudden. Like the past itself, reaching out to grab her and drag her back.

She straightened, reached for her pouch of tobacco. The routine – rolling the cigarette, lighting it, taking that first, heady drag – helped. And the pain in her body – not yet numbed by the tablets – had its uses. It distracted her. In her head, she made a list. Phone the editor. Drive to the hospital. Sit outside a meeting.

She wouldn't think about Cillian Larkin.

Martha struggled into a short green dress, a pair of black leggings and her Doc Martens, which she tried and failed to lace. She left her hair down because she found it too heavy to lift in the circumstances.

She covered the worst of the bruising on her face with a layer of foundation, located the biggest, darkest sunglasses she owned, left a voicemail for the editor and left the apartment.

She drove to the hospital and thought about Cillian Larkin.

The way he hadn't sat on the couch. He'd been about to, Martha felt sure. And then he'd remembered. All the things that had happened on that couch. The conversations they'd had. All the ways they had been there together. He had stopped just short of the couch, then sort of reversed until he was sitting on one of the kitchen chairs instead. But there were memories there too. Cillian, straddling the chair the wrong way around, his long hands draped over the back of the chair, as Martha cut his hair, the tickle of his breath warm against the skin of her arm as she snipped at the fringe that hung into his eyes like fraying curtains.

'Don't take too much off,' he'd say.

'I'll take as much off as I like.' But she never took too much. It had been dark then, his hair, the grey only beginning to make itself understood. Now it was almost all grey. A metal grey. It needed a good cut. It had always needed a cut, no matter how often she had taken the scissors to it.

He was no beauty. His nose was long and narrow and his bushy eyebrows held a suggestion of mono-brow and his cheeks bore the faded scars of a virulent strain of teenage acne. But, she'd had to concede – and not just when she'd been drinking – that there was something about Cillian Larkin, although quite what it was was difficult to put your finger on. The height, she supposed, might have had something to do with it. The brown eyes were wide and fringed with those annoyingly thick, dark eyelashes that men take for granted and women covet. He'd been mad about eye contact so that you felt sometimes, when he looked at you, like you were the only person in the world. Martha had always looked away first.

He seemed the same, mostly. Same clothes – straight navy jeans, plain navy T-shirt, black leather jacket, runners – but different too. In their last few months, he had looked worried. Fearful. She had resented that look, knowing what it was he was worried about. Fearful of.

The details were coming fast now, hurling themselves at her, as if she hadn't decided not to think about him.

She thought about him. She came out with her hands up, gave herself up to it. Perhaps it was time. Overdue even. Maybe she needed to take those thoughts out of storage, look through them before she committed them to black plastic bags, tied them with string at the top, said goodbye.

She'd never said goodbye.

Not in the traditional sense.

Now, she thought about the fine lines that fanned from the edges of his eyes. About the fact that they were longer now. How they deepened and spread when he laughed. And the way he used to laugh. With his mouth open so wide you could see all the way back to his larynx. And his mouth. The way it formed itself around his words this morning, slow and quiet, stirring memories of that same mouth, long ago, moving around her body, slow and insistent and thorough. 'If you're going to do a job, you have to do it right,' he'd said, lifting his head from between her legs when she got impatient with his pace, squirming beneath him. Then bending towards her again, with his

75

mouth, as if they had nothing but time. As if there was all the time in the world.

The driver in the car behind pressed his hand on the horn, left it there. Martha glanced up in time to see the traffic light change from green to amber, then red. She was surprised to see that she was almost at the hospital. The car behind was still beeping. She thought about thrusting her hand out the window, giving him the finger, but it seemed too much of an effort and, besides, the noise was helpful in its way. The way it filled her head and left no space there for anything else.

At the hospital, Martha stood in front of the directory and tried to work out where Tara's room might be. Katherine had told her which floor. Was it the third? The letters of the words seemed to shift and blur. Martha closed her eyes, shook her head, looked again. Or was it the fifth floor? St Colmcille's ward? That seemed to ring a—

'Martha?' The voice was familiar although it must have been nearly two years since she'd last spoken to Cillian's sister. At her child's christening, and the less said about that particular fiasco, the better.

'Joan. Hello. How are you?'

'Are you looking for your friend? Tara Bolton, isn't it? I was on the phone to Cillian earlier. He told me what happened at the bank. Terrible business.' Joan shook her head. She looked the same: short brown hair framing a round, youthful face, belying the fact that she was Cillian's senior by eight years. She wore no make-up or jewellery other than a fine gold band around her wedding-ring finger which had, Martha remembered, belonged to Cillian's mother. Her uniform was an immaculate white, her shoes a soft black leather, comfortable as slippers. In her hands, a clipboard. Behind her ear, a pen. She looked like someone you would call in an emergency. Someone whose presence in a room would make people feel somehow safer.

'Tara, yes, I wasn't sure . . .'

'She's in St Columba's ward, on the fourth floor.' Joan smiled. The smile held a trace of wariness, Martha felt. As if she was remembering the last time she'd seen Martha. Falling against the baptism font, unsteadying it, then trying to right it by reaching for the rim, only to unsteady it further still, causing it to crash to the ground and break into a fair few stony pieces.

Joan's baby boy – Naoise – had begun to cry those long, insistent cries peculiar to babies, and Martha had left shortly after that.

Joan's eyes rested briefly on Martha's face. Martha could see her taking in the surplus-to-requirement sunglasses, the shadow of bruises visible beneath the thick layer of make-up. Had Cillian told her everything that had happened at the bank? Probably not, for surely Joan would have made some reference to the bruises. For a brief moment, Martha wanted to tell her. That she hadn't been drunk and fallen over. That she hadn't had a drink for one year, four months, two weeks, four days. That she was different now.

She didn't say any of that. Instead, she gestured towards the bank of lifts. 'Thanks, I'll . . .'

'I'll grab a lift with you. I'm heading to the fifth floor,' said Joan, looking at the notes on her clipboard now, not looking at Martha's face and thinking the worst.

In the lift it was just the two of them. Joan pressed the button for the fourth and fifth floors. Martha studied the numbers on the screen, waited for the lift to move. She had always found social interactions difficult without the benefit of alcohol. Especially when she was around people who knew her when she drank. Since that day, when she'd quit, it was sometimes like learning how to *be* in the world, all over again.

Joan did not appear to notice her discomfiture. Nor was she a person who found silence awkward.

The lift groaned upwards.

'How's little Naoise?' Martha finally came up with.

'Not so little anymore. He's a big, bold three-year-old these days.' She whipped out her phone, touched the screen a couple of times and presented it to Martha. The similarity was uncanny. Naoise was the image of Cillian.

'He's lovely,' Martha said.

'You wouldn't say that if you'd seen him the other day in SuperValu. He took off all his clothes and ran through the fruit and veg aisle. It's his latest thing. Streaking through supermarkets.' Joan laughed so Martha did too, and when she stopped, the silence in the lift seemed deafening.

They were edging past the second floor now.

'You won't stay too long, will you?' said Joan. 'Tara's doctor reckons the post-traumatic stress is severe so it's best to keep things . . .' she looked at Martha with a sort of an apologetic smile, 'quiet, you know?'

Martha nodded, much too emphatically. 'Of course,' she said. Then, after a pause – they had just inched past the third floor – she said, 'And Joan, I . . . I just wanted to . . . I mean . . . the last time I . . .' She stumbled along the sentence, her voice straining as if her throat had constricted. That sometimes happened too, when she met someone she hadn't seen since the old days. The old her. She supposed it had something to do with shame. And anxiety. A potent mix.

'That's all water under the bridge,' said Joan. Martha hoped the water reference was unintentional.

'Oh, I saw your piece in the *Herald* last week,' Joan said then. 'About becoming a humanist celebrant, wasn't it?'

'Yeah, a friend of mine recently qualified as one.'

'It was really funny.'

'Thank you.'

'I'm glad to see you're working again. And Cillian's moved on too. He's really happy in Donegal. Everything worked out for the best in the end.'

The lift jerked and the doors slid open. Martha had to stop herself running out. Joan put one hand against the door to stop it closing. With her other hand, she pointed at a closed door along the corridor. 'She's in that room,' she said.

'Thanks,' said Martha, but the lift doors were already shutting. In the narrowing gap, she saw that Joan had taken the pen from behind her ear and was scribbling furiously on the clipboard, as if her meeting with Martha had never happened. Or had made no impression on her day.

Why would it? They had all moved on.

Martha approached the door that Joan had pointed to, knocked on it, waited and then, when nothing happened, she turned the handle, pushed at the door. The handle banged against the wall and the door swung back towards her. Katherine, who had been dozing in a chair beside the bed, jerked.

'Sorry, Katherine, I didn't mean to startle you.'

'Martha. I'm so glad you're here,' said Katherine. She looked exhausted, the skin on her face straining against the bone beneath. Damp strands of hair hung, listless, around her face.

'Maybe she'll respond to you.' Katherine nodded towards the bed, where the blankets covered Tara's head and the outline her body made against them was a small, tight circle.

'She must be melting under there.'

'If you pull the covers down, she only pulls them back up.'

From the bed, there was no sound. No movement. Katherine stood up, stretched. Martha could hear the pull of her bones.

'Have you been here all night?' she said.

Katherine nodded. 'I kept thinking she'd wake up and leap out of the bed, you know? Insist on getting out of here.'

Martha nodded. She had thought the same thing.

'What did the doctor say?'

'He thinks it's post-traumatic stress. Which might be true if it was someone else. But Tara? She was on that train that derailed and a plane that made an emergency landing. Not a bother on her.'

Martha remembered what Tara had done both times. She'd got on the next train, the next plane. She'd kept moving. She had never stopped moving, not since Martha had met her on her first day at school.

'Has she . . . spoken to you?' Martha asked.

Katherine shook her head. 'Not really. She hasn't even asked for her phone or laptop.'

'Jesus.'

'I know.'

On the table by the window was a bottle of Coke. Martha used to drink a lot of Coke. It was a handy drink for hiding things in. Things like vodka. Vodka didn't have a strong smell. And a vodka and Coke just looked like a Coke. Nobody passed any remarks when she drank a Coke.

She looked away. 'Where's your mother?' she asked Katherine.

'At mass. She's throwing novenas at the problem.'

Martha grinned even though it hurt her face.

'Besides,' Katherine went on, 'she says she can't look at Tara like this. She says it's too unnatural.'

That was the word Mrs Bolton had said that day, way back in 1993, when Ireland eventually agreed with Europe that adults who make love to other adults of the same sex, in their own safe homes, in their own sweet time, were no longer in danger of being arrested. Jailed. 'Unnatural,' said Tara's mother, shaking her head. 'Grown men doing God knows what to each other. It's just . . . unnatural.' Tara and Martha had been sitting at the kitchen table. Martha had opened her mouth to say something but Tara caught her eye, shook her head in her small, discreet way.

In the end, neither of them had said a word.

'Why don't you go home for a while?' Martha said to Katherine. 'I'll stay here with Tara.'

'Are you sure?'

'I promise I'll ring you if there're any developments.'

'Thanks, Martha.' Katherine lifted her coat from the back of the chair. 'I need to get to the bank, see what's what. The phone's been ringing off the hook all morning.'

When Katherine was gone, Martha pulled the chair closer to the bed, sat down. A vase of lilies on the locker beside the bed leaked their cloying scent into the hot dryness of the room. Martha leaned towards her friend.

'Tara?'

No answer.

'Tara?' She said it louder this time, accompanied the word with a gentle poke to the shoulder. Then another, not so gentle.

Nothing.

Martha stood up, picked up the vase, put it in the corridor on the floor, closed the door firmly on the misleading delicacy of the blooms. Next, she threw open the window, waving her hands to encourage the chill January air inside. 'There,' she said. 'Isn't that much better?'

Still no response, even though Tara loved lilies and detested draughts.

Martha stood at the head of the bed. She curled her fingers around the edge of the blanket, pulled it down to reveal her friend's flushed face. Already, Tara's usually shiny, silky hair had the dull, limp appearance of someone who had been in a hospital bed for a long time.

The woman in the hospital bed seemed like a different person to the woman Martha had picked up from the airport only two days before.

*   *   *

Martha had driven from the airport to Tara's apartment in Malahide where Tara had dropped her bombshell, albeit in her usual calm, collected way.

'I've been seeing someone.'

'What?' Martha nearly choked on her tea.

'Don't say what, say pardon.' Tara parodied her mother. Her impersonation was immaculate.

'A fling?'

Tara shook her head slowly.

'You mean you're having a relationship with somebody?'

Tara nodded, slower still.

'I can't believe it,' said Martha.

'It's not *that* preposterous.' Tara's tone was a little injured now.

'No, of course not, it's just . . . you took me by surprise, is all.'

'I was a little surprised myself, to be honest.'

'What's her name?'

'Mathilde.'

'What's she like?'

'She's French, she loves knitting, skiing, historical fiction, has a pathological interest in the female orgasm and she owns a cafe in London. That's how I met her. Do you want to see photographic evidence?' Tara asked.

'I do,' said Martha, as Tara whipped out her phone, her fingers a blur as she tapped at the screen. 'There,' she said, handing the phone to Martha. On the screen, a photograph of Tara on a deserted beach standing beside a beautiful brunette with bright blue eyes and long, athletic legs. Martha couldn't see her feet because they were immersed in the frothy surf but she was sure they were beautiful too; Tara was a stickler for good feet.

'She's stunning,' said Martha, mostly because it was true and also because she was momentarily rendered dumb in the face of Tara's uncommon enthusiasm when it came to, well, relationships. Stuff like that.

Tara was protective about her sexuality. She'd never really come out. Not in any formal sense. 'My sexuality is nobody's business but my own,' she'd said. 'You don't go around telling people you're a heterosexual, do you?' Martha conceded the point.

Tara had gone out with only a handful of women – and only after she moved to London – and had not invested in any long-term relationships. 'I don't have time,' she'd said once, when Martha brought it up.

Her relationship with Mathilde was new ground. Unfamiliar terrain.

'I'm happy for you, Tara. It all sounds great.'

'There's a catch.' Tara set her cup on the coffee table and looked at Martha, her face grave.

'What?'

'She wants to get married.'

'To you?'

Tara glared at Martha. 'Stop being fatuous, Martha. She wants to have a wedding. Invite our families.'

'Might be best if you tell your family you're gay first.'

'Can't you be serious for once?' Tara stood up, went to the kitchen and found a tin of tuna fish which she opened and began eating with a fork. This was her version of comfort eating, which was probably why she was so skinny.

'Do you want some?' she asked.

'Don't you have any chocolate biscuits?'

'Any what?'

'Oh, never mind. Go on. I promise not to say anything glib.'

Tara stood in the kitchen until the tuna tin was empty, then returned to the couch, sighed a tuna-fish sigh that Martha managed to avoid by pressing herself against the back of the couch.

'She proposed to me. She had a ring and everything.'

'Where is it?' asked Martha, peering down at her friend's fingers.

'Well, that's just it. I only wore it when I was with Mathilde. I didn't mean anything by it, it's just . . . I hate having to explain myself to people, you know that.'

Martha nodded. She knew.

'Then, the day before yesterday, she showed up at Heathrow. I was checking in for a flight to Milan. She'd had a meeting at the airport and thought we'd have time for a coffee before my flight.'

'And she noticed you weren't wearing the ring?'

Tara nodded. 'We had a fight. We never fight. It was horrible. And in public.' Tara covered her face with her hands and Martha was terrified she might cry. Tara didn't believe in crying, felt it was a waste of make-up. Martha knew she should hug her friend. Or touch her arm at least. But they weren't huggers or touchers as a rule and doing either now might make the situation worse.

'Mathilde couldn't believe I hadn't . . . come out to my family. Christ, I hate that term. Come out. Coming out of the closet. That's worse. We don't have closets in Ireland, I told her. We have wardrobes. Except you never hear about people coming out of those.' Tara's voice was becoming as thin as her argument.

'Take a breath,' Martha said, forgetting about the tuna.

Tara closed her eyes and breathed in and out, several times. She could be so literal sometimes.

'OK, go on,' said Martha, trying not to sound impatient.

'Well, we sort of made up and she went to kiss me and . . . we were in the middle of Heathrow airport, for God's sake . . . there were people everywhere and . . . I pulled away from her and she just looked at me and said, *I see*, in this really quiet voice.'

Tara lifted her head. Looked at Martha, shook her head. 'She said I was the first gay homophobe she's ever met.'

'You didn't tell her how you feel about the word gay, did you?'

'I thought it best not to.'

84

Tara managed a weak smile and Martha was glad. They sat for a while, in the kind of silence that never bothered them.

'I should have told you. Ages ago. About Mathilde,' Tara said.

'It doesn't matter.'

'I just . . . it was all so new to me, and I wasn't sure if—'

'You don't have to explain.'

'I rang her when I landed in Milan. Then again after my meeting. I was going to . . . you know . . .'

'Apologise?'

Tara nodded. She didn't like admitting she was in the wrong. Probably because she rarely was.

'I left messages but . . . and then, when I arrived back in Heathrow, I found myself scanning the crowd in Arrivals because sometimes she meets me off the plane and the place was mobbed and there were all these people, kissing and hugging each other, and one couple in particular. Two women. Maybe in their fifties. And they just looked so . . . sort of . . . unselfconscious, as if it was the most normal thing in the world that they should be together, in public, and when they stopped kissing, one of them said, "I missed you so much." Anyone could have heard her. And I started to cry. Like, proper crying. Out loud.'

'In the Arrivals hall?' Martha was shocked.

'I couldn't stop once I got going.'

'Jesus.'

'A security guard came up to me and asked if I was OK. And I told him I'd just found out . . . just that minute . . . how . . . fond of Mathilde I was. I thought it would be a more gradual thing, you know? But this was like someone hit me on the head with, I don't know, a mallet or something. Something heavy at any rate . . .'

'Fond?'

Tara looked at Martha. Her expression was solemn. 'I love her.' It was nearly a whisper. 'Like the way you loved Cillian. That much.'

It had been strange. Tara mentioning Cillian. They never talked about him, not usually. Part of Martha's 'new beginning' that Tara had referred to after everything had come to a head.

'Move on, Wilder,' she'd said when Martha mentioned his name on occasion. 'There's nothing to see here.'

Tara slumped against the back of the couch, as if her bald revelations had sapped her of her usual reserves of energy.

'The security guard – his name is John, by the way – took me for a coffee. Obviously, I was anxious about airport security but he said not to worry, he was due a break and one of his colleagues would cover for him, and I told him everything. Can you believe that?'

Martha could not. Sharing confidences was not one of Tara's traits. And certainly not with random strangers.

'We're following each other on Twitter now,' Tara said. 'He's sent me a few links about, you know, telling people like . . . your family, that you're . . . I suppose . . . about your sexuality. Then he booked me on the next flight to Dublin and . . . here I am.' Tara raised her arms in a sort of 'Ta-Dah' gesture, and while her smile was of a diluted quality, it was there. It was definitely there. Martha was relieved to see it.

'Does Mathilde know you're here?'

'No. I thought I'd get everything done, then fly back to London tomorrow evening and surprise her and . . . you know . . .'

'Live happily ever after?'

'Maybe.' This non-business-related optimism was unprecedented.

'So,' said Martha. 'What's your plan?' Tara perked up at the mention of a plan, as Martha knew she would.

'We're going to tell my family.'

'We?'

'Yes.'

'Why do I have to?'

'Katherine first,' Tara continued, her voice gathering strength. 'I've arranged for us to meet her at the bank tomorrow. At noon. We'll take her for lunch, then go to see my mother.'

'Ah, not your mother too?'

Martha could see Tara steeling herself before she nodded firmly.

'Don't you think—?' Martha began.

'It has to be all or nothing. It's the only way Mathilde will believe that I . . . you know . . .'

'Love her?'

'Yes.'

'Oh, fine,' said Martha, shaking her head.

'I knew you'd say yes. Thank you,' said Tara, and she leaned towards Martha and gathered her in her arms as best she could and hugged her and, after a moment, Martha hugged her back. The sensation was strange. They stayed like that, on the couch, with their arms around each other for much longer than Martha had anticipated. It was not unpleasant. She felt liquid and light-headed. Feelings she usually associated with drinking. But she wasn't drinking. She was sober. She supposed it was a moment. For both of them. A good moment. She held onto it. Wanted to make it last.

Except the good moment didn't last. Of course not. Because now Tara was in a hospital. On a weekday. When she should be behind her enormous walnut desk in her enormous corner office on the top floor of the enormous office space she rented in the enormous office block in London's reassuringly expensive South Bank, speaking with authority into one of her phones, broker-ing some highfalutin deal or other. Maybe buying more Internet companies. And then, after work, she should be at a little-known but fabulous bistro in some trendy on-the-cusp-of-gentrification part of London, having dinner with Mathilde, celebrating Tara's long overdue disclosures to her family. Martha knew Katherine would be fine about it. And while Mrs Bolton might have repaired to a church to throw novenas at Tara's revelation, she would have gotten over it. Eventually.

Tara had told Martha she was gay – although she didn't actually use that word – on the day that Martha got drunk for the first time, two weeks before her fourteenth birthday.

She was home alone that Sunday. Her father was in Pretoria, reporting on the inauguration of Nelson Mandela. 'The first black president of South Africa, Mo,' her father had said before he left. 'That's no small thing.'

Her mother had taken Martha's brothers to Sunshine House.

Martha's mother took great trouble with her appearance any time she went to Sunshine House. She went there a lot. One of their most dedicated volunteers. On every committee, at every meeting, every event. She read to the kids, did arts and crafts with them, brought the few who could manage it on nature walks around the grounds, told them the names of the wild flowers growing in the hedgerows.

Martha had been relieved to note that since her mother had begun volunteering there, six years earlier, she'd been better. Perhaps better was too strong a word. She'd been busy. Distracted. She had less time to wonder what Martha was up to.

Martha laid her careful plans.

That day was the annual memorial service at Sunshine House. For the kids who had kicked the bucket. Martha wondered where the term *kicked the bucket* came from. She would look it up in the school library the next time she was there for detention.

She didn't say *kick the bucket* in front of her mother. She didn't say anything. She was busy pretending to be sick. While her mother was in the shower, she mixed bread and milk into a thick paste in the basin that was kept in a cupboard in the utility room and used for vomiting into. She considered the sodden mess at the bottom of the basin, then crumbled an Oxo beef stock cube into it, which lent it a more authentic colour. She diced half a carrot and threw it in. Her mother put carrots into nearly everything she made. The final touch was drenching the substance with a good dose of vinegar, giving it that credible sour stench. She carried the basin to her bedroom, set it beside her bed. In the bathroom, she filled a hot water bottle, then got into bed and pressed it against her face for as long as she could manage.

James and Mark had forgotten that today was the day for the memorial mass and hadn't allowed themselves enough time to come up with a plausible excuse as to why they couldn't go. They gave her daggers as they trudged towards the car. Martha waved – weakly – from her bedroom window.

'Are you sure you're going to be alright, Martha? Your temperature is very high. Perhaps I should stay?'

'No! I mean, that thermometer is old. It's probably not very accurate.' The thermometer had shown a reading of a hundred and five which, under normal circumstances, would have meant that Martha was either dead or dying. She'd depended on her mother's general air of abstractedness but still. She'd gone too far by putting the thermometer directly on the hot water bottle when her mother had briefly left the room.

She always went too far.

She hadn't any specific plans for the day. She figured Amelia wouldn't mind her missing the memorial mass since they'd never really known each other. Besides, she'd been to all the other memorial-this-that-and-the-others so, in karma terms, her account was in credit, surely?

She had a vague idea that she wanted to get drunk. But that wouldn't be much fun if there was no one there to bear witness.

She rang Tara.

'I thought you were going to Amelia's memorial,' Tara said in her bossy-boots voice.

'I'm sick. Do you want to come over and get drunk?'

'I thought we were going to get drunk after the exams?' Tara was a stickler for making plans and adhering to them.

'That's not for another month at least. I'm bored. And I want to practise.'

'OK.' Practising was up there with studying, in Tara's immaculately kept book. That was why she was so good at the tuba.

Martha was in charge of mixing the drinks. Her father's bar in the basement had a large selection and she knew what went with what. 'I think we should start with brandies and ginger. Ginger is good for settling your stomach.'

'But your stomach is not unsettled,' Tara said.

'Not yet,' said Martha, handing her friend a large tumbler full to the brim. Tara spat her first mouthful out. Martha drank hers.

'Can you make me one that doesn't taste like alcohol?' Tara asked as Martha approached the bar once again.

'A vodka and lime, coming right up,' Martha said.

'That's not too bad,' Tara conceded as she braced herself and took a sip. 'What are you having?'

'Whiskey sour.' It was her dad's favourite drink. She poured a measure of whiskey into a cocktail shaker, squeezed half a lemon on top of it and added some sugar. Then she put the lid on and shook it with a great deal of alacrity and deft wrist movements. She poured the lot into a cut glass tumbler, topped it with ice and a slice of lemon, then added a cherry for good measure. The procedure took less than a minute.

'You'd never think you were the worst in the class at home economics.' There was a note of admiration in Tara's voice that gave Martha a warm, fuzzy feeling. Although that might be the whiskey hot on the heels of the brandy.

They lay on a rug on the floor of the basement that Martha's dad called the snug and Martha's mother called the den. They talked about Katherine, Tara's sister, who was moving out of home the following day.

Into a flat.

They dreamed of the day they could move into a flat.

'Do you think Katherine's done it?' Martha asked idly.

'With who?'

'Anyone.'

'No way. I don't think she's ever had a boyfriend.'

'Have you done it?' Martha lifted her head off the rug, looked at her friend.

Tara shook her head. 'I'd tell you if I had.'

'Have you done your economics homework?'

'No.'

'Don't lie.'

'OK then, yes,' said Tara, crumbling as Martha had known she would. 'I did it last Thursday.'

'But it's not due till tomorrow.'

'I know. I couldn't help it.'

'Can I cog it?'

'Ah, Martha, you know I don't—'

'Pretty please with a cherry on top?' Martha lifted the cherry from her glass, waved it towards Tara's face.

'Oh, fine,' Tara said, slapping Martha's hand away.

'Thanks. And I promise I'll change it around a bit so it won't be as good as yours.' Martha knew that Tara panicked if she lost her footing at the top of the class.

'I don't know why you just don't do it yourself. You're clever.'

'It's easier this way.'

'But now you're not going to know what external economies of scale are.'

'I'll manage.' Martha stood up too quickly, had to steady herself against the wall before she could make her way to her father's record collection, which nobody was allowed to go near, although her father made an exception for Martha. She thought jazz might be good. Jazz seemed an appropriate soundtrack to drinking, she felt. She thought it might have something to do with the haphazard rhythm of it.

She slid the record – Billie Holiday, one of her father's favourites – out of its sleeve and settled it on the turntable before lifting the arm, resting the needle along the first groove. She loved the crackly sound before the music began. That sense of anticipation.

'I think I'm going to be sick,' Tara said, after Martha insisted she try a peach schnapps.

'Can you do it into the basin in my room?' Martha said. 'It could do with a top up.'

'Aren't you drunk yet?' Tara asked later, with a combined sense of admiration and curiosity.

'I'm not sure.' By now, Tara had been sick twice and the basin in Martha's bedroom was more than half full. Martha made her tea and mentioned toast, although that never materialised.

'I don't *get* alcohol,' Tara confessed, shaking her head. 'It tastes horrible. And makes your head ache. And your stomach ache.'

'Don't forget the hangover bit. You've still that to look forward to.'

Tara groaned. Stretched herself across the couch and covered herself with a wool cardigan belonging to Martha's mother.

She looked at Martha with bloodshot eyes.

'What about you?' Tara asked.

'What about me?'

'Do you get it?'

'What?'

'Alcohol. Being drunk.'

Martha shook her head. 'Not really.' This was the first lie Martha ever told Tara and she felt the sting of it. Felt bad about the telling of it. Because she *did* get it. Alcohol. Getting drunk. Right from that very first time, she got it. Understood it. What it could do, inside your head. How it could make the world look different. Better. How it could transform possibilities into certainties.

'I'm going to be a journalist,' she told Tara.

'I know. You've said it before. Millions of times.'

'No, I mean *really*. Like, I'm going to be a brilliant fucking journalist. The best.'

'Better than your dad?'

'Just as good as him.'

It made things easier to say, alcohol.

'I like girls.' Because Tara said it so quietly, Martha knew what she meant at once.

'You don't fancy me, do you?'

'No!'

'You don't have to sound so outraged. Why wouldn't you fancy me? What the fuck is wrong with me?'

'You're my best friend. That's what I mean.'

Martha's face flushed with colour. She reached for her glass and drank deeply.

'You won't tell anyone, will you?' said Tara.

'Who would I tell?' said Martha, in her matter-of-fact voice.

'Thanks, Martha,' Tara said before she threw up again, on the deep pile rug that covered the floor between the couch and the fireplace. Martha cleaned it with bleach, which was what scuppered her in the end. Her mother detected the smell straightaway when she returned with Martha's brothers from Sunshine House. Following her nose, she soon came upon the scene, pointing at the circle of milky pink in the middle of the once entirely blood-red rug.

'You've been drinking,' she told Martha, now pointing at the bar she had never wanted her husband to install, where Martha realised she had left their glasses, an empty packet of Mikados and a half a bottle of beer with a cigarette butt floating on the top. 'And smoking,' her mother added when her gaze slid down the bottle. 'I don't know which one is worse.'

'Dad lets me take a sip of his drink sometimes,' Martha said, trying to steer her mother's anger towards her father, who was better able for it, especially at times like this when he wasn't in the country. She noticed her words now. How they slurred into each other, like they were drunk themselves. That was interesting, she thought. The effect of the alcohol on speech. Not brilliant, no. But interesting all the same.

'On the day of Amelia's memorial service. How could you?'

Martha wasn't sure what Amelia had to do with it. She didn't dwell on it. Her mother carried her sister into most conversations. In her arms. Like she was still four years old. Which, Martha supposed, she still was.

'Wait until your father gets home and hears about this.'

She carried the basin from her bedroom to the kitchen. Even the sight of its foul contents couldn't induce Martha to vomit.

Right from the beginning, she had the stomach for it.

Her mother couldn't wait in the end. For her father to get home. She went to her bedroom and rang him, in his hotel bedroom. The phone rang and rang but she kept redialling, the tip of her finger red from her efforts. When she eventually got to speak to him – she rang his colleague who gave her the name of the bar around the corner from the hotel where he thought Peter might be, which turned out to be the exact place he was – Martha, listening in on the phone in the kitchen, heard him say that girls would be girls and teenagers would be teenagers and Mo would be Mo.

Tara's hand tugged at the bed cover, pulled it back over her head. The movement startled Martha, brought the mean confines of the hospital room back into focus.

'Are you awake?' she said.

'No,' came the muffled voice from the bed.

'What are you going to do? Hide in here for the rest of your life?'

'I don't want to talk.'

'In general? Or to me in particular?'

Tara made no response.

Martha rubbed her eyes, winced at the pain the action produced, tried to think of something she could do that might help. She poked her finger against Tara's arm even though it had yielded no results earlier. Still, it was all she could think of.

'Stop it,' Tara finally said, reefing the covers away from her face and turning towards Martha.

'There's no need to be so snippy.'

'This is serious, Martha. I've got PTSD, you know.'

'You'll be right as rain in no time. Your mother's chanting a novena as we speak.'

'Jesus, your face,' said Tara, lifting her head off the pillow, which Martha took as a good sign.

'I know. This is when I miss having a Facebook page. I'd say I'd get a fair amount of likes with a mush like this.'

'This is not one of those times when you can make me laugh and everything will be fine.' The head was down again, the eyes shut tight.

'I don't see why not.'

'You should go.'

'You haven't told me the plan yet.'

'There is no plan.'

'There's always a plan. Mathilde, for example. Where are we on that particular enterprise?'

Tara shook her head, her eyes still closed. 'It's too late for all that. You don't come out when you're thirty-five. I'm too old for this shit.'

The uncharacteristic deluge of negativity momentarily stunned Martha. It was like dissonant chords, vying with each other.

'You should at least ring Mathilde. You were supposed to meet her last night in London, weren't you? She'll be worried.'

'*No!*' Tara sat up this time, reached for an oxygen mask hanging on a rail beside the bed, breathed deeply into it.

'Jesus, sorry, Tara, just . . . you know . . . relax and . . . it'll be OK.' Martha stood up. She had gone too far. She always went too far.

The door opened and Mrs Bolton stepped inside, smelling of incense and peppermints. 'Oh, good, you're awake. That'll be the novena to St Christopher. He's very reliable.'

Tara's eyes swivelled to her mother's face. She pulled the mask away from her mouth. 'You have to tell Martha to go, Mum,' she said, louder than necessary, given the size of the room. 'She's . . . not helping. She's insisting that I'm fine and I'm not fine, I'm not fine, I'm not fine, I'm—'

'Sssshhhh,' her mother said, hurrying towards Tara, pulling her into her mountainous bosom. 'It's alright, love. I won't let anyone upset you.' She glanced at Martha and gestured towards the door with her head.

'I was just trying to help,' Martha said.

'I think you should go,' Mrs Bolton whispered and while there was a trace of an apology in her tone there was also authority.

Martha should go.

She stepped towards the door, grateful for the rubber soles of her Doc Martens that made no sound against the awful porridge-coloured linoleum.

Tara was whimpering now. 'I just need to sleep. I'm so tired, Mum, I've never been so tired . . .'

Martha stepped into the corridor, closed the door behind her. She stood there, not moving yet. Fear gripped her. It was like the fear the morning after a night's drinking. When you can't quite remember what you've done but you know it's not something good.

Eight

'Do you know if he will regain consciousness?' A man's voice. Tobias guessed around forty. A garda, Tobias thought. Not a Dubliner, with that accent. Somewhere northern. Tobias had not travelled around the island much, despite the decades-long span of his residency in the country. He wasn't as proficient as he should have been at identifying the various accents. Something suggested Donegal. The man on RTÉ who read the news every night at 6.01 p.m. was from Donegal, Tobias remembered. He'd read that somewhere. Where was it? Oh yes, the *Irish Times*. When? Last year. Summertime? No, it was just after he'd moved into the nursing home and that was nearly a year ago so it must have been spring. Early spring. March, perhaps. Yes. March.

And so on and so forth went the thoughts around Tobias's head. He concentrated on them, allowed them to lead him along, as if by the hand, to the next one and the next and in this way it was possible to keep thoughts of other matters at bay.

He was cursed with one of the finest memories of anyone his age and many younger. It had always been thus. Under ordinary circumstances, this was not problematic. He was adept at corralling his thoughts. His memories.

But here, in a hospital, which is where he supposed he must still be, lying in a bed, in a coma, according to the doctors, his memory seemed to have gained the upper hand. It was leaking everywhere. All of a sudden. Surprising him with the vividness of its colour, its attention to detail. His response to these memories that ran like film reel through his mind, someplace behind his eyes, surprised him. The strength of it. It seemed almost . . . overwhelming. There was little he could do in the face of such persistence. Still, he did what he could. Like concentrating on the voices.

Now Mr Ryan – a consultant, although just what his area of expertise was Tobias had yet to discover – spoke to the man who might be from Donegal. The tall man with the quiet voice. Tobias knew he was tall because . . . well, he didn't know why he knew he was tall. Perhaps he was short and rotund? But Tobias would wager – were he a betting man, which he was most certainly not – that he was tall. There was an air of authority about his tone. Tobias thought he might be a police officer.

Mr Ryan was using medical jargon to camouflage the fact that he did not know the answer to the man's simple question.

'. . . and that, Detective Larkin, taken in conjunction with the blunt force of the trauma to the . . .'

A detective then. Close enough.

'It's important that I speak with him when he comes to,' said the tall man with the quiet voice who might have hailed from Donegal.

Mr Ryan again, his tone detached as he spoke about Tobias as if Tobias wasn't even there.

And perhaps he wasn't. Not really.

'. . . and its position at the frontal lobe of the—'

'So you can't tell when he might regain consciousness?'

'It's not as simple as that,' said Mr Ryan.

'Is that your way of saying you don't know?' If Tobias had been a different kind of person, he might have warmed to the detective with the quiet voice from somewhere to the north of the island.

Tobias didn't hear Mr Ryan's reply, if indeed the consultant deigned to respond to the detective's blunt question. Instead, he felt a tug, like a hand slipped inside his, pulling him, and he had no choice but to allow himself to be dragged along. He knew there was no point in resisting it. The tug of memory was too strong. When he looked back, he saw himself lying on a hospital bed, his eyes closed in a way that seemed final. He looked frail and inconsequential, the outline of his body making little impression on the stiff white sheet covering him. The voices became distant until they were echoes of voices. Memories of voices. And then they were gone and he was a boy again, in Dresden, and the war was raging around Europe but it hadn't come to Dresden.

Not yet.

'You're the man of the house now, young man,' the officer said to Tobias. The one who came to their front door with the envelope.

Tobias's mother began to cry as soon as she saw the soldier. She batted the envelope away, as if she thought that the news mightn't be true if she didn't open it. If she didn't read the words.

She handed Tobias the baby – Greta was four months old then – and leaned against the door like she might fall if she didn't.

Greta cried too and Tobias rocked her in his arms and blew warm breath onto the soft folds of skin at the back of her neck, as he had seen his mother do, to make her giggle. His brothers – Bruno, who was seven, and Lars, nine – were fishing for salmon at the Blue Wonder bridge on the banks of the Elbe with their friends. They would cry later, when Tobias put them to bed, and he would tell them to stop or he wouldn't read them a story but it wouldn't make any difference.

Tobias thought he might cry too. Later. When everyone had gone to bed and he was alone in the kitchen. But he didn't.

Perhaps it was because of what the soldier had said. Perhaps it was because he was the man of the house now. After all, he was nearly fourteen.

On clear nights, you could hear the bombs fall to the north, towards Berlin. Tobias's mother said they wouldn't attack Dresden but when he asked why, she didn't say.

The Youth Movement kept him and his brothers busy. Distracted them from hunger and cold. Even after he'd eaten, Tobias felt hungry. The hunger was a part of him now, as solid as a limb. He queued for bread, for potatoes, for vegetables. Sometimes there was meat, thin fillets of grey flesh of dubious origin. Most days, Tobias's mother managed to make broth which Tobias spooned into four bowls. Cut the bread if he had managed to find any. Bruno always finished his meal first. Glanced around the table with his bright blue eyes that enticed people to give him more than his fair share. Tobias stirred the thin soup in his bowl, lifted a sliver of meat with his spoon, slipped it into Bruno's bowl when his mother's head was bent towards the baby, suckling at her breast. He put his finger on his lips. *Ssshhh.* His mother said everyone had to get their share. Bruno winked at him and stuffed the meat into his mouth, swallowing it without appearing to chew. Lars noticed but said nothing. At nine, he understood how seven-year-olds might need more than their fair share.

Greta often cried after her feed as if she, too, were still hungry. His mother wrapped the baby in a shawl and held her close to her thin body, rocking her until Greta fell asleep. She put her in the cot, still wrapped in the shawl. Tucked an old coat over her. His father's old coat. Sometimes she told Tobias and his brothers one of her stories. They all loved her stories. Especially when she drew the pictures that went with them. Tobias knew he was too old for stories. They went to bed early most nights. It was too cold not to.

Tobias wondered when the war would end.

In the mornings, the net curtains stuck to the windows. Tobias lit a fire if there was wood, his breath collecting in clouds before his face. When he looked in on Greta, asleep in her cot, her hands were always in tiny fists on either side of her head, cold as ice cubes. Tobias held each one up and blew on them before he tucked them inside the rough wool of his father's coat. They ate hunks of bread for breakfast, mugs of hot water. School started at eight o'clock. Bruno always held Tobias's hand, Lars dragging his feet behind them. 'I don't want to go to school.' His teacher – Fraulein Horowitz – had left the year before. 'She didn't even say goodbye to us,' Lars had said that day after school, when she never appeared. He'd struggled not to cry. His mother told him to be quiet. Told him never to mention Fraulein Horowitz again, if he knew what was good for him.

'I'll ask Herr Smidt if you can come on patrol with us tonight,' Tobias sometimes promised Lars. 'So long as you go to school and stop complaining.'

That usually worked. Lars longed to be as old as Tobias so he, too, could learn to shoot with the Hitler Youth, could sit in the fire trucks with the sirens blaring and climb ladders and put out fires with the massive hoses that the boys were shown how to use.

Lars would grin at his brother then, whack him on the arm with a playful fist. Tobias would grip the peak of Lars's cap, pulling it down over his eyes, turning Lars around and around and pushing him towards his classroom. Lars staggered and laughed and Tobias waited until he was inside his classroom before he headed towards his own school where they would begin the day as they always did, with the salute and the chant that felt more like a prayer, albeit one that was never answered. Except you couldn't say that. Not out loud. You couldn't say anything. He recited it, same as everyone else. In a loud, certain voice with his head high, as if he were proud. As if the Russians weren't coming.

His mother cried at night when she thought they were asleep. The cry was muffled and Tobias – lying in his bed – heard her and knew she was pressing her face into his father's pillow so none of her children would hear her.

He held his hands against his ears when he heard her. That's what he had been doing when the sirens sounded that night.

Lying in bed, holding his hands against his ears, trying not to hear his mother crying.

It was ten o'clock. Tobias had heard the sirens many times before, a mournful wail that ripped through the night air and made his ears ring like a bell. He pulled himself from sleep, from the warmth of his bed and dressed quickly in the cold darkness of the bedroom he shared with Lars and Bruno. He woke them, helped Bruno with the stiff buttons of the coat that stretched across his skinny chest, the two sides barely reaching now. Already he could hear Greta's frightened cries and his mother's voice, soft and low, soothing her as she pulled her clothes on.

Tobias dragged a box from underneath his bed, lifted his father's gun out of it, wedged it into the waistband of his trousers. He always took the gun on nights like these. He'd never used it but the solid weight of it against his hip granted him some comfort. He picked up the suitcase they kept at the front door of their terraced house for the nights they spent in the cellar of the apartment block five doors down. It contained crackers and water, a few stubs of candles, some clothes and books, a pack of cards, a nappy for Greta. He took Bruno's hand and opened the door.

'Do you think it's a false alarm?' Bruno asked the same question on each of these nights.

'Yes, of course,' Tobias said, as he always did.

Lars and Bruno followed their big brother out the door onto the narrow road where already a strong current of people flowed, moving in the same direction. 'Stay close by me,' said Tobias to

Lars, as he took Bruno's hand and checked his mother was behind them, the baby clutched in her arms, now too tired to cry.

Already the place – a stale-smelling rectangle with cement walls and floor – was full. Tobias fought his way through the crowd who, ten minutes before, had been fast asleep in their beds, dreaming perhaps about peace. Or a cake made with real eggs. Or coal burning in a fireplace.

They were awake now. The air was thick with too many people in too tight a space. It was difficult to catch your breath. Two ancient, stooped men used every ounce of their energy to shut the door of the cellar, their arms taut and their hands flat against the door with their efforts. Greta cried when the door banged shut, stopping briefly to suckle at her mother's breast. Tobias took off his coat and slipped it over his mother's shoulders to afford her some privacy. She caught his eye and he nodded and looked away, not wanting to draw attention to his mother's state of undress, wanting to protect her modesty. He felt that's what his father would have done.

The lights flickered before they went out. Tobias knew he was too old to be afraid of the dark but the darkness in the cellar pushed against his face and seemed to pull the air away with it. He concentrated on Bruno's breath, which he could feel against the skin of his hands, wrapped around his brother's small body.

They waited. In the dark, time made no sense. Nothing did. Not even the war which seemed to Tobias like time itself: relentless, constantly moving to some place in the distance that nobody could see.

They heard the bomb before they felt its impact. A thin screeching sound. Briefly, Tobias thought about the fireworks his father had bought once, years ago. He had set them off in the park at the bottom of their street on New Year's Eve. Tobias had watched them soar, cutting the sky in two with their dazzling light. An orchestra of sound exploded in the cellar, discordant and frantic, some of it muffled as mothers pulled children against the fabric of ancient coats and worn-out dresses.

The impact of the bomb – which fell somewhere to the east of where they sheltered – shook the walls of the cellar, made a sound that seemed too big for the space they occupied and Tobias imagined the foundations of the block shifting beneath them and each apartment overhead, the rooms filled with ordinary things, teetering on the edge of the building. When the noise subsided, Tobias opened his eyes, separated himself from his brothers, rubbing dust from their faces, the shoulders of their coats. 'You alright, Lars? Bruno?' Lars nodded furiously without looking at his older brother. Tobias had told Lars to be brave and that's what he was trying to be. Bruno was too young yet to know how to be brave. Or how to pretend to be, at any rate.

'I want to go home now, Tobias. Can we go home now? I'm scared, Tobias, I want to—'

'We'll go home in a little while, OK?' Bruno looked at Tobias with his enormous blue eyes in his small white face and nodded. 'Where are you going?' he said then, as Tobias stood up.

'I have to—'

'You don't have to do anything except stay here with your family,' his mother hissed. She put her hand on his arm. 'You can't leave, Tobias. It's too dangerous.'

'I'll be needed at the fire station, you know that. Don't worry, Mama, we've been training. I know how to be careful.'

'NO!' His mother screamed the word and the baby jerked in her arms, awake again, crying again. 'No,' she shouted again. 'You must not go, Tobias. I forbid you to go.' Her face was red. Furious. Almost accusing. For a moment, Tobias hesitated. The boy from the house two doors up from Tobias's pulled at the shelter door, opening it an inch, peering outside. Tobias couldn't remember his name. Kai? Or perhaps Karl.

'Come on, Tobias, we'd better get a move on,' he said.

Tobias peeled his mother's fingers from around his wrist. 'I have to go. It is my duty.'

'Duty is what got your father killed.'

'You don't mean that.' Tobias glanced around but people were too busy with their own fear to pay much attention to them.

'You will die out there.' She was crying now and Tobias reached for her hand, squeezed it.

'I won't. I'll be careful. I'll be back soon.'

'Do you promise?' It was nearly a whisper.

'I swear on my life.'

He glanced at his brothers, wrapped around each other like puppies in a basket. He put his hand on the baby's head, her soft curls damp and hot against his fingers. He did not bend to kiss his brothers. Not in front of everyone.

He would regret that.

Later.

Out in the streets, it was clear that this wasn't like the other times. This time, the bomb had come for them. Dresden was on fire.

It was like a depiction of hell that Tobias had seen in a religious book in his grandmother's house when he was a small boy. The heat was like a wall that you couldn't scale. People ran, crying and screaming. Mostly women and children together, or children on their own crying for their mothers, or mothers on their own screaming for their children.

Tobias ran through the streets, following a line of fellow fire officers, trying not to look, trying not to see. They were needed at the hospital where the roof had collapsed, Kai – or Karl? – told him.

The fire turned the night sky into howls of furious orange. Flames billowed from every window, every door and the smoke it produced was thick and black.

As the fire tightened her grip, sucking oxygen from the night air, running became difficult, then impossible. Tobias slowed to a jog, then a walk, then he stopped. He leaned against a wall, recoiled from the bright heat of the brick. He stood there and now he looked. Now he saw. An old woman, stumbling from a building, tearing clothes from her body as the fire licked her with treacherous tongues. The air was scorching, it burnt his nostrils, the inside of his mouth.

Tobias ran again, against the rush of people churning through the streets. He concentrated on getting to the hospital. Many of the roads were impassable; he kept having to turn back, find a different way.

Only one section of the building was intact when he got there. Herr Smidt, who was in charge of Tobias's unit, was at the front of the building, shouting to be heard.

Their job was to evacuate the patients – the ones who were still alive – to the section of the hospital that remained. And to salvage as much medical equipment and medicine as they could.

Tobias got to work. Everything he saw seemed shadowed by sound. The noise of the fire was like cymbals clashing. And on the fringes of the sound were the flames, the heat, the smell. People everywhere, dead and dying, their tiny, shrivelled corpses stiff and smouldering.

He held the damp blanket that Herr Smidt had given each of them against his face. He moved on, looking for another survivor.

Up ahead, something fell from the top storey of the burning building. It was a man.

Along a corridor, a small boy lay quiet on a blanket. Maybe Bruno's age. A narrow bone poking out of his knee where the rest of his leg should be. A deep, bloody gash down one side of his face. Tobias didn't look at the bone. Or the gash. He lifted the boy, wrapped his damp blanket around the boy's head. He was grateful that the boy made no sound. He was as light as a bag of feathers.

It was this boy who saved Tobias's life. Tobias never knew his name, what age he was, where he lived. But the boy saved Tobias's life as surely as if it were he who had lifted Tobias, carried him away from the burning city.

Tobias reached the part of the hospital that still remained – which was a ward on the ground floor at the back of the building. He looked for a space to deposit the boy, found one near the wall, beside a woman who looked like she might be kind. Tobias turned and headed towards the door.

'Sir?' It was the boy. His voice was small. Tobias turned back.

'Do you know where my mother is?' the boy asked.

Tobias shook his head and the boy began to cry.

Tobias moved towards him and then he stopped. He could hear something.

It was a sound. Not like the sound the fire made. This sound was clear. Like a screech.

Outside, Tobias could hear people. Running. Screaming. There was an anticipation in the room, like a breath held. Something was coming for them. Something else.

Tobias dived towards the boy, covering his small, broken body with his own as the bomb fell, exploded, made the world shake once more so that all the bones in Tobias's body felt like they would shatter with the force. He kept his eyes shut, held on tight to the boy whose skin was slick with sweat. There was a smell coming from the place where the rest of his leg used to be. Like old meat.

The heat inside the ward was like an animal, hurling itself against the bars of a cage. Tobias could feel the oxygen draining from the room, like water down a plughole. He knew they had to leave, knew there was nowhere for them to go.

He picked the boy up, hauled him across his shoulders as they had been trained to do during the drills at the fire station. The handle of the door was too hot to touch. Tobias pulled at the cuff of his jacket, wrapped the threadbare material around his hand and pulled open the door. Outside, more of the city burned, the long orange flames dancing up the sides of buildings, swallowing everything whole.

Much of the hospital was rubble now. Under an iron bar lay the body of a boy. Kai. Or Karl. Tobias didn't need to touch him to know he was dead.

His father always said, in an emergency it is important to have a plan and stick to it.

Tobias's plan was to find somewhere safe to put the boy, return to the shelter, get his mother, his brothers, his sister, head for the river maybe. They could hide along the bank, perhaps. Immerse themselves in the water, protect themselves somehow from the heat and the flames.

It wasn't much of a plan, Tobias knew, but the thinking of it, the concentration of his mind on it, helped him put one foot in front of the other, make some progress, instead of standing by and waiting and watching.

Tobias ran. 'Are you bringing me to my mother?' the boy asked. 'Yes,' said Tobias.

There was nowhere safe to put the boy so Tobias carried him – heavier now – to the street where his home was and where his family was.

Except they weren't there. Along the side of the street where Tobias had lived with his mother and his brothers and his baby sister, there was nothing. Just burning mounds of bricks and wood and shattered glass and pieces of a world that seemed far, far away – a smouldering book, a pair of broken glasses, a doll with matted hair and vacant, staring eyes, a blackened saucepan, broken cups. Ordinary things from ordinary lives that now seemed somehow extraordinary to Tobias. He laid the boy in a doorway on the other side of the street where the buildings were, for the moment, intact. He hauled at the rubble covering the cellar where he had left his family, but the debris scorched his hands and the smoke it produced – black and toxic – threatened to overcome him.

I swear on my life. That's what he had told his mother. What he had promised her.

He sat beside the boy. He didn't remember how long he sat there. Perhaps he slept. There was daylight in the sky when he looked up. That seemed impossible to Tobias. Daylight. The world, turning its face again towards the sun, as if nothing had happened.

The boy was dead.

Tobias gathered him in his arms and rocked him like he wasn't dead, like he was rocking him to sleep the way he used to rock Lars. And Bruno. And baby Greta.

Tobias didn't know the boy's name. He should have asked the boy his name. He laid him on the path, pulled the blanket over his head. He wiped tears from his face. He was glad his father couldn't see him now. Crying for a stranger. When he hadn't been able to save his own family.

He hadn't been able to come up with a plan.

And the promise he'd made to his mother, broken, in pieces, like the buildings all around him.

'. . . let me know as soon as he wakes up – that would be helpful.' The man again. The detective. There were people who might share a confidence with a voice like that.

'Cillian?' A woman's voice now. The sister-in-charge, Tobias knew, although just how he had acquired this information, he could not say with certainty. She seemed to know the detective. A wife, perhaps? A girlfriend?

'Ah, Joan, I was just on my way to look for you.'

'Are you still able to come for dinner next week? Naoise has been talking about nothing else.'

'I'd love to but I'm not sure now. The Super is throwing

everyone he's got at this bank robbery case. I'd say I'll be working day and night for the foreseeable.'

'Well, call over whenever you're free. I'll give you a doggy-bag if you can't stay.'

No, not a lover. Perhaps a sister?

'Thanks, sis.'

The affirmation of his calculation gave Tobias a small degree of pleasure, which he conceded was foolish but, at his age and especially in the circumstances in which he now found himself, he felt he could permit it.

'Does this mean you're not going to Donegal to see Stella at the weekend?'

Donegal! Another – small – victory.

Tobias could hear the detective's hair rub the collar of his shirt as he shook his head. He deduced that Cillian had neglected his barber in recent times.

'Stella will be disappointed.'

'I phoned her yesterday to tell her. She's fine about it, she has a lot on at the moment with her sisters.'

'You know, for an intelligent man, you can be fierce stupid at times.'

'What do you mean?'

Then the woman, speaking again. 'I saw Martha earlier.'

'Aye, so did I.'

A pause then in their conversation. Not a comfortable one, Tobias felt, although, what did he know of relationships?

The rustle of starched fabric. Tobias thought it might be Joan folding her arms across her chest, preparing a speech perhaps. Some advice maybe. She seemed protective of this man. More like a mother than a sister.

'What is it?' the man – Cillian – said.

'Nothing, I just hope . . . everything's going well for you now – it'd be a shame if—'

'Listen, Joan, Martha happens to be a witness in a case I'm investigating. That's it. There's no need to be worrying about me.'

Tobias found himself wondering who Martha was and then felt foolish. What business was it of his?

'I'm not worrying. I'm just . . . I'm glad you met Stella, that's all. She's . . . solid, you know? You can depend on her. You could do with a bit of that in your life.'

'How's my wee nephew?'

'He's grand now that he got over the igloo melting. And I'm fully aware that you're changing the subject.'

'I'd better get back to the station.'

The creak of shoe leather as Joan – Tobias presumed – rose on the tips of her toes and then the rustle of starch again as she pulled him against the stiffness of her uniform. Hugged him. Tobias was quite certain that was what was happening and – oddly – it both warmed and saddened him. The closeness of their bond seemed deeper than he had imagined bonds between grown-up siblings might be. Not that he had imagined much. Just sometimes. The idea caught him unawares and he wondered – briefly – what it might have been like, if things had worked out differently.

Nine

A meeting was going on at the station when Cillian got back from the hospital. The Super said he wanted everybody's undivided attention on the bank robbery case. 'I've gotten the green light for overtime so I don't want to hear about plans for the weekend or family commitments or any bollox like that, yeah? Not till we put this thing to bed.'

Cillian Larkin didn't mind. And he knew Stella didn't either, no matter what Joan said. 'Sure, you'll be home for good soon enough,' she'd said yesterday when he rang her. 'I'll have my fill of you then, won't I?' She laughed her comic-book laugh – *hahaha* – and Cillian felt relieved that Stella understood about his job. How important it was to him.

After Martha, Cillian hadn't planned on getting involved with anyone. When he'd applied for the transfer to Donegal, he had been after a quiet life. Quieter, at least. Quiet thoughts. He wanted to do his job well, fish with or without any degree of success, read good books, drive to Bray when he had a weekend off, spend time with his nephew and with his sister, Joan, and her husband, Tony. He did not want this new life to be tinged with anything else. Anyone else.

Stella had said she felt the same way. Was after the same thing. Work and family and – when she had time – a day spent on the bank of the river Owenea, between Ardara and Glenties, where – the locals claimed – you could see the salmon leap.

'I really like fishing.' That was one of the first things she'd said to him. He remembered thinking this strange because he'd met her at the Donegal Angling Club and had thus made certain assumptions of the members in terms of the hobbies they enjoyed.

She had rung the station a few days later, asked for him, wanted to know if he would come into her classroom. Talk to her kids about his job. He liked that. The way she called them *her* kids. He agreed and, afterwards, she had asked him to go for a drink with her. 'Some time,' she said, and he liked that too. The casualness of it. A drink rather than a date. He said yes. When they went for a drink – the following week – she drank Diet Coke, and when he asked her about it, she shrugged and said she was working the next day and it sounded so reasonable the way she said it. So obvious. Cillian felt something then, although it was only later he identified the feeling as relief. There would be no need to worry. With Stella.

Stella knew about Martha and Cillian knew about Patrick, but neither had gone into the details of their past relationships. 'I wasted enough time on that fella,' Stella had said and her tone was matter-of-fact. She had drawn a line, stepped over it, moved on. Cillian felt buoyed by this possibility. The possibility that he could do the same.

And he *had* moved on. He had moved to Donegal. Left Martha behind him. It had been difficult at first. For a good while. Sometimes, he wished he'd never met her. Things had been simple before he'd met her. He had been someone who thought mostly about work. Then he met Martha and, afterwards, things were different. Everything – every thought – was tinged with Martha. What she would say, what she would think, how she would look the next time he saw her, the sound of her laugh when he told her some amusing work-related anecdote, the raise of her sceptical eyebrows when he held his hands apart to demonstrate the length of the fish he had nearly caught.

It hadn't been easy. To stop thinking about her. To move on, leave her behind. But he had managed it in the end. Not all of a sudden. Not one particular day or night. It had been a gradual thing. And it had taken a long time.

After he had phoned Stella, Cillian knew he could put her to one side and concentrate on the case. That was the nature of their relationship. It suited him. Suited them both, Cillian felt.

The roadblocks they'd set up had yielded nothing so far, but a jeep that looked like the one the gang had driven away in had been found burnt out near Wavin Lake, close to Balrothery. Cillian waded through tedious hours of CCTV footage to get one clear shot of the jeep's number plate, which turned out to be a fake. Forensics hadn't been able to get anything useful from the car. Only the butt of a cigarette nearby which happened to be the same brand of cigarette enjoyed by Jimmy Carty.

Apart from that, nothing.

Cillian sat at his desk and trawled through records of stolen vehicles but the jeep wasn't listed. He then studied the log of telephone calls made to the station in the last week. He wasn't looking for anything in particular, just seeing if something jumped out at him. It was tedious work and he was about to get himself a strong coffee when he saw something that made him pause. It was a telephone call from Mrs Flanagan in River Valley, who was known to them all at the station, being a regular caller both in person and by phone. She was harmless enough, a nosy neighbour who had managed to get her hands on the reins of her local Neighbourhood Watch scheme which, coupled with her fertile imagination and pessimistic tendencies, made her a regular caller to the station with a variety of crime-related theories. She had a particular fixation on HiAce vans and had accused almost every plumber, electrician and carpenter, who dared to drive such a vehicle in her vicinity, of suspicious activity over

the past several years. Which was probably why her phone call –
logged three days ago – had received only perfunctory attention.
Cillian read her report, then picked up the phone.

'Mrs Flanagan? Detective Larkin here at—'

'Ah, Cillian, how are you, love? I haven't heard from you in
ages.'

'No, I've been—'

'Are you ringing about my neighbour's jeep?'

'Yes, I—'

'They're in Lanzarote at the minute, the Mitchells. Second
time in the last twelve months, if you wouldn't be minding.
And himself on the dole. I ask you! Of course, her mother finally
died last summer so maybe she left a few quid behind, you
wouldn't know and of course, I wouldn't *dream* of asking . . .'

'So, you noticed their jeep had gone, did you?'

'What? Oh, yes, they took a Swords Cab to the airport so
their jeep was in the driveway. They bought it second hand but,
still, it's only two years old and—'

'And when did you notice it was gone?'

'What? Oh, yes, well, I was dusting the window sill in the
front room last Thursday. It must have been coming up to half
seven in the evening because I saw Mr Mulligan walking down
the road – he usually goes to the library on a Thursday evening
and gets back in time for *Coronation Street*. He had the books in
a SuperValu bag – he says he reads five books a week. Five! I ask
you—'

'And that's when you noticed the jeep was gone?'

'I'm getting to that, Cillian.'

Cillian waited.

'And that's when I noticed the jeep was gone,' said Mrs
Flanagan then.

Cillian waited some more.

'And I know that her son – he's married with three children

115

over in Boraimhe – sometimes borrows it but I didn't see him coming to take it. Usually I'd spot him, just out of the corner of my eye, like. Or hear the engine start. People say I'm very . . . what's the word . . . ?'

Cillian could imagine a few.

'Observant, that's it. I'm observant.'

'Do you have a number for the Mitchells?'

'I do, love. Mrs Mitchell wrote down her new number for me on the back of a flyer before she jetted off. It's here someplace, just hold on a . . .'

Protracted rustling now.

'I have the number,' said Mrs Flanagan, reading it out. 'She wrote it on the back of Lenny's flyer.'

'Lenny?' Cillian sat up straighter.

'Leonard, I suppose. But we all call him Lenny. A lovely fellow. He's a window cleaner – he was here last week, left my patio door so clean I nearly walked through it: I thought it was open.'

'Lenny Hegarty?'

'That's him. Does he do your windows too?'

'You've been very helpful, Mrs Flanagan.'

'Have I?'

'Better observational powers than some of my colleagues.'

'Only doing my civic duty, Cillian, you know that.'

'Well, keep up the good work.'

'Over and out,' she said before she hung up.

Cillian rang Mrs Mitchell in Lanzarote who confirmed that, no, her son hadn't borrowed her jeep, which should be parked in her driveway in River Valley. She wasn't best pleased to find out that it was not.

'Did you get your windows cleaned last week? Before you went on holidays?' asked Cillian when she'd calmed down.

'Well, Lenny was up alright – he's our window cleaner – but I can't remember if it was last week or the week before. Why?'

'Did you tell him you were going on holidays?'

'God, I don't know, it was . . . oh, wait, yeah, I did. He said he'd been to this resort before. He recommended an Irish pub. They play traditional music in the evening. Fiddles and that. And then the fry-up in the mornings. It's like a home from home.'

Cillian looked up Leonard Hegarty on the computer. He was on the system but it was petty stuff mostly. What interested Cillian was the company Lenny kept. He was a known associate of Jimmy Carty's. He noted Lenny's address and left the station.

Lenny's car wasn't in his driveway in Swords Manor. Cillian parked further up, on the other side of the road, adjusted his rear-view mirror so he could see the house. He settled down to wait. There was a lot of waiting in his line of work although he hadn't known that as a young boy, dreaming of being a detective. He had always wanted to be one, which was strange because there were no guards in his family. His father – whom Cillian had only a vague memory of – had been a carpenter and his mother – who had died two years after his dad when Cillian was ten – a housewife.

Eventually a car pulled into Lenny's driveway but it was his girlfriend, Natasha, and Cillian didn't approach her, didn't want her telling Lenny, putting him on the defensive. He checked his phone to see if Martha had phoned back. He had rung earlier, just to see how Tara was doing.

He decided to call it a night, the long wait in the car making itself felt across the backs of his shoulders and down his cramped legs.

If things had gone to plan, he would have been on the road to Donegal by now. Instead he was in his car driving west instead of north. To his own house in The Ward in north County Dublin – that he had leased to a fire-fighter friend of his when he'd moved to Donegal.

Cillian had bought the house in The Ward nearly three years ago. Just after he'd been promoted to detective.

The estate agent had called the house a 'fixer-upper'.

'More like a "faller-downer",' Martha had told him when he took her to see it.

The house – a subsiding stone cottage crowned with a sodden straw roof gaping with bald spots – was situated in what Martha called 'the middle of nowhere' but what Cillian referred to as 'halfway between Finglas and Ashbourne'.

'The good thing is the windows are so dirty you can't see the countryside,' Martha had said, rubbing a pane with the cuff of her jacket, an act which had no discernible effect on visibility.

'Can't you say anything positive?'

'Yes.' She'd rummaged in her bag, taken out a bottle and two glasses. 'I brought wine.'

Cillian tightened his grip on the steering wheel, shook his head, as if he might dislodge Martha from his mind in this way. He concentrated on Stella. Pictured her in his head. Small. She was definitely small. Petite, he supposed some people might say. There was a plump softness to her body which Cillian still found unsettling, after the taut length of Martha. He'd always felt that Martha's body had to be navigated carefully, whereas Stella's felt like pillows you could sink into. He remembered the first time they'd slept together, thinking that thought. And wondering how long it would take before he stopped comparing every woman he met – every person, actually – to Martha bloody Wilder.

It was nine o'clock by the time Cillian pulled up in front of his house. He killed the engine, listened to it idle away, looked at the stone cottage. Oddly, when Stella had mentioned *home* the other day on the phone, it was this place that had come to mind. He had leased it out for the past two years but whenever Cillian stepped back into it – to replace a floorboard or paint a room – the sensation of being home was strong, despite the evidence of his tenant's belongings in every room.

The townhouse he rented in Mount Charles outside Donegal town looked pretty much the same as when he'd moved in, he realised. Stella said he hadn't put his stamp on it. Apart from his few toiletries in the bathroom, his books in a pile on the floor beside his bed and his fishing rods propped in a corner of the hall, it could have been anyone's house.

Niall – the fire-fighter to whom he had let his house when he left Dublin – had kindly agreed to let Cillian stay in the spare room during his six-month secondment to Swords. Cillian halved his rent, lent Niall his fishing rods when he wanted them and cooked his speciality – chicken tikka masala – when he had the time. It was an arrangement that suited them both.

What Cillian enjoyed about living out here was how dark the dark got. On a clear night, like tonight, the sky was lit with stars, the light from the closer ones clear and uncompromising, others glowing in clusters, like lamplight. Now, as he looked up, he saw a shooting star arcing across the sky and he smiled as he remembered Joan, years ago, pointing out his first one, telling him he could make a wish. He took his keys out of the ignition, lifted his work files from the passenger seat and got out of the car. The cold was sharp and immediate and he thought about the boy – Roman – somewhere out there.

'You can make a wish on that, you know.' The voice came from the step at the front door and startled him.

'Who's that?' He looked around, peered through the darkness towards the voice.

'It's me.'

'Stella?'

She moved towards him, stopped short of him. 'Surprise,' she said, smiling.

'How did you . . . find me here?'

There was some truth to what Martha had said. About the house being in the middle of nowhere.

'I took a few wrong turns but I got here in the end,' she said. In the dark, her teeth seemed very white and very long. She was wrapped in a wool coat with an enormous collar that she had turned up against the cold. A scarf was wrapped around her neck and her arms were wrapped around her body. In spite of these efforts, her teeth chattered. The noise it produced sounded loud in the darkness.

'Are you going to let me in?'

'Sorry, of course, I'll just get my . . . keys and . . . you took me by surprise, that's all. I wasn't . . . expecting you.'

'A nice surprise, I hope.'

'Yes. Of course. Of course it is.'

She leaned towards him, wrapped her arms around his neck, kissed his mouth. Cillian wondered if Niall were in. He wouldn't mind Stella staying. Not at all. It was just . . . well, Cillian would have liked to run it past him. He pulled away from Stella, whose eyes were still closed.

'Stella?'

Her eyes snapped open. She smiled. 'And don't worry about Niall. I rang him during the week. Let him know I was coming.'

'Really? How did you—?'

'I rang the fire station. He said it was fine. In fact, he's gone away for a few days so we have the place to ourselves.'

'Oh . . .' Niall hadn't mentioned any plans. Cillian hoped his tenant hadn't felt obliged to absent himself. He wasn't even sure Niall knew about Stella. Had he mentioned her?

'It's so nice to finally be here,' she said, waving towards the house. 'It looks a lot more . . . homey than I would have thought.'

'Come on inside, you'll freeze out here.' Cillian moved towards the house, stopping to pick up her bag, which seemed bigger than an overnight case. 'How long are you planning to stay?' he asked.

'We're on midterm break so . . .' she said, without finishing the sentence.

Cillian turned on the lights in the hall, the sitting room and the kitchen as he made his way towards the spare room – his bedroom now – at the back of the house where he set her bag.

Her suitcase.

When he returned, the lights were off and the lamps were on and Stella was crouched at the fireplace, lighting both ends of a Firelog she had brought. Cillian had to agree that in the soft lamplight, with the fire taking hold, the cottage did have a homey feel to it. A lot homier than the townhouse in Mount Charles.

Stella stood up, put the guard in front of the fireplace and turned towards him, still smiling.

'I thought it was Sandra's engagement party tonight,' he said.

'Selene's, you mean? And no, that's not till next month.' Stella was the middle child of seven – or was it eight? – children, all daughters. It was hard to keep track. Their names all began with the letter S – Susan, Sarah, Sorcha, Selene, Sadie and . . . he couldn't remember . . . oh, Sam, was it? Short for Samantha, he supposed. Seven of them in total. He was fairly sure. Stella said her mother had overcome a lisp in her mid-twenties and she thought that might be the reason for the prevalence of S names for each of her mother's seven – eight? – daughters.

'Tonight is Saoirse's first wedding anniversary, remember? They're just having a small party in their house.'

Oh, yes, Saoirse. Eight so.

There was always some occasion when it came to the Bennett sisters. Three of Stella's sisters were married with children, one was married and expecting her first child, one was engaged to be married, another had recently discovered an engagement ring in her boyfriend's toolbox that slid onto the finger she and her sisters called 'the wedding finger' perfectly and, while she had replaced it in amongst the nails and screws and spanners, it was, the sisters knew, only a matter of time. The remaining sister – the youngest, Cillian felt sure – was doing what was referred to as a *strong line* with a local politician. With an election looming, it wouldn't be long before he made an honest woman of her, as Stella's parents phrased it, the electorate being more trustful of young bucks like that whose cards were marked.

'Saoirse understood when I told her I couldn't make it. She knows I haven't seen you in ages.' Cillian thought he detected an emphasis on the word. *Ages*. But that wasn't true. Was it? He had travelled to Donegal two weeks ago, hadn't he? But there was an expectant expression across Stella's face and he felt obliged to say something.

'I'm sorry, work has been—'

'I understand,' she said. 'You've been busy.' She walked over to him, put her hands on his shoulders. 'I won't get in your way,' she said. 'I'll make you a few home-cooked meals. You look like you could do with some looking after.'

'You told me I was self-sufficient, remember?' She had added *for a man* at the end of the sentence.

Stella studied his face. 'You're not annoyed with me?' she said. 'For surprising you like this?'

'No.' It came out faster than he'd intended. He didn't think he was annoyed. Wrong footed, maybe. He moved towards the kitchen to check provisions. See what he could rustle up. An omelette maybe. He thought there might be a box of eggs.

'Good,' Stella said. 'It's just . . . well, I've missed you. There! What do you think about that?' He opened the fridge, scanned the shelves.

'I've been eating on the hoof the last couple of days so I don't have a lot of grub in, I'm afraid,' he said, and it was entirely plausible that he mightn't have heard her, with the sound of his rummaging and the distance between them. It was just . . . he'd been busy. He hadn't had time to miss her. 'And Joan keeps threatening to feed me so I haven't done much shopping.' He stood up, turned around to look at her.

'Oh, good, I'm really looking forward to seeing Joan again,' Stella said. 'I'll make something for dessert.'

'Well—'

'The signal's not great here, is it?' Stella scrolled down the screen of her iPad with her finger.

'The thing is,' said Cillian, 'I don't know if I'll be able to make it to Joan's. With work and everything. This new case. I'll be flat out, I'd say.'

'OK, look,' said Stella, setting her iPad aside. Her tone was brisk. The school teacher calling her class to heel. 'Why don't we just make the most of the time we have now? Hmm?'

Cillian nodded. 'Sure,' he said. 'I'll phone for take-out. There's a lovely Indian in Ashbourne that delivers—'

'No need,' said Stella, standing up. 'I made lasagne. It's in the boot of the car.' She paused and her look was expectant so he said, 'Great.' He'd told her that lasagne was his favourite food when she'd asked him once. Months ago. The effort she'd gone to. On the drive home, he'd been thinking about a hot shower, a mug of tea and a read of his book in bed before he got a few hours' kip. But Stella had gone to trouble. He should be more grateful.

He *was* grateful.

She had just taken him by surprise, that was all.

'I'll get it, pop it in the oven. Why don't you go and freshen up?'

In the bathroom, he manhandled himself out of his clothes, took a quick shower and towel-dried his hair – which could do with a cut – ran his hand along his face – which needed a shave.

He walked into the bedroom. Stella must have unpacked while he'd been in the shower. Her clothes hung in the wardrobe, a bottle of perfume, a collection of nail polishes and a couple of magazines on the locker beside the bed. The window that he had opened was now closed and the radiator made the groaning noise it made when it was turned on, which it never was because, otherwise, Cillian found the room stifling. He could hear Stella moving around in the kitchen now, filling the kettle, opening a press. He heard the low hum of the oven, pre-heating, and another low hum which was, he presumed, Stella herself. Humming a tune to herself. She sounded happy. She had made an effort, travelled all this way. With lasagne. He left the window closed, the radiator on and put on the jeans that Stella had bought him a while ago.

'How did you know my size?' He had been surprised to find they fit perfectly when she'd insisted he try them on. He struggled to find clothes that fit his tall, lanky frame, which was his reason – his excuse – to darken the doors of as few clothes shops as possible.

He pulled a T-shirt over his head, pushed his feet into a pair of flip-flops and walked downstairs. 'There you are,' Stella said as he walked into the kitchen. She had changed too. She must have done that while he was in the shower. Now she wore a dressing gown – although it probably had a fancier title than that, with its delicate shade and shiny material. Silk perhaps? Satin?

'You must be tired,' he said. 'After the journey.'

She laughed, then pulled at the belt of the dressing gown to briefly reveal a complicated red-and-black all-in-one bodice-type thing, with no obvious buttons or zips or anything else that might suggest a way in. She wrapped the dressing gown around her again, tied the belt. 'I'm not a bit tired.'

She stepped close to him, encircled his waist with her arms. Through the flimsy material, he could feel her heart and it was

racing and it made him feel bad. He knew he wasn't the romantic type. *Thank Christ*, Martha had said when he'd admitted it.

Stella set the table in the dining room. She lit tea lights,
arranged them along the sideboard. In the centre of the table,
two long red candles flickered.

'You sit down, I'll dish up,' she said before disappearing into
the kitchen, leaving Cillian sitting at the table with the candles
and the matching napkins. He felt strange. Like a visitor in his
own house. It had been a strange week. He supposed it might
have been partly because of Martha. Seeing her again. She had
never arrived at his door unannounced. And definitely not with
homemade food. A bottle, perhaps. Always a bottle. He'd never
seen her in a dressing gown, flimsy or otherwise.

Entirely naked or fully dressed, that was Martha. No half
measures.

Stella came back into the room, handed him a glass of
Prosecco. He wasn't much of a Prosecco drinker. Stella and her
sisters always drank Prosecco, Cillian noticed. Probably because
there was always something to celebrate: engagements and hen
nights and weddings and babies and anniversaries.

Cillian accepted the glass, touched it against hers and they
drank. He knew Stella would drink one glass and if she took a
second, she wouldn't finish it. He had seen her on the way to
the bottle bank, her empties in one small cardboard box,
comprising mostly glass jars that had contained olives and pesto
and soya sauce. He knew he would never get up in the middle of
the night and find her downstairs, passed out on the couch. He
liked knowing that. The certainty of it.

'You look deep in thought there,' Stella said when she sat
down.

'Oh, just thinking about work stuff. It's been a . . . funny
week.'

'Funny?'

'Busy, I mean.'

He told her a little about the case – the bank robbery – and she in turn supplied him with details of the field trip to the castle in Donegal town with her 'kids' and Cillian could almost hear the click of things falling back into place, things getting back to normal. It was only natural that Martha should be in his head, with the week that was in it. Him coming across her after all this time.

He felt better after the food. Less . . . wrong footed. He'd probably just been hungry, despite the curry he'd eaten in the Star at lunchtime. *Hollow legs*, Joan used to call him when he was a kid, asking for second helpings and then thirds.

After dinner, Stella rummaged in her handbag, drew out a small square parcel wrapped in brown paper and tied with a gingham ribbon. 'That was the manliest ribbon I could find,' she said, handing him the parcel. 'It's just something small, something to mark the occasion.'

He managed not to say, *What occasion?* Could almost hear Martha giving him maybe as much as six-and-a-half out of ten for cop-on. Her expression would have been bemused.

Instead, he accepted the parcel. 'I don't have anything for you.'

'It's nothing,' she said. She leaned across the table, put her hand on his shoulder. Her fingernails, always painted, were red tonight. As red as one of Naoise's fire engines.

'I know we haven't seen each other much these past few months,' she said, 'but we met exactly a year ago today, would you believe.'

He felt shock. That so much time had passed between them. Inside the wrapping paper, a box containing a pair of silver cufflinks in the shape of fish. 'They're lovely,' said Cillian, who had never worn cufflinks and wasn't entirely sure how to go about attaching them to a shirt.

'They're salmon, the jeweller said,' Stella told him, leaning towards him.

His phone rang.

'Sorry, I just have to . . .'

'Go ahead,' said Stella, straightening. She watched as he fished his phone out of the pocket of his jeans. He looked at the screen.

It was Martha. He walked into the small room off the kitchen, which had been his office before he transferred to Donegal. He closed the door.

'Hello,' he said.

'It's Martha Wilder,' she said.

'I know.'

'How do you know?'

'Your name came up on the screen.'

'Oh. Right.'

A pause then.

'I got your message just now,' she said. 'I had put my phone onto silent at the hospital. I'm just leaving now.'

'No worries. I was just ringing to see how Tara was?'

'I don't think she appreciated my visit.'

'Why not?'

'She's gone mental.'

'Is that the official diagnosis?'

'The doctor confirmed she's got that traumatic thingy-majiggy.'

'Post-traumatic stress disorder?'

'It sounds so serious when you put it like that.'

'It's probably just a short-term thing. It often is. And Tara is made of stern stuff.'

'I think if I could just slap her in the face a couple of times, she'd snap out of it.'

'Maybe let the professionals handle it.'

'Did you catch the baddies yet?'

'Still working on it.'

The door opened and Stella stood in the doorway. 'You want some coffee, baby?'

She never called him baby.

He pointed at his phone to indicate – unnecessarily, he felt – that he was still on a call. Stella nodded and left.

Martha said, 'Sounds like you're busy there, I'll let you go,' and she hung up without any further ado and it felt like a gust of wind had blown through the house, knocked things over.

'Who was that?' said Stella. In all the time – a year apparently – that he'd known her, Stella had never asked him who he'd been on the phone to.

Ever.

'Martha Wilder.' There was no need to lie.

'Oh,' said Stella, pushing at her cuticles with a fingernail in a way that looked painful. 'I didn't know you two were still in touch.'

'We're not.' He gave a brief account of Martha and Tara being at the bank and Tara now in hospital. He didn't mention that he had been in Martha's apartment. It was already a bit . . . awkward. That he had not mentioned Martha when he initially told her about the robbery.

Stella didn't comment on that. Instead, she looked at her watch. 'It's late to be calling,' she said. 'Was she drunk?' Her question was matter-of-fact. Almost rhetorical. She had seen the YouTube footage. Everybody had.

'I don't think so.'

Stella opened her mouth then closed it again, as if she had decided against saying whatever it was she had been about to say. Cillian was glad. He didn't want to talk about Martha. Besides, there was nothing to talk about. He had already thought about her much too much today and now he was anxious to get the day behind him.

After they'd eaten, Stella stood up, removed the fancy dressing gown – a kimono, perhaps: was that what they were called? – with a studied casualness. Cillian scanned the complicated red-and-black all-in-one bodice-type thing but still could not locate any buttons or zips. She took his hand, led him to his bedroom. 'This is another bit of your anniversary present,' she said, turning towards him as she reached the edge of the bed.

'I feel bad, not having anything for you,' he said.

'Oh, but you do,' she said and ran her hand down his T-shirt, unbuttoned his jeans, unzipped them, slid her hand under the waistband of his boxer shorts, took hold of him.

This was an aspect of Stella that he had not quite acclimatised to. It was an unexpected part of her, he felt. He thought it might be because of her job. If you had to guess what Stella did for a living, there was a good chance that you might go for school teacher. There was something school ma'am-ish about the way she held herself. Straight. Unbending. She wore her hair short and dyed it dark brown three times a year. Manageable, she called it. And the way she dressed – an almost prim femininity with emphasis on A-line skirts, court shoes and high-necked blouses. It was like a uniform which, when removed, signalled the end of something. Like the ringing of the school bell to dismiss class.

Stella had waited until maybe the third or fourth time they had sex before she revealed her predilections. She adopted a sort of breathy voice, fluttered her lashes in a way that made Cillian think she might have something in her eye and spoke in heavily accented innuendo. Cillian felt he was playing opposite her in a film except he didn't have a script. Didn't know his lines.

He knew he wasn't what Stella would have called an *adventurous* lover. He felt she would have preferred one of those. She was fond of props. Blindfolds, fake feathers in dubious colours, massage oils in various fruit flavours – she favoured summer berries — and ribbons to tether wrists and ankles to bedposts or, if no bedposts were available – as none were in his rented house in Mount Charles – she improvised with door handles and window catches and the like. The ribbons, as harnesses, were ineffectual but Stella seemed unconcerned with their shortcomings in this regard. Instead, she thrashed about on the bed as if she were swaddled in metal chains and whimpered in a sort of baby voice that Cillian was not to touch her *there* and under no circumstances should he lick her *there* and whatever he did, please, please, please, oh no, no, no, don't kiss her *there*.

It took Cillian a good while to get used to the drama.

Martha had called him a *robust* lover.

'Robust? That doesn't sound great.'

'It is what it is,' she'd said, in her matter-of-fact voice. 'Now stop talking and take your clothes off.'

In all other areas, Stella was, well, standard, he supposed. Although standard was no way to describe a person. What he meant was she was a normal person. Not that her sexual preferences were *ab*normal or anything. They just took you by surprise, that was all. Took a bit of getting used to. Besides, they didn't spent too much time in bed. Between Cillian's work and Stella's job and their family commitments, there wasn't all that much time to indulge the various sexual sagas Stella came up with.

The arrangement suited Cillian down to the ground.

'Does Stella mind? You being in Dublin for six months?' Joan had asked when he took her for dinner shortly after his secondment began.

'Not a bit.'

'Really?'

'She's glad of the free time, to be honest. She's busy doing the lesson plans for the resource hours she'll be taking on in September. And then one of her sisters is getting married so she's—'

'Another one?'

'Aye. They're all at it.' He'd smiled but Joan did not smile back. Instead, she shook her head. 'And what about you and Stella? Have you talked about . . . the future?'

Cillian shook his head. 'Stella's getting over someone,' he said. 'She doesn't want a big deal of a thing. And neither do I. It's just nice to have a bit of company from time to time. It suits us both.'

Except that, now, here she was. In Dublin, in his home, with her fancy dressing gown and her homemade lasagne and her suitcase that was much too big to be a weekend bag. And no mention of a departure date and her squaring it all away with Niall, without either of them saying a word to him.

Stella – perhaps sensing his confusion in relation to the complicated bodice, and maybe everything else – took off her shoes, her glasses, got into bed and steered him towards a cleverly concealed zip at the front of the thing. She did not produce feathers or ribbons or blindfolds or suggest a narrative involving, for instance, a nurse and a patient and, for a while, everything was grand.

Afterwards, Stella propped herself up on her elbow, traced circles on his chest with the tip of her fingernail. 'I've been thinking,' she said, then paused, looked at him. Her brown eyes were nearly black with pupil. Outside, Cillian could hear what sounded like the hoot of a barn owl, eerie and still. He was seized with an urge to pull on his jeans, his flip-flops, to go into the garden and see if he could spot it.

Stella nudged him. 'Are you listening to me?'

'Yes,' Cillian said. 'Sorry.' He tucked his hands behind his head, looked at the tongue and groove ceiling he had spent a weekend putting in last summer. It had been a painstaking job but now, lying here, the wood glowed amber in the lamplight, gave the room a sort of gentleness that Cillian associated with the house that he would soon leave again.

'Well, just about you coming home to Donegal. Another two weeks and you'll be back for good.'

Cillian nodded, waited.

'I'm just . . . looking forward to it. That's all. I'm very . . .' she sat up in bed so he couldn't see her face anymore '. . . fond of you, you know.'

'I'm fond of you too,' he said, and it wasn't a problem, saying it, because it was true. He *was* fond of Stella.

Stella turned around, took his hand, smiled at him. 'And when you get back, we can . . .'

'I'll have to get this case sorted first.'

'I know. You keep saying.' There was a shrill edge of impatience in her voice now.

'Sorry, Stella,' Cillian said. 'I just want everything to be clear, you know?'

'Jesus, Cillian, it's not like I'm asking you to marry me or anything.' There was a pause then. A clammy, expectant one, like the pause between the crash of thunder and the flash of lightning.

Then, 'You should see your face,' and Stella laughed – *hahaha* – and nudged him in the ribs with the point of her elbow. Cillian laughed too. He felt tired.

'All I meant,' Stella went on, her voice straining now with the kind of patience she reserved for her senior infants, Cillian felt, 'is that we can do things. Together. Like a proper couple. When you get back. That's all.'

She waited for him to say something. He fished around, then, 'Right.'

'For starters,' Stella said, 'you can dance with me at Selene's wedding. You'll be the only man there who can dance.'

Cillian laughed. 'I thought Selene and Eddie were taking salsa lessons. For the first dance malarkey?'

She snorted. 'You can't make a silk purse out of a sow's ear. I should know. God knows, I tried to with Patrick.' She threw herself back against her pillow with a deep sigh.

'Are you OK?' Cillian had taken Stella's account of her break-up with Patrick – we outgrew each other, it was a mutual decision – at face value.

Stella looked at him, struggled to produce a weak smile. 'I'm fine . . . now.' A studied emphasis on the *now*. Then, as though she had given herself a stern talking to, she sat up, rearranged her pillow and settled herself against it. She smiled at him like the last bit of their conversation had never happened. 'Who taught you to dance, anyway?'

His phone rang again and he made a dive for it. Stella shook her head and sighed, got out of bed, headed for the bathroom. He was glad. He wouldn't have to say it now. Say her name again. Say that it had been Martha Wilder who had taught him to dance. Two years ago. In the back garden of this house.

He picked up the phone, jabbed at the answer icon.

'Hello?'

It was the station.

'Yeah?'

'We picked up the young lad. Roman Matus.'

'Where?'

'Not far from Blessington.'

'Is he alright?'

'Well, he's not the happiest bunny in the hutch but he's in one piece, just about.'

'I'm on my way.'

Ten

Who – the fuck – calls a grown man *baby*. For. Fuck. Sake.

Martha flung her phone towards her handbag on the passenger seat. It missed and landed on the floor. Then it began to ping, letting her know she had a voicemail. She harboured an acute desire to take her foot off the accelerator, use it as a hammer to flatten the phone.

She didn't bother trying. Only because she knew she couldn't reach the damned thing.

She gunned the engine and roared out of the hospital car-park.

The day had become night without Martha noticing. She had spent a long time at the hospital, for all the good that had done. She didn't want to go home. Instead, she drove with no particular destination in mind, rolling cigarettes with one hand which she smoked one after the other. The February night was full of the threat of rain. Martha didn't mind that. She liked winter, once Christmas was in her wake. Christmas was adept at reminding people like her of all the things they had squandered.

In winter, there was no need to be out and about, doing energetic things like women in tampon ads. In winter, it was perfectly acceptable to pull the blinds down at four o'clock in the afternoon, wrap yourself in pyjamas and slipper socks, drink too much tea, watch too much television. It was expected, almost. Although, in recent months, Martha hadn't been watching too much television. She had finally admitted to Tara what she'd been doing, when her friend had phoned from London last week.

'How are you?' Tara had asked.

'Fine,' Martha said.

'Can you elaborate?' Tara was keen on particulars.

'On a scale of one to ten, ten being grand and one being fairly toxic, I'd say I'm a six.'

'It's not like you to be so positive.'

'Maybe a five-and-a-half.'

'What are you up to?' Tara had asked.

'The usual. The freelancing work is getting steadier now, a few more—'

'No, I mean right now. What are you doing right now?'

'I'm talking to you on the phone, you dope.'

'Just before I rang. What were you doing?' Sometimes Tara could be pedantic.

'Well . . .'

'Go on.'

'I . . .' Martha hesitated again, feeling exposed. This was her first time saying it out loud. 'I appear to be writing a book.'

'I thought so,' said Tara, who loved being right and almost always was.

'Why did you think so?'

'You used to talk about writing one.'

'I was usually pissed.'

Tara didn't comment on that. Instead, she said, 'How good is it?'

'Well, I don't know, do I?'

Tara said nothing. She often said that silence was one of the best weapons in a business woman's arsenal.

'OK, then. It's . . . I think it's . . . I mean it's not too . . .'

'Sorry to interrupt but could the next sentence be a complete one? It's just, I've got an incoming call from Tokyo that I need to attend to.'

'Fine,' Martha snapped. 'It's . . . alright.'

'Alright?'

'Yes. Alright.'

'Excellent,' said Tara, as if Martha had used another word. A better word.

'What's it about?'

'Don't you need to attend to Tokyo?'

'Let me worry about that.'

'It's about a woman.' Martha paused there.

'Go on.'

'I *am* going on. Give me a second.'

Tara said nothing.

'The thing about the woman . . . I mean . . . she's a . . . well, she's going through . . . that is to say . . .'

'She's an alcoholic?' Tara said.

'No!' said Martha, quickly. 'She just has . . . an uneasy relationship with alcohol.'

'Is it fiction?'

'Of course it's fiction. It has a happy ending, for starters.'

They went on to discuss other matters but, later, when Martha hung up, she felt relief. That she had said it out loud. To herself as much as to Tara. That's what she was spending the winter doing. She was writing a novel. And not drinking. Those two things seemed unlikely bedfellows. And, since she had said it out loud to Tara, credibility had grabbed hold of the idea, held it up to the light.

The car's headlights cut a narrow gorge through the road ahead, and in the shadows the hedgerows appeared grotesque and misshapen, like some hideous, relentless creature. You could drive for hours along the network of winding, narrow roads threaded through north County Dublin beyond the airport and never get anywhere. At one point, the twisting road Martha was on seemed familiar and it took her a moment to realise she was driving towards Cillian's house. She turned left at the next crossroads, then left again so that she was moving in the opposite direction now.

She often did this. Drove. Since she had stopped drinking, her life had become smaller and, in many ways, that was a relief. Sobriety had brought clarity. Not at first – of course not. But later. She knew what she wanted to do now. She wanted to stop talking about writing and write. She knew who her friends were now. Tara, mostly. And Dan, still.

The others turned out to be just people she had drank with. People she had worked with. And after work, drank with. Now, she went to her orchestra practices. Most weeks. Sunday mornings had been something of a revelation. How quiet the world was on Sunday mornings, in her new, small life. Something almost precious about them. She thought it might have something to do with the realisation of how many she had wasted.

But now, the dark, endless roads seemed to be mocking her, and the smallness of her life seemed as narrow as the light thrown by the headlamps.

She could call in to Dan. He was one of the few people Martha knew who did not mind people calling in without prior arrangement. 'Although you're the only person I know who actually does it,' he clarified. Dan lived in a pretty little mews in Sandymount, all high-ceilings and bright, spacious elegance, with a secluded terrace at the back where he could drink pints of Creme de Menthe and parade naked, if he felt like it, which he sometimes did.

And it would take ages to drive to Sandymount and that was a good thing; she was safe in the car. Driving. Distracted.

But then she remembered that Dan was at an exhibition opening in Berlin tonight. By now, he would have drunk his body weight in schnapps and swelled his German Twitter followers by about a gazillion.

She would ask him to go and see Tara when he got back tomorrow. Tara, despite herself, had liked Dan. Right from the start. It was Martha and Dan – the couple – she harboured grave misgivings about and, of course, her observation – along the lines of *this will end in disaster* – was, in the main, accurate.

The urge to somehow *fix* Tara was compelling and childish. To stamp her feet and say, *Stop it*, and cross her arms and frown until Tara agreed to be her old self once again. Martha needed her to be her old self. She relied on her in a way that she hadn't quite understood until now.

She had looked for contact details for Mathilde but she didn't know her surname or the name of her cafe. She had typed a string of words into her search engine – Mathilde, French, cafe, London, Tara, knitting, lesbian – but had so far come up with nothing.

How good is it? That's what Tara had said about the book Martha was writing. The quietness of her conviction. It was nearly better than a crystal glass of Scottish single malt. Martha remembered feeling something close to elation. Yes, elation, she didn't think that was too strong a word, even for her.

And then today, in that mean, antiseptic hospital room. Tara talking to her mother as if Martha wasn't even there. *You have to tell Martha to go.*

And Joan. The nodding certainty of her smile. *Everything worked out for the best in the end.*

Martha ended up parked outside her parents' house. The lights were off so she knew her mother wasn't there. She checked her watch. Seven o'clock. She was probably at one of her fundraising committee meetings at Sunshine House.

She fumbled for the set of keys she still had, let herself in, closed the front door and leaned against it, savouring the familiar smell, the habitual weight of the house settling around her. Even after all this time, she still thought of it as her father's place. Still felt his absence there. It was in the quietness of the kitchen now, the missing piles of papers and books strewn about the place no matter how many times her mother told him to keep his stuff in the office. It was in the yawning emptiness of the huge chair that still sat at his desk, the stuffing oozing along the seams as if the chair was in the process of giving up the ghost.

Her mother had wanted to throw the chair out last year, when the skip was there, after the landscaping job. Martha had told her she'd take it but, the truth was, there was no room for it in her living room because of the couch.

In the end, her mother kept the chair. Said nothing as the skip was hauled onto the back of a truck and driven away, even though there was more than enough room in the skip to accommodate the chair.

'Thanks, Mum,' Martha had said that day.

Her mother shook her head, folded her arms tight across her chest. 'You'll have to get rid of that ridiculous couch of yours if you want the chair, Martha. I can't have it cluttering up the house indefinitely.'

The bar in the basement had been dismantled, removed, a few short weeks after he'd died, although, at the time, those weeks had seemed longer than Milton's *Paradise Lost*.

That's where Martha wrote, on these nights when she stole into the empty house. In the room where the bar used to be. Perhaps she felt his ghost there. Or was it the ghost of the drinks he had drunk there?

Memory was a strange beast, separating the father you had adored as a child from the man you observed from more distant, adult shores.

Martha turned on her laptop, checked her mails. One from the editor of the *Irish Times Magazine* asking her to do a piece on regret. *Just 1,000 words. I need it in a week. I know you can turn it around.*

Martha could have done with the commission but regret was bad enough without having to write about it. She wrote a one-word reply – *No* – then added a *Thank you* at the end. Pressed Send.

A memory sliced through Martha's head then, sharp enough to cut. This often happened here. In her father's house. 'Stay in the moment,' the instructor had said at the first – and last – mindfulness class that Martha had attended last year. It was a difficult thing to achieve in this place. This house. The past had the upper hand here.

It was her first piece of writing. The first piece she could remember, at any rate. Martha was seven years old. The piece was entitled 'My News'.

Today is Wednesday. It is a snoey day. I like sno. My friend's name is Tara. I have two brothers. When I grow up, I'm going to be a writer like my daddy. I like my daddy. He is fun. I like playing chasing at school cos I never get caught.

Martha had written it in pencil with her left hand although she could write just as well with her right. Her teacher – a sweet fossil of a lady who lied about her age so she could avoid retirement – stuck a gold star on top of the page and told her to keep up the good work. Martha knew that Olly Clyde would chase her home after school that day. He hated anyone getting gold stars. He hated people with red hair. He hated girls who were taller than him. Even at seven, Martha was the tallest in the class. She had hair the colour of a spring carrot and a father who was sometimes on the telly. Olly Clyde – who lived with his grandparents – took particular exception to Martha Wilder. She wasn't scared of him even though her best friend Tara's big sister said that he had strangled a cat and had made a knife out of wood, sharpened to a point with flint. But no amount of knives and dead cats could make up for the fact that his legs were short and pudgy and no match for Martha's long, strong stride. She reached her front door a full minute before he rounded the corner at the top of her road, red-faced and out of breath. She'd waited until she was sure he could see her before she gave him the fingers.

Her mother was not having a lie-down that day. Instead, she was in the kitchen chopping vegetables for dinner. She didn't look up when Martha entered the kitchen. 'How was school?'

'Fine.'

'What did you do?'

'Same as usual.'

'Who did you play with in the yard?'

'Tara.'

'Get changed out of your uniform, like a good girl.'

Martha liked the name of the road where she lived. Yellow Walls Road. It had something to do with sailors, in the olden days, draping their yellow sheets over the walls along the street to dry. She had her own room and her dad had let her choose whatever paint colour she wanted. She chose blue. She said, 'Blue is not just for boys,' when her brothers challenged her on it. Her father had pushed his fingers through her blunt fringe. 'That's my girl,' he said. She did her homework standing at the whitewashed desk at the window of her bedroom. Sums, reading and spelling. Her teacher said they should ask their mothers to listen to their spellings. Instead, Martha covered the words with her hand, spelled the word out loud, then took her hand away to check if she was right. She had her homework done in less than ten minutes. She took her uniform off and hid it on the floor of her wardrobe because her mother liked her bedroom to look tidy. Her brothers – who shared a room not because they had to but because they wanted to – were four years older than Martha and had a sign on their bedroom door that said 'No Girls Allowed', which Martha ignored. Not that she wanted to go into their bedroom. She just wanted them to know that she could and she would, any time she wanted.

Her father had swayed a little as he stepped into the house that evening. 'I bring glad tidings,' he bellowed.

'Did you bring sweets too?' her brother Mark shouted from the floor of the den where James had wrestled him to the floor and was sitting on him.

'You're late,' said her mother.

'If you kiss me, I'll tell you my news,' he told her, sweeping her dark hair from her neck and kissing the lobe of her ear.

'Would you stop that,' she said, moving away from him and opening the oven door to haul out a chicken. 'Look, it's dried up now. After all my effort.'

'Why didn't you eat it? When it was ready?' He reached into the fridge, got one of his beers out. He drank half of it out of the bottle, standing at the open fridge, then tipped the rest into a glass.

'We were waiting for you. You'd said you'd be home hours ago.'

'What's your news, Dad?' asked Martha, picking a roast parsnip off a dish. He grinned at her.

'Only the best, Mo.' Her father was the only one who called her Mo, no matter how many times her mother told him not to. Martha didn't mind.

'The newspaper want me to cover the election in America.' He burped loudly, then caught Martha's eye and the two of them giggled.

'You're going to America? Again?'

'It's work, baby. Good work. A bit of reporting for RTÉ as well. It's a great opportunity.'

'How long?'

'A few weeks, maybe. Definitely not longer than a month.'

'A *month*!'

'I'll be the man of the house when you're gone,' said Mark, crawling into the kitchen as best he could with James sprawled on his back. He was alluding to the fact that he was born twenty-two minutes before James which meant that, in this contest at least, he had won.

'Sit at the table,' her mother demanded, and everyone did. Her father lit a cigarette. Her mother moved her food around her plate with a fork in the absent-minded, lethargic way she had.

Martha was starving and roast chicken was her favourite, dried up or not. She asked for seconds. 'No,' said her mother. 'The leftovers are for tomorrow. I don't want to be stuck cooking again.'

'Dad, I got a gold star for my news today,' said Martha when she had finished. 'Do you want to read it?'

'Sure I do, Mo.'

'Her name is Martha.' Her mother got up from the table and gathered the empty plates, scraping the remains of the food into the bin. The noise made Martha's teeth shudder. She thrust her copybook towards her father and he read it out loud, raising his voice to be heard over the terrible scraping sound.

Her mother swung around when he'd finished. 'What do you mean, you have two brothers? What about your sister? Why didn't you say you have a sister?'

Martha didn't think her mother would mention Amelia today. She had seemed fine. Downstairs chopping vegetables instead of having one of her lie-downs. In her clothes instead of her pyjamas and dressing gown. Her hair brushed and neat today. Shiny even. Like she'd washed it earlier.

'Ah, leave her alone, Miriam, she's only a kid.'

Her mother turned on him then and Martha wished she had one of those teleporters they had on *Star Trek* that could beam you to another place.

'And so was Amelia. Just a kid. You remember, don't you, Gerry? You remember Amelia? Martha's twin sister.'

'Of course I do, love.' He reached for her, covered her hand with his own. She snatched it away as if he had burnt her. Martha could see that her eyes were bright and that she would cry soon. 'She might have been with us for only four years but that does not mean we can forget her.'

Her father walked towards her again, his arms outstretched. 'Don't come near me,' her mother said, dumping the plates on the counter and opening the kitchen door. She glared at Martha. 'Snow has a W at the end. And you have two brothers *and one sister*. Don't ever forget that.'

Martha sometimes wondered what it would have been like to have a twin. A proper twin, like Mark had James. Instead of having one who was born with spina bifida and who died in a place called Sunshine House on the day before she was supposed to be four. Martha didn't think Sunshine House sounded like a place where people could die. Her only clear memory of Amelia was the day of her funeral, when she lay in a box in the sitting room. Amelia looked like she was asleep so Martha poked her skinny little arm with her finger to wake her up and her mother had slapped her hand away and said, *Stop that*, in a low hiss that made Martha feel like crying except she didn't. Her father took her out to the garden and pushed her so high on the swing she could see the walls along the street that used to be draped with yellow sheets but were not anymore because the sailors had all sailed away.

After dinner, her mother went to bed and her father took a bottle of whiskey into his office and closed the door. Martha could hear him pouring the whiskey and lighting a cigarette before thumping his fingers against the keys on his typewriter.

Her brothers were watching *Dr Who* on the telly in the den. They told her to get out when she sat on the couch because it was too scary for a baby like her. She stayed until it was over then put herself to bed. She brushed her teeth but didn't say her prayers like her mother told her to because her father said that heaven and God were like the tooth fairy or Santa Claus for adults. Martha wasn't quite sure if her dad believed in the tooth fairy or in Santa Claus. She was pretty sure he didn't believe in God or heaven. He never said it when her mother was around because her mother often said she would see Amelia again in heaven and that she couldn't wait. Martha wondered when she would go and see Amelia in heaven and if she would come back. She didn't think so because Amelia never came back. She was sure that if Amelia did come back – even for a day – her mother would be happy and smile and be glad when Martha got a gold star in school. Through the bedroom wall, she could hear the strike of a match along the bumpy side of the box and knew that her mother was lighting the candle on the table where all the photographs were. There was one with Martha in it as well, near the back of the table. Martha and Amelia were dressed in matching green skirts and polo necks. They looked the same in the picture except that Amelia was smaller.

In the photo, they stood together on the couch in the den and there was a hand, right at the edge of the photograph. Martha knew it was her mother's hand because of the rings and because of the way it stretched towards Amelia in case she fell.

Martha read a chapter of *Well Done Secret Seven*. Her father had bought her all fifteen books in the series on his way back from London last week. Her mother said it was too much for one little girl and her father said a girl could never have too many books.

When she turned off the lamp beside her bed, she pulled the duvet over her head and shut her eyes tight. Even so, she was sure she could hear the Daleks rattling along the landing, look-ing for her. She knew if she told her father he would carry her on his hip around the house, looking behind every door and in every cupboard until they were certain there were no Daleks lurking in the shadows. But she knew he wouldn't hear her call-ing him through the doors of her bedroom and all the way down the stairs, into his office. And she didn't want to get out of bed in case the Daleks heard the creak of the floor beneath her foot and came to exterminate her. So she stayed under the duvet with her eyes shut tight and told herself that if there were no such thing as God or tooth fairies or Santa Claus, then there was probably no such thing as Daleks and that maybe there was no such thing as Amelia anymore because she was supposed to be in heaven but if there was no such thing as heaven, then where could she be?

Martha left the house before her mother arrived home. Easier that way. No need for explanations about the bruises on her face. Her mother was a worrier. Also a pessimist. She would assume the worst before Martha got a chance to explain.

Martha supposed she couldn't blame her. She had been an accident-prone drinker.

Eleven

'Take off your watch. Do you have a phone?'

'No.'

'Stand straight. Hold your arms out to the side.'

The guard didn't tell Roman his name. Nor did he look at the boy as he issued his instructions. He ran his hands along Roman's arms, down his chest, his legs.

'Open your mouth.' Roman could see stiff grey hairs poking out of the man's nose. Feel the man's breath – hot and stale – against his face. He pushed a stick inside Roman's mouth. Like an ice pop stick. Scraped it against the inside of his cheek. Put it into a sample bottle.

'Turn your pockets out. Take the laces out of your runners. And the belt out of your trousers. Put them in this bag.'

His fingers were pushed, one by one, onto a piece of inky sponge then pressed into individual boxes on a form.

'Sign there.'

Roman signed.

'Follow me.'

Roman followed the man down a corridor. He wondered if he would be put in a cell. He had seen prison cells on the telly. His feet felt heavy. He kept walking.

He wasn't sure which garda station he was in. He had sat in the back of the police car, kept his head down. The car had jerked to a stop and Roman looked but they were at the back of a building he didn't recognise. He was led inside between two guards.

Now, he was in a small, airless room. The walls were painted a dull grey. There were no windows and the fluorescent tube overhead filled the room with a harsh white light.

In the centre of the room, there was a table, two chairs on one side, one chair on the other. The guard pointed to the single chair and Roman sat on it. The guard left. Roman heard the rattle of keys, the door being locked and the sharp clip of the man's shoes against the floor, growing fainter.

Now the only sound he could hear was his breathing. It sounded loud. Fast.

Roman shifted in the hard plastic chair. He had pins and needles in his legs. He couldn't remember when he had last eaten. He didn't feel hungry. He didn't feel anything.

He jumped when the door opened. Two men entered. Roman recognised one of them. Cillian Larkin. He stooped his head as he walked through the door. Roman had met him a few times at the youth club. He had taught him how to play chess. He was OK. Decent. He nodded briefly at Roman, moved towards a machine in the corner that looked like a DVD player. He pressed a button on it. A red light came on and in a small monitor on the wall behind the machine, Roman could see himself now. He looked smaller on the screen. He looked like a scared little kid. He sat straighter in the chair, folded his arms across his chest, pressed his hands into his armpits to stop them shaking.

Cillian looked at his watch. 'It is twenty-three hundred hours on Friday the twenty-first of February, 2014. The suspect, Roman Matus, has been cautioned. Present at this interview are Detective Cillian Larkin and Detective Michael Murphy.'

The two detectives sat down on the other side of the table. Cillian leaned forward. 'Your mother's outside. She can sit in on this interview, since you're a minor.'

Roman shook his head. He hadn't known she would be in the bank on Wednesday morning. Her face, when she saw him. The way it fell. The shape his name made on her mouth. Like she couldn't believe it was him. Like she still thought the best of him.

He could get through this, he thought, so long as he didn't have to see her face.

'You have to say it out loud. For the tape,' Cillian explained, pointing towards the monitor.

'No,' said Roman. His mouth was dry.

'Speak up,' said the other man. Detective Murphy.

Roman cleared his throat. 'No,' he said again. 'I don't want her here.'

Cillian looked at his file. 'And I see you've waived your right to a solicitor.'

'Yes,' said Roman.

Cillian shook his head. 'That is a bad idea, Roman. Do you understand the seriousness of this crime? Armed robbery? Possibly attempted murder? We can place you at the scene and we have witnesses who will say they saw you with a gun in your hand. We've taken your fingerprints. We'll know in the morning if your prints are on the gun that was used to shoot the victim, Mr Hartmann.'

Roman knew they would find his prints on Jimmy's gun. He hadn't worn gloves. It hadn't occurred to him.

If it hadn't been for the drawing, they might have gotten away with it. Roman wouldn't owe Jimmy anything anymore. They'd be quits. Jimmy had given his word.

Jimmy had found it at the bottom of the old man's safe deposit box, after he'd filled the pockets of his trousers, his shirt, his jacket with the neat bundles of notes he'd lifted from the box.

'Don't touch that,' the old man had barked when Jimmy'd reached for the drawing. Jimmy had ignored him, slid the stiff piece of paper from the clear plastic folder it was in. Roman glanced at it. It was a charcoal drawing. They'd worked with charcoal in Art last year. It was a drawing of a woman kneeling in a field, holding the body of a man.

'Come on,' Roman had said. 'You got what you wanted. Let's go.'

'Don't fucken tell me what to do, you little runt,' said Jimmy.

'That is mine.' The old man's voice was loud then. Any louder and it would have been a shout. 'It is not for the likes of you.'

Jimmy had grinned. 'Maybe this little scribble is worth a bob or two and if it isn't, I can always use it to wipe my arse, can't I?' He put the drawing back inside the folder, slid it inside his jacket.

That was when the man had pushed himself out of the chair with his good leg. Threw himself towards Jimmy. Jimmy shoved the man away from him so that he fell, landed on the floor. Jimmy reached for the gun that he had tucked into the waistband of his trousers, pointed it at the man's head.

Roman hurled himself at Jimmy. 'Get off me,' Jimmy had shouted, reaching for Roman's hair, his eyes. His fingers clawed and pulled at the boy's balaclava. He reefed it off.

Roman reached for the gun in Jimmy's hand, wrapping his fingers around the handle that was slippy with sweat. The old man shouted in a language Roman didn't understand. The muzzle of the gun pointed this way and that. Jimmy's fingers tightened around the trigger. The gun went off. The old man stopped shouting.

'Will he be OK?' Roman asked Cillian. 'Mr Hartmann?'

'A bit late to be concerned about the man's welfare now, isn't it?' said the other policeman. There was contempt in his voice. Roman couldn't blame him.

'Who were the others? At the bank?' the man barked at him.

Roman did not reply. He knew what would happen if he told the truth. To him. To Mama. He knew what Jimmy was capable of.

The silence in the room stretched like elastic. Cillian took his phone out of his pocket, swiped at the screen and pushed the phone across the desk towards Roman. 'How well do you know this man?'

It was a picture of Lenny. Roman shrugged. 'I don't know him,' he said. Inside his chest, his heart thumped like a judge's gavel. What did the police know? And would Jimmy think that it was Roman who'd told them whatever it was they knew?

'Did you start working for Jimmy Carty when you moved into his house? Or was it later?' Cillian said.

Roman concentrated on an ink spot on the desk in front of him. Cillian sounded so certain of everything. Roman wished he felt certain of anything.

He shook his head. 'I don't know what you're talking about.'

He knew the exact day. It was the *one clean break* day. That's how he remembered it so clearly.

Roman had gotten used to things, he supposed. Uncle Lech being dead and the shabby room at Jimmy's house and the telling of the lies to Babcia on the Sunday-night phone call and Mama not having time to do anything anymore except work and sleep. He didn't like it. But he was used to it.

But nothing stays the same. He should have known that. One wrong move and everything tumbles down, like the houses of cards Roman used to make when he was a kid.

Mama fell on her way home from work late one night and broke her arm. One clean break. That's how the doctor in the hospital had described it, like it was a good thing.

That's when he had started working for Jimmy.

She slid on a glassy slick of ice that she would have noticed if she hadn't been so tired. She was always tired now.

She fell at the edge of the footpath, one foot lifted in readiness to cross the road, so that when she landed, it was in the shallow curve of the gutter at the edge of the road. Roman imagined her lying there. In the gutter. With her eyes closed, the scooped-out concrete of the gutter almost like a hammock around her. The pain in her arm – trapped beneath her body – and her ankle where she'd torn ligaments did not make itself known until later.

'Your mother got lucky. It's a clean break,' the man in the white coat at the hospital said, after they'd spent hours sitting in hard plastic chairs in an overcrowded, overheated room that smelled of stale bodies and damp clothes.

'I need to be at work in two hours,' Mama had said.

The doctor looked at her then, as if he had just noticed her. As if he hadn't known she was there until now.

'What do you do?' the doctor asked, placing the nib of his pen on another interminable form attached to a clipboard.

'I'm a cleaner.'

Roman stuffed his hands into the pockets of his jacket. Made fists of them while the doctor scribbled the word in one of the blank boxes. She didn't even seem to mind. The word. Saying it. Out loud. To strangers. To this self-satisfied man to whom Roman and Rosa were just two more people in a long procession of the walking wounded on whose behalf he would fill in forms that night.

Roman minded. 'What are you getting your ma for Mother's Day, Roman?' Ian Flynn had shouted at him in the classroom, in front of everybody. Roman ignored him. Not that that ever worked. Not with Ian Flynn.

'A scrubbing brush,' Ian roared, his face creasing with his donkey laugh, his stomach quivering like an enormous jelly.

'Maybe you could get *your* mother a cure for disappointment,' piped up Meadhbh from the door of the room. 'I'm sure she needs one after spawning an idiot like you.'

Roman had felt two things, equally and urgently. He felt

grateful. That Meadhbh was his friend, his best friend, actually – well, his and Adam's.

He felt shame too.

'I'm a cleaner,' Rosa said. She kept it short and simple.

'Well, I'm afraid your cleaning days are over for the time being. Six weeks at least in plaster. And you need to keep the ankle elevated. Give the ligaments a chance to knit. You'll just have to take it easy, eh? Get someone else to mop the floors, am I right?'

Rosa nodded, as if his suggestion were an option. As if there were somebody else she could count on to mop the floors in her stead.

One clean break and the cards they had been dealt came tumbling down, lay where they fell.

There was no safety net. No social welfare payment coming their way. No medical card. No sick leave.

There was nothing.

The rent was due on Friday. Roman opened their cupboard in the kitchen when they returned to the house, after he'd helped Mama get into bed. There were two tins of chopped tomatoes, half a packet of pasta, a cup of rice, a few scoops of porridge oats, two mucky potatoes, a jar of instant coffee.

At ten past nine in the morning, Rosa's mobile rang. Mrs Mulligan. 'I don't appreciate being let down like this,' she began when Roman answered the phone. 'You're already ten minutes late and if you're any later, I'll have to postpone my hair appointment.'

'This is Roman. Rosa's son.'

'Oh.'

'And you can fuck right off.'

'How *dare* y—'

Roman hung up. The sense of satisfaction was short-lived. Mama would be angry. Mrs Mulligan was a weekly job. Thirty euro that could be depended on. That's what Mama would say. As if anyone could depend on thirty euro. Roman filched two slices of bread from the Lithuanian couple's cupboard, as well as a chunk of their cheese. He made a sandwich and left it on a plate, along with a glass of water, on the locker by her bed. She looked young when she was asleep. Sort of innocent, as if she had no idea what one clean break meant for them. Roman went to school. The afternoons, evenings and nights were long enough. School was a distraction. And he had his friends. Meadhbh and Adam. The other kids left him alone because of Meadhbh and Adam. Meadhbh mostly. Everybody liked Meadhbh. The few muffled comments here and there about him being a foreigner, or the smell of the weird food in his lunchbox, him not having a dad, him not having Nike high-tops, his hair being too long, his trousers too short. Nothing major. Nothing the other kids – even the Irish ones – didn't get from time to time. Nothing he couldn't handle.

The next day, the bill from the hospital arrived. It was addressed to his mother but Roman opened it. A hundred euro. Roman tore it into small pieces, put it inside an empty egg box in the green bin. He went to school. When he got home, Mama was still in bed. She struggled into a sitting position when he opened the door, and he saw the fear in her eyes, the way it drained when she saw that it was Roman at the door. He sat on the edge of her bed, careful to give her plastered arm, her swollen ankle, a wide berth. 'We need to come up with a plan,' Roman said. 'While you're getting better.'

Mama shook her head. 'I don't want you to worry about things like that. That's my job.'

'The rent is due tomorrow, isn't it?' Roman said.

'I have it put by,' she said, nodding towards the wooden box that her grandmother had given her when she was a girl. It was supposed to be a jewellery box.

'What about next month's rent?' said Roman. Mama's fore-head was damp with sweat. Her hair, hanging like greasy curtains around her face, was dull and limp. The doctor had given her a plastic covering to put over the plaster on her arm in the shower but she hadn't used it yet and Roman didn't suggest that she should. He didn't think she'd be able for the walk down the hall to the bathroom. Climbing into the bath, standing on her swollen ankle under the shower, trying to wash herself with one hand. Roman didn't think she'd be able for any of that. She had only broken her arm but it seemed to Roman like she had done more than that, like she had broken something inside herself, something essential.

She looked exhausted, like a wrung-out cloth.

She shook her head. 'I don't want you to worry, Roman. I'll speak to Jimmy and—'

'No!' The word came out louder than he'd intended.

'What do you mean, no?'

'Just . . . I mean . . . I'll talk to him, OK?'

'It's not your responsibility, Roman.'

'You said it was you and me, Mama. Against the world. Didn't you?' Mama's smile was weak but there. She nodded.

Roman was in the kitchen when Jimmy came in.

'. . . and the doctor at the hospital said she might be able to go back to work in three weeks. Maybe even less.' Roman's face flushed at the lie but Jimmy didn't notice. He was busy shaking his head, slowly, like he was sad. Or disappointed. 'Look, Romeo, if it were up to me . . . but the bank manager doesn't want to hear excuses when it comes to the mortgage, am I right? He won't give a flyin' fuck about you or your sad little story, will he?'

Jimmy looked at Roman. Waited, like he was expecting a response. Roman shook his head. 'And you know, apart from the rent, your sweet mama owes me a not insignificant sum of money, let's not forget.'

Roman didn't mention the fact that it was Lech who had owed the money. There was no point. Not with Jimmy.

'And I know I'm a bit of a pushover, especially when it comes to the fairer sex, and, let's face it, they don't come much fairer than Rosa, am I right?' Jimmy smiled and nudged Roman in the ribs. Hard. 'But I'm not runnin' a charity here, know what I mean?'

Roman took a breath, steadied himself. 'I will get a job.'

'A little runt like you?' said Jimmy. 'No offence, kid, but no one's going to be offering you a job any time soon.'

'I could wash cars.' Roman had seen people – men, granted – at traffic lights with brushes and pails of soapy water, swiping at the windscreens of the idling cars before the drivers had a chance to tell them not to.

Jimmy laughed again. He was always laughing. Loud laughs with no humour in them. 'No right thinking man is going to let an underage immigrant within a mile of their wheels. Fuck knows what damage you'd cause.'

'I'll do anything, Jimmy.' Roman knew he shouldn't beg. He had told himself to keep calm. To talk to Jimmy man-to-man. Now, here he was with the begging bowl in his hands, shaking it under Jimmy's nose.

Jimmy studied Roman like he was a page in the *Racing Post*. 'Well . . . I suppose I could . . . maybe there *is* something you could do for me.'

'A job?' Roman felt something leap in his chest.

Jimmy shrugged. 'Yeah. I suppose. I've an opening coming up in my . . . business. I need a delivery man. Someone I can trust.'

An image of the small brown-paper packages that Jimmy used to slip to Uncle Lech swam to the surface of Roman's mind. Jimmy hadn't called them deliveries then. 'I've a little something for your uncle,' he'd say.

A little something.

'I can do that,' said Roman and his voice was filled with the kind of conviction that belonged to a man. A delivery man.

'I'll tell you what, I'll give you a trial run, see how you go, alright?' said Jimmy. 'As a favour, yeah?'

Roman nodded. 'I won't let you down.'

Jimmy looked amused. 'Seems like you're the man of the house now, young Romeo, wha'?' He laughed, sat down and put his feet on a kitchen chair. 'And I *know* you won't let me down. Will you?' Jimmy's pale blue eyes bore into Roman's face like a drill. 'I won't,' Roman said. He knew he wouldn't get a second chance. He'd have to be good. Be the best delivery man Jimmy had ever had.

'And this is top secret, yeah?' Jimmy tapped his nose with his finger. 'Just between you and me. No need for your mother to worry her pretty little head about it, OK?'

Roman nodded. 'How much will you—?'

'We'll get to that, son. All in good time. A trial run first. Then we can talk turkey.'

Upstairs, Roman told his mother that she wasn't to worry about anything. That Jimmy had agreed to cut them some slack. 'You can just concentrate on getting better, Mama, OK?'

Rosa struggled out of her covers, sat on the edge of her bed. Her face was grey and pinched. He could tell she was in pain, just from looking at her face. She had painkillers but she didn't like to take them. There was a woman who worked in the nursing home who was addicted to painkillers. She didn't want to take any chances. She didn't mention Lech in that conversation but Roman knew she worried about drugs. Addiction. Running in the family like eye colour or height.

'I don't want you working for Jimmy.'

'I'm not working for him. Maybe just a few odd-jobs. Only until you're better.'

'No, Roman,' said Rosa, quieter now.

'Don't worry. Everything will be OK. You'll see.'

Rosa shook her head. 'Things were supposed to be different here. In Ireland.'

'Things are different.'

'Better, I mean. I wanted things to be better for you.'

'I know.'

'Jimmy will get you into trouble.'

'I can handle myself.'

'You're just a boy.' But there was resignation in her words. She knew too. Their options were limited.

Roman handed her a cup of coffee, told her to get back into bed. She was exhausted. After the hospital. And working all the hours before she fell.

Roman sat at the small, rickety table in their room, finished his homework, thought about being a man. A delivery man.

It would only be for a little while. Until Mama's cast came off. Until they got back on their feet. Again.

One clean break, the doctor said.

Sometimes that's all it took.

Cillian sat in his chair, waiting, like Roman was going to tell him everything.

Roman said nothing.

He wondered how long he'd been sitting in the chair. Despite the stuffiness of the room, he felt cold.

He wished things were different. It was like wishing on a star. Or throwing money down a wishing well. Pointless.

Cillian pulled his hand down one side of his face. The dark shadow of his bristles crackled against the skin of his fingers.

When Cillian stood up, the room seemed smaller, the ceiling lower. He crammed his hands into the front pockets of his jeans, leaned his back against a wall. 'If you don't talk to me, Roman, I can't help you. It's your choice.'

'What's going to happen now?' Roman asked. Cillian picked the papers from the desk, shuffled them, gathered them with a paperclip.

'We're going to have to keep you in custody,' he said. 'This is a very serious crime and you're not cooperating so we don't have any choice. There'll be a hearing. Maybe tomorrow. You'll more than likely be remanded in custody unless . . . well, unless anything changes.' Cillian paused there, waited. But Roman didn't say anything. Kept his head down, concentrated on the ink spot on the table.

He wouldn't be going home tonight. He had known that, of course he had. But it was different now that it was happening. Everything was different now.

'Interview ended at . . .' The other policeman consulted his watch. 'Twenty-three forty-five on Friday the twenty-first of February, 2014.' He stood up, indicated that Roman should do the same.

The boy's fear was liquid now, roaring through his veins like blood, pulsing against his temples, the narrow frame of his chest. Cillian was wrong. He didn't have choices.

Choices were for other people. People like Meadhbh and Adam. They'd be walking home from school tomorrow. Laughing at something stupid Adam said, sharing a bag of chips or a Pot Noodle and never thinking about all the choices they had.

Babcia said self-pity was a terrible waste of time.

Still, he felt it now.

He put one foot in front of the other, moved towards the door. This is how he would manage, he thought. One step at a time. He wouldn't have to make any decisions or decide where to run to next because there were no decisions left to be made, no more running to be run. In a way, it was a relief. Not to have to decide. Not to have to run.

But Roman didn't feel relief. There was only the fear.

Twelve

It still irked her when she woke up the following morning.

Fuck sake.

Want some coffee, baby?

The voice, while distant, had had a distinct northern twang. Cillian had probably met her in Donegal. She must be staying with him. Or maybe she'd moved in? Into that wreck of a cottage in the middle of nowhere, God help her.

She distracted herself by examining her collection of injuries in the bathroom mirror. The bruises around her ribcage were particularly impressive. She ran her fingers along the palette of colours. In some places, her skin was so dark it seemed unlikely it would ever return to normal.

She applied her make-up carefully but, even so, it would be impossible to avoid her family's questions. Her mother was insisting on taking them to lunch after the memorial service.

'Try not to be late, Martha,' her mother had said on the phone earlier. Her tone was filled with low expectation.

And Martha wouldn't have been late if she hadn't stopped at the hospital before the service.

On the surface, Tara seemed improved. No longer under the covers, pretending to be asleep. But still in bed, her hand clamped around the oxygen mask beside her. Mrs Bolton offered to leave when Martha arrived but Tara insisted that she stay. 'You won't be here long, will you, Martha?' Tara had said. 'You're going to Sunshine House today, aren't you?'

Surely a person with proper, honest-to-goodness PTSD would not remember that kind of detail? Although it was Tara, so perhaps it wasn't out of the question.

When Mrs Bolton left the room to freshen the water in the vase where the stinking lilies still bloomed, Martha took her chance.

'Have you spoken to Mathilde?' she asked.

Tara shook her head. 'She told me not to contact her.'

'Only if you weren't going to tell your family about the two of you.'

'Well, I didn't. And I'm not going to.'

'Jesus, Tara, this is ridiculous.' Martha wanted to shake her. She knew she probably shouldn't.

'Can you please stop haranguing me?'

'Haranguing? Seriously? Who says that?'

'The doctor said I have to avoid stress.' There was the hand, reaching for the mask again.

Still, Martha persisted. 'Discarding a perfectly good relationship sounds pretty stressful to me.'

'Well, *you* did it,' Tara said, glaring at Martha.

'Exactly.'

Martha scorched out of the hospital car-park. She should slow down. Two more penalty points and she'd lose her licence. Again. Although the first time had not been an innocent accumulation of forgotten speeding fines and illegal parking. 'Driving under the influence.' It seemed like the judge had shouted it from his bench. It had made an arresting headline in the next day's newspapers.

She drove five kilometres shy of the speed limit and tried not to worry about Tara. She was made of stern stuff, wasn't she? She'd snap out of it soon.

Martha's family took up most of a pew in the little chapel on the grounds of Sunshine House. If her father or Amelia were there, they might have filled two, because no doubt Amelia would have married, produced grandchildren for their mother, like Mark had done. Martha always imagined Amelia as the good girl. Perhaps because she had only been four when she died. She would have been the type of daughter who never forgot Mother's Day, who gave thoughtful, beautifully wrapped birthday gifts. She would have named her first-born daughter Miriam, for their mother, and it would have been Amelia who insisted on extending her happy and comfortable family home to include a granny flat where their mother could live, in her dotage.

Martha wondered if her mother imagined these things too.

She crept up the side aisle of the chapel into the small space at the end of the pew beside Mark, whose eyes were closed, although Martha suspected exhaustion rather than devotion; fatherhood had taken him by storm. She lowered herself into the seat beside him and would have gotten away with her late arrival had it not been for one of Mark's twins – Amelia – waving at her and pulling at her grandmother's sleeve. 'There she is, see? Over there. There's Martha.' As if there had been a discussion earlier about the possibility of Martha not arriving on time. Or at all.

Afterwards, her mother said, 'That was lovely, wasn't it?'

'What was?'

'The memorial service.' Her mother's voice was strained with barely contained impatience.

'Yes. Sorry. I wasn't sure . . . Yes, it was.'

'I *did* tell you what time it started, didn't I?'

'Yes, sorry . . . I had to—'

'Are you coming to the restaurant for lunch? I included you in the booking.'

'Of course. I'm looking forward to it.' This wasn't, strictly speaking, true but Martha felt she owed her mother on these occasions. Perhaps making up for the times she hadn't bothered going. Or worse, the times when she had, when she'd been drinking.

They drove in convoy to the restaurant. Martha used the time to come up with a valid excuse as to why she had to leave in an hour.

It wasn't that she wasn't fond of her family. She was just uneasy in places where alcohol could be obtained with a raised finger.

Her brothers and their wives – Helen and Anna – and Mark's two little girls – four-year-old twins, Amelia and Alice – were already sitting around a large table when Martha arrived.

The passing years had done little to diminish how identical James and Mark were. They had aged in exactly the same way: the beginnings of soft craft-beer paunches around their middles, matching widow's peaks that appeared to be retreating at the same pace, the same patch of coarse grey hair springing like heather through the triangle of white open-necked shirts. Their features were cherubic: round, open faces, pale blue eyes, small, shallow dimples and deep – matching – clefts in the centre of their chins. Everyone agreed they took after their mother while Martha and her father had been the tall, angular ones who looked like they might upset a table laden with crockery in their attempts to negotiate their place.

Helen was pregnant. James had announced it at the last family dinner that Martha had attended. 'We're pregnant,' he had said, beaming at the head of the table where their father used to sit.

'Is it twins?' asked Mark, always competing.

'I think this family has been plagued by enough twins, don't you?' said James, nodding towards Mark and Martha.

The thing was, Martha had never felt like a twin. She felt a little . . . separate.

'I'll need to go at three.' Martha leaned towards her mother during a heated debate between Mark and James about the ending of the director's cut of *Blade Runner*.

'Could you at least wait until we've ordered before you start talking about when you want to leave?'

'No, it's just . . .' Martha found it difficult to make herself understood when she was amongst her family. Like she was on one end of a transatlantic call, they on the other, with nobody taking account of the time delay.

There was a very definite, very loud chorus of *nos* when the waiter asked if they would like to see the wine list.

I'm driving.

A little early for me, I'm afraid.

I'm on antibiotics – this from Mark. Nobody asked him what for. He was a longstanding, devout hypochondriac.

The waiter nodded when they finished, glanced at Martha, as if waiting for her reason, then left with the wine list, undisturbed, under his arm.

The silence that followed was a little awkward. James – a keen keeper of the peace – whipped his wallet out of his pocket from which he plucked a colour 3D photograph of their baby, accompanied by much detail of the technology involved. Everybody said that the baby was the image of Helen – which would have been ideal – when in fact he was a ringer for James (and Mark, obviously), right down to the snub nose (which was cute on the baby) and fivehead (which is what they called James's – and Mark's – enormous forehead).

'Why are you wearing your sunglasses inside?' Amelia – the inquisitive one – asked. Alice – the resigned one – studied Martha before returning her attention to her pasta.

'Because your smile is so bright, I need to shield my eyes from it,' Martha said.

'I'm not smiling now,' said Amelia, fixing Martha with her best sombre face.

'Eat up, Amelia,' Anna said.

Martha felt a sort of expectancy around the table.

Conversation lulled, loaded forks paused halfway to mouths, water glasses were returned to the table. An explanation was required, Martha felt. She took off her sunglasses. 'You should see the other guy,' she said, grinning, even though grinning hurt.

There was a synchronised intake of breath.

'Oh my God!'

'That looks painful.'

'Fudging hell,' said Mark; Anna didn't permit cursing in front of the children.

'What did you do?' her mother asked.

'It's not as bad as it looks,' said Martha.

'You weren't . . . ?'

'No!'

This came out loud enough to attract the scrutiny of other diners. Martha put her glasses back on and looked at her mother and brothers, in whose faces she could detect the familiar trace of doubt. This was the thing about families, Martha thought. They had you pegged, no matter what you did. She had never made any sort of declaration. There had been no announcement about her decision not to drink. No confidences shared about her realisation that she was someone who had an uneasy relationship with alcohol. For a long time, they hadn't even mentioned it although, of course, they'd noticed. It was like they were holding their breath. Like they couldn't quite believe what was right there, in front of their faces.

She supposed she couldn't blame them. She had thought about it the other day. Thought about gathering her sobriety in her arms, throwing it onto the counter of the Pound pub. Exchanging it for one drink. Then another. And another.

'No,' she said again, quieter this time. 'I was at that . . . bank situation in Swords the other day.'

'Goodness, the one that got held up?' said Helen, one hand cupping her mouth, the other laid protectively across the tiny swell of her belly.

'Yes.'

'Leave it to our Martha to be in the thick of the drama, eh?' said James, swilling his water around his glass as if he were aerating a fine wine. He smiled when he said it but there was a hint of accusation. Martha supposed she only had herself to blame. She had form.

'What does "held up" mean?' enquired Amelia through a mouthful of penne.

'Don't speak with your mouth full,' said Anna, tucking a linen napkin into the collar of Amelia's dress. Martha winked at the little girl, who winked back, albeit with two eyes rather than the traditional one.

'Anyway, I just happened to be in there with Tara and—'

'Tara's home?' said Mark, who had always harboured – unfulfilled – notions about Tara.

'Will you let her finish?' said James, who had harboured similar notions.

Martha picked up her glass of water. 'Maybe we should change the subject?' she said, nodding towards Amelia, whose eyes were full of questions she was getting ready to ask.

'Is Tara alright?' Mark persisted.

'Well, she . . . she's in hospital actually.'

'Oh my gosh!' said Mark.

'What happened to her?' asked James.

'No, it's . . . it's nothing that bad. Nothing serious I mean, I mean, she's fine. Really. Just a bit . . . shaken, I suppose.'

Now Mark was Googling the bank raid and James was talking about the inefficiency of the guards and Anna was picking a tube of pasta off the floor and Helen was nodding and pretending to listen to James, and Mark told them the name of the man who had been shot and her mother shook her head and said how lucky Tara was that she hadn't been badly injured.

But she had been injured, Martha realised, sitting there. And it *was* bad. Because Tara wasn't herself. Some part of her – an important part – had been removed, as surgically as an appendix.

A waiter bearing a tray full of martinis passed close enough for Martha to reach out, lift one. One martini. Just the one.

'Are you alright, Martha? You're very pale all of a sudden,' Helen said.

Martha reached for her water, drank it in one gulp. 'I'm fine, thanks.'

'But the bank robbery happened three days ago,' her mother said. 'Why didn't you tell us?'

'I didn't want to worry you,' said Martha. Her mother nodded, allowing the observation. She was a champion worrier. A persistent headache could be a brain tumour. Forgetting the name of a substitute teacher you had for three months in primary school was symptomatic of early onset dementia. Any type of blemish on your person was, more than likely, the beginnings of a rash that would lead to bacterial meningitis. Or viral. Whichever the fatal one was. Even her tendency to worry was fraught with worry, stress being such a significant factor now in so many cancers malignant ones, obviously.

'Amelia used to come up in bruises like that,' her mother said now, nodding towards Martha's face. 'When she'd get her injections. Her arms would be covered in them, the poor child. Not that she ever complained. There was one time when she . . .'

Dessert arrived eventually. Martha finished her tiramisu before everyone else, eating the same way she had drank, which is to say that she only stopped when there was nothing left.

Now, the little girls were discussing their ballet class.

'Mum said I'm the goodest in the class,' said Amelia.

'And me,' chimed Alice. Amelia sighed a long-suffering sigh which made them laugh.

'You know, your granddad was a great dancer,' said Martha, leaning towards the girls. 'He taught me how to waltz.'

'I didn't think boys could dance,' said Amelia.

'Not all of them,' said Martha. 'But some can.'

'Yes, your granddad wasn't a bad dancer,' her mother conceded. 'When he was sober,' she added, under her breath.

'What's sober?' asked Amelia. You could never get away with anything with Amelia. Martha loved that about her.

'Better eat your ice-cream before it melts,' Anna advised.

Now James and Mark – who ran a dry-cleaning business together – were telling their mother about a new shop they were planning to open.

'. . . never been a dry cleaner's there before but my market research showed that—'

'*I* did the market research, James.'

'You *started* it and then *I*—'

'Only because I had to attend that boring bloody conference in—'

'You *volunteered* yourself. You said you'd never been to Leeds, remember?'

'Why would I bloody well want to go to Leeds?'

And on it went. Martha wondered how they ever got any actual work done but they did, somehow.

Anna was telling Helen about a great yoga class she had attended when she was pregnant with the twins and Amelia wanted to know where she and Alice had *been* before they were in Anna's tummy and Martha thought about her father, dancing with her in the kitchen one Christmas Eve, and about the last time she had danced. The night she had taught Cillian Larkin how to waltz.

*   *   *

He had cooked dinner for her that night. He liked to cook, used it as a way to unwind after work.

'This is pretty domesticated, isn't it?' he'd said.

'Don't go getting any ideas.'

'Still, it's been a year.'

'Not until next Thursday.'

'So you *do* know.'

'Fuck off.'

'How would Madame like her steak?'

'Bloody.'

Cillian had turned his back to her, poked at the meat on the barbecue. From her vantage point, she could study him, unde-tected. She drank him in, like a cold beer on a hot day. There was something deliciously untidy about him. Perhaps because of the length of him. Or his dark, thick hair that grew out as well as down, if left untended, which it often was.

He wore cut-off jeans. Nothing on his feet. She could see blades of grass poking between his toes. His T-shirt was so old the writing on it had faded away. 'It's my lucky T-shirt,' he'd told her when she'd offered to burn it. He claimed that Kurt Cobain had taken it off his back at the Point Depot in 1992 and Cillian had caught it, worn it ever since.

'Have you ever even *washed* it?'

'I'm not going to dignify that with an answer.'

Nobody believed him about Kurt Cobain. Well, Martha didn't anyway.

She thought about the T-shirt then. Brushing against his smooth, sallow skin, covering his wide, hairless chest, not quite reaching the top of his jeans so she could see the small of his back, the delicious hollow of it.

Martha lifted her glass and swallowed a mouthful of wine. Cleared her throat.

'You OK?'

'Fine.' She looked away, collected herself. Sometimes, she felt her physical attraction to him was overwhelming. Something beyond her control. She struggled to contain it. It felt like trying to get a lion into a shoebox.

'I know you were staring at me.'

'Don't flatter yourself.'

'It's my bum in these jeans, isn't it?'

'You have no bum in those jeans.'

They ate at the rickety wrought-iron table Cillian had found in his sister's attic and repainted. According to Joan, it was the table where their parents had sat when his mother told his father that she was pregnant with Cillian. Martha noticed that Joan often spoke to Cillian about their parents. Anecdotes. Like a photo album he could flick through in their absence.

'How did she manage to raise you? She was eighteen and you were only ten.'

'She told my mother she would. So she did.' Cillian made it sound simple. A matter of promises made and kept. Sometimes, when Cillian talked, Martha felt something curious. Like anything was possible. She was almost always able to put it down to the drink, the next day.

Cillian had bought the house a little over a year before. Just after he'd been promoted to detective.

A year later, the garden was improving quicker than the inside of the house. 'I'm better outside,' Cillian said and Martha thought this was an accurate observation. There was something untamed about Cillian. He didn't look as comfortable when he was in an enclosed space, always bending his head through doorways.

'How's your steak?'

'Fine.' It took her by surprise, every time. How good he was at cooking. Nothing fancy, mind. Chocolate cake, T-bone steak, served with the mushrooms he picked in the woods at the back of the house, fried on a pan with butter and garlic. That kind of food. Martha – who didn't happen to be an enthusiastic eater – ate whatever Cillian cooked. It was always tastier than she expected.

'Have some salad.'

'No.'

'It's good for you.'

'What's that got to do with anything?'

'Do you want more baked potato?'

'I want more wine.'

She held out her glass. Cillian poured.

'How's work?'

'Fine.'

'I saw your report on *Primetime*. About the asylum-seekers. I thought it was really good.'

'Thanks.'

Cillian mopped up the juice from the meat on his plate with a crust of bread. He sat back in his chair, looked up. She followed his gaze and was startled by the number of stars. There were certain things about the countryside that were proving not as awful as she'd feared. Not that she lived here. Of course not. But she was here quite a bit, all the same.

The quiet, for one thing. You could hear yourself think. If that's what you happened to be doing.

And on a clear night like tonight, there were stars.

'There's Orion's belt,' said Cillian, stretching out his long arm and pointing towards the constellation.

She knew he was going to say that.

Before he said it.

She knew.

'Remember what we always say,' Tara had reminded her, when it looked like she and Cillian were going to make it past their one year anniversary. 'Familiarity breeds contempt.'

But sometimes, familiarity could be ... well, nice, she supposed. Saved you the bother of second guessing.

'There's Orion's belt,' he said, as she knew he would.

Martha smiled, reached for her wineglass.

'How's the case going? Did you catch the baddies yet?'

His face when he smiled. Especially here, outside in the dusk, with the lengthening shadows smoothing the edges. Yes, his nose was too long and his bushy eyebrows held a suggestion of mono-brow and his cheeks bore the faded scars of a virulent strain of teenage acne. But when he smiled – which was more often than not, Martha felt – something happened to his face. Something good. He looked happy. No. Content. Martha didn't know anyone else who looked like that.

'I caught a few this week. But apparently there's more.'

'At least you'll never be out of a job. A bit like a funeral director.'

'That's a comfort.'

Martha's wineglass was empty. Again. She didn't want to reach for the bottle. Be seen to be reaching for the bottle. Instead, she excused herself and went inside to what Cillian called the powder room but which was just a room bearing a toilet with a chain flush and a rusting claw-footed bath that Cillian swore would be beautiful again, some day.

She sat on the edge of the bath and fished a miniature bottle of vodka from the inside zip section of her handbag. She kept a selection of them in there – along with tissues so the glass wouldn't clink and give her away – for emergencies.

Not that this was an emergency.

But Cillian could get funny sometimes. About how fast she drank. Or how much.

He sometimes commented on her drinking and she didn't like it, and they were having such a lovely evening, she didn't want to spoil it by drinking the last of the wine, then having to go inside and hunt down another bottle while he looked at her in that way he had. That concerned way.

This way was better. She tipped the contents into her mouth. Swallowed hard.

There was no smell from vodka but she brushed her teeth anyway, with the travel brush she kept in her make-up bag.

'I'm getting a lot of work done on the house this summer. Make it . . . more homey, y'know?'

'Less of an outhouse, you mean?'

'I've been thinking . . .' He stopped then, looked suddenly shy, his thick fringe spilling across his forehead.

'What?'

'Well, the house, it's a bit big for one person.'

'Cillian, it's a two-bedroomed cottage. You're not going to get lost in it any time soon.'

'The bed. That's pretty big.'

'Well . . . yes, that is a big bed.' Martha felt the familiar rush of blood around her body, a pulse beginning between her legs. She'd never been like this with anyone else. She'd always liked sex but she'd taken it, left it, not dwelled on it. All Cillian had to do was say *bed* or graze his fingers against hers as they both reached for the pepper shaker or just arrive in a room in his awkward, lanky way and she'd be off, thinking about him in all manner of compromising positions.

Impure thoughts. That's what they'd called them in school, those worrying nuns.

'It's even bigger when you're not in it.'

'What?' Martha dragged her thoughts back to the conversation.

Cillian sat forward in the chair that looked too small for him – although most chairs looked like that. He dragged his hands down his face, took a breath. 'What I'm saying is . . . I'd like you to be in it. In bed with me. More of the time. Actually, all of the time.'

'What about work? We'd get nothing done. Dublin would be like Gotham City, with the baddies running riot.'

'I'm being serious.' He reached his hand across the space between them, put it on her leg. 'I want you to move in with me. Or at least think about it.'

For a moment, Martha said nothing. Instead, she poured the last of the wine into her glass. Already the empty bottle was distracting her. The fact of it. She always liked to know where the next drink was coming from. And the next.

'Martha?' He took his hand off her leg, waved it in front of her face like he was attempting to wake her from a trance. She shook her head.

'Sorry, I just . . . you took me by surprise there.'

A part of her – a not insignificant part – wanted what Cillian wanted. She'd thought about it, thought about how lovely it would be. He was a strangely gentle man despite the rangy heft of him. And he could lift things. Her sofa, for instance. The one that was too big for her living room. He'd said it was too big. She'd bought it anyway. And then he stopped saying it was too big and somehow got it up the stairs of her apartment building where the lift never worked. All the way to her apartment on the third floor. He eased it in through the door. Slid it into position. He wasn't even out of breath.

'Joan wants me to dance with her at the wedding,' Cillian said then, like nothing had gone before. 'I still can't believe she's getting married.'

'It's a pity Naoise can't walk yet. He'd make such a cute page-boy, wouldn't he?'

'He's criminally cute, alright.'

'When you say dance, do you mean proper dance? Or are you

talking about your version of the eighties disco dance with the shuffley legs and sticky out arms?' Martha said.

'No, proper dancing. Like a waltz or something. She said it's traditional. The father of the bride dances with the bride apparently. Except there's no father of the bride. So she's asked me.' He sounded worried. He was one of those people who could do things. Without being shown. He'd re-thatched the roof on this ridiculous cottage, for fuck sake. Although he later admitted to watching a YouTube tutorial. He tuned in Radio 4 on her digital radio without being asked. There was nothing IKEA could throw at him that he hadn't been able to assemble. He could replace a string on her violin even though he had never played a musical instrument and, when she asked him to buy tampons on his way over to her apartment, he knew to get tampons *and* Panadol *and* a slab of dark chocolate.

He just knew.

And now here he was, not knowing. Not knowing how to waltz.

'There are tutorials on YouTube,' Martha offered.

He shook his head. 'It's not something easy like making an igloo.'

'I suppose I could teach you,' she said slowly.

He looked at her and she saw his surprise. 'I didn't know you waltzed.'

'I don't as a general rule. But I know how to. My dad showed me.' She didn't mention that he'd been pissed. It was after a trip to Bonn. He'd attended some ballroom dancing thing, one of the nights. They were mad about waltzing, the Germans.

'It'll only take a minute.' She stood up. Marched towards the grass.

'Take your shoes off,' Cillian called after her. 'Your heels will sink into the ground, it's still soft from the rain.'

Martha took her shoes off.

They stood in the grass, in the field he called the garden. They stood beneath the canopy of stars that punctured the dark of the sky where no clouds dared. She arranged his arm around her waist, fitted one of his huge hands into the small of her back, the other in an upright L-shape, so she could slip her hand between his thumb and forefinger. It had no right to feel so dainty there, her hand, and yet it did.

They began to move, she whispering one-two-three and his hips hard against hers and they turned and they turned, there, in the garden, in the dark, with the moon glancing against their bodies and she hummed the 'Emperor Waltz' and wondered if this is what people meant when they said, *It's good to be alive*.

It was good to be alive.

That night.

It was good.

She'd got up after he'd fallen asleep. Opened a bottle of wine, careful not to wake him. He'd wonder why. Was she thirsty? Was she stressed? He'd want to know.

They were exhausting, the questions.

The truth was, she liked drinking. Better still, she liked drinking alone. It was like a hobby, although not one that she talked about. She'd be the same if her hobby was ten-pin bowling. She wouldn't tell a soul.

She sat in the room that would some day become a den, if Cillian's plans saw fruition – which, she had to admit, they usually did. Tipped the wine into a mug that could be passed off as tea if he woke.

He'd say, 'Can't sleep, Martha?' He said her name like it was a question that could never be answered.

He didn't wake but she worried that he would, and that took the good out of it. When she finished the bottle, she brushed her teeth and got back into his big bed, careful not to wake him.

She lay there, staring into the dark, and she knew. That she wouldn't be able to move in with him.

In the sober light of morning, she told herself that it was because of her work. The unpredictable nature of it, the way she needed to come and go at odd hours. And the novel she sometimes thought about writing. She'd need her own space for that, wouldn't she?

But that night, lying in Cillian's big bed, with the empty wine bottle hidden in her handbag and the mug she had used to drink it rinsed and dripping on the draining board in the kitchen, she knew. That she couldn't live like this. Live with him.

She was better on her own, never having to explain.

Much better.

Martha thanked her mother for lunch, bade her brothers and sisters-in-law goodbye and gathered her nieces in her arms, kissed their sticky vanilla ice-cream cheeks and reiterated her offer to babysit, which was politely but firmly declined. She supposed she couldn't blame Anna and Mark. For most of the little girls' lives, she had not been ideal child-minding material.

'Keep in touch, won't you?' her mother asked, lifting Martha's hair away from her face to inspect the bruising at closer quarters. 'And stay out of trouble. Please? I'm getting too old to be worrying about you.'

Thirteen

Tobias could not tell how much time had passed, only that it had. One night. Perhaps two. Or more. He thought it might be the afternoon. There was a sag in the air that he associated with afternoon, those hours between the first tentative light of dawn and the dark certainty of night that stretched and stretched.

He sensed Rosa in the room rather than heard her, although it wasn't until she stood beside his bed that he knew for certain she was there. He recognised her quietness. And her scent. Lily of the valley, he thought.

He could hear the rub of Rosa's shoes as she walked around to the other side of his bed, faint against the floor. She still favoured the right leg. Had done so since her accident late last year. Most of October and November she was gone. Nobody told him where she was and he hadn't asked. It was not his place to do so. It was only when she returned, her wrist and ankle still swollen from her fall, that he conceded – privately – the impact of her absence.

He had missed her.

To Rosa, he merely said they had much catching up to do and told her to be at the library the following Thursday at their usual time.

He heard the creak of the chair beside his bed as Rosa sat down. He could feel her tension; it was like a physical presence in the room.

When she spoke, she whispered, as if she were afraid someone might find her there. Instruct her to leave.

Tobias was certain that he was ill enough to warrant a 'next-of-kin-only' visitor policy but perhaps they had relaxed that policy when they realised there was no one else.

He couldn't make out exactly what she was saying. If he could, he would have told her to speak up. Speak clearly. Something about her boy. How he didn't want to see her. She had sat outside the room where he was being questioned. She wanted him to somehow know that they were in it together.

That's the way it's supposed to be. I and Roman. Against the world.

Tobias could smell the sour heat of her despair and forgot to correct her.

Roman and me.

Jimmy knows that I know. He says he will hurt Roman if I say anything. I know he will.

Rosa cried then. The sound of her cry startled Tobias although it was a cry he associated with her – a quiet cry, one that didn't want to draw attention to itself.

The sound dimmed, became distant like a door had closed against it and he was a boy again and it was Dresden that was weeping. Dresden that was burning still. People ran like tributaries to the Elbe. Some waded into the depths of her icy water, submerged themselves beneath her grey, churning surface. Not all of them re-emerged as the fast-flowing river took her toll. Some lay in the mud of her bank, rolled in it until they were indistinguishable from the stinking, sodden earth. Some just sat there and stared at their city. At Dresden, burning. These people looked stunned, as if they did not believe what was there in front of their eyes. What was as real as the war itself. All the long years of it.

Tobias ran. Along the east side of her bank, in the direction of the flow of her waters. He had no plan, no provisions, no people.

He kept running.

Even years later, when he thought about that time, after the bombs dropped, he could never recall how long he ran. How far. He ran until he stopped. Hours that felt like days. That felt like his whole life.

He ran through the rushes, trying to keep out of sight of the planes that continued to roar through the low-hanging clouds, the glare of their lights sweeping along the river, along the banks, training their guns on people who moved and even on those who didn't.

Any time he slowed, he thought about his mother in the cellar. Dead now, her burnt body perhaps still clutching baby Greta to her breast. He saw the blackened remains of his little brothers, wrapped around each other like cubs in winter.

He had not saved them. Had not saved anyone. Only himself.

He ran on.

He finally stopped when his hunger and his exhaustion became big enough to banish all other thoughts from his mind. He was in a thick knot of woodland. It was difficult to know how far he had come. He sheltered behind the trunk of an oak tree which cut the worst of the wind. He lay on the forest floor. Already he could feel the damp seep through his clothes.

He did not eat. He must have slept.

When he awoke, there was a gun pointed at his face. A hand grabbed his shoulder, reefed him to his feet, shook him.

'Who are you? What are you doing here?' The man was tall. Gaunt. He had a ferociously angular face. He was old but his body, while thin, retained a measure of sinewy strength.

Tobias shook him off, pulling his father's gun from the waistband of his trousers. His father had taught him how to shoot the gun. He had never used it before. Now, he cocked it at the man. 'You shoot me, I'll shoot you, understand?' he said in a voice he barely recognised as his own. His voice had finally broken and his first thought was of his mother, who had laughed these past months when his voice had gone from a screech to a growl during the course of a single sentence. 'Your voice will break when it's good and ready, Tobias,' she'd told him, ruffling his fringe the way he always told her not to.

His father's gun felt too big for his hand. Too heavy. Still, he didn't lower it. It was a woman, in the end, who stepped between them. An old woman with a ragged shawl around her shoulders, wearing boots that seemed much too heavy for her twig-like frame. Her eyes were swollen into slits, the whites red and veiny, like she'd been weeping.

'There will be no killing of our own,' she said in a voice that was as ragged as her shawl. 'If you want to shoot each other, you will have to shoot me first.' It was almost an invitation, the way she said it. The tall man lowered his weapon, never taking the hard blue of his eyes off Tobias's face. Only when the gun was by his side did Tobias tuck his father's weapon back into his trousers.

There were about ten of them. All running from Dresden, just like him. Old men and women mostly. A few boys Tobias's age. They studied Tobias as if he might know something they didn't. As if he might have come up with a solution.

'Where are you going?' he asked them.

The old woman pointed south. 'I've been telling them. We should go back. We need supplies.'

'There are no supplies. There's nothing left.' This from a boy about the same age as Tobias, with blood drying on the front of his shirt. He sat on a wet rock, his face buried in hands that were blue with cold.

'If we continue on, we'll freeze to death. And starve.'

'If we go back, we'll burn.'

Nobody said anything after that and Tobias sat back down, not wanting to draw attention to himself. The group continued arguing amongst themselves and Tobias had the curious sensation that he wasn't there at all. That he was perhaps already dead, unnoticed and unnoticeable. Another part of him – the part that had run and run until he could run no longer – knew that he was alive, that he would do anything to stay alive for reasons that were now beyond his comprehension.

They boiled water in a blackened pot a woman produced from a straw bag over a fire fed with thin branches the blood-stained boy had cut from trees. The rabbits Tobias caught and skinned did not go far and Tobias felt hungrier after the food than he had been before. The old woman who had stood between Tobias and a bullet handed him a hunk of bread, hard as a rock. Tobias tried not to cram the whole lot into his mouth, chewed it for as long as he could, anxious to make it last. She took her rag of a shawl from around her shoulders and offered it to Tobias who shook his head. 'Take it,' she said. 'You are young. You have your whole life ahead of you and the night will be bitter. I have my coat.' She pointed at her ill-fitting coat, none of the buttons matching.

Tobias stretched the shawl on the ground and lay on it. The fire had been doused so its flames would not give them away but the old woman lay beside him, her back to him. 'We'll keep each other warm,' she whispered.

When Tobias opened his eyes the next morning, the woman was staring at him. Her eyes were milky blue and her lips were parted. Tobias knew she was dead but a vague warmth persisted from her body, as if some essence of her remained. Tobias found himself unafraid. Perhaps this was what happened when you survived. It left you unafraid. He was not afraid of this old woman who lay dead beside him. Instead, he felt a sadness deep inside himself that stretched and stretched and threatened to burst out of him and he swallowed hard and closed his eyes and allowed the last of her to warm him.

Later, Tobias tried to dig a hole with his bare hands but the ground was hard, unrelenting and his fingers too stiff with cold to make much headway. In the end, the tall man carried the old woman to the river, lay her on the bank and rolled her in. The river accepted her swiftly, carried her away.

The decision was made to keep to the river, head back to Dresden. The sky had issued no sound during the night, so perhaps the planes had finished their work. There would be no more bombs. Tobias didn't think any of them really believed that. People had said the Allies would never bomb Dresden. *The Florence of the Elbe*. They had been so certain.

Tobias followed the others. In the distance, he could see the city – his city – glow beneath great plumes of black smoke.

Now, looking into the past, seeing that young, rudderless scrap of a boy, Tobias wants to say, Stop. Go back. Turn the other way. But then again, what would have happened if he had ventured away from Dresden instead? Something worse? It was wartime, after all. Happy endings were in scarce supply.

Instead, he walked on, followed the others. He didn't remember how far he walked before it happened. In his memory, it seemed endless, the walking. The insistence of one foot in front of the other. And again. And again. Like life itself, the walk. Relentless.

He stopped when the others stopped. Craned his neck to see what they saw. It was an airman. He was injured, huddled at the base of a tree. One leg lay at an unnatural angle from his body. Blood poured down his face from a deep cut on the side of his head. Pieces of his parachute were snagged on the bare branches of the tree, the fabric straining south in the biting wind that swept down the river.

The tall, gaunt German shouted at the airman, stabbed the muzzle of his gun towards him. The airman tried to raise his arms over his head and the tall man spat at him and Tobias saw the saliva sliding down his face, turning pink as it mixed with his blood. The tall man squatted in front of the airman, roughly pulled the man's jacket off, his belt, his hat.

Then he looked at Tobias. 'Do you have any bullets in that gun of yours?'

Tobias nodded, removed his father's gun from the waistband of his trousers, offered it to the man who shook his head. 'You must do it, it's your gun.'

'Do what?'

The only noise was the river on his right, intent on her journey south. Tobias looked at the airman, who was talking now, fast and urgent. Tobias couldn't understand what he was saying but the tone was undeniable. A pleading tone.

'He's Polish. He's one of the bastards who killed your family,' the tall man shouted at him. Tobias hadn't mentioned his family but such a story could be assumed of any of them. He thought about Greta's pink face. How soft her skin felt between his fingers when he gently pinched her cheeks. The way she laughed like she would never stop. And how her laugh made the rest of them laugh, no matter what the day had brought.

He straightened his arm, pointed the gun towards the man, who was shouting now, a steady stream of words, getting louder. Some of the words were German. Tobias heard the word for 'wife', the word for 'children', the word for 'baby', the word for 'love', the word for 'home'. The Polish man had a wife. Three children. Another one on the way. He loved his wife. He loved his children. He wanted to be a father. He wanted to go home. He was crying now, his head bent towards his chest like he didn't want them to see his tears. His shoulders moved up and down with the force of his cries, heavy with resignation.

Tobias hesitated. Could feel his arm lower.

The tall man thundered towards him, lifted Tobias's arms

until the gun, which he held in both hands, was trained on the man.

The airman knew then. That he would be dead soon. His cries quietened. He wiped the tears on his face with a filthy hand. He looked at Tobias, waiting. Tobias could see him waiting in the hard set of his shoulders, in the clenched fists of his hands, along the lines of his ruined face.

'This is your chance, boy,' the tall man said.

Tobias cocked the gun. The man flinched.

'Do it for the Fatherland.'

Tobias's mouth was dry. He trained the gun at the man's neck. Could see a pulse jump there. Imagined what the man might look like afterwards. Imagined him dead.

The airman looked at Tobias, his hands still in the air. Then he closed his eyes and Tobias saw him take a breath and he knew that if he didn't do it now, do it immediately, he wouldn't be able to do it at all.

He pulled the trigger. The shot unbalanced him and he staggered backwards.

The noise was sharp, enormous. It seemed to reach up into the bare branches of the trees, make them shudder. Tobias opened his eyes. He had missed. The tall man shouted at Tobias, grabbed his arm, pulled him, trained the muzzle of the gun inches now from the airman's head so that Tobias could see the mud entrenched along the folds of the man's ears, could see the pink veins threaded through the whites of the man's eyes. His mouth was frozen on a word, on one of his few German words: wife or children or baby or home. One of those words.

Tobias fired again. The bullet lodged in the side of the man's neck and blood spurted from the wound and it was bright red. It was the brightest red Tobias had ever seen, and there was so much of it.

The man's eyes dulled and something like a smile crept across his face, as if a part of him were glad. Glad perhaps that the war was over.

At least it was for him.

'Rosa? You OK?'

Tobias felt the draught of another person arriving into the room. Rosa stood up. Tobias heard the legs of her chair rasp against the floor.

'I go now,' she said, even though she was adept at the future tense. The same as the present tense, Tobias had explained, with the word 'will' inserted before the verb. *I will go*. She had understood almost immediately.

'What will you do?' Tobias had asked, as an exercise. 'In your future?'

'I will look after my son.'

'What else?'

'I will go to work.'

'What else?'

She had paused then. Tobias had drummed the fingers of his good hand against the wood of the table in the library.

'I will improve my English and buy a flower shop and Roman and I will move into our own apartment and it will have a balcony with a chair where I can sit and watch the sun set.' She'd laughed her small laugh when she said that, as if it were a wish rather than a statement, and he'd nodded curtly, as if it were a statement rather than a wish.

'Rosa? You OK?' It was the man. The detective. Tobias focused on his voice, grabbed at it, allowed it to bring him back into the room, into the present.

He could usually manage his thoughts. Quell them, when it became necessary.

It was different here, in this narrow hospital bed with the

inconvenient tubes and the antiseptic smell. It seemed as if his memories had taken him hostage. Were holding him to ransom.

'Here.' Tobias could hear the detective rummage in his pocket, pull something out. It must have been a tissue because then he heard Rosa blow her nose, her small *thank you* afterwards.

'I've been looking for you. Did you get my message?'

'The nurse told me to turn off my phone,' said Rosa.

'I called into your house. Had a little chat with your landlord.'

'Jimmy?' Fear gripped her voice.

'Why are you protecting him? He's going to hang Roman out to dry.'

A pause, then, 'I don't know what you mean.'

'Look, Rosa, you and I both know that Roman's a good kid who got mixed up in a bad situation.'

'Yes. He is a good boy.'

'Help me to help him. You recognised Jimmy's voice, didn't you? At the bank. You can help us identify him?'

Rosa said nothing. Tobias could hear the *tick tock* of the detective's watch.

'I can protect you, Rosa. You and Roman. You just need to trust me.'

When Rosa exhaled, Tobias could hear the shake of it. 'Have you heard when the hearing will be?' she said.

'Not till the day after tomorrow, I'm afraid. Monday, three o'clock.'

'He won't talk to me.'

'I'll keep an eye on him, Rosa. He'll be OK.'

'Thank you.'

'I haven't done anything. You won't let me.'

Rosa said nothing but perhaps she might have nodded. One

of the nurses came in – they were always coming in, prodding and poking him. The detective left.

'Cheer up, love,' the nurse said to Rosa, as if they were in the middle of a conversation. 'He could wake up. Any minute. It happens. I've seen it happen.'

He could not hear Rosa respond. Perhaps she had smiled her quiet smile instead.

Tobias knew that Rosa did not think he would awaken. They were cut from the same cloth, he and Rosa. Or was it Rosa and he? He was appalled to find that he did not know for sure, felt it was part of this process he was embroiled in.

This slipping away.

Fourteen

When Martha got home from the restaurant, Dan was standing at the entrance to her apartment block, holding an enormous bouquet of roses in one hand. In the other, an egg tray accommodating twenty-four Cadbury Creme Eggs, which happened to be Martha's favourite confectionery, although even she found the sight of twenty-four of them challenging.

'For you, my precious,' Dan said, managing only a small bow, constricted as he was by his wares.

'Why?' Martha couldn't help smiling. Few people could, in Dan's vicinity. It might have been his huge blue eyes, or his short, blond hair, immaculately cut in a pageboy style. Or perhaps it was his short legs and long feet which lent him a clownish air, an impression encouraged by his dress sense.

Today, he wore a brightly coloured short-sleeved shirt – patterned with some class of exotic fruit (lychees, he told her, shaking his head at the enquiry) – and linen shorts to his knees. His only concession to the bitterness of winter was to don woollen socks, which he wore with brown leather sandals.

He looked about twelve. He would be thirty-nine on his next birthday.

'They're first and foremost a *get well soon* token,' said Dan, 'following the recent traumatic events at the bank.'

'And secondly?'

'Happy anniversary, darling.' Dan thrust the flowers towards Martha. His smile, always wide, widened.

'I'm not sure it's appropriate for us to celebrate our wedding anniversary while we're waiting on our divorce.' Martha needed her two hands and much of her arms to accommodate the flowers.

'Two years,' he told her, holding open the door to her apartment block and ushering her inside. 'It's not nothing.'

They by-passed the lift with its habitual *out of order* sign and climbed the stairs.

'You *do* remember that we were only married for four months of those two years?'

'Four months and three days, actually.'

'How can you be so sure?'

'You broke my heart, sugar plum fairy. Clean in two.' He stopped on the landing, placed his hand on his chest, affected a pained expression.

Martha fumbled inside her bag for her keys. 'Are you sure you're not gay?'

'Well, I'm bi-curious on my Facebook profile but no, I don't think so.'

'Your heart's on the other side,' Martha told him.

Martha and Dan Hennessy had met through work, although Dan didn't have a job, as such. He was the only child of a famous and reclusive British painter – Daniel Hennessy – equipped with an enormous trust fund and an ability to opine on his father's body of work to any radio station, television network, newspaper or magazine who asked him, for a fee. TV3, where Martha had managed to secure some – very – menial work in their admin. department after her fairly spectacular fall from RTÉ's grace, had asked Dan to appear on their late-night arts programme to talk about his father's latest painting which was entitled *The Past, The Present, The Future* and was, in the main, a series of lines and blobs and squiggles and smudges. Martha thought it was pants and so, it turned out, did Dan and it was on this common ground that the seed of their relationship dropped.

That the seed took root and produced a riot of ground cover was mostly thanks to a robust and shared interest in what Dan called socialising and Martha called drinking.

Martha had noticed Dan on her way out of TV3 that evening. He was at a vending machine, hitting the side of it with the flat of his hand in a way that had little impact on the wares inside. A can of Coke teetered on the edge of a shelf, behind the glass.

'You need to be firm with it,' Martha told him, slipping her foot out of her boot, in a way that Dan confessed – later – made him feel both afraid and aroused.

Martha hauled the machine away from the wall, moved her hands along the back of the machine, selected a spot then hit it – once – with the heel of the boot.

She fished the can out of the mouth of the machine, handed it to Dan with a curt nod, then put her boot back on and moved towards the exit.

'Wait,' Dan called.

Martha turned. Scowled. 'What?'

'I must take you for a drink.'

'Why?'

'To thank you.'

'No need.'

'I must take you anyway.' Dan confessed – later – that his manhood – which is how he referred to his penis – went from half-mast to full steam ahead when he said *take you*.

'Why?'

'Because you are beautiful and I am thirsty.'

Martha was thirsty too.

They got married, two months later, in Las Vegas. Like most of their activities, the wedding was unplanned and executed with scant regard to detail and consequence.

Las Vegas was no place for sobriety. Martha had realised that when she and Dan first arrived. They had taken a wrong turn and ended up in an alleyway towards the back of their massive, glittery hotel. There was nothing glittery about the alleyway where they'd found a man sitting on a kerb, wearing nothing but a pair of Calvin Klein underpants, his arms wrapped around his skinny frame, crying quietly into the hard bone of his knees. He'd lost everything, he told them.

'Even the shirt off your back?' Up until that moment, Martha had presumed this was just an expression. A figure of speech.

She got drunk, and stayed that way, pretty quickly after that. Vodka with a dribble of tonic. No messing around. Vodka was a reliable beverage. You could depend on it to blunt the edges in a timely manner.

Their hotel room was bigger than Martha's apartment.

'Did they upgrade us?' Martha wanted to know when they opened the door.

'What?' asked Dan who, after a trek to the other side of the room, was rummaging through the mini-bar. He tossed her a baby bottle of vodka and she caught it in her left hand.

Dan looked at her with naked admiration. He loved that she could do things he found difficult. Catching was one of those things. So was swearing. And fixing the leak in his kitchen sink. 'It just needed a new washer,' she had said.

'I don't know what a washer is,' Dan confessed.

'Give me strength,' Martha said.

The pair had decided on the plane over to set a limit for themselves. An amount in excess of which they would not gamble. They shook on it and ordered mini bottles of Champagne to go with their breakfast because they were on their holidays or because it was their first holiday together or because they were nervous flyers or because . . .

Just because.

After the Champagne was finished, they'd ordered orange juices which Dan sweetened with a bottle of duty free gin. They proposed frequent and progressively bizarre toasts.

'Here's to the hairdresser who gave me a bob in the March of 1994,' said Martha. 'I hope he's rotting in a Turkish prison.'

'Is he Turkish?' enquired Dan.

'No.'

Martha was at the blackjack table on Day Two when she reached her limit. By then, the vodka had its arms around her and she played on. She lost five hundred dollars in two hours.

Martha and Dan had planned to take a trip to the Grand Canyon. They'd planned to go trekking. See the sun rise across the desert.

Instead, after five days of drinking and gambling and eating potato chips and hotdogs and cookies the size of their faces, interspersed with fitful sleep and vague attempts at sex, Martha and Dan decided it would be a hell of an idea to get married in the little church behind the Kentucky Fried Chicken restaurant at four o'clock on a Wednesday morning.

So that's what they did.

Back in Dublin, at work and relatively sober, Martha attempted some analysis of the situation. She wondered about the authenticity of the marriage. After all, the man who'd married them had been dressed as a minion from *Despicable Me* for reasons Martha appeared to have deleted from her memory bank.

She did that a lot back then.

Deleted things.

The morning after they'd returned, she had found Dan asleep on her oversized sofa in his usual brightly coloured short-sleeve shirt and linen shorts, the telly blaring and a bottle of whiskey – what was left of it – clutched in his hand.

She supposed it was their sofa now.

She looked up *annulment* on her computer. She'd have to make an application to the High Court. Or the Circuit Court. One of those. She'd have to get a solicitor. She'd think about it after lunch. She went to Grady's, ordered a toasted sandwich and threw back a couple of vodkas and tonic. It looked just like a sparkling Ballygowan, which was handy because her colleagues – she was now temping in a small market research company – were getting a bit holier-than-thou about people drinking at lunch-time. They looked at her when they said *people*.

Fuck them.

By the time she got back from the pub, the vodkas had done their work and she'd forgotten about the annulment and the circuit-court-or-was-it-the-high-court and the getting of a solicitor.

Martha helped Dan move the rest of his stuff into her apart-ment the following weekend. 'Do you mind if I hang that in the sitting room?' he said when she picked up the only artwork he'd brought with him.

Martha looked at the small charcoal drawing. It was the face of a woman. A beautiful woman, her hair long and dark and her face small and pale. In her eyes, a reflection of – Martha moved her face closer to the drawing – snow. A field of snow. At the edge lay a boy in a soldier's uniform.

'It's called *I See You*,' said Dan, when Martha looked up.

'Who's the artist?' said Martha, searching the drawing for a signature but finding none there.

Dan shook his head. 'Nobody knows.' He grinned at her, then poured generous measures of whiskey into the heavy crystal tumblers he had taken out of a box. 'We'd better get this down us first,' he said. 'Before we ring our parents.'

They drank in a methodical manner, both of them reaching for a refill at the same time.

Afterwards, Martha rang her mother – her father was holed up somewhere writing his memoirs, which he'd been working on for the best part of a decade – and Dan rang his father – his mother had left years before – and they told these people their happy news and held their phones at arm's length during the subsequent reactions. But at least it was official now. Telling people made it official.

Nothing much changed.

If she ever compared Dan to Cillian – which she never did because she tried hard never to think about that lanky fucker – she might have expressed relief that Dan wasn't judgemental. He never commented if she opened a bottle of wine at lunch-time on a Saturday. And a Sunday. No snide, *Is it not a little early in the day?* comments, thank you very much. Nor did he so much as glance in her direction when she opened a second one. Or poured vodka into her favourite tumbler when she got in from work. Or say, in a pseudo-caring voice, *You OK, Martha?* Dan didn't say anything about the regularity with which she went to the bottle bank. Usually at night because, well, that was the handiest time for her to go, wasn't it? In fact, he offered to go himself. Without a murmur about the weight of the bag or the clink of the bottles.

Theirs was not a conventional marriage. No tedious furniture shopping – Martha had everything they needed – and no arguments about domestic chores: neither of them did any so there was nothing to argue about. On the days Martha went to work, Dan stayed in bed. When she rang in sick, she stayed in bed too. In the evenings, they talked about whether they would eat out or order in.

Spontaneous. That's what they were.

They drank until the small hours, then fell asleep.

They never fought.

*   *   *

They still didn't, despite the separation. Three more years and they'd be eligible for a divorce in Ireland. Or, as Dan put it, they could *divorce with love.*

'Nobody divorces with love,' Martha told him.

'If you insist that we get divorced, then I insist we do it with love.'

Martha had to admit that Dan did most things with love. He couldn't help himself.

'Fine then,' she snapped.

Still, she had to admit the flowers were cheerful. They brightened the room. As did Dan. Theirs had always been a comfortable bond. More in keeping with old friends than lovers.

'You don't think *I* have an uneasy relationship with alcohol, do you?' he had asked with genuine surprise when she told him, that day, about the decision she had made to never drink again.

'Probably.'

'Gosh.'

Still, he soldiered on, although he never drank in Martha's company now. She was grateful to him for that, and for the companionship he supplied with his trademark ease.

Martha sighed.

'What troubles you, my precious petal?'

'I'm worried about Tara.'

'Perhaps she might grant me an audience? I could visit her tomorrow.'

'See if you can weasel contact details for Mathilde from her. I think if Mathilde talks to her, she might come round.'

'There's something else. I can tell.'

'There isn't.'

'There is.'

'There isn't.'

'There is.' Dan could do this for hours.

'Cillian was here.'

'Cillian? I thought he had repaired to the wild west. Donegal, wasn't it?'

Martha nodded. 'He's only here temporarily. He's working on the bank job.'

'Did he ravish you?'

'Of course not. He's with someone else now.'

'And how do we feel about that?' Dan asked, picking up one of Martha's long white hands and stroking it the way he stroked his cats.

'We don't feel anything about that,' said Martha, snatching her hand back. 'We are merely mentioning it.'

'I suppose he's still dashing.'

'He looks the same.'

'Dashing then.' Dan looked at his watch. 'I have to go. I have to pontificate on a radio panel in an hour.'

Martha felt something like panic catch hold of her. She knew if she asked Dan to stay, he would. She didn't ask him.

'You OK?' He put his hand on her sleeve at the door, tugged it gently.

'Yes. Of course. I'm fine. Why wouldn't I be?'

'Such a prickly little soul.'

'Goodbye, Dan.'

'Call me if you need me.'

'I won't need you,' she barked at him.

When he left, the apartment seemed flooded with silence. Like a weight. A tsunami of silence. When the water pulls back, before the waves hit.

She stood in the dark of the hall and listened to it, this ominous silence. It was not unfamiliar, the sound, but it had been a while since she had heard it. Felt it.

She had been doing fine.

Now, it felt like someone had pulled aside the boulder of the cave she had been holed up in and she was blinking in the glare of the light.

She had been fine.

She thought about tequila. She had never rated its taste but she had appreciated its efficiency. How effectively it would swipe at the silence, chase it away.

She could drive. She'd be at the Pound in five minutes. Her fingers stopped inches short of the hook her car keys were hanging from. She didn't know how long she stayed like that, in the dark, in the hall, reaching.

In the end, she played her violin. Pulled it out of its case, ran her hands over the cracks. She played every piece of music she had: Vivaldi, Mendelssohn, Dvorak, Tschaikowsy, Bartok. When she finished, she played them again, louder.

Her neck, arching towards the instrument, ached. The strings bit into the pads of her fingers. The small of her back begged her to stop, as did her neighbours, banging on the walls.

She played on, into the silence, filling it with sound. It was not as effective as tequila. It took longer. A lot longer. Afterwards, she crawled into bed with her clothes on. She was too tired to feel victorious. She did not feel victorious. Because tomorrow was waiting for her. And the day after that. And all the days after that, in a line, waiting for her.

If Tara were here, she would say, 'It's just one bad day.'

It hadn't even been that bad.

Just that sense of disturbance. Of the earth shifting beneath her feet. Changing. But she had already changed. She had been good. It should be easy now. Easier.

Why wasn't it easier?

Fifteen

'Lenny, you're looking well.' Cillian walked up the driveway towards Lenny's house as the man opened his front door. Lenny twisted his head, scowled at Cillian. 'What the fuck do you want?'

'I'm very well, thank you for asking. And how's your good self?'

'I'm busy.' Lenny tried closing the door. Cillian put his hand on it.

'Busy washing Mrs Mitchell's windows, by all accounts,' said Cillian.

Lenny's hand dropped away from the door. 'Who?'

'She's still in Lanzarote. Spending most of her time in that bar you recommended. Still, she was a bit miffed when I told her about her jeep.'

'I don't know what you're talkin' about.'

'Can I come in?'

'Do you have a warrant?'

'Do I need one?'

'No!'

'Because I can get one within the hour, as you know. Or you can just let me in and we can have a chat.'

'What about?'

'Won't take long.' Cillian stepped inside, closed the door and strode towards the kitchen. Behind him, he could hear the reluctant tap of Lenny's shoes against the tiles as he followed.

'How's Jimmy these days?' said Cillian, sitting at the table.

'Haven't seen him,' said Lenny, leaning against the kitchen counter.

'No?' Cillian's eyes swept around the room. 'Where were you last Wednesday?'

Lenny glared at him. 'Do I need a fucken solicitor?'

Cillian smiled. 'A pillar of the community like yourself, Leonard? I hardly think so.' On the wall behind Lenny's head, there was a corkboard, cluttered with the usual stuff that corkboards were cluttered with. Bills and takeaway menus, a freebie calendar from the bookies, opening times for the local gym, an old Irish pound note. But in the top left-hand corner, half hidden behind a flyer for a new dry cleaners', was a charcoal drawing. Of a woman. She reminded him a little of Joan. Perhaps because of her uniform. He was sure it was a nurse's uniform, albeit one from a different era. The nurse was bent over the body of a man in a field. A soldier. Other than the two of them, the field was empty, edged by bare branches of trees reaching gnarled limbs into a dark grey sky that threatened rain. The grass was long gone, replaced by flattened mud.

Cillian couldn't help noticing the gentleness of the nurse's arms around the soldier who, on closer inspection, was only a boy, perhaps seventeen years old. Even the way she touched the boy's neck, checking for a pulse with the tips of her fingers, was somehow tender. One word, *Meeting*, was printed in small, neat lettering in a corner of the drawing.

Something about the drawing looked familiar, although Cillian couldn't put his finger on it.

'I was here,' said Lenny, folding his arms across his chest. 'With my girlfriend, Natasha. All day.'

'Sweet,' said Cillian. He took his phone out of his pocket, checked the screen and stood up. 'Well, it's been lovely but I should get back to work.'

'About time you did something useful,' said Lenny, heading out of the kitchen towards the front door. Cillian followed him, then paused halfway down the hall. 'My jacket,' he said.

'Fuck sake,' said Lenny, already holding the door open.

Cillian moved back into the kitchen, out of Lenny's eyeline. He already had the phone on camera and he held it towards the drawing, took a photograph of it, before he grabbed his jacket from the back of a chair and left the kitchen.

'Next time, I'll bring Custard Creams to go with our tea,' said Cillian, stepping outside.

'I'll report you for harassment, Larkin. I know me rights.'

'OK, then, chocolate Hobnobs it is.'

Cillian got into his car. In the rear-view mirror, he could see Lenny watching him, his face devoid of his usual charm offensive.

On the way back to the station, his phone rang and he reached for it. It was Stella. 'I know I'm not supposed to ring you when you're at work,' she said.

'Is everything OK?' said Cillian.

'Everything is great. I'm in town, buying you a lovely shirt and tie to wear to Joan's on Monday night. To go with your new cufflinks, of course. What time is she expecting us?'

Joan, on hearing that Stella was visiting, had insisted that Cillian take some time off work to bring her over for dinner.

'Ah, you're very good, Stella, but you don't have to trouble yourself. I *have* shirts. And ties.'

'Do you? You never seem to wear them.'

'I do.' Only when it was absolutely essential. Funerals and weddings, in the main.

She'd barely been here for twenty-four hours. It felt longer. Cillian felt shabby, thinking that. It was the case. He was flat out. And she was still vague about when she might leave. He thought he could relax a bit more if there was a departure date.

Up until her arrival at his house, Cillian would have said he'd known Stella for a few months. They were friends. He was pretty sure he had never called her his girlfriend. And he didn't think Stella would refer to him as her boyfriend. He was too old to be anybody's boyfriend.

Except, now, it seemed he was. Had been for a year.

Somewhere along this train of thought, while Stella was talking '. . . and I said to Selene that if Eddie's mother didn't want to wear the cerise pink hat to the wedding, then . . .' it came to Cillian. Where he had seen a drawing like the one in Lenny's kitchen.

'Sorry, Stella, I have to go,' said Cillian.

'Oh.'

'I'll see you later.'

'What time?'

'I'm not sure.'

'Will you ring me?'

'I'll do my best.' He hung up before she could say anything else. Went into Contacts, found her. Her phone went straight to voicemail.

Martha Wilder. Leave a message.

Cillian drove back to the station and was sitting at his desk with a mug of coffee when she arrived. Mick held the office door open and was about to motion her inside when she strode right past him. Immediately, the office seemed smaller. Dingier.

'Nice digs,' she said, looking around. The room housed a splintering wooden desk, a plastic chair, a rusting ceiling fan, an ailing potted plant and a small square window – open – that looked onto a small square yard filled with wheelie bins, weeds and one menacing-looking crow.

Cillian smiled. 'I would have got the Febreze out if I'd known you were coming.'

Martha opened an enormous handbag, rummaged arm-deep in its depths. 'I brought the drawing you mentioned in your voicemail. It's in here somewhere.'

'I only meant you to send me a photograph of it.'

'You piqued my curiosity,' she said. He nodded. She had always been curious. He supposed that's what had made her so good at her job.

'Besides,' she went on, 'I needed a distraction. I'm writing a brochure for a health food company and it's making me queasy.' She pulled a frame from her bag, set it on the table between them.

Cillian studied it. While it was different to the one in Lenny's kitchen, there were similarities. This one used charcoal too. And the woman. The nurse. He was pretty sure that she was the same woman. In Martha's one, the artist had drawn only her face, catching her beauty in the delicate slant of her cheekbones, the fine line of her jaw. Cillian moved his face closer to the drawing. In her eyes, he thought he could see a reflection of snow. A field of snow. At the edge, a young man, lying on his back. No more than a boy really. A boy in a soldier's uniform.

'It's called *I See You*,' said Martha, sitting on the chair on the other side of his desk. 'It was a gift from Stan,' she said. 'I mean Dan.' She smirked and he nodded, conceding the jibe.

'He gave it to me when he left. I told him it wasn't traditional for people to give each other their possessions when they split up but he insisted.'

'Oh,' said Cillian, looking up. 'I didn't know that you'd split up.'

'Yeah, marriage was another of those considered decisions I made when I was on the sauce.' Martha grinned a sudden, unexpected grin and Cillian grinned back, as if it was contagious, which, in fairness, it was.

'This one is only a print. Dan says the original is worth a small fortune which, for ordinary people, is probably fairly sizeable.'

Cillian took out his phone and showed Martha the photograph he had taken earlier in Lenny's kitchen. 'What do you think of that?' he asked. She took the phone from him, brushing her fingers against his in the transaction, and he sat a little straighter, crossed his arms and felt somewhat foolish, although he couldn't say exactly why. Martha peered at the screen. The bruises on her face were not as vivid as before although the array of their colours was vast, like autumn leaves. Her skin, while pale, held no trace of the grey of the previous day. But her skin had always been pale without make-up.

He thought about her comment, *When I was on the sauce*. She had piqued *his* curiosity with that. Although she had always piqued his curiosity.

Strands of her hair lifted in a sudden breeze through the window. They blew against his face and he brushed them away.

'Sorry,' said Martha, setting the phone on the desk between them. 'It runs amok if I don't restrain it.' She gathered her hair in both hands so that, for a moment, her neck was exposed and Cillian was reminded of its slender length.

She pushed as much of her hair as she could fit down the back of her jacket.

She handed Cillian his phone. 'That's interesting,' she said.

'It looks like the same woman, doesn't it?' said Cillian. 'In both of the drawings.'

Martha nodded slowly. 'Yes,' she said. 'Yes, it does.'

'Do you think they were drawn by the same artist?'

Martha considered this. 'If that's the case, it's quite a find, Cillian.'

'Why?'

'Nobody knows who the artist is. He – or she, but it's broadly believed to be a he – drew ten of these, all in charcoal, apart from one which is a charcoal drawing of a house over a shop, but with a vase in the window, full of flowers that are painted this really vivid red. That's the only one that doesn't feature the woman, the nurse. Six of the drawings are privately owned and four are in art galleries. I mean international galleries. MoMA, Guggenheim; the big guns. If what you've got there is the genuine article,' she nodded towards his phone, 'then this is a big story. Where did you get it?'

Cillian shook his head. 'I can't say right now.'

'I have Jelly Babies in my handbag.'

Cillian laughed. Martha had found it amusing, he remembered. His penchant for the people-shaped jellies. 'You're too tall for Jelly Babies,' she had said.

'Is anything known about the artist?'

Martha shook her head. 'Not really. There's speculation of course. That maybe he's German. That maybe he fought in the Second World War. And that he lives – or lived, more likely – in Ireland after the war.'

Cillian thought about Tobias Hartmann. According to the system, he was a German national, although he had lived in Ireland for decades. Not quite old enough to have fought in the Second World War. He would have been only fourteen when the war ended.

'You look like you're in pain,' said Martha. 'Are you thinking thoughts?'

'Trying to.'

'I'll leave you to it.'

'How's Tara doing?' he asked.

Martha shook her head. 'I was in earlier. I brought the FTSE 100 index but even that didn't rouse her.'

'She just needs some time,' said Cillian.

'You're not going to say something like, *Time is a great healer*, are you?'

Cillian shook his head, grinning. 'I know how you feel about the humble cliché.'

Martha stood up.

Cillian stood too, looked at her. 'Listen, Martha, this stuff we were talking about, it's . . .'

Martha nodded. 'I know. Top secret. I won't say a word about any of it.'

'Thanks,' said Cillian. Even though neither of them owed the other anything anymore, he knew he could trust her on this. There were some things you just knew.

There was a knock on the office door and the Super barged in. 'I'm not disturbing yiz, am I?' he barked.

Martha picked up the framed drawing from Cillian's desk, slid it inside her bag. 'I'd better let you get back to crime-busting,' she said.

'Ah, Martha Wilder, how are you?' the Super roared at her then. 'My ex-wife is a big fan of yours. That piece about the custody battle over the boxsets in particular.'

'I hope it was helpful?' said Martha.

'Well, now, *I* didn't read it, obviously. I'm more a sports pages kind of a bloke. I just happened to glance at the article, in the dentist waiting room the other day. Molars, bane of the existence. Anyway, your woman, the ex, she took the lot. Even *Fargo* and she feckin' hates the Coen brothers.'

Cillian stood up. 'I'll see Martha out, boss. Then I'll be in to you, OK?'

They walked towards the front door of the station. At the entrance, Cillian stopped. 'Thanks for your help, Martha.'

'Buy me a family bag of Maltesers and we'll say no more about it.'

'So Wilder's back on the scene, wha'?' said the Super when Cillian returned inside. He was a notorious gossip, as well as a keen, if covert, reader of women's magazines.

'She's helping us with our enquiries,' he said.

The Super smirked. 'Is that what we're calling it these days?'

Cillian ignored him, told him instead about Lenny and the stolen jeep and his visit to Lenny's house that morning. He didn't mention the drawing on the cork board. He wasn't sure where he was going with that. Probably nowhere. Still, it wouldn't do any harm to call in to Mr Hartmann's nursing home. Take a look through his stuff. If he was the artist, there might be something there. Drafts or sketches. And if that was the case, then maybe he kept a drawing in his safety deposit box at the bank. An insurance policy. Or maybe he kept it for plain old sentiment? Jimmy or Lenny could have taken it along with the money and Lenny was just the sort of dope who would keep it.

It was a long shot.

'So that's it?' said the Super. 'All the tax-payers' money you earn and that's all you've come up with so far?'

Cillian nodded. 'Afraid so.'

'No wonder Wilder dumped you,' said the Super, turning and heading down the corridor.

His office still smelled of her. That peculiar mix of tangy lemon and woody tobacco and mint. He left the door open and pushed the window as wide as it would go but her scent lingered and it was difficult to concentrate, the way it moved around him, like pieces of their past, snippets of their nights. Their days. Not all of their days had been bad. Some of them had been pretty good.

He had liked Martha Wilder pretty much from the start. And then, he had loved her.

It happened one day. One ordinary day. It wasn't a big thing in the end. No grand event, like the first time they had sex – after their first date, just inside the front door of her apartment. Or when they went on their first mini-break together – Belfast. Martha wanted to see the port. 'I love ports. The stink off them. Anything could happen in a port.' Cillian had convinced her to visit the Giant's Causeway which she'd declared 'too fucken beautiful'.

'You're too fucken beautiful,' he'd told her that day as the light from the lowering sun glanced through her hair, setting it on fire in a way she would have called *odious*, had she known. He'd said it in an Ian Paisley voice to take the weight out of it. And he knew it would make her laugh, his Ian Paisley impression. She laughed and even though he loved her laugh – a low rumble, like thunder – it didn't happen then. Not right then. She walked out to where the causeway met the sea, scooped water into her cupped hands and threw it over him. 'I think we should get you back to the hotel,' she said. 'Get you out of those wet clothes.'

Oh, the sex. Glorious was not a word that Cillian Larkin often had cause to employ but glorious it was just the same. She tasted of cigarettes and wine and even though he neither smoked nor drank wine, he did not seem able to get enough of her. Of the taste of her, the smell of her skin, the weight of her hair, slipping like rope through his fingers. The sound she made when she came. Like someone trying not to make a sound. There was something contained about her. Potent.

And yet it was not this part of their relationship that made him fall in love with her in the end.

It turned out to be the day she bought the sofa. That great, squashy sofa that was too big for her apartment but she bought it anyway.

'I'll come with you, if you like,' he'd offered. He was supposed to be going to a conference. Instead, he was asking a woman if he could go sofa shopping with her.

He hated shopping.

'OK,' said Martha. 'But only if you agree not to voice any opinions on my choice of sofa.'

'I don't generally have opinions on sofas, to be honest,' he said. 'I couldn't even describe mine if you asked.'

'I didn't ask.'

'I think it's blue.'

'It's green.'

'I won't say a word.'

'And you'll throw in lunch, like you said?'

'When did I say that?'

'Will you?'

'Yes.'

'Someplace that serves chips and wine?'

'Of course.'

'OK then. I've to file some copy first so don't distract me for an hour.'

He made coffee in her kitchen, poured some into the Dalek mug he had bought for her last Christmas. She had bought him the exact same one. It said, *Make me tea or I will exterminate you.* No sugar, no milk, leave the teabag in. He carried it into her office, set it on her desk beside the mousepad and left, closing the door quietly behind him. He texted his boss.

Can't make conference. Something important came up.

He read the paper at the kitchen table, which was where he always sat when he was in her apartment, on a comfortable chair, with a cushioned seat and armrests. He always sat on this particular chair, although he had not made a conscious decision in this regard. Had not declared it *his* when he had first sat on it, six months earlier. Martha always sat on the opposite side of the table. Perhaps it was their version of a commitment, in a relationship where work came first for both of them.

'I love my job,' she'd told him, early on. There was a faint warning in her tone.

'I love mine.'

'Good,' she'd said.

A week could go by without them seeing each other because of work commitments. And then they'd see each other and Cillian would come away from her wondering how he could have let a week go by. Gradually, the gaps shortened and the time they spent together lengthened. Neither of them had requested this. It hadn't been a discussion. But it had happened nonetheless.

The sound of her fingers tapping against the keys of her laptop was familiar. He realised he liked it. Something quietly insistent about it.

The sofa had to be squashy. And red. And velvet. 'I want it to be like the one in the Gryffindor common room,' she explained to the man in the furniture shop on Capel Street. Her tone was matter-of-fact, like there was nothing odd about a woman – a grown-up – with a serious job, a woman who had interviewed criminals and got them to admit to things they had denied in courtrooms, a woman who sometimes got texts from the leader of the opposition – *Is a pint out of the question?* – to want the same couch that Harry, Ron and Hermione squabbled on during their formative years at Hogwarts. The man – who had come out of the shop and greeted them when he noticed them peering in the window – nodded and said, 'I have just the thing,' as if he were no stranger to the seating preferences of an avid Potter fan.

'Are you Oliver Cassidy?' Martha asked, nodding towards the sign above the shop door. She always wanted to know who was who, Cillian noticed.

'He was my father, I'm called after him,' said the man, smiling as if he'd just remembered something and the memory was a good one. 'He died five years ago.'

'I'm sorry,' said Martha and the man shook his head like he disagreed. 'Ah, he had a good innings, as he'd say himself. And a good life, for the most part.'

The sofa fulfilled all Martha's criteria, although no measuring tape was needed to work out that it was too big for her apartment, a bald fact that Cillian made no reference to. Martha appeared diminutive when she sat on it.

'Why don't you take your shoes off and put your feet up?' Oliver Cassidy suggested. 'Take your coat off too. I find it's best to sit on a couch the same way as you would at home. You'll get a better feel for it, yes?'

Martha – who disliked getting her size sevens out in public – surprised Cillian by taking the man up on his suggestion.

'And you, sir?' He turned to Cillian, gestured towards the other end of the sofa. 'Would you care to try?'

'Oh, no, it's not for—'

'It's really comfortable, Cillian. Have a go,' said Martha.

He sat down at the other end.

'Put your feet up, sir, like your wife here.' Oliver nodded towards Martha with a smile across his broad face as if she were someone he'd known for years and hugely approved of.

The word *wife* settled on Cillian in a not unpleasant manner. He was surprised Martha hadn't picked Oliver up on it. Perhaps she hadn't heard him. He kicked off his runners and lifted his legs onto the couch. His feet found hers and he trapped one of them between his and massaged her toes. She caught his eye and scowled but did not pull her foot out of his reach. Oliver disappeared into a room at the back of the shop, telling them not to rush into a decision, warning them that a purchase of a sofa was a long-term commitment, they should consider every aspect, put themselves in different positions, wonder if they could see themselves sitting there in ten years' time, which was the length of the guarantee, even though the sofa would last much longer than that, he assured them.

Martha looked at Cillian. 'Ten years? That's about a third of the rest of my life, I'd say.'

'You reckon you're shuffling off your mortal coil before you hit sixty-five? Seems a little premature.'

'Not if you take the wine, fags and sausage rolls into account.'

'You have a point.'

'Are they my socks you're wearing?' she asked.

'Sorry. I didn't bring a spare pair to your apartment yesterday.'

Martha blushed, which he knew she hated. She said it made her hair seem even redder. And while she referred to herself sometimes as Big Foot, Cillian knew she could be a little sensitive about the length of her limbs and their attachments.

Cillian waved a foot at her. 'Look, it doesn't fit. The heel is halfway down my foot.'

'What?' She looked confused.

'I figured you were blushing because you thought your socks fit my feet.'

'Oh.' She looked at his raised foot, shook her head. 'No. And I'm not blushing, why would I be blushing?'

'Right.'

'I was just thinking . . . you might want . . . I mean, I have a few spare drawers in my place, you could . . . if you wanted to . . . it might be handy . . .'

'Are you offering me a drawer to put my smalls in? At your apartment?'

Oliver returned with two delicate china cups on saucers, which he handed to them. 'I was making a pot anyway,' he explained. 'I'll be at the desk doing a spot of paperwork if you need me, alright?'

Martha thanked him, pushed her finger through the cup's tiny handle. 'I'll have to buy the couch now,' she said, taking a sip of tea.

'Do you like it?' Cillian asked.

'I love it.'

'And the size . . . you don't think it's too—?'

'No.'

'Great. And yes, a drawer would be . . . handy. Thank you.'

Martha's smile always took a while to get going. It started as a twitch at the corners of her full, red lips before spreading slowly across her mouth and onto her face, during which time she shook her head, as if denying it. 'Grand. I'll sort that out.'

They sat on the couch with their china cups and their shoes and jackets discarded on the floor beside them and drank their tea and said no more about that or any other matter. They were the only customers in the place and the scratch of Oliver's pencil against a page in a ledger was the loudest sound in the shop.

That was when it happened.

A thought rose to the surface of Cillian's mind. Burst. Like an air bubble. And the thought was a simple one, as sometimes the best thoughts are. And it was simply this:

Happiness.

Which, Cillian acknowledged, was more like a feeling than a thought but that's what he thought nonetheless.

That's when it happened. That exact moment. And he knew, despite the few relationships he'd had over the years, that it had never happened to him before.

There was no anxiety attached to the feeling. Nothing attached to it at all. It was just there. A stand-alone feeling.

Oliver accepted the card Martha handed him. 'You can pay a deposit now and the balance when it's delivered, alright?'

Martha shook her head. 'I want to pay it all now. While I have the cash in my account.'

Oliver nodded and assured her that she and Cillian had made a wise decision and, in his sonorous voice, it sounded profound and true. Martha smiled at him as if she thought so too.

'Cillian?' She was pulling on her jacket now, glancing at him over her shoulder.

'Yes?' Cillian raised himself into a sitting position. He was still absorbed by the thought – the feeling, he supposed – that had barged through the door of his head. That had answered, 'Indefinitely,' when Cillian had asked how long it would be staying.

'Are you coming?'

'Yes.' He struggled out of the couch, shoved his feet into his runners, shook hands with Oliver – something he had never done before when leaving a shop – and walked outside to where Martha was waiting for him. The crowds – thicker now – moved around them, like a coordinated flash mob.

'Why are you looking at me so funny?' Martha leaned towards him with the look he most associated with her. Her curious look. He cleared his throat.

'I . . .'

'Are you hungry? You look hungry.'

'Yes. Yes, I think so.'

'You think so? How can you not know for sure? You either are or you're not.'

He reached for her then, pulled her against him. 'I am,' he said.

'Oh,' said Martha.

And when he kissed her, she kissed him back instead of pushing him away and referring to her views on Public Displays of Affection, which she might ordinarily have done.

Perhaps she sensed that there was something out of the ordinary about the day.

Something extraordinary.

He pushed his hands through the thick flow of her hair, kissed the pale skin of her neck, before he collected himself, stepped away from her.

She looked at him as she adjusted the scarf around her neck, her serious green eyes fixed on his face, like she knew. But then she shook her head and said, 'I don't know what's gotten into you, Cillian Larkin.'

Cillian shrugged, even though he knew what had gotten into him. Martha Wilder had gotten into him. Had crept up on him, slow and careful, like a B-side on a single that you always knew was there but never got around to playing. And then one day, you flip the record on the turntable, lay the needle down and there it is. The song that turns out to be the best thing about the single. The best thing about the band. But it's more than a great song. It's more than a set of notes positioned haphazardly along a score. It's like the song was written for you. Is about you. Tells the world who you are. Tells *you*.

And when the song ends, you lift the needle again, place it back on the groove, play it again.

And again.

Sixteen

The hearing on Monday morning was in a small room in the courthouse. Mama was there. She'd worn her best clothes: a skirt and jacket. Not quite matching but close enough. The charity shop had tried to pass it off as a set but Roman had put it under scrutiny, managed to knock five euro off the asking price. Mama had been embarrassed at his haggling. She hated drawing attention to them.

She had taken the time to blow-dry her hair today, instead of plaiting it as she usually did. 'Easier for work,' she'd told him when he'd asked why she always tied it up. He thought of her then, bent over a stranger's toilet bowl, scrubbing at their shit stains with a long handled brush that could never be long enough for a job like that.

She waved frantically at him and he nodded, grateful when the guards on either side of him marched him towards the top of the room, indicated a line of chairs, sat him between them. He couldn't see his mother then. Could almost pretend she wasn't there.

He hoped she wouldn't have to say anything. He imagined her on the stand, saying something awful like, 'My son is a good boy.'

She might cry and Roman would want to put his hands over his ears so he wouldn't have to hear the sound. It was the worst sound in the world, his mother crying.

The hearing was nothing like the court cases he had watched on the telly. Nothing much happened. Guards spoke in clipped monotones, using vocabulary Roman was unfamiliar with. 'The defendant was apprehended at twenty-three hundred hours near Blessington. He resisted arrest and was subsequently . . .' The voices droned on. Hot air blasted from two ancient storage heaters and the man in charge – was he the judge? – wore no wig, no black gown and smiled a lot, as if he were somewhere else, listening to something else entirely. Something lovely. Like his numbers being called out by that woman who does the lottery on the telly on Saturdays. Roman couldn't remember her name. She had long wavy hair and wore tight dresses – that was all he remembered. He didn't know why he was thinking about her. Why he wasn't concentrating on the hearing. It was going on and on. He tried to tune back in when he realised he was thinking about the woman who called out the lottery numbers and about the man who might be the judge and why he wasn't wearing a wig and a gown like judges did on the telly. Nobody mentioned the old man. If he was alive or dead.

If he died, would Roman be charged with murder? He hadn't asked Cillian that.

He wondered if Meadhbh knew about the hearing. If she believed that he had shot the old man.

She probably wasn't thinking about him at all. Why would she be? It wasn't like she was his girlfriend. It wasn't like he'd said anything.

He'd thought about it. About saying something. The day of the party. Everybody was going. Mama told Roman he could go so long as he had all his homework done and got a lift home with Adam's mother. Mama was much better by then. She had returned to some of her jobs. The house cleaning jobs. The women didn't seem to mind Rosa cleaning their toilets with only one hand, so long as the bowls were spotless afterwards.

And she could go back to the Moon & Stars, Penneys and the nursing home, once her cast came off. Which meant that Roman could stop being a delivery man for Jimmy.

'I've a job for you,' Jimmy had said that evening.

'I've been invited to a party,' said Roman. He immediately wished he hadn't mentioned the party.

'Lookin' to sow your wild oats, are you? My little Romeo.' Jimmy laughed. Roman didn't say anything. He knew he'd have to do the job.

'I need you to do a little drop for me and you going to the party will be the perfect cover story, won't it?' Jimmy winked, his smile wide and toothy.

Little drops.

That's what Jimmy called them.

One more little drop. Maybe his last one.

It was Meadhbh's party. Her fifteenth birthday party. Roman wished he were six months older than her instead of the other way round. Adam was fifteen too although you'd never think it. He'd plucked at Meadhbh's bra strap, visible beneath the thin fabric of her shirt, pulled it before releasing it so that it snapped against her skin in a way that, Roman felt, must hurt. Instead of telling Adam he was immature and stupid, Meadhbh chased him around the classroom and, when she caught him, she wrestled him to the ground and sat on him. Adam pretended to struggle. He ended up tickling her and when she tickled him back, he laughed way too loud. Adam was always doing stuff like that these days. Real kid's stuff. Roman and Meadhbh never carried on like that. They talked about books mostly, when it was just the two of them. They both loved books. Roman wrote fan fiction. Stories about Hermione. Meadhbh was the only person who knew. She had read one of his stories and told him it was good. She told him that he could be a writer some day.

He had changed the subject. It had been one of the happiest days of his life.

'So,' said Meadhbh, sitting on the desk and putting her feet on the edge of the chair where Roman sat. The left side of her left shoe pressed against his thigh in a way that was sort of alarming. He shifted over on the seat, producing a narrow gap between her foot and his leg. 'What are you wearing to the party?'

'It's not for another week,' Roman had said. He knew exactly what he was wearing. His black jeans. Mama had already washed them and they were in his half of the drawer, ironed and ready. The Gryffindor hoodie Mama had given him the Christmas before Lech died. It still mostly fit him, if he pulled up the sleeves. The runners from TK Maxx that almost looked the same as Converse.

'I can tell you what I'm wearing, if you like,' said Adam, jumping onto the desk beside her, sliding along the top of it till his hip bumped against hers.

'Don't bother,' said Meadhbh, taking her feet off Roman's chair and pushing herself off the desk with her hands. 'I'm not sure I could take the excitement.' She smirked at him, shook her head. Roman made sure he didn't look at her as she walked away.

Adam looked. He kept looking till Meadhbh slid into her seat near the top of the classroom.

'I'll have the delivery for you at eight,' Jimmy had said.

'I'm supposed to be at the party at eight,' Roman reminded him.

Jimmy laughed. 'No self-respecting party starts at eight, my son,' he said. 'Now, as I said, I'll give you the gear at eight. Yer man said he'll be at the pick-up spot at ten o'clock.'

'Ah, Jimmy—'

'At ten o'clock,' Jimmy kept going, raising the volume of his voice so Roman would know he was supposed to be listening, not talking. 'It's only round the corner from your little girlfriend's gaff so you'll be able to nip out and back and no one will be any the wiser, am I right?'

Roman nodded. There was no point telling Jimmy that Meadhbh wasn't his girlfriend.

Jimmy assumed Roman had done all kinds of things with all kinds of girls.

'Make sure he gives you the full whack for it. Not like last time. I'm not running a credit union here.'

'OK.'

'And you're to come back here with the money. I don't want you going back to the party with it. Someone might nick it.'

Roman reckoned the party would be nearly over by the time he had dropped off the money and come back but there was no point in mentioning it. He'd seen Jimmy mess people up. He had glimpsed him, through the crack in the door that led into the garage one day. Jimmy, with a strip of cotton wrapped around the knuckles of his right hand, beating the face of a man held up by Tommy and Lenny on either side of him. He'd done it in the middle of the afternoon, when Mama and the Lithuanians were at work. They'd put masking tape over the man's mouth so the neighbours wouldn't hear. Men scream like girls when they're in that kind of pain, Roman found out. The three against one kind.

At first, everything went according to plan. He collected the brown parcel from Jimmy and left the house. Meadhbh's party was in her house. Roman thought he would like a house like Meadhbh's one day. A house with a piano that people knew how to play, a garden that bloomed in the summertime, where people sat and read. Or just thought about whatever it was that people who lived in houses like these thought about. A house with photographs and copies of famous paintings on the wall.

One print in particular caught Roman's eye. He peered at it but the artist's signature was not there. Meadhbh told him it was called *Flowers* and that nobody knew who had drawn it. It was a charcoal drawing of a terraced brick building on a main street that reminded Roman of Swords main street, an old-fashioned paper and sweet shop on the ground floor and two sash windows above, both filled with roses in a vase. The flowers were the only thing in the picture that were painted. A bright red. Nearly crimson. There was something sort of startling about them. Alive.

Roman hoped that Meadhbh would like the basket of bath bombs from the Body Shop. Fruity ones. He'd seen her smelling them in the shop a few weeks ago, returned on his own the next day. The woman in the shop remembered him. Gift wrapped the bath bombs. Threw in a tube of body lotion that smelled of watermelon. For free.

'What are you getting for Meadhbh?' Adam had asked the day before.

Roman had shrugged. 'Not sure yet.'

Most of his class was at the party. Roman played pool with Adam. He won. Then he beat Meadhbh in darts. In one five-minute game of FIFA, he scored fifteen goals and no one had topped it yet. And then, when they stood in a circle and danced to 'Sing' and sang the words out loud, Meadhbh had looked right at him when she sang the line about finding someone and taking their hand. He knew it was just a song, just a line that everybody was singing, but the way Meadhbh looked at him when she sang it, it felt like she was singing it just for him. It felt like a true and certain thing.

She held her hands out in front of her and he grabbed them all of a sudden, without stopping to worry about whether or not he should. And now they were spinning, the two of them, around and around, and when they stopped they staggered like spinning tops before they collapsed on the sofa in the corner, and the muscles in Roman's face ached from laughing.

And then it was five to ten and Roman couldn't delay any longer. He had to go. He didn't bother with his jacket. He didn't want to draw attention to the fact that he was leaving. As he pulled the front door behind him, he could hear somebody suggest a game of dares and his heart clenched in his chest in a way that hurt, but it was the good kind of hurt and he imagined how Meadhbh's lips would feel against his and, in his imagination, they were soft.

The man was waiting on the corner where he should be, the shadow of a cherry tree thrown across his face, making it featureless. Roman bent low, pretended to tie his shoelaces while scanning the street for any signs of trouble. He couldn't wait to get rid of the package. He could feel it in his pocket, the rectangular bulk of it rasping against his leg in the tight jeans. An uncomfortable reminder of the difference between him and Meadhbh. Not even the thought of the crisp twenty euro note pulled taut in Jimmy's hand could ease the discomfort of it. He knew Meadhbh wouldn't understand. Her mam gave her twenty euro for tidying her room.

He rose to his feet, reached inside the pocket of his jeans, wrapped his fingers around the packet.

He stood there, felt himself sort of flooded, all of a sudden, like he had been lying down for ages and then stood up much too quick. In some way, he felt he was standing on the edge of his life, looking down at it. He felt a strange sense of certainty, like he was in charge of everything. He was calling the shots. This would be his last drop, he decided. Mama would go back to work properly next week and Roman would get a job doing something else. Delivering newspapers maybe? Something safe. They would save up, him and Mama. Move out. Into their own apartment maybe. Things would be different from now on. He would tell Jimmy to go stuff himself. They were nearly all paid up, him and Mama. Soon, they would owe Jimmy nothing. Roman would return to the party and kiss Meadhbh. On her lips. Keep on kissing her even when the standard ten-second countdown had petered out.

He had practised on the back of his hand. Loads of times. He would kiss her tonight and he would make sure it was a good kiss.

A great kiss.

'What the fuck took ya?' the man – a skinny affair with pockmarks denting the drawn skin of his face – hissed at Roman when he appeared beside him.

Roman was used to this reaction. They always looked like they'd been waiting ages.

Roman put his hand out for the money. 'Always get the money first,' Jimmy said. 'Those fuckers'll fleece ya if ya give them half a chance.'

The man's smile was gappy, like a kid's, and the teeth that remained had a stained, listing quality, as if they weren't staying long.

'Listen, tell Jimmy I'll pay him double the next time, I'm having a . . . bit of a cash-flow situation . . .'

Roman shook his head, took a step back. This sometimes happened. Jimmy would be angry. The tip of his nose would turn white and pinched. He'd look around the room for something to throw. The man made a grab for Roman. Roman dodged him like he was on the basketball court, dodging his mark. Then he ran as if he were running towards the opposition's basket, stuffing the packet back into the pocket of his hoodie. The man ran after him for a minute, then stopped, bent low with his hands on his knees, his breathing loud and wheezy. Roman kept running. He ran until he reached Meadhbh's house, then he stopped. He knew he should keep running until he got to Jimmy's. Jimmy'd be waiting for him. He wouldn't be happy when he heard.

Instead, Roman stopped outside Meadhbh's house. He thought about the game of dares. If it had started yet. He still had that strange sense of certainty. Of being in charge of his life. He would insist Jimmy pay him. Pay him anyway, no matter what had happened. Roman had kept up his end of the deal. It wasn't his fault things hadn't worked out, was it?

The front door of Meadhbh's house opened and two people came out holding hands, darting towards the side passage where some privacy was granted by way of two potted bay trees, one at either side. Roman crept up the driveway, using the Range Rover as cover. It was a boy and a girl. He could make out their silhouettes. The girl leaned against the side of the house and the boy pinned her there with his arms on either side of her, his hands spread against the brickwork. Then he cocked his head at a curious angle and swooped towards her face. Roman heard the kiss rather than saw it. It made a wet smack of sound. It did not sound like a good kiss. Certainly not a great kiss. When the boy came up for air, the girl giggled and that's when Roman knew.

It was Meadhbh.

And Adam.

Adam and Meadhbh.

Roman didn't go back to the party. Meadhbh would return his jacket to him on Monday morning at school. He knew she would. By then everyone would know. About Meadhbh and Adam. Going together. Meadhbh would say that she and Roman were still friends but everything would be different. Adam would have a special signal he would give to Roman when he wanted to be alone with Meadhbh, which would be pretty much all the time, Roman knew. He knew that because if Meadhbh was his girlfriend he'd want to be alone with her pretty much all the time.

He ran home, wasn't even breathless when he got there. He felt like he could run the length and breadth of Ireland and not be out of breath. Like there was an energy inside him and if he didn't keep moving, he might explode with it.

'How'd it go?' Jimmy asked. Roman wasn't even afraid of telling him about the deal. He didn't care about Jimmy and the tantrum he was about to throw. It was only when he reached inside the pocket of his hoodie and realised that the packet was no longer there that fear began to make its presence felt, wrapping itself around his body like the tentacles of that enormous jellyfish that had stung him last summer.

Jimmy didn't have a tantrum.

He didn't shout.

Or throw anything against a wall.

He remained in his seat. He didn't look at Roman. When he spoke, his voice was low and soft.

'You fucken owe me, Roman. You owe me big time.'

Roman nodded. He knew. 'How much?' he asked.

Jimmy leaned forward, close enough for Roman to see the network of red veins threaded through the whites of his eyes. He shook his head. 'You owe me, Roman,' he said again, as if Roman hadn't heard him the first time. 'I'll let you know when it's payback time, yeah?'

'But I—' Roman knew that payback for Jimmy always involved interest. A lot of it.

Jimmy pointed a long nicotine-stained finger towards Roman's face and Roman tried not to flinch. Tried not to look afraid. 'Shut. The. Fuck. Up.' Jimmy was doing that thing he did with his voice sometimes. Talking low, almost a whisper. Smiling as he talked, as if he was saying something funny.

Now the smiley-winning-lottery-numbers man who must be the judge but didn't look like a judge was talking and Roman struggled to concentrate.

'. . . no option but to recommend that this young man remain in custody until such time as . . .'

Mama didn't cry. Instead, he heard the scrape of her chair against the floor, the pitch of her voice, louder than usual. 'I want to go with my son,' she said. It was like a declaration, the way she said it, an order, and he knew what it would have cost her to stand up and announce herself like that. To draw attention to her pale face and red eyes and the fear that shrouded her like a veil.

Roman was pulled to his feet by the guards on either side of him, their hands wrapped around his upper arms. In this way, he was led briskly from the room. From the corner of his eye, he saw Cillian talking to Mama. Heard him saying, 'Do you understand?' at the end, speaking slower than he normally would, probably because of his Donegal accent. But she understood a lot now. Since she'd started those English lessons with the old man in the nursing home.

The old man. He was alive, Cillian said at the hearing. Still in a coma. But alive. Roman was glad that the old man knew, at least. That Roman hadn't shot him. That he had tried to stop Jimmy shooting him.

There was some comfort in that, however small.

Now he was in the back of a police car and there was a wire mesh between him and the two guards in the front and the car was moving, through Swords and then away, leaving Jimmy and school and Meadhbh and Adam and home . . . and Mama. Leaving them all behind.

Seventeen

A swirl of the air around his bed as the door opened. He could smell lemon and mint and something else. The woody smell of tobacco.

'There he is.' He recognised Joan Larkin's voice. The sister-in-charge.

'Oh. He looks . . . different than I remembered.' Tobias could not put a face or a name to the other voice. Low. Feminine.

'He's lost weight.'

'Do you think he'll . . . ?'

The sound of window blinds being adjusted. Perhaps opened. Or closed. Tobias couldn't tell.

'Hard to tell in these cases, Martha. And he's elderly, which doesn't help.'

Martha. Tobias remembered the name from a conversation a few days ago. Or perhaps longer? It was getting harder to keep track of time. Almost impossible.

'I suppose I should . . .'

'You can stay if you like. He doesn't get visitors. Apart from a Polish woman. Rosa. She works at the nursing home where he lives. Lived.'

'Is she the one whose son . . . ?'

'Roman, yes. He's in custody. There was a hearing this morning, far as I know.'

'Cillian mentioned him. He doesn't think the boy—'

'Well, you know Cillian. Always ready to believe the best of people.'

The silence that followed Joan's statement was, Tobias felt, full of something. Not quite awkwardness but, certainly, there was little ease in it.

He could hear Martha rummage in her handbag, the crackle of foil as she eased a – he could smell the mint, stronger now – chewing gum? Yes, chewing gum, into her mouth. He imagined her there, not quite looking at Joan, concentrating on the chewing of the gum to ease the not-quite-awkward silence.

Martha stayed where she was, after Joan left, standing near the door. He could hear her shifting on her feet, could hear her hand working its way through her hair. Long, he thought. Tangled.

'Oh, fuck it.' Strangely, the expletive did not offend him in the usual way. Possibly because of his . . . situation. This feeling of suspension, of floating in a tide that was going out. Or maybe it was the way the word slid from her mouth, something habitual and matter-of-fact about it.

She dragged a chair near the head of his bed and sat down. Silence then, apart from her fidgety breath.

'This is ridiculous,' she said. The thump of a bag against the floor. Too heavy for a handbag. Perhaps one of those computer bags. All the young people carried them nowadays, their backs and shoulders bowed with the weight. She was stretching now. He could hear the muscles in her neck and back pull and strain.

A long sigh then. Something resolute about it. The moan of the chair beneath her, the pull of a zip, rummaging, the chair moaning again. A pause and then the scratch of a pencil on paper, which he found confusing – what was she doing? And why was she doing it here? – but comforting also, reminding him as it did of the time he had spent skating the pared tip of a pencil across a page. He had never felt more present in the world than when he was drawing. There were times when he did not feel deserving of such a feeling, for it was a good feeling, close to happiness, he was certain. But it gripped him like an addiction, and he had no choice but to keep drawing. It was something he could not help.

He did not think Martha was drawing. It was slower, more deliberate. He thought she might be writing. He did not wonder what she might be writing. Instead, he concentrated on the sound of the pencil, the soft rub of it against the paper and he imagined it as a lullaby, like the ones his mother used to sing to baby Greta, who listened as she struggled to keep her eyes open.

She always fell asleep in the end.

Tobias followed the sound, saw it as a path he was walking along, down, down, down, the path leading to the place in his mind where he kept her.

He dreamed of Mary Murphy.

It was the smell that Tobias remembered most when he arrived back in Dresden. A dense, acrid smell that clung to his clothes, his hair, crawled under his nails, his skin. The streets of the city were filled with rubble and vague possibilities of people. Bits of people. Tobias was careful not to step on them. He wandered rather than walked. He had no destination; there was no place for him to go. In the Altmarkt, a bonfire of bodies burned, the heat from the flames almost impossible to contemplate as more and more bodies were collected on wooden handcarts and thrown on the blaze.

The zoo had been bombed and someone said there were lions roaming the streets. Tobias wondered what it would be like to see a lion emerging through the thick clouds of smoke that hung like curtains across the city. He thought he would like to see one. He wandered through the streets but saw no lions.

He had no memory of how he felt as he roamed through the city that had been home. Now, home was just a word. A mythical word that came from one of the stories Mama had read to him when he was a child. He was a ghost, haunting a place that was no longer there.

A truck pulled up alongside Tobias. The passenger door opened and a boy, not much older than Tobias, wearing a Luftwaffenhelfer uniform jumped down. He pointed to the back of the truck. 'Get in,' he said.

Tobias did as he was bid. In a way, it was a relief to have an order to follow, a place to go.

The truck was crammed with other boys just like him, with blackened faces and deadened eyes. Tobias squeezed himself between two of them and felt the pain in his fingers as they began to thaw with the heat of so many bodies so close together.

The boys discussed where they were going. Most thought they were being sent to the Russian front. Someone knew for a fact that the Red Army was only thirty-five miles north of Berlin now. That created a momentary pause. They had all heard the stories about the Russians.

They took no prisoners.

Tobias said nothing. He closed his eyes but did not sleep. He found himself unable to care where the truck was going, only that it was going. Leaving Dresden in its wake.

He was flotsam, borne on a tide that was neither ebbing nor filling. Just moving. Perhaps west to the allied front. Perhaps north to be thrown to the Russians.

All Tobias knew for sure was that he would never return to Dresden.

The truck stopped every so often. The boys jumped out, pissed in hot arcs at the side of the road, spat their phlegmy spits. Tobias, who had never travelled this far out of Dresden before, looked at the landscape. At the white glare of the frozen fields, separated by lines of trees, their bare branches reaching towards the sky like hands begging for mercy.

He did not know where they were when the attack happened. Or how long they had been driving. Perhaps a day. Perhaps longer. The drone of an airplane, faint at first. The truck swerved towards the side of the road, flinging the boys against the canvas wall like stones from a slingshot. The driver shouted at the boys – *Get out, get out* – and they piled out of the truck and ran blindly in all directions as the plane, low now, strafed the truck, the road, the fields.

Tobias ran and, when one of the bullets made its mark, there was something close to relief in it. When he fell, he fell in slow motion. He could no longer hear the screams of the other boys. He remembered the sensation of air, rushing past his face. He remembered thinking it was not unpleasant, the sensation. He lay where he fell. The road was cold against his skin but the blood running down his face was warm. He closed his eyes.

When he opened them, a face was hovering over his. It was her face.

What Tobias remembered most about Mary Murphy was her eyes. Dark blue. Almost navy. She was hovering above him and, at first, he thought perhaps he was dead and she was an angel.

'Leave him, he's a fucking Nazi.'

She turned and shouted over her shoulder. 'He's only a boy. If we leave him here to die, we'll be just like them. And this war will make even less sense.'

'We don't have room for him.'

'We'll make room.'

She half-carried, half-dragged him to a makeshift ambulance. He remembered her arms around him, the warm, sweet smell of her sweat as she pulled and pushed him. He wanted to tell her to leave him be. But the sensation of being borne by her, the feel of her arms wrapped around him, was something he had no power to resist.

When Tobias came to, he was in a bed, one of many beds arranged in rows with sheets strung around some of them. Later,

Tobias realised that the soldiers in those beds were dying. Nearly dead. And he was glad, then, about the sheets.

'Don't say anything.' That's what Mary Murphy said to him. That first day, when he came to. 'The soldiers won't know you're a German if you don't say anything, alright?' Her face was beside his; she was whispering as she changed the bandage around his head. 'The bullet only grazed you,' she told him. 'You'll be grand before you're twice married.' When she laughed, she closed her eyes. He looked at her face. He thought he'd never seen such a beautiful face. The clear softness of her skin, the shape of her mouth, the slender line of her jaw.

'Don't cry, love,' she whispered to him. 'It'll be OK.' He was ashamed to feel the hot leak of tears from the corners of his eyes. He blinked them away.

He said nothing. He slept deep, dreamless sleeps. He ate his rations and did not ask about the other boys in the truck. What had happened to them.

The nights were the worst. Men, stoic in the daylight, whimpering in their sleep, calling out for their mothers, screaming as they saw, again and again, the horrors of the war they had been fighting, perhaps wondering what it had all been for.

In spite of this, Tobias felt something close to calm for the first time since the bombs had dropped on Dresden.

It was because of Mary Murphy. Every day he listened for the soft step of her shoes as she made her way along the beds. Held his breath as she drew near. He pictured her face before he saw it. Closed his eyes and saw her there. She slipped her hand around the back of his head, lifted him so he could drink the water from the cup she held with her other hand.

'There now,' she said, as she returned his head to the pillow. 'There now.' Her voice was a whisper, brushing against his ear. He could listen to her forever.

He listened to her stories, memorised them so he could take them out later when she was gone, listen all over again. The things she told him felt like a secret between them, never to be told.

Even though Tobias never spoke, he felt like she was the only person in the world who knew him. Knew he was there. That he existed.

When she removed the stitches in his head, he knew it was only a matter of time.

'This might hurt,' she said. There were so many things he wanted to say. To tell her. How she had given him back something of himself that he'd thought was lost forever. How she was the best part of his day. Of every day.

He said nothing.

He would regret it.

Every day.

Eighteen

On Monday night, Cillian drove to Joan's house, where he and Stella were expected for dinner. Stella was still talking. Now something about another of her sisters. Saoirse, he thought. A papier-mâché love heart her husband had made her for their first wedding anniversary. He'd presented it to her at the party they threw to celebrate. The party that Stella had missed the night she'd arrived. That seemed like a long time ago. Cillian now knew that paper was the traditional gift for one-year wedding anniversaries. '. . . and he painted it in the Donegal colours – you know the way she's mad about the GAA? I asked him how long it had taken him to do and he said . . .'

The car was stuffy – Stella liked the heat up high – and Cillian pulled at the tie around the collar of the shirt that Stella had bought him. The damn thing was like a noose, strangling him. He tried to concentrate on Stella's voice. '. . . and Saoirse decided that, from now on, she'd try to visit her mother-in-law every second Friday, even though the nursing home is on the far side of Killybegs but then Selene suggested . . .'

Cillian's visit to Tobias Hartmann's nursing home had yielded little. There were barely any personal effects in the small bedroom where he had lived for the past year. Two stiff shirts hanging in the wardrobe, a book of razor blades in the bathroom, a nail file. In a drawer, two tins of shoe polish: brown and black. A shoe horn. On top of his bedside locker, a plastic bottle of prescription pills. A book about ancient Rome. There were no photographs on the walls, no keepsakes or mementos, nothing to suggest a life that had been lived. It could have been anybody's room. In the end, Cillian had to concede that he had no evidence to connect the old man lying in a coma in hospital with the drawing he had seen in Lenny's house. The hunch was a dead end. He was glad now that he hadn't mentioned it to the Super. He would have said that hunches were about as much use to him as his divorce lawyer.

He noticed that Stella had stopped talking. He glanced at her. She was looking at him, smiling.

'This is nice, isn't it?' she said, putting her hand on Cillian's leg as they inched along the Stillorgan dual carriageway.

'Being stuck in traffic?'

Stella laughed – *hahaha* – and in the stuffy confines of the car, the noise was shrill.

'I just meant it's nice, you and me, going to your sister's, spending some time together, like a proper couple, you know?' Her hand was massaging his thigh now. He picked it up, squeezed it and, after a reasonable amount of time had passed, returned it to her lap.

She still hadn't specified when she might go home, although the schools reopened next week so she'd have to be back by then.

Wouldn't she?

'Are you alright?' Stella said.

'Sorry, yeah, I'm fine. Just a bit . . . tired, I suppose.'

'You've been working too hard. I've hardly seen you.' There was an undertone of accusation in her voice.

'I'm sorry but I did tell you, when you arrived, that I had to work.'

'Och, don't mind me,' she said, waving her hand dismissively. 'I might be a wee bit hormonal. I'm waiting on my visitors. They should have been here by now.'

'Your visitors?'

'You know.' Stella lowered her voice. 'My *period*.'

'You're not . . . late, are you?' He was always careful.

'Ah no. Not really. Although in fairness you can usually set your watch by me, I'm that regular.'

'So you *are* late?'

'A few days. Nothing to worry about.'

'A few?'

'Five.'

Five. Five days. That was late. Cillian's grip on the steering wheel tightened so that the bones of his knuckles strained against his skin.

Martha had had a 'scare' before. Before he had realised how bad things were. How bad the drinking was. It was one of the only times she had cried. 'I haven't been taking folic acid. Our baby could have spina bifida, like Amelia.'

Our baby.

He had held Martha tight, breathed into the soft mesh of her hair and told her it would be alright. Everything would be alright. He thought about a baby with bright green eyes. A girl with red pigtails that flew behind her when she ran.

Our baby.

Martha took the folic acid after that. 'Just in case,' she said, and she smiled at him and it was like a question, her smile, and he kissed her mouth and that was like an answer and, for a while, everything seemed possible. Happiness, all that stuff. Until he found out how bad things were and nothing seemed possible anymore.

'Look,' said Stella, returning her hand to his leg again. 'It's probably nothing. And if it's something, you know, we'll deal with that too, won't we?' She smiled sweetly at him, leaned in to lay her head on his shoulder. 'You know, it's funny, it feels like we've been together for years.'

'Sorry, Stella, I can't . . . I just need to change the gear there.'

She moved back into her seat and he put the radio on and she hummed along to a tune Cillian had never heard before while the car edged along the road, making little headway in the traffic. A muscle leaped against Cillian's temple. 'I'll stop by the chemist on my way home,' he said when the song ended. 'Pick up a pregnancy test.'

'Och, no, don't bother,' said Stella, shaking her head. 'They're wild expensive, those things. And anyway, as I said, my visitors are probably on their way.'

It was a relief to get to Joan and Tony's house, which was a charming bungalow on the outskirts of Bray with views of the mountains at the back of the house and snatches of the Irish Sea at the front. Cillian usually loved visiting his sister and her family.

When Joan wasn't there, he completed DIY jobs which Tony passed off later as his own. 'I can't be a nurse who likes ballroom dancing *and* is bad at DIY,' Tony said when he'd first enlisted Cillian's help in this regard. Cillian was pretty sure his sister knew about Tony's DIY shortcomings. Very little got past her.

Tonight he felt like a visitor in his sister's house. Which he was. He just hadn't felt like one before. He supposed it was because of Stella, who *was* a visitor.

'Where's Naoise?' Cillian asked as Tony led them to the bright, busy kitchen at the back of the house.

'Don't even think about waking him up,' Joan warned him, her face pink from the heat of the rack of lamb she had been seasoning. 'He was like a Duracell bunny today. I had to take his batteries out.'

'Oh, what a shame. I was looking forward to meeting him. I *adore* children.' Stella's smile was wide and her hand, which she placed on Cillian's arm, was clammy.

'So do I,' said Joan, hugging Stella whom she had met, twice before, in Donegal. 'Especially when they're asleep.' Stella laughed and laughed.

'Here, sit down, love,' said Tony, pulling out a chair when she finally stopped. 'I've made my famous French onion soup for starters.'

Joan stuck a ladle into the soup tureen on the table. 'Small print: may cause flatulence. You'll be in the spare room tonight, Tony.'

Cillian smiled. He had seen the way his sister looked at her husband sometimes. Brief, occasional glances but in it he could see their story. He knew there'd be no one in the spare room tonight. He was glad for his sister. She had made sacrifices in her life.

'So,' said Tony, tucking an enormous linen napkin into the collar of his T-shirt and digging in. 'How's work going, detective?'

'Very busy,' said Stella at once. 'When he came home before six the other night, I thought he was an intruder, *hahaha.*'

The word – *home* – landed on Cillian like a cold raindrop that drips down your neck.

'Are you cold, love?' asked Stella, pinning his hand to the table with one of hers.

'No,' he said, pulling his hand away and reaching for his glass. 'I'm grand.'

'You're a bit pale as well. I hope you're not coming down with something.'

'You're wasting your time there, Stella. That fella would tell you he's grand even if he was *dying*. Wouldn't you, Cillian?' Joan winked at him over the rim of her wineglass.

Cillian groaned. 'Please don't trot that story out,' he said.

'Oh, what story?' said Stella. 'You have to tell me now.'

Joan always told the story like it was an amusing anecdote. Cillian didn't remember it like that.

It was the night of his sister's first college ball. Joan – who had deferred her nursing degree for three years after their mother died – had finally started the course the previous September in Letterkenny.

She'd been looking forward to the ball for weeks.

'A ball,' said Stella. 'How romantic! Who did you go with?'

'Oh, some scrawny little fella. Kevin someone-or-other.'

Kevin Pendergast: the only boyfriend Cillian ever remembered his sister having, until she met Tony when she was forty-six.

'That must be Kevin,' Joan had said that night when the doorbell rang. Cillian, thirteen then, remembered the unfamiliar sound of Joan's high heels against the wooden boards on the staircase, how the sound had echoed all around the house that seemed bigger, now it was just the two of them.

'I thought he was a bit flushed alright when I was leaving, but of course he insisted he was OK,' said Joan, shaking her head towards Cillian.

Mrs Campbell always got a mention in the story. The hero of the piece.

'If it weren't for Mrs Campbell . . .'

'Who's Mrs Campbell?'

'The next-door neighbour. She was very kind to us after Mum died. And thankfully she had a key to the door,' said Joan. 'She'd made gingerbread for Cillian but I think that was just her excuse to put her head around the door. Check in on him. She knew I was out that night.'

Mrs Connolly had had to push and push at the kitchen door to get it open. Cillian was slumped against the door, unconscious by then, a dead weight.

'I got to the hospital at around nine o'clock that night and Cillian came to the next day, at around eight. The first thing he said was, "What's for breakfast?"'

She left out the bit about Cillian's heart stopping – at 03.07 – and a doctor from Pakistan – who happened to be in Cillian's ward on his rounds at the time – performing CPR on him for thirteen minutes – a minute for every year, Joan said – and if he hadn't been in Cillian's ward on his rounds at the time, Cillian's heart would have stopped and not started again.

'He was mostly grand by the time he came to, thank God. The antibiotics were getting the better of the meningitis by then.'

Joan had cried when Cillian woke up in the hospital. Cried and cried into the fleshy shoulder of a nurse who let her. Who told her to take as long as she needed. When she stopped, she sat in a chair beside Cillian's bed, took his hot hand between her cold ones. She said, 'Sorry.' She whispered it, over and over.

Cillian had misunderstood. 'Am I going to die?' he asked.

Joan had shook her head. 'No.'

'Why not?'

'Because I won't let you.'

It wasn't until a few weeks had passed that Cillian realised.

'Why did you break up with Kevin?'

'I . . . it's not really . . . I mean . . . it's complicated, Cillian.'

Joan had dropped out of her nursing course then. Sold their parents' house. Moved them to Donegal town where they had family. A support system, Joan had called it. She completed a carer's course by distance learning. She took a job in a local creche, worked in the mornings while Cillian was at school. He always remembered her being there, in the house, when he got up in the morning, when he left to go to school or Gaelic practice, when he returned.

Joan was there.

When he was older, he knew why. It wasn't that complicated after all. Joan had made a promise to their father first. Then their mother. She felt she had breached it that night. The night that Cillian nearly died.

Kevin – who went on to become an orthopaedic surgeon – wrote to her for a while. Joan never wrote back. Cillian supposed it was easier to keep promises like Joan's without other people around.

Without complications.

Complications were other people.

Later, Stella insisted on seeing the climbing frame that Tony had built for Naoise.

'From scratch,' Tony said, as he led Stella out of the dining room towards the playroom.

Joan smiled at Cillian. 'I think he almost believes it himself,' she said.

'What do you mean?'

'I know you did it. And the bathroom cabinet. And you rehung the kitchen door, didn't you?'

'No! I mean, sure, I gave him a dig out but . . .'

Joan laughed. 'Your secret is safe, kiddo. Besides, I think it's kind of sweet.'

Cillian grinned. 'He's a good man, your fella.'

Joan studied him. 'So. You and Stella. Must be serious – you haven't brought a woman over here since Martha.'

'You sort of insisted, as I recall.'

'It would have been rude not to invite her over when she came all this way to see you,' said Joan. 'So is it?' she added.

'Is it what?'

'Serious? With Stella?'

Cillian pushed his fringe out of his eyes. 'I didn't think so.'

'But?'

'She's late.'

'How late?' Joan always took everything in her stride.

'Five days.'

Joan sat straighter in her chair. 'Has she taken a pregnancy test?'

241

Cillian shook his head. 'She only just told me in the car on the way over.'

'And . . . what will you do? If she is, I mean?'

Cillian shook his head. 'I don't know.'

'How does Stella feel about it?'

'She doesn't seem too put out by the idea.'

'Maybe she's right in a way. I mean, look at me. I didn't plan to settle down. Definitely didn't plan on having a baby. I thought I was too old by the time I met Tony. But Naoise turned out to be the best thing that happened to us in the end,' said Joan, smiling now, as she often did when she talked about her family.

'Yeah, but me and Stella, we're not . . . I mean, you and Tony, you were pretty sure from the start, weren't you?'

Joan hesitated before she spoke again. 'Is it because of Martha?'

'What do you mean?'

'Is she the reason you're reluctant to move on?'

'No, of course n—'

'Because Martha moved on, Cillian. She dumped you. Remember?'

He remembered.

'Is this a fucking intervention?' Martha had shouted that night. He'd arrived at her apartment unexpectedly with Chinese food. Wanted to surprise her. It was their anniversary, of sorts. Eighteen months. A year and a half. Not that he was going to say it. 'You soppy cow,' she'd say if he mentioned it, and then she'd grin at him without ever knowing how beautiful she was. Already, he could taste her.

He took the stairs to her apartment three at a time.

He hadn't seen the nine o'clock news. Hadn't seen Martha's report. The bag of Chinese food was warm against his hands. She would say, 'Should we eat first? Or get the sex out of the way?'

'Best to get the sex out of the way.'

Her violin was in three pieces on the hall floor. She loved that violin – it had been her grandfather's. She had always said no when he asked her to play him a piece of music. 'You think I'm better than I am,' she told him one night, nearly a whisper. 'You'll be disappointed.'

'Martha?' He put the food on the hall table and picked up the pieces of the violin with careful hands. Perhaps it could be put back together? In the kitchen, she was a lot of the way down a bottle of vodka. She wasn't bothering with tonic or ice or lemon. She wasn't even bothering with a glass, was drinking it from the neck. In her hand, a remote control pointing at the television. She barely registered his arrival, concentrating instead on the television screen where she was interviewing a politician outside the Dáil. The Minister for Health, Cillian saw.

She asked him a question that Cillian could not make out. Neither could the minister. 'I can't understand you,' the minister said.

'Perhaps I should say it in Spanish?' slurred Martha, a sly reference to his latest affair with his live-in nanny from Barcelona.

'Libel is an expensive business, Martha,' he said, walking – briskly – away.

'So is adultery,' she roared, tripping along in his wake, waving the microphone towards the back of his head before becoming entangled in her own feet – her size sevens – and falling down a set of three concrete steps.

The crack as her head hit the path was sharp.

Martha jabbed at buttons on the remote, played the segment again. She turned up the volume and shouted along with the words, 'Libel is an expensive business, Martha.' She laughed then, a high, mirthless laugh.

'Let me take a look at your head,' said Cillian, putting his hands

243

on either side of her face. There was a lump on her forehead and sore-looking scratches down the side of her face. She laughed again.

'You're always trying to fix me, Cillian Larkin.'

'I think you should put some ice on that bump.'

'I got fired.'

'I'll make you some coffee.'

'I broke my violin.'

'It's a fairly clean break. I reckon it can be salvaged.'

'You think everything can be salvaged.'

'You should eat something.'

'I want more vodka.'

'I think you've had enough.'

That's what did it. Five words. *I think you've had enough.* That's what kicked the legs of their relationship out from under them. There were times when Cillian wondered if it had been worth it.

Would he say them again if he could go back?

He supposed he would.

'Is this a fucking intervention?' she shouted. 'Because it's come at a very inconvenient fucking time. I'm trying to get drunk here.' This time she splashed the vodka into a glass, drank it in one long, gulping motion, then sat on the couch that was too big for the room and passed out.

Cillian switched off the television, got a blanket from the bedroom. He put her in the recovery position and tucked the blanket around her. He moved her hair back from her face, loosened the top button of her shirt and put a bucket on the floor beside her and a glass of water and two Panadol on the coffee table beside the couch. He slipped off her shoes. Her size sevens. On a note he wrote:

'I don't want to intervene. But I do want to help. I love you. We can sort this. Call me when you feel better.'

He waited for a while, worried that she might throw up in her sleep.

Then he left.

Martha didn't call.

Cillian did. He left messages, emailed her and, finally, rang the buzzer at her apartment. There was no answer. He didn't use his key.

A week later, he received a large brown bubble-wrapped package in the post. By then, the segment was all over YouTube. Someone had put music to it, turned it into a rap, with a close-up of her face as she tumbled down the steps. Her expression was one of surprise. As if she couldn't believe it. Couldn't believe she was falling.

Inside the parcel were things he had left behind in her apartment. Ordinary things like socks, a box set of *The Wire*, a pinstriped tie he kept for emergencies, a toothbrush, a packet of razor blades, a book on fly fishing.

At the bottom was her key to his house.

A brief note, written on a yellow stickie. *I think that's everything. Martha.*

The writing was not like hers. It was written in small capital letters. It left nothing to the imagination.

He stopped calling.

He concentrated on work. There was a new case. There was always a new case. He was grateful for that. Joan got married and he danced with her, the way Martha had shown him.

He concentrated on work.

She wasn't on the news anymore and part of him was glad about that. It might have distracted him from the job. Seeing her face.

He had put her in the recovery position.

That's how he had left her.

On her couch.

In the recovery position.

Nineteen

The pecking order was clear from the beginning. The pecking order was always clear. There was the leader, his followers, the hangers-on, the outcasts.

The leader was short and stocky. There was something barely contained about him. Like an active volcano, ready to erupt at a moment that could never be anticipated. He was seventeen, long black hair and a face that would have been pale had it not been for the clusters of spots that spread from the bottom of his neck to the top of his forehead, many of them raw red or bleeding from picking and scratching.

One of the staff had introduced Roman to the boys earlier, at dinner.

'This is Roman Matus,' the guard said. They didn't call themselves guards but that's what they were, all the same, with their keys jangling from a metal ring attached to their trousers.

The guard introduced Roman to the leader first, as if he, too, knew the pecking order. The boy – Marcus – stood up, extended his hand. 'Ah, Roland, my uncle Jimmy told me to expect you. Asked me to extend his warmest wishes for your continued rude health.'

'It's Roman,' the guard said. Marcus ignored him.

'Your uncle Jimmy?' Roman said, as the boy pumped the hand that Roman had offered.

'Jimmy Carty? You two are acquainted, I understand? He

says to tell you that your mother's fine. He's taking real good care of her.'

The boy winked at Roman, resumed his seat as the guard continued the introductions. The room seemed to shrink, the walls pressing in on him, making it hard to breathe. He nodded at each of the other boys in turn until the guard had finished, couldn't remember any of their names. Beads of sweat bloomed across his upper lip and he struggled not to wipe it, not to draw attention to his fear. His weakness. The guard nodded towards an empty seat near the end of the table, between a fat black kid and a skin-and-bone Romanian with thick-lensed glasses.

The outcasts.

Roman sat on the chair, made a great play of being hungry, concentrated on eating, stuffing food into his mouth. It tasted neither good nor bad. It tasted of nothing as he sat there and ate and thought about Marcus, the leader, being Jimmy's nephew, being in Trinity House, being locked in with him. He knew it was not a good thing but wondered how bad it might be. He didn't know. He didn't know anything. All around him, the sound of the other boys. No one spoke to him. It would be up to him to speak first. To announce himself, so that they could categorise him. A follower, a hanger-on, an outcast. He knew how the system worked. He said nothing. Kept eating. After dinner, he went to his room.

He tried to formulate a plan but all he came up with was to keep to himself, keep quiet, keep out of trouble. That sounded like advice a father might give. When Roman was younger, he had assumed his father would arrive. One day. There would be a knock on the apartment door in Puck and Roman would answer it and there he'd be. His father. Standing there, smiling. And Roman would know it was his father because . . . well, he would just know. People knew things like that, didn't they?

Everything was different now. He was different. Besides, how could anyone find him here? In this room that locked from the outside.

There wasn't much in the room. A bed, a locker, a wardrobe. The window was small and square, set high in the wall, the glass divided by three bars. Through it, he could see only cloud. He lay on his bed and watched the clouds edging past.

In the morning, the rattle of keys, the click of the lock, the door swinging open.

The place was set up to resemble a normal house. One like Meadhbh's or Adam's. There was a kitchen, a dining room, a room with a telly and a room that they called a games room, with a pool table and a PlayStation and a bookshelf.

The sound of doors being opened, shut, locked, unlocked echoed along every corridor. It was not like a normal house.

The games room was where the other boys hung out after school. When Roman arrived there, the leader was bent across the pool table, expertly sliding the cue back and forth along the V he had made between his thumb and forefinger, the followers and hangers-on laughing at something he had said.

Roman made his way along the wall, kept his eyes on the ground, made no sound. He stopped near the bookshelf. There were about ten boys in the room. Aged between fifteen and seventeen, Roman guessed.

Marcus hit the white ball with the tip of his cue, potted two reds and straightened, looked at Roman.

'Look what we have here, boys. A Polak who *reads*,' he said, smiling and moving towards Roman.

The cue stick was tucked under his arm and when Marcus stopped the tip of it was inches from Roman's neck.

'Perhaps you could start a book club, Roland?' he said to Roman. 'Wouldn't that be a pleasant way to pass an evening, boys?'

The followers smirked and the hangers-on laughed, too loud. The outcasts concentrated on the television screen, relieved that their numbers had swelled, giving them better odds.

Roman told himself to say nothing. To ignore Marcus. Instead, he ignored his own advice. 'My name is Roman,' he said.

'Do I look like somebody who gives a shit what your name is?' Marcus stepped closer to Roman, whispered the words so close to his ear that Roman could feel flecks of spittle land on it.

'Everything alright over there, lads?' The guard – a bulky man with a bald head and a white face, vast as a vacant car-park – looked towards them.

Marcus smiled. 'Just talking to Roland here about the possibility of starting a book club.'

'A book club?' The guard looked dubious.

'We'll talk about it some more later, OK, Roland?'

He was pretty sure he wouldn't stand a chance against Marcus. Roman was nearly as tall as him but Marcus had bulk. And he had his followers. And hangers-on. That was like an army compared to what Roman had.

Roman didn't think he was a good fighter. He had only ever fought one time.

The first time Pieter Adams had called Roman a bastard was when Roman was seven. Babcia was in the kitchen, hacking a head of cabbage with an enormous knife, when Roman returned from school that day. Asked her what it meant.

'Who said such a terrible word?' Babcia let go of the knife. It clattered against the wood of the table. She put her face in her hands and shook her head. She'd probably start crying next. Babcia cried about everything. She always said the same things when she cried about Mama. The high hopes she'd had for her. Before The Trouble.

Roman wasn't sure what The Trouble was but he had an idea that it might be something to do with him. Or maybe his father.

Once, he asked Babcia if she had known his father. 'Ha,' Babcia spat. 'Your own mother barely knew him. A fly-by-night, that fellow. Here today, gone tomorrow.'

Pieter had several theories, all of which he liked to share with Roman and the rest of the class.

By the time Roman was eleven, he knew what *bastard* meant. And *illegitimate*. They were words that Pieter had hissed at him so often, Roman no longer heard them. But then, Pieter came up with a new word.

Whore.

'You don't know who your father is because your mama's a whore.'

Roman couldn't let that go. Not that. 'I'll fight you after school. Usual place.'

There was an initial sense of satisfaction following the declaration. Pieter was the one who picked the fights. That was the way it had always been.

Roman's declaration was issued with calm conviction, before he turned and walked away, whistling, as if he hadn't a care in the world.

As if he could beat him.

There weren't many rules attached to the fights. You showed up, faced your opponent in the middle of the clearing, where the grass no longer grew with the weight of so many feet. Pieter's gang counted down from five. And then it began. They didn't usually last long, the fights. Pieter was the biggest boy in the class. It was the kind of big that would, in later years, run to fat. People said Roman was small for his age. Mama said he was only eleven years old; he had plenty of time to grow.

Roman didn't wait for Pieter's gang to finish the countdown. He charged, bent his head, rammed it into Pieter's chest. Pieter, taken by surprise, staggered backwards and

Roman knew that this was probably his only chance. He kicked Pieter's shin, pushed his hands into the solid wall of his chest, put what weight he had into the push, kept running and pushing until Pieter toppled backwards, his head connecting with a bare branch, stretching from a cluster of trees like an arm. A helping hand. Pieter lay on the ground, his hand clamped to his head and blood oozing thickly between his fingers. Roman had a moment to feel it. The upper hand. The sensation of a wrong being righted. The sweet feeling of victory.

And then Pieter's gang surrounded him, held him by his arms, dragged him towards Pieter, who had staggered to his feet, thick lines of blood oozing down his face, giving him a wild, savage appearance.

'Look what you did,' Pieter said, pointing to his head as if Roman might not have noticed the blood.

'Good,' shouted Roman. Then he spat at Pieter although it was a pathetic spit that did not go anywhere near Pieter's face. 'And I'd do it again if you had the guts to call your little boyfriends off.'

Pieter curled both hands into fists. 'Hold him,' he had said.

'What's going on over there?' the guard asked at breakfast on the third morning.

Roman bent to retrieve his fork that Marcus had elbowed off the table. He'd waited until Roman's hand was leaning against the floor before he flattened it with his boot and Roman cried out in pain.

'Are you alright, Roland?' Marcus asked, poking his head under the table, smirking.

'Sorry,' Roman said to the guard as he returned to his chair. 'I was just picking up my fork and I . . . banged my head off the table, that's all.' The pain in his hand, hidden beneath the table, was loud as a scream. Roman clamped it between his legs, used his left hand as best he could to butter his toast.

He sat through his afternoon classes, ate dinner, watched television and waited for the bell to ring for bedtime. He couldn't have told anyone what he ate for lunch or for dinner or what programme he'd watched. He moved from one thing to the next. He felt like a ball in a pinball machine, falling and landing, then falling again.

He tried not to think about Mama. About Meadhbh. And Adam. They were part of a place that seemed a long way away now. A place that he couldn't go back to.

He thought about the man at the bank – Mr Hartmann. He was so old. And the bullet had spun him around, tore through his body. How could somebody that old survive something like that? Sometimes he imagined that the old man *did* wake up. *Did* recover. Remembered everything that had happened at the bank that day. What would Jimmy do to Rosa then? What would he get Marcus to do to Roman? Saliva pooled in his mouth like he was about to throw up.

'Are you alright, Roman?' One of the guards – a woman – put her hand on Roman's arm as he passed her in the hall. 'You're very pale.'

'I'm fine,' Roman said. 'Thanks.' He moved on. The realisation that he was alone, that he had never been so alone, settled on him, heavier and heavier, as the second hand crept along the clock face in the games room.

There had been other small incidents. Nothing that any of the guards noticed. Someone shoved him against the wall of the corridor as he made his way to his classroom. As Roman bent to gather the books that had fallen from his bag, someone kicked one, sent it sliding down the corridor. Roman picked the books up, continued on his way as if nothing had happened. Running on the basketball court during PE, someone hooked a foot around his foot, sent him sprawling. 'Are you alright, Roland?' One of Marcus's gang bent down to where Roman lay on the ground, looked around before landing a kick in Roman's stomach, leaving him winded and coughing.

'Get up there, Roman,' called a guard from the sidelines. 'No histrionics, please. This isn't football.'

Now, in the games room, Marcus and his gang were gathered in a corner, bent low over a coffee table, playing cards. Marcus glanced at Roman, sitting by himself on the couch, winked, returned to the game.

Roman thought about the days. All the days that stretched in front of him. He didn't know if he could manage them. All the days.

He had to.

Roman had seen Jimmy hurt a woman. A drug addict who couldn't pay. He had punched her face, then walked away, massaging his fist with the fingers of his other hand. He hadn't watched her fall, didn't turn as she hit the ground. He had hit her like she wasn't a woman. Like she wasn't a person. He had done it and walked away, like it cost him nothing.

Roman's breath seemed to be stuck in his chest. He stood up. Left the room. He asked if he could take a shower. He didn't want a shower.

He wanted to go home. It was such a childish thought. He knew that. He did not allow himself to cry in the shower. He bit his lip hard, concentrated on the pain and didn't cry. He squeezed shampoo into his hand, rubbed it onto his hair.

The door into the bathroom opened. It didn't lock but there was a light that went on, on the door outside, when someone was in there. Nobody was supposed to come in when the light was on.

'Who's there?' Roman's voice sounded like the voice of a younger boy. It sounded afraid.

Roman heard the soft creak of rubber soles against the tiled floor. He stood there, under the shower, held his breath. A shadow appeared on the other side of the shower curtain. A silhouette. Then the curtain was yanked across, the rings screeching against the bar, and there was Marcus, standing there, saying nothing, the suggestion of a smile across his narrow face. His eyes travelled halfway down Roman's body, then he smirked and shook his head. 'I'd say you have the ladies begging for more. A lot more.'

Roman wanted to cover himself with his hands. He didn't. Instead, he stood there, straight up, his arms rigid by his sides. He could feel goosebumps erupt all over his skin. He was scared but he didn't want Marcus to know, because fuck him.

'What do you want?' he said. His voice sounded reasonable, like he was fully dressed, having a normal conversation with a normal person in a normal place. The smirk slid from Marcus's face. He lifted one hand towards his face as if inspecting it. Between his fingers, Roman saw the dull glint of a razor blade. He took a step backwards, the hard metal circle of the shower dial digging into his back. Marcus leaned towards him.

'Do excuse me,' he said, reaching behind Roman and turning the water off. In the hot, dripping silence that followed, Roman could hear a commotion outside in the corridor. 'That's one of my boys, having a convenient epileptic fit,' Marcus said, nodding towards the door. 'Keep the guards busy while you and I have a little chat.'

'What about?' It took effort to keep his voice even. To keep the shake out of it.

'I thought we could talk about your mother, for starters. She's coming to see her golden boy tomorrow, according to my sources.' Marcus smiled, flicking the blade between his fingers as he spoke.

Roman said nothing. In his temples, the back of his throat, his ears, he could feel his blood thumping.

Roman shrugged. 'So what?'

Marcus stepped closer so that Roman could see the line of blackheads clustered along the bridge of his nose.

'What are you planning to tell the bitch?' Marcus's voice was a whisper now. A hiss.

'I already told Jimmy. I won't say anything.'

'Jimmy says he doesn't trust you.' The blade was between the tips of Marcus's fingers now, inches from Roman's face. Roman forced himself not to look at it. He took a breath.

'Jimmy doesn't have much of a choice, does he?' It was only when he said it, out loud, that he realised the truth of it.

Yes, Jimmy had Mama as his bargaining chip, but Roman had something too.

He had the truth.

A flicker of surprise crossed Marcus's face. Roman took the opportunity to sidestep him, reach for his towel hanging on a hook just outside the cubicle. Marcus twitched at the sudden movement, snatched at Roman's arm, pulled him out of the shower with one hand, the blade in the other.

Inside Roman's head, a switch flicking. Like a trip switch when a fuse blows. He had reached some boundary inside himself. The outer limit of what he could manage. What he could take. And what he couldn't. He launched himself at Marcus, who stumbled backwards, looked for a moment like he might fall but then grabbed onto the edge of the wash-hand basin, righted himself. Roman bore down on Marcus, could feel the grunt of his breath on his face. 'Come on,' he roared at Marcus. 'You want to cut me? Go ahead. Fucking do it.' His breath was coming in bursts, his chest heaving with it.

Marcus glanced towards the door. 'Shut the fuck up,' he hissed. 'They'll hear you.'

'I don't care,' shouted Roman. He didn't. He was beyond caring. He raised his arm, made a fist of his hand and landed a punch on Marcus's face. It was a good punch. Marcus staggered back, hit the wall then sprang forward, the hand that held the blade stretched in front of him. Roman heard the cut rather than felt it. It was a sound like a page getting ripped from a book. His face felt hot and wet and he put his fingers to his cheek, looked at them. It was only when he saw the blood that the pain made itself felt. A searing type of pain. He brought his hand again to his face, ran his fingers along the gash. It went all the way to the corner of his eye and he blinked and now everything was turning first pink, then red and the pain was intense now. It burned a path down his face, hot as a furnace. With his good eye, he saw Marcus coming for him again and he turned to run for the door and Marcus's hands were on him now, pushing him, and his bare feet slipped against the bathroom tiles, wet with condensation, and he fell forward and the last sound he heard was that of his head – the side of his head – cracking against the edge of the wash-hand basin and he saw the floor coming towards him now, rising to meet him. He closed his eyes and braced himself for the impact.

Twenty

'Excuse me, I'm looking for Mary Murphy.'

That's what Tobias said in the end.

The house on Swords main street was exactly as Mary Murphy had described it. The paper and sweet shop her father ran on the ground floor, the living quarters over the shop, redbrick with sash windows and net curtains, behind which one could make out a vague outline of flowers in a vase. She had told him they were artificial flowers that had been there for as long as she could remember. She told him a lot about her home. Her country. As if, in the telling, she was preserving it in some way. Keeping it safe until her return.

She was determined to throw away the artificial flowers when she got home. Replace them with fresh ones.

She said that life was too short now for things that weren't real.

The flowers in the window were artificial.

It was raining. It was always raining in this country, Tobias thought, although Mary had been right about the softness of it against your face, how it released the smells of the earth, sharpened their potency.

Standing outside the shop in the rain, Tobias thought about what he would say to her.

He drew his father's pocket-watch from its place in his waistcoat, glanced at it. Ten o'clock in the morning. He was due at work at noon. In the two months he'd been working at Mr Goldstein's

257

watch repair shop on Little Britain Street, he'd never been late. Never missed a day, even when he'd been sick, never received any complaints from customers or from Mr Goldstein himself. He intended to keep it that way. Truth was, he was grateful for the job. And for the bedsit that Mr Goldstein rented to him in the house next door. He'd got the job four weeks after he arrived in Dublin. After he had taken the ferry to England, another one to Ireland.

April 1946 he had arrived. He had been transferred to a prison in Hamburg after he was discharged from the hospital. He had spent a year there while the Allies decided what to do with him. It wasn't the worst kind of place. It had been a printing factory, located on the outskirts of the city. Partially bombed during the war, but a section of the stone building had endured, like a trib-ute to everything that was good about Germany. That had been good about Germany.

He had shared a cell with four other German prisoners of varying ages and experiences. They passed the time playing cards and swapping stories of war. Tobias said little and, being the youngest, his silence was, for the most part, indulged.

At times, he felt as unknowable to himself as he was to his fellow prisoners. He could make no sense of the past and strug-gled to imagine the future. Perhaps this was why he allowed Mary Murphy to take a seat in his head. Perhaps this was why he dreamed of her. Everything else was like a scab over a wound; he didn't want to pick at it, make it bleed again.

'It's got no pretensions to grandeur, mind,' Mr Goldstein had said that day when he showed Tobias the bedsit after he'd offered him the job.

'It will be fine,' Tobias said, following Mr Goldstein out of the shop and down the street.

Mr Goldstein stopped all of a sudden and Tobias narrowly avoided walking into the back of the diminutive man. Mr

Goldstein had reached an age that was impossible to guess at. Somewhere between seventy and a hundred was the best Tobias could come up with.

He looked at Tobias, allowed his eyes – still a defiant brown, as if they had given time her marching orders – to travel across Tobias's face, the lines across his forehead multiplying and deepening as he did.

'I know you're not Austrian, son,' said Mr Goldstein.

Tobias shook his head. There seemed little point in doing anything else.

'I don't care where you're from. I never did care about that sort of thing. I'm a businessman, understand? I'm looking for a hard worker, someone with a bit of know-how up here.' He pushed a long, narrow finger against his shiny, bald head. 'Understand?'

Tobias nodded. Waited.

'Is that the last untruth you'll ever tell me?'

'I'm sorry sir, I didn't—'

'Answer the question, please.'

'Yes.'

'I don't care about the past. My business is time. Fixing it, getting on with it. Understand?'

'Yes.'

'I don't want to talk about what happened, who did what to whom. That's in the past and we're all about the future, boy. What are we about?'

'The future.'

'That's it.' The old man turned again, continued down the path with surprisingly long strides on such short, skinny legs, his arms swinging like he was on parade.

Tobias worked six days a week, noon till closing. Mr Goldstein liked to open up by himself in the mornings. Said it was his favourite time of the day. He stood at the corner of the street, keeping an eye on things along Capel Street as he smoked the first of the day's five cigarettes, crushing the lit end between his fingers when he was finished and slipping it into the tin box he kept in his trouser pocket. He smelled of tobacco, and although Tobias never smoked, he grew fond of the smell.

At night, in the bedsit, Tobias used the utensils available to him – a small gas stove, a frying pan and a kettle – to make dinner, which usually turned out to be bread and cheese and mugs of tea. The coffee in the corner shop was terrible and he'd grown used to the bitter taste of tea.

In his free time, he improved his English, studying Mr Goldstein's newspaper of the previous day, underlining words he didn't understand, which Mr Goldstein took pleasure in explaining in the afternoons. 'I like to see a young man with ambition,' he said. Tobias didn't think he had ambition. But he wanted to be able to talk to Mary Murphy when he saw her again. Like she had talked to him.

He didn't know what he would say if she asked him why he had come to Ireland. He had no family here. No family anywhere.

He could say that he wanted to thank her. And that was true. She had saved him in ways that he struggled to explain.

He wanted to tell her that he was no longer the boy she had cared for.

He was a man now.

He wanted to let her know how she had made the future seem . . . possible once again. Because what is the future, only the plans we make and Tobias's plans were filled with Mary Murphy.

He wanted to tell her that he . . . he wanted to say many things. He was not sure if he could find the words.

And now here he was, so close now, standing outside her house.

* * *

'Excuse me, I'm looking for Mary Murphy.' After all the lines he had rehearsed, this was the one he ended up saying.

'Who are you?' Tobias's first impression of the man behind the counter was that he seemed like someone who looked older than he was. He couldn't say why exactly. There was a hard set to his face, as if the muscles there were unaccustomed to expressing themselves. The sleeves of his shirt were rolled up to a pair of bony elbows, revealing sinewy white arms roped with raised blue veins, as if he'd recently carried out a job that was physically demanding.

'I'm . . . Tobias Hartmann.'

'That means nothing to me, son.'

'Are you Mary Murphy's father?'

The man nodded, moved to a brown box on the floor, hauled it onto the counter and reefed it open with a Stanley knife. He had a pronounced stoop when he walked, like the weight of the world had overcome him.

'Your daughter . . . Miss Murphy . . . she nursed me when I was injured. During the war. I . . . I was passing and I wanted to thank her.'

The man stopped what he was doing – lifting magazines from the box, arranging them on a shelf – and sat down suddenly on a stool Tobias hadn't noticed before, tucked behind the counter. 'I told her she shouldn't go,' he said, his voice smaller now. He shook his head and laughed a short, bitter laugh. 'I don't know why I bothered. She never did anything I ever told her and that's a fact.' He reached into the pocket of his trousers, took out a cigarette, lit it and closed his eyes as he inhaled. Tobias thought perhaps it was his cue to talk but then the man went on, as if Tobias wasn't there. 'Working for the Brits. After everything that's happened in this God-forsaken country.' He shook his head as he spoke, kept shaking it, even when it seemed like he had nothing else to say. Then he glanced at

Tobias, pulling hard on the end of his cigarette. 'A good nurse, was she?'

Tobias nodded. 'Yes. And she was kind. To everyone. And brave. She was so . . . brave.'

The man shook his head. 'Just goes to show you. Bravery's no use to anyone in the end.'

'So.' Tobias cleared his throat. 'Is she here?'

The man shook his head, stood up and crushed the butt of his cigarette into an ashtray on the counter. 'The Brits got their pound of flesh out of her, then sent her home with TB at the end of the war. She died last Christmas, God rest her soul.'

Last Christmas. Tobias remembered Christmas Day in the camp in Hamburg. They had marked it with a football game in the concrete square of the yard. Took off their jackets, used them to mark the goals, despite the bitterness of the cold. They warmed soon enough running around. Tobias remembered laughing when he scored the winning goal and they hoisted him onto their shoulders and bore him around the yard. He had been laughing and Mary Murphy had been dying. He had been warm and laughing and full of hope and plans for the future and everything was about her. All his hope. His plans. They had all been about Mary Murphy. And she had been dead all along.

'I'm very sorry for your loss,' Tobias said. He offered the man his hand and the man hesitated then shook it. After that, Tobias couldn't think of anything further to say so he bought a newspaper and left the shop. In his pocket, the photograph. The black and white one that a soldier had taken of her in the hospital. The soldier had tucked the photograph inside his jacket pocket. Tobias had slipped his hand into the pocket one night. Taken it.

In the photo, she is turning her head, her mouth is parted, as if she is about to say something. Tobias thought perhaps he should give the photograph to Mary's father. But he left the shop with his hand in the pocket, his fingers wrapped around the photograph as if he were safeguarding it, although for whom or from what, he couldn't say.

The rain had stopped but the clouds hung heavy and grey to the west and it was only a matter of time before it would begin again. Outside the bank, there was a bench. Tobias sat on it, on the sodden wood of the seat, and remained there. He thought how lucky poets and writers were. They had words to express themselves. Tobias had no words. Just an emptiness inside him where words should be. It was like all the things he had done, the things he had failed to do, were here now, inside him some- how. He had reached his destination to find . . . nothing. Nobody. He sat on the bench as people moved along the street, around him, past him, like he wasn't there at all. The emptiness inside him swelled and surged until it seemed it would swallow him whole. Part of him welcomed that notion. And part of him knew that he didn't deserve to feel like this. Hollow. He had no right to mourn for Mary Murphy. She had never been his. She had been a dream. The kind of dream a child dreams. Full of impossible hope.

He stood abruptly. He would open a bank account. Today. He had time. Mr Goldstein recommended regular saving. That was the way to a secure future. A little bit put by every week. He would do it here. In Swords. He would walk to Swords once a week, maybe take the bus if it was raining. He would pass by the house where Mary Murphy had grown up with the flowers in the window that would always be artificial now. He would allow himself to think of her, briefly, as he passed, and then no more.

Twenty One

Early morning. Cillian's favourite part of the day. The hiss and spit of the coffee machine and the creak and settle of the house around him. He poured coffee and stood at the patio doors, watching the pale light of morning slip across the night, ease it away.

Stella walked into the kitchen, pulling the strings of her dressing gown – kimono? – around her waist. She snapped on the main light and Cillian blinked in the sudden brightness.

'Did I wake you?' he said. Her face glistened with a fresh coat of make-up. He didn't think he'd ever seen her without it.

She shook her head. 'I thought we could have breakfast together.'

'I was about to leave. And I've already eaten. Sorry.'

'A banana?' She eyed the banana peel on the table. 'That'll not get you far.'

'I never eat much in the morning.'

'You need fattening up,' Stella said, opening the fridge and reaching for a box of eggs.

Cillian stood up, rinsed his cup in the sink. 'How are you feeling?' he asked. Perhaps her 'visitors' had arrived during the night?

'Never better,' said Stella brightly. 'What have you got on today?'

'Just, you know, the usual.' Today was the second anniversary of Paulie O'Sullivan's death but he had never told Stella about the boy before, so he made no mention of it now.

'I'm going to spend today shopping, before I head home in the morning.' Stella said. She was setting the table now. For two.

'You're going home?'

'Ah, look at your wee face.' She was beside him now, wrapping her arms around his waist. Her perfume gathered like a cloud around him; dense and sweet. 'You don't mind, do you?' she said, her voice muffled against his jumper. 'It's just . . . I said I'd help with the favours for Selene's engagement party and I need to get myself ready for school starting back next week and . . .'

'Yes! I mean, no, of course I don't mind, I . . .'

'And you'll be home too. Soon. Won't you?'

He nodded, disentangled himself from her. 'Listen, I think it's time you did a pregnancy test.'

'Gosh, you're keen, aren't you?' She laughed – *hahaha*. 'I'm only a few days late, Cillian.'

'Seven. Seven days.' He tried to keep the edge out of his voice.

'OK, OK, I'll pick one up.' When she kissed him, he tasted lipstick.

He got the call about Roman on the drive to work.

'Fuck sake,' Cillian shouted down the phone. 'I *warned* them about Jimmy's nephew. They *knew* Roman was a target.'

'It could have been worse – he's not going to lose the eye apparently.'

'Has his mother been informed?'

'Yes.'

Cillian felt relief. That he hadn't had to tell Rosa about her son. He remembered Paulie's mother. Her face when he'd told her.

*   *   *

'Put the gun down, son,' Cillian had said to Paulie that day. 'It's not too late.' In the distance, the drone of a siren. The gun looked huge in Paulie's white, skinny hand. He pointed it at Cillian. His eyes were black with pupil and already his face had the caved-in features of an addict.

The boy's finger tightened against the trigger and, before he pulled it, he ran towards Cillian, shouting, and his face was so alive in that moment, filled with fury and noise.

In the report, it would say that Cillian discharged his weapon at 15.36. Cillian did not remember pulling the trigger. He remembered the boy. The way he had stopped running. Like he had frozen in place. In time. Like he was suspended against the indifferent grey of the February sky. He was dead before he hit the ground, the sound of the shot still ringing in Cillian's ears, the weight of his gun hot in his hand.

The boy was fourteen years old.

The Super said Cillian didn't have to tell her. Paulie's mother. About her son. He told him to go home after the ambulance staff had cleaned and dressed the bullet wound on Cillian's arm. He'd send somebody else.

Cillian remembered every detail of Mrs O'Sullivan's face when he told her. The grey, almost green pallor of it. She shook her head, she kept shaking her head, kept shouting, *No no no*, as if, in this way, she could change everything. By the sheer force of her will. A mother's will.

Behind her, in a frame on the hall table, a photograph of Paulie – Cillian recognised the boy's heart-shaped face – in shorts and a T-shirt on a beach, holding a cone with ice-cream plastered all over his face, dripping down his arm. He was maybe three years old in the picture. His mother beside him, leaning towards him with a tissue in her hand, her other hand on his small three-year-old shoulder.

*   *   *

'Cillian?'

Cillian looked up from the computer screen. His colleague Mick stood at the door of his office, a concerned expression across his face.

'What is it?' said Cillian.

'I said the boy's mother is here to see you,' said Mick.

'What boy?' For a moment, he thought it might be Paulie O'Sullivan's mother.

'Rosa Matus. Roman's mother,' Mick said.

'Oh. OK. Tell her I'll be right out.'

He shut down the file he had been studying, forced himself out of the office to the reception area where a mother was waiting for him. Another mother. This one hadn't lost her boy but she probably felt like she had.

'Rosa. Sorry to keep you waiting.' Rosa looked different today. Her mouth was set in a rigid line, her usually pale face was flushed and her grey eyes were dark, almost black.

She rounded on him. 'My son was attacked,' she said. 'What are you going to do about it?' Cillian could feel the heat of her anger coming off her in waves. He stepped towards her.

'Come on in here,' Cillian said and he led her into his office, closing the door behind him. 'Sit down,' he said, gesturing towards a chair.

'Don't tell me what to do. I've had enough of being told what to do.'

Cillian pushed the chair towards her and she stood for a moment, glaring at him, daring him to tell her to sit down again. Cillian sat down and, after a while, so did Rosa. 'He should never have been put in that place,' she said. 'Roman needs to be at home. With me. He's just a boy, he's my boy and—'

Cillian leaned towards her, his elbows propped on his desk. 'Rosa,' he began.

'You were right,' she said, her voice quiet now. Deliberate. 'I *did* recognise Jimmy's voice. At the bank.'

Cillian said nothing. Waited.

'And he has a scratch on his neck. I saw it. That woman, the one with the long red hair, she scratched one of their necks that day. Hard enough to draw blood. When she was trying to save her friend.'

'Martha?'

'Yes, you can ask her. She'll tell you it's true.'

'Why didn't you say that? Before?'

Rosa shook her head. 'I was scared. I'm always scared. Roman is the brave one. I know my Roman did not shoot Mr Hartmann. I'm sure it was Jimmy. But Roman won't say because he thinks he is protecting me. But it is I who have to protect him. I am his mother.'

She looked at him then. 'So, can you arrest Jimmy? After what I've told you? About the scratch?'

Cillian sighed. 'I need something more concrete.'

'What if Mr Hartmann wakes up?'

Cillian nodded. 'Yes, if he is able to identify Jimmy, if Jimmy was the one who shot him . . .'

'He was. I know it.'

'. . . then his testimony will certainly be valuable,' said Cillian. 'But the chances of a man that age recovering from . . .'

Rosa nodded. Stood up.

'Where are you going?' Cillian said.

'I need to be with my son.'

'I'll drive you.' He leaned towards his computer. 'Give me a minute to close this down.'

Rosa stood up, pulled her coat tight around her narrow frame.

When he had logged out of the system, Cillian pulled his jacket on, grabbed his keys. He held the door open for Rosa but she had stopped in front of the wall where he had stuck printouts of various information relating to the case. She was peering at the printout of the photograph Cillian had taken at Lenny's house. There was a frown on her face. 'What is it, Rosa?' said Cillian.

'Is that Mr Hartmann's?' she said, pointing at the printout.

'What makes you think that?'

'It looks like one I saw in Mr Hartmann's bag a while ago. He asked me to hand him his briefcase. I'd had my cast taken off but my hand was still a little weak and I dropped the case. His papers scattered all over the floor and when I was picking them up I noticed a drawing, just like this one. Not exactly the same but the same woman. Except she was sitting by a fireside. And she was wearing a dress, not a uniform.' Rosa touched the face of the woman in the photocopy. 'Her eyes are exactly the same. And there was a word, printed also, at the bottom left-hand corner of the page, just like here.' She pointed to the word *Meeting*. 'And it was a different word. *Home*, I think. Yes, *Home*, I'm pretty sure.'

'Was it an original?'

'I don't know. It didn't look like a photocopy.'

'Did you ask Mr Hartmann about the drawing?'

Rosa shook her head. 'Mr Hartmann is a very private man. I asked him little.'

Cillian sat at his computer again. 'I need you to put that into a statement,' he said.

Afterwards, Cillian drove Rosa to Temple Street hospital. There was a guard on duty at the door into intensive care. Another on the main door into the hospital. Rosa looked at him before she went inside and now he saw hope crowding into her face. 'You can get him, can't you?' she said. 'You can arrest Jimmy?'

'I promise that I'll keep you informed of developments,' said Cillian. He nodded towards the hospital entrance. 'Tell Roman I was asking for him, won't you?'

'Thank you, Detective Larkin.' Rosa stood up, stretched her hand towards Cillian and he shook it, felt the dry roughness of her skin, and something else. A wave of protectiveness towards this small, thin woman who was still standing, still being a mother, despite everything.

Cillian headed to the courthouse with a fairly flimsy file. He knew that the grounds for the issuing of a search warrant for Lenny's house were threadbare but the court clerk had a soft spot for him. 'I wouldn't do this for just anybody, Larkin,' she said, shaking her head but handing him the warrant.

'I really appreciate it.'

'How are you ever going to thank me?' She fluttered her eyelashes at him.

Cillian grinned. 'Thank you, Trish.'

She shook her head. 'I was hoping for more.'

'Thank you very, very much,' he called over his shoulder as he left the building at a jog.

It took Cillian another hour to gather a team of guards outside Lenny's house. 'I know what I'm after,' Cillian told them, 'but you lot stay and go over the place with a fine tooth comb, you never know what else Lenny's got in there.'

Lenny let them in with bad grace. 'I told you, Larkin, you're wastin' your time.' He followed Cillian into the kitchen, watched him pull the thumbtack out of the little drawing, lift it off the cork board with gloved hands. 'What the fuck?' Lenny said and Cillian could see beads of sweat glisten on his forehead.

'This is very impressive, Lenny,' said Cillian. 'You've a real future in art, I'd say.'

'That's Natasha's. She did one of those evening classes.'

'Oh, really? Where?'

'I don't know, do I?'

'Phone her,' Cillian said. 'I'd love to do that course myself.'

'She . . . she doesn't have her phone with her.'

'Well, she can always ring me if she wants to know where her drawing is, alright?' Cillian slipped the drawing into a plastic evidence bag and left the house.

Now he was at the lab, filling in the paperwork to have the drawing forensically examined. He looked at his watch. Already afternoon and nothing from Stella. Part of him was glad. The part of him that didn't want to know. The same part that had been relieved this morning. When she'd said she was leaving.

He opened the window of his office, breathed.

After this case, he would take some leave, he decided. He needed to sort himself out. Take some time to think. He couldn't think at home with Stella there. It was like being on a train that never stopped, never slowed, that roared through the station you wanted to get off at.

He would take some leave. Bring Naoise fishing. Take him to a movie.

The Super had told him to take leave after Paulie died.

Cillian shook his head. 'I need a change. I need to get out of here. Out of this city.'

'Fuck sake. What are you? Little Bo Peep after losing your sheep? You just need a break, Cillian. That's all.'

Cillian did not respond. The Super sucked air through his teeth, shook his head. 'Look, Cillian, you're one of the best on my squad. Don't fuck that all away because of some junkie kid playing cops and robbers.'

'Jesus – the kid's barely cold in the ground yet.'

'Just take some time off. Get some sleep. Eat red meat. Get laid. You'll be grand.'

'But I—'

That's an order.'

Cillian stayed in his house. Where he thought about Martha. About ringing her.

He went to Joan's house where classical music played on the radio and the sound of the violins brought Martha to mind and he dragged his hands down his face and felt heavy with tiredness in spite of the week's leave and the early nights.

'I need to get away,' he told Joan.

'Not too far,' she said. 'I'd miss you if you went too far.' She cupped her two hands around one of his. He remembered holding her hand at their mother's funeral. She'd told him to be brave and tightened her grip on him when the men lowered the coffin down with thick rope.

'There's a position coming up in Donegal town.'

'Lot of fishing in Donegal,' Joan had said.

'Yeah.'

'What about the house? You've done so much with it.'

'Ah, it's just bricks and mortar, when all's said and done. I'll rent it out, maybe.'

He locked the door on the fixer-upper stone cottage he had bought. A faller-downer, Martha had called it.

But he had fixed it up in the end.

It was everything else that had fallen down.

Twenty Two

'Hello?' It was less of a greeting. More of a question. 'An inter-rogation,' Tara had called it once.

'I don't want people to get the impression that I like small talking on the phone,' Martha had told her.

'I'm fairly sure they won't get that impression,' Tara had said.

It was a number she didn't recognise – although, with the freelance nature of her work now, that was not unusual. She answered it.

It was Cillian Larkin. They had been a couple who spoke regularly and at length on the phone on the days when their work commitments didn't allow them to see each other. Now, his voice on the other end of the phone seemed strange as well as familiar. 'Oh. Hello,' she said again, after he'd announced himself, although now there was no question mark after the word, only a pause.

It sounded like Cillian was outside somewhere. Walking. She could hear traffic in the background, his breath down the line. 'I managed to get my hands on that drawing I told you about.'

'A spot of breaking and entering?'

'Something like that.'

Martha continued walking towards the music shop. She needed an E string for her violin – it had snapped last night – and a diversion from the stultifying piece she was writing about Valentine's Day for a women's magazine.

'A conversational piece is what we're after,' the editor had said. 'Just give us your thoughts, OK? A bit of humour, obviously. But mostly positive stuff, yeah?'

Martha had gritted her teeth but agreed. She needed to eat, after all.

'I'm going to need to have an expert look at the drawing. To authenticate it.'

'If you need it in a hurry, Dan could probably give you a preliminary opinion.' Martha sidestepped a man holding the hand of a jerky-legged, sticky-faced toddler, who carried a rattle that he shook with great enthusiasm. As the noise faded, she could hear it again, this time coming down the phone line. She stopped. Looked behind her. She saw a bin truck near the bottom of the main street, then heard its rumble down the line.

It took her a moment to see him, walking his long, swingy-armed walk, talking into the phone.

'Did you get dressed in the dark?' she asked.

'What do you mean?'

'You're wearing odd socks.'

She saw him stop, check his socks. When he looked up, he was grinning.

Martha stopped in front of him. 'At least your shoes are on the right feet,' she said.

He smiled his crooked smile. 'There you are,' he said, like she was exactly the person he wanted to see. She remembered that about him. She supposed it was something to do with charm. It was not a characteristic she had been burdened with.

She hung up, put her phone in the pocket of her parka.

'Your bruises are fading,' he said. 'How's the rib?'

'I can do everything except housework.'

'So it's business as usual?'

'Pretty much.'

Now he was looking at her in that way he had. A sort of

unhurried way, like he had nothing else to do, nowhere he needed to be. Martha felt the heat of her blood rushing into her face. She hated this about herself. Her propensity to blush when there was no need for it. She looked at her watch. The universal signal. *I have things to do, places to be.*

'I ducked out of the station for a quick coffee,' Cillian said then. 'Do you have time for one?' And Martha, who had just had a coffee, who should have been returning to her apartment to work, said, 'Sure,' and they began to walk again.

They did not discuss where they might go for this quick coffee. They simply walked up the main street of Swords, turned in to the Plaza and ended up in the Wooden Spoon. It was the café that Martha had always considered theirs, even though it annoyed her when couples made such proprietary claims.

Cillian reached for the handle, the tinkling sound the door made as he opened it for her like an announcement. That they were here again, after all this time.

'Bakewell tart?' Cillian asked her when the waitress came to take their order. Martha nodded, knew he would order the apple tart, cold, with no cream, which he did. There was something a little *Twilight Zone* about it. Like they had travelled back to one of their Sunday afternoons. Sunday afternoons had often been good. Better than Sunday evenings, when Martha would get twitchy, looking for an excuse to open a bottle, while Cillian would come up with reasons why she shouldn't.

There hadn't been many Sunday afternoons, with the demands of their jobs, but now, sitting here again, it felt like they had been here only last Sunday and the Sunday before that and the one before that.

It felt familiar.

It felt good.

Cillian put a forkful of apple tart on her plate and she put a forkful of Bakewell tart on his, as they had always done, and they ate in silence and even the silence was familiar.

'So you reckon Dan wouldn't mind coming down to the station? To take a look at the drawing?'

'Throw in a pair of handcuffs and he'll be there quicker than you can say, *Book 'em, Dano.*'

Cillian nodded. 'He wouldn't . . . ?'

'Blab?' said Martha. 'No. He knows what I'm capable of.'

Cillian smiled. 'So . . . you're still friends . . . you and Dan?'

'Yes.'

'Is it not a bit awkward? Being friends with your ex-husband?'

Martha laughed. 'I never thought of Dan as my husband. Not even when we were married.'

'I couldn't believe it. When I heard you were married.'

'Neither could I, to be honest.'

They both laughed at that.

'How's Tara?' Cillian asked then.

'I'm going in this evening. Dan was in earlier. He said Tara didn't want to see him, which is strange. Tara loves Dan, despite herself.'

It was Tara's mother who had persuaded Tara to let Dan in. 'I told her I'd had a bout of PTSD myself,' Dan had told Martha, when he rang earlier.

'You never had PTSD,' Martha said.

'I did so! That time I got chased by the koala in the bush.'

'What was he going to do? Hug you to death?'

'Those things are *vicious.*'

Martha looked at Cillian. 'They're moving Tara to St Pat's at the weekend, if there's no change.'

'That's not good.'

'No.'

Dan, however, had managed to get Mathilde's surname and contact details from Tara's phone. 'Did Tara not mind giving you that information?' Martha had asked.

'Eh, no.'

'You stole it.'

'I think *stole* is a harsh word.'

But despite phoning and leaving messages, there had been no reply from Mathilde.

A woman pushing a complicated double buggy negotiated her way past their table. Even though Martha pulled her chair as far as it would go towards the table, the side of the pram knocked against the chair, and Martha's handbag, hanging by its strap from the back of the chair, fell, spilling its contents on the floor. 'Oh, I'm so sorry,' said the woman, bending down, reaching for safety pins, cigarette papers, a tuning fork, a stock of pens and pencils, all with teethmarks at their tops. One of the babies in the buggy began to cry, the other abstaining for a moment before joining in. 'You go on,' Cillian told her, taking Martha's handbag from the woman. 'You've your hands full there.' The woman apologised again. When she wheeled the buggy away, Martha saw her notebook lying on the ground beside Cillian, open on the page. The page where she had written her reasons. Her six reasons. Two of them a name. His name.

Cillian closed the notebook, handed it to her. 'You're still writing lists,' he said, scanning the ground and putting the last of the detritus – a pouch of tobacco, several hair grips, a block of rosin, a parking fine – into her bag.

'Oh, that's an old one. I wrote it ages ago. The day after my father's funeral.'

'I hope you didn't mind me calling in that day.'

'You were good to come. I never . . . I never thanked you.'

'There was no need.'

*   *   *

They had waked her father.

Everyone came. Family, friends, colleagues, rivals, neighbours. The drink flowed. Nobody mentioned cirrhosis. Cirrhosis of the liver. People said he was a great man. A brilliant writer. Loved the craic. A party man. Always in the thick of it. Social. Gregarious.

Martha nodded at the people who said these things. She nodded and shook hands and accepted condolences and drinks from people who told her what a great man her father had been and how often he had spoken of her and how proud he had been of her.

'A chip off the old block, this one,' said her uncle Sebastian, clapping her too hard on the back and nodding towards the tumbler of Scotch in her hand. 'Same poison as her old man.' He roared laughing, like he'd said something funny.

She drank and tried not to look towards the coffin in the middle of the room where her father lay, silent and grave and absent.

Nobody would ever call her Mo again.

Dan took charge of the bar. He was an attentive barman, Martha thought. He remembered people's names and the drinks they were drinking. 'Same again, James?' he'd say, pressing a clean glass against the brandy optic. He drank steadily throughout that long day, without ever seeming drunk.

Drink. That was what she had in common with Dan. The thought surfaced in her head, without warning. Like a fully formed sentence you have no recollection of writing. It was just there, all of a sudden.

Martha slipped into the back garden, sat on the swing. She held her glass between her knees, pushed her feet against the grass, began to swing. She thought about Amelia. Wondered, would she be sitting on the swing next to Martha if she had lived? Swinging beside her, with a glass of whiskey trapped between her knees. The evening was cooling now, the street-lights coming on, puncturing the fading light of the day.

And then she'd heard his voice.

'Hello, Martha.'

She was facing away from the house so she didn't see him. But she knew who it was all the same. That melodic voice. The soft Donegal accent he refused to lose, despite his years in Dublin. Typical of him to come. She remembered thinking that. To be the better person.

She could feel the drink when she lifted herself off the swing. Could feel it inside her head, toxic and familiar. She thought she might throw up. She knew she wouldn't. Not in front of Cillian Larkin. Wouldn't give him the satisfaction. She turned her head. Saw him. She hadn't seen him since that day. In her apartment. More than six months ago. His face was so familiar. She couldn't believe how familiar his face was.

'Listen, I won't stay long. I just . . . I was sorry to hear about your father. I wanted to let you know. See if you were OK.'

'I'm fine.' She was careful with her words. Didn't want them to sound slurred.

'Good. That's . . . good. I know how much he meant to you.'

'He died of cirrhosis of the liver. Did you know that?' She hadn't realised she was going to say that. She'd thought she might mention Dan. *My husband, Dan.* Something about Dan. *Not every man thinks I've had enough, see?*

And now here she was, spilling her guts instead. Telling him things he didn't need to know. Giving him ammunition. Confirming everything.

'I'm sorry, Martha. I really am.' For a moment, Cillian looked like he was going to walk towards her. She stiffened, wrapped a hand around the chain of the swing. She thought she could take everything else that this long, relentless day threw at her. Her father in the coffin, the very fact of him being gone, being dead, the cirrhosis and nobody mentioning it and everyone getting pissed, Dan serving drinks at the bar her father had built, like a monument to what would kill him in the end.

Martha could take it all, she knew she could. But if Cillian touched her. If he put his hand on her.

'You alright, gorgeous girl?' It was Dan. He had abandoned his post, was going to rescue her from this moment.

Her relief was tinged with disappointment and she was confused and put it down to the day. The relentlessness of it.

'This is Dan,' Martha mumbled in Cillian's direction. Cillian stretched one of his arms towards Dan, shook his hand. The Long Arm of the Law, Martha used to say when he reached for her, pulled her against him. She had to stand on her toes, she remembered. Coax him down before she could put her mouth on the pulse that jumped against the warm skin of his neck, in spite of her height.

'I'm Martha's husband,' declared Dan. They'd been married nearly four months by then. 'And you are . . . ?' Dan liked referring to himself as a husband. Martha thought it was because of people's reactions. Their surprise. He didn't look like a husband, they told him.

'Cillian Larkin.'

'Ah, the detective! Homicide, yes? Do you have a gun? And a catchphrase? You've got to have a catchphrase, am I right?'

Cillian smiled at Dan. Martha recognised it as his patient smile, the one he reserved for questions like those, for people like Dan.

Dan smiled back. A wide, open smile that suggested nothing could go wrong. But his eyes were bloodshot and she noticed how he used the side of the swing set to steady himself.

All of a sudden, she was sober.

She stood up. 'I have to go,' she said.

'Sure, baby. Hey, I'll come with you,' said Dan, wrapping a clammy hand around the back of her neck.

'I'll see you, Martha. And . . . sorry again about your dad. I really am.'

Martha hadn't cried all day. Or the day before. Or the day before that. Not even at the hospital.

'You're in shock,' Tara had said. But she didn't feel shocked. Just . . . a sort of numbness. A sensation of watching from the sidelines. Watching herself, and all of them, going through the motions.

Now, she felt like she might start. Crying. And if she started, she might not stop.

She nodded at Cillian and headed for the house, walked through it with her head down so no one could engage her. She made it to the front door, walked outside and opened the taxi app on her phone. 'I can drive,' said Dan, hard on her heels.

'No, you bloody well can't.'

'Why are you shouting at me?'

'You're over the limit.'

'I've only had a few little tipples.' He placed his hands across his heart, like he was swearing an oath.

'You've had at least six gins.'

'So this is how it feels to have a nagging wife.'

'This is the first time I've ever mentioned your drinking. That hardly classifies as nagging.'

'Fine. We'll get a cab.'

'Let's walk towards the Dublin Road. It's too cold to stand around.' She didn't want to be there when Cillian came out of the house.

They ended up in the field in Donabate. A plot of land. They had been at a wedding in the Waterside hotel last spring and had taken to the beach at two o'clock in the morning, with a bottle of wine. It was Martha who'd spotted the For Sale sign and it was Dan who'd bought it for her the following day.

'I'll build us a house there,' he'd told her when he got the deeds. He waved them like a flag in his hands, a flourish of ceremony.

They'd promptly forgotten all about it.

Martha never worked out why she decided to go back that day. The day of her father's funeral.

The field was overgrown by then, the grass up to Martha's knees. In one corner, the blackened remains of an amateur campfire, a few empty crisp packets and a dozen flattened cans that had once contained a brand of beer she'd never heard of. There was something familiar about the scene. The remnants of something.

'Are you sad?' Dan wanted to know. 'You look sad.' His face registered alarm. He wasn't a fan of sadness.

Martha shook her head. 'I'm tired,' she said.

'It's been a long day,' Dan said, kicking a stone and watching it fly through the air, landing against a tin can. The noise it made was sharp. Martha looked at Dan. His face seemed empty, devoid of anything other than his eyes, his nose, his mouth. It was like looking at a stranger's face.

'You never say my name.'

'What are you talking about?'

'When you're talking to me. We've been married for four months and you never say Martha. I don't think you've ever said it.'

Dan looked confused. 'Why would I say it?'

'When's my birthday?'

'Why are you—?'

'The date. What is it?'

'It's . . . the twelfth of something, isn't it? The twelfth of March, that's it! Isn't it?'

'No. And I don't know yours.'

'Why do we need to know that stuff? That's not important.'

'What is important?'

'You're upset. Let's go home. We can open a bottle of wine and—'

'Tell me. I need to know. What's important to you?'

Dan rubbed his eyes. 'I think you need some sleep. I think that's important.'

'We're stuck, Dan. You and me. We're stuck.'

'And some food. When was the last time you ate? Come on.' He tried to put his arm around her shoulder but she shrugged him away, moved towards the hedge that separated the field from the sandy path that led to the beach.

'I bought this field for you, Martha Wilder.' He was behind her now. She felt the heat of his breath on her neck. 'I will ring a builder tomorrow. And an architect. And ... I don't know ... a plumber maybe. Plumbers are fairly vital, I'd say. And I will build a house here for you, Martha Wilder. And I will say your name in every sentence I utter to you, from now until death does us part. OK? OK, Martha? Martha Wilder?'

She turned around, shook her head. Felt a rush of affection for him. 'It's not your fault, Dan.'

'What's not my fault?' He had his hands in the pockets of his linen shorts now, was shifting from one foot to the other.

She knew he wanted to leave this place. Leave this conversation. Get back to the apartment. Open that bottle of wine. Part of her wanted that too. It would be easier than this sobering realisation.

The empty field.

The empty cans.

'I've made a mess. I lost my job.'

'You'll get another one.'

'You make it sound like it doesn't matter.'

'It doesn't.'

'I loved my job.'

'You'll love another job.'

'I drink too much.'

'So do I. We're Irish – that's what we do, remember?'

'I lost my job because I was drunk.'

'Yes, but you're a YouTube sensation, don't forget.'

'It's not funny.'

'It is a bit, my love. I mean, Martha.'

'And my dad . . .'

'He was a great man.'

'He drank too much.'

'So did Brendan Behan, and he turned out alright.'

'He was always drunk. He died when he was forty-one years old.'

'Could he have written *Borstal Boy* sober?' Dan swiped at the screen of his phone, typed something. 'And your birthday, Martha Wilder, happens to be next month. Is that why you mentioned it? You were worried I'd forget? What would you like? You can have anything you want.'

Martha looked towards the sea. To her left, Lambay Island. She'd heard there were deer there. And – strangely – wallabies. Cillian had told her that once, long ago, so she supposed it must be true. Now, in the failing light, it loomed like a dark shadow against the grey of the sky that threatened rain. She imagined it could be spectacular when the sun rose behind it, spilled her colours across it, at the beginning of a brand new day.

Martha looked at Cillian, her notebook in her hand. 'I know I wasn't exactly . . . hospitable to you that day. I think I hated you a bit back then. You knew the truth about me before I did.'

'I was just . . . worried about you. Trying to, I don't know, help, I suppose.'

Martha put the notebook on the table. 'You did help,' she said, her voice quiet.

'How come I'm listed twice?' Cillian nodded towards the notebook.

Martha shrugged and smiled. 'I'm superstitious about lists, remember? They have to have an even number.'

Cillian nodded slowly, like this was a reasonable explanation. For a moment, they said nothing. Martha felt exhausted. She also felt full to the brim of an alarming kind of energy. She thought it had something to do with the truth. The telling of it. To Cillian. She picked up her mug. The last of her tea was still warm. When she glanced up, Cillian was looking at her as if he, too, had something to say. Some truth to reveal. The table between them seemed smaller than before. She felt closer to him. Close enough to see the small, almost-faded scar at his hairline – skateboarding accident, aged nine – the tiny flecks of green circling the pupils of his eyes and the dark shadow of stubble blooming above his wide, soft mouth.

She took it all in. Drank it in. It was intoxicating somehow. Like a shot. Several shots, one after the other. The silence between them was like an irresistible melody and it made her want to move. To lean towards him, put her mouth on his, spread her fingers along the smooth skin of his neck. She could spend the afternoon kissing him. The evening. The night.

And then his phone rang and Martha looked at the screen as he pulled the mobile from his pocket and saw the name of the person who was calling right there on the screen and it was Stella. 'Sorry, I have to take this.' Cillian said.

Martha examined her watch. 'I need to go anyway,' she said. She stood, and moved towards the door, as if everything were normal and ordinary and Tara was in London and Cillian was in Mount Muckeridge or Mount Charles or wherever the hell he was supposed to be and the door of the Pound pub was firmly closed. Locked. Boarded up.

She turned at the door. Cillian was talking on the phone now, not looking towards her. She felt the heat of her blood in her face again and she turned away, walked out of the cafe, and even when she was safely outside, her skin burned with the memory of her face as she sat in the cafe opposite him. The want in it. The ache. For all the things she could not have. And the useless knowledge that she had them once. And she had let them go.

Twenty Three

'Roman?' The voice seemed far away. Like an echo of a voice. He moved towards it. It felt like he was swimming. Up and up, towards a distant surface. He held his breath, could feel his lungs strain inside him. He broke the surface and breathed, could feel something warm against his skin and thought it might be the sun.

'Roman?' The voice was closer now and the warmth on his skin was a hand. He recognised it. It was Mama's hand, on his forehead, running down the side of his face, resting on his shoulder. His mama's hand. He thought he had never felt anything so soft. So warm.

'Don't cry, Roman, it's OK now. Everything is OK now.'

He didn't want her to see him crying but, now that he had begun, he couldn't stop. His shoulders heaved with the force of his cries, tears stormed down his face, hung from his jaw before dropping onto his chest. Mama wiped them away with her hand. Her soft, warm hand.

'I'm sorry, Mama,' he said. 'I let you down.'

Now she cupped his face with both of her hands. Shook her head. 'No,' she said. She smiled at him then but her smile was edged with a kind of sadness. Roman could see it. He closed his eye. He didn't want to see her sadness. He had done everything he could so that she would not be sad.

'It is I who should be sorry, my Roman. You have never let me down,' she said, bending low to him so he could feel her breath against his cheek.

He put his hand up to his face, felt the bandage covering his eye, the side of his face. 'What is . . . ?'

'You won't lose your eye. They thought, at first, that you might but you won't. Isn't that good news?'

A nurse yanked at the curtains around his bed. 'Oh, we're awake, are we?' she declared. She looked at Rosa. 'Could you step outside for a few minutes, Mum, while we examine this young man.' It was a statement rather than a request. It was the way most people spoke to his mother, Roman thought. The people in the Citizens' Information Office, the tax office, the social welfare office. They barely glanced at her. They made assumptions based on forms she had filled in and the quiet way she stood, like she was waiting to be dismissed.

Rosa shook her head. 'No,' she said. Her voice was low but deliberate. 'I will stay here with my son.'

Roman waited for the nurse to insist but she only sighed and shook her head before dragging her trolley towards the bed, picking up a thermometer and inserting the nozzle of it into Roman's ear. His mother picked up the clipboard hanging at the end of the bed. Without asking the nurse's permission. Scanned the notes on it. 'What does this mean, here?' Rosa asked the nurse, pointing at a line of what looked to Roman like scribbles across the page. The nurse, wrapping a black band around Roman's arm, glanced at the clipboard. 'It's a note about the stitches,' she said. 'He's had fourteen.'

'Will they leave a scar?' his mother asked. The nurse nodded. 'Maybe,' she said, 'but it will fade in time.'

When the nurse left, Rosa pulled the curtains around the cubicle once more, sat on the chair beside his bed. 'You have to talk to me,' she said. 'You have to tell me everything and then I can help you, OK?'

The need to tell her – tell her everything – swelled inside him. He thought if he opened his mouth, everything would spill out. The whole story. He pressed his lips together, shook his head.

'I know it wasn't you,' Mama said. 'Who shot Mr Hartmann.'

'How do you know?' She seemed so certain and, even though he couldn't tell her the truth, it was something. To hear her say it. To hear her believe it.

'I know you, Roman,' she said. 'You are a good boy.' When Mama smiled, her face changed. 'I know it was Jimmy and that you won't say it was because you are afraid of what he might do to me. I was afraid too. But I'm not afraid anymore.'

'Why not?'

'Because I have you. It's you and me. Remember? Against the world.'

'Why do you never talk about my father?' Roman hadn't known he was going to ask that. But the words were out now. He couldn't take them back.

'Oh, Roman.' She shook her head, lowered it.

'I'm sorry, Mama.' Roman reached his hand towards her. Touched her arm. 'I didn't mean to make you sad.'

Now she smiled. 'You never make me sad, Roman. You're the happiest thing about my life. The best thing.'

Roman didn't know how he could be the best thing. All the trouble he'd caused.

'Roman, I . . . I know I should have told you about your father, but . . . the truth is, I don't know a lot about him and I didn't want you to think . . . He was stationed in Puck for two weeks while the boat he worked on was being repaired. I worked in the cafe then, down by the port. And one day, he came in and ordered a coffee and then he asked me out and said he wouldn't leave until I said yes.'

'So you went on a date?'

'I suppose so. Yes. He said he was going to whisk me away. To Rome. That's where he was from. Rome.'

'What happened then?'

'He took me to dinner every night after my shift. And afterwards, we'd go dancing. He was a fantastic dancer. And we'd walk. We'd walk for hours, the two of us, just talking and laughing. He could tell a good story, your father. I suppose I should have known.'

'Known what?'

'Just . . . I suppose . . . that none of it was real. None of his plans for us.'

'Why not?'

'Well, he came into the cafe, as I said, every day for two weeks, until one day . . . he didn't. I went down to the port that night after work and his boat was gone and so was he and that was that.'

'Oh.'

Mama looked at Roman then, put her hand on the curve of his shoulder. 'I don't regret it, Roman. I don't want you to think that I do. Those two weeks, they were . . . I was happy. And then, you were born, nine months later, and that was the best thing that ever happened to me. You were the best thing that ever happened to me. You believe me, don't you?'

Roman nodded slowly. 'So my father . . . doesn't know about me?'

Mama shook her head. 'I'm sorry, my love. I tried to contact him. When I . . . when I found out that you were on your way. But . . . I didn't know the name of the boat or the company he worked for. I didn't know anything in the end.'

'What was his name?'

'Alessandro Romano.'

'Is that why you called me Roman?'

Mama nodded, her face flushing pink.

'I like my name.'

'I like it too.'

She bent towards him, cupped her hands around his face, careful not to touch the bandage across his eye. 'When Mr Hartmann wakes up, he will tell the police the truth,' she said. 'I know he will.'

Roman felt something grab hold of him. Hope maybe. He wasn't sure. It was the way she said it. Like *she* was sure.

Her phone rang and she reached for her handbag, fished it out, answered it.

'Hello?'

'Yes, this is Rosa Matus.'

'No! But—'

'I don't—'

'But can't you—?'

'OK, yes, OK. I will come straight away.'

And Roman knew, the way some part of him had always known, that things would not work out. That everything would not be OK. He saw it in her falling face, the way she let the phone drop into her bag, the way she didn't look at him.

'I have to go now, Roman.'

'Where?'

'I'll be back, my love. As soon as I can.'

'Where are you going?'

She stood up and he could see her arranging her face before she lifted it towards him. She didn't want him to know that things would not work out. That everything would not be OK.

'It's Mr Hartmann. He's . . . The nurse said that he . . .'

'He's going to die, isn't he?' said Roman. His voice sounded flat. Disinterested. His heart hammered against the wall of his chest.

Rosa shook her head. 'No! I mean, there's no way to tell for sure, is there? He could . . .' She stood up. Picked up her coat from the end of his bed.

'Mama? What did the nurse say? Tell me.'

Rosa looked at Roman then. Her eyes were a darker grey now, against the white skin of her face. She opened her mouth and Roman knew that what she said now would be the truth.

Her voice, when she spoke, was quiet. Steady. 'The nurse said I should say my goodbyes.'

Twenty Four

When Martha got home from her coffee with Cillian, she sat on her sofa. It seemed vast. Even bigger than usual. She thought it might be because of Cillian. Seeing him reminded her of how much space he had filled. How empty the spaces were after he'd gone.

She should get back to her Valentine's Day article. She thought about cleaning the bathroom instead. Or maybe the kitchen. Certainly not both. It could only be one or the other.

Instead, she grabbed her coat and her keys and drove to Dan's house.

She saw him through the window in his sitting room when she pulled up in the driveway. He was kneeling on the floor, waist-deep in what he would later call IKEA-gate. Much later. When his sense of humour returned.

Every inch of floor was covered in screws, pieces of wood, sheets of glass, handles, nails, brackets, a measuring tape, a selection of calculators, two coffee pots – both empty – a bend-able ruler, a step-ladder and lavender-scented tea lights: an impulse buy when Dan had finally reached the sanctuary of the checkout.

'Did you not get a hard hat?' she asked when he let her in.

'The man in IKEA told me I wouldn't need one,' said Dan indignantly.

'Why on earth did you buy a self-assembly cabinet?' Martha

asked, stepping over a brand new toolbox crammed with brand new tools.

'Because . . . that's what people *do*, isn't it?' Dan said.

'People, yes. But you? Did you even read the instructions?'

'It's thirty-two pages! Of course I didn't.' Dan pointed a shaking finger at a set of instructions that looked like they'd been crumpled into a ball and thrown at something.

In front of him stood what could be the beginnings of a cabinet, in a Picasso painting perhaps.

'All the tools I bought,' said Dan, shaking his head. Martha didn't have the heart to tell him about the Allen key and screwdriver that came with each flatpack and were, pretty much, all each assembly required.

'On the plus side,' she said, 'you don't have to open the door to reach inside it. Look.' She slid her hand through the gap between the two doors at the front of the cabinet, wiggled it about.

'It's not funny.' Dan looked dejected.

'Do you want me to help you?' said Martha

'No, thank you.'

'Do you want me to do it for you?'

'No, thank you.' His voice was smaller now.

'I won't ask again.'

'OK, then, fine, have it your way,' said Dan, unstrapping a – brand new – tool belt from around his waist and throwing it on the couch before throwing himself there too.

'The first time's the worst,' said Martha, glancing at him.

'Do you mean that, in time, I could do it myself?' A slender ray of hope lit Dan's face.

'I wouldn't go that far.'

He threw himself back against the couch again, although he could not maintain his black mood for long. After two minutes, he lifted his head up. 'I suppose I could make you some tea.'

'That would be lovely.'

'Although I only have an echinacea, thyme and liquorice blend.'

'Fuck sake.'

By the time Dan had gone to the corner shop, bought Barry's tea and chocolate Hobnobs, Martha had dismantled the cabinet and arranged the various screws into neat piles along the floor.

'I'm missing screw 2B,' she said. 'Do you know where that is?'

'Are you actually being serious?'

'It looks like this.' Martha showed him the picture in the instruction manual.

'I think something rolled under the chaise longue when I dropped the hammer on my foot.'

Later, when she was finished, they sat together on the couch, Martha working on her laptop while Dan read their star signs from the *Daily Mail*. Every so often, Dan gazed at the cabinet with equal parts admiration and regret.

'You know that print you gave me?' Martha said. '*I See You*'.

'It was the least I could do, my sweet, after you agreed to squeeze the boil on my—'

'Stop it.'

'Yes, I am familiar with the print. What about it?'

'Cillian is working on this case and—'

'CSI Donegal?'

'Yes. I met him today. By chance. We went for coffee.'

'Curiouser and curiouser.'

Martha ignored him. She got her phone out of her laptop bag and showed Dan the photo of the drawing that Cillian had sent her.

'Do you think this one could have been drawn by the same artist?' she said.

'Oh my gosh,' said Dan, taking the phone and peering at the screen. 'Where did you find this?'

'I'm not at liberty to say.'

'This is *so* James Bond – Daniel Craig era, obvs.'

Martha ignored him. 'Well? Do you think it's by the same artist?'

'At first glance, I would say most definitely. It's the same woman. The nurse. Of course it could be a copy. I'd have to see the original to comment comprehensively.'

'Cillian asked if he could pick your brain, such as it is.'

'Might I have to testify?' Dan looked both thrilled and terrified.

'I wouldn't say so. He's just after a preliminary opinion.'

Dan studied Martha's face. 'What's going on? Does Cillian know something about the identity of the painter?' he demanded.

'No, and you're not to mention this to anyone, OK?'

'You know I would sooner die than betray your confidence.'

'Do you have to be so dramatic?'

Dan didn't respond, perhaps presuming that the question was rhetorical.

'He wants you to go down to the station.'

'Oh my days!' Dan's hands flew to either side of his face. 'I shall go at first light. That's when I'm at my freshest.'

In the olden days, Dan would have said, 'This calls for a stiff glass of port,' or some other alcoholic beverage. Now, he handed her a chocolate Hobnob and said, 'So. Any word from Mathilde?'

Martha shook her head. 'Her phone keeps going to voicemail when I ring.'

'Maybe,' said Dan, 'you should stop phoning her and just write to her. You're a good writer. When I read you, it's like talking to you, except better.'

'Why better?'

'Editing,' Dan said.

Martha sighed. 'I suppose I could try.'

'And if that doesn't work, I could go to London. Manhandle her over here,' said Dan, flexing his arm to reveal no muscle tone whatsoever. 'Tell her it's make or break. Time to get her cards on the table. Leave no holds barred. Pull all punches.'

'Have you run out of idioms?'

'No, I just thought that was enough to be getting along with.'

'Tara doesn't even seem to care that she could be transferred to St Pat's.'

Dan gasped. 'The asylum?'

'We don't say asylum anymore.' Martha sighed. 'I wish she'd just . . . snap out of it. Everything feels so . . . strange recently. Nobody is where they're supposed to be, you know?'

Dan gave her a sharp look. 'You haven't been anywhere you're not supposed to be, have you? Like the pub?'

'What would you do if I said I'd thought about it?' She kept her tone light.

'I'd sit on you until the thought went away. Now, pop on your shoes and coat. I'm taking you out.'

'I don't feel like going out.'

'There's a Sean Scully exhibition in the Hugh Lane Gallery,' said Dan, ignoring her.

'You know he annoys me.'

'Exactly. Annoyance is one of the best forms of distraction and you, dear heart, are a woman in need of distraction, yes?'

Dan strapped sandals onto his besocked feet and stood up. He looked unconcerned, as if Martha had never mentioned the possibility of a drink after all this time.

Disappointment and relief flooded her body. Equal in quantity. It was confusing.

Twenty Five

It seemed impossible that so much time had passed.

The grave was overgrown, as if no one had touched it since he last came.

He came once a year, on the ninth of May, which was her birthday.

He thought about her every day.

She had nearly made it. Mary Murphy.

Tobias summoned her into his mind, like he was calling her.

Mary.

There she was, her hair as long and dark as it had been in 1945. It framed her small, pale face in a way that was so delicate.

So alive.

And her eyes. Dark blue. Almost navy. Full of impossible hope.

He fished the photograph of her out of his pocket, the paper worn and thin from the march of time on it.

In the photograph, she was turning, her lips parting, about to speak. Many times, he imagined what she might say.

He remembered the way she said his name. She spoke like she was reciting a poem. Or a song. He imagined her saying his name again, like it was a sweet song that she might sing.

Tobias sat on the lip of the grave, stretched his arm towards the headstone and scraped at the soft moss that grew there. He pulled at weeds that grew along its base.

The rose bush he had planted years before was still thriving and the swollen buds were opening again, releasing a trace of the scent they would produce come the summer.

Tobias glanced around the graveyard, made sure no one was in earshot before he said it. He always said it. Her name. Just her name.

Mary Murphy.

He felt foolish saying it out loud. It was like a pact between them now. If he failed to say it, he would let her down. He would disremember her, and everything she had done in the war would have been for nothing.

It had taken him many Sundays to find her grave. The first time he found it, he had shouted her name. Perhaps even cried it. People stared. He hadn't shouted after that.

Now, he put his hand on the warm stone beside the date – 27 December 1945 – and spoke her name.

He finished weeding the grave, although it was, by his standards, a rudimentary effort. He worried that some of her family might find him at the grave some year, on the ninth of May. He had never prepared an explanation for his attendance there.

Or at least none that made any sense.

Tobias took off his jacket and mopped his brow. It was unseasonably warm. The usual crowds gathered around the headstone of Michael Collins, leaving balloons and flowers on the grave to wither. Tobias opened the satchel he always carried, took out the sketch pad, his tin of charcoal. He preferred drawing with charcoal, liking the starkness of it, the way it got on his fingers, reminding him of the work he had done. He didn't need to consult the photograph anymore. Hadn't needed to for years. He drew her from memory, although, he acknowledged, she had no real place in his memories. She was not his. But she was there all the same.

He drew her as she was in the photograph. Half-turned towards him, lips parted, about to speak.

'You've some talent there, sir.' The voice was clipped. Perhaps British. Or Anglo-Irish. Tobias turned and nodded at the man. A handsome man of rigid bearing and a wool suit.

'You're an artist.' It was a statement rather than a question. Tobias shook his head.

'May I?' The man extended his arm and Tobias handed him the drawing of Mary Murphy. The man studied it with great concentration. Tobias stood up, took the watch from the breast pocket of his waistcoat beneath his jacket and glanced at it, so the man might think he was in a hurry. He wasn't to know that Tobias had closed the shop. That he closed it on this day every year. He wondered what Mr Goldstein, who had sold Tobias the shop before he died, would have made of that. The shop closed on a perfectly good working day.

'It's exquisite. Quite extraordinary. The attention to detail. And the emotion. So contained. So potent.' The man looked up, smiled at Tobias and removed a business card from his wallet. 'Malachy Hemingway. No relation to Ernest, I'm afraid.' He allowed himself a small chuckle and Tobias imagined he introduced himself thus on a regular basis. The comment, followed by the small chuckle. He accepted the man's card, followed by his hand, which he shook briefly. He wasn't fond of speaking to people on the ninth of May. It was his day. His and Mary's. He visited her, drew her face, walked from the cemetery in Glasnevin to his flat in Little Britain Street, drank two glasses of whiskey and went to bed.

It was a day of routine that had not altered over the last almost twenty years and he didn't want to waste time speaking with anyone, regardless of their familial links to literary icons or otherwise.

Tobias looked at the card. It was good quality, embossed with a painting by Daniel Hennessy, if he was not mistaken. In fussy font, it proclaimed that Malachy Hemingway was an art dealer with offices in London, Dublin and New York. Tobias nodded, returned the card to the man.

'Have you sold much of your work?'

Tobias allowed himself a small smile, shook his head. 'It's a hobby.'

Malachy continued studying the drawing, then jerked his head up, bored his eyes into Tobias's face. Tobias took a small step back.

'Would you be interested in showing me your work?'

'Why?'

'I might be able to sell some pieces for you.'

Perhaps it was because he had nothing to lose. He had countless versions of the very same drawing of her face. Sometimes he drew her on a battlefield, a figure approaching the wounded and the dead, carrying a medicine bag, coming through trees that were always bare. It was always winter in Tobias's drawings. He thought perhaps it was because of the cold during the winter of 1945. He had thought he would never be warm again, after that winter. Sometimes she was in a field hospital, tending to a soldier. On rare days, he drew her sitting on a bench by a body of water. The Grand Canal. Her face untroubled by war. It was fanciful, he knew, but he imagined that she might have sat there had she lived.

Perhaps he agreed because of Malachy himself. His cheery optimism seemed in direct contrast to Tobias's disposition and, while it was forceful, it did not appear to be forced. He must have been one of those people for whom optimism was not a chore, Tobias thought.

Or perhaps it was because of the uniformity of Tobias's daily routine, the small space he occupied in the world. This was something different. New. It appealed to him in a way he could not understand. He did not consider himself to be a man of ego, although, yes, he took pride in his work as a watch repairman, of course he did. He handed Malachy the drawing.

'It's so unlike anything else out there. Who are your influences?' Malachy peered again at the drawing.

'My influences?'

'I mean, what other artists do you admire?'

Tobias remembered his mother then. How she illustrated her stories with sketches. The blur of pencil in her hand, the worlds she created for them. He shook his head. 'Nobody you would have heard of,' he said.

Tobias wrote down the telephone number of the shop and Malachy promised to call when he had news, which he declared would be sooner rather than later.

Tobias smiled when Malachy left. Artist! Oliver Cassidy, who owned the furniture shop on Capel Street, would get a kick out of that. Scribbles. That's what Oliver called them. When he liked one, he asked Tobias if he traced it from a book, then laughed his donkey-bray laugh before taking the chessboard down from the press in Tobias's bedsit and setting it up on the footstool they set between them.

'Tobias?'

'Mary?' He strained towards the voice, struggled to lift the lids of his eyes.

He saw her face. Older now, her dark hair shorter and streaked with grey. Lines around her navy eyes, deepening with the beauty of her smile.

A sound then. Like an alarm ringing. High-pitched and urgent, it surged against him, like a tide.

A door thrown open, the hot air lying like a rough blanket over him stirring now, lifting like a weight, and there was freedom in it and he could feel himself lifting too. Coming away.

He thought Rosa might be there. He smelled her familiar lily-of-the-valley smell, and he breathed her in and the scent brought his mother to him as surely as if it were she who had opened the door, stepped inside.

'*You said you'd be back soon,*' she whispered. Her hand on his forehead was soft and cool.

Voices now, all around him. He could hear the nurse. The furious rattle of her trolley, the flat smack of her rubber soles against the floor. 'Get Mr Ryan,' she barked. Her huge, fleshy hands on him now. On the withered folds of his neck, her fingers pushing against the jugular, feeling for him there.

'Goddamnit, where's the crash team?'

'They're coming.'

'What's keeping them?'

A weight now, pushing down on his chest, rhythmical, almost soothing. He reached inside himself, like someone leaving a house, glancing into each room, switching the lights off as he moved towards the door. He hesitated there, the metal of the handle cool in his hand, the door ajar.

'We're losing him.' There was angry frustration in the nurse's voice. She was not the kind of woman who lost people, Tobias felt. Not that kind of nurse. He wanted to tell her it was alright.

It wasn't her fault.

It was just his time.

It had been a long time coming.

He felt heavy with effort and yet curiously light at the same time, like the white, fluffy dandelion seeds Bruno and Lars used to blow on, scatter them to the air, watch them lift away.

Now he could feel the gentle weight of Rosa's thin arms gathering around his neck, the tickle of her hair, unrestrained by its habitual plait, against the worn-out skin of his face. He could taste the salt of her tears. Tobias wanted to tell her not to feel sad. He did not feel sad. He was grateful. That she had been his friend. He wished he had told her that.

He could feel himself moving now towards the small square of window. Outside, the light was fading. He saw the pale outline of the moon, struggling to make its presence felt as the lowering sun threw the last of her colours against the palette of the sky.

Twenty Six

Mathilde never rang Martha. Nor did she respond to the email Martha had deliberated over. Instead, she appeared, like Napoleon from the island of Elba.

Martha was holed up in her apartment, writing, with scant attention to day or night, her novel gushing out of her now like blood from an open wound.

She heard a noise.

It sounded like a stone hitting her window.

Pesky kids, she muttered, lifting her laptop off her knees and tossing it onto the oversized sofa. She strode into the kitchen, thrust her head out the window and noticed that she was not alone. The heads of a number of her neighbours also poked from various windows across the facade of the building, like gargoyles. Martha looked down.

On the manicured lawn at the front of the building stood a petite brunette, wearing a long cashmere coat over a baggy T-shirt and tracksuit bottoms, tucked into Ugg boots. Beside her, an overnight bag. Her hands were filled with stones.

'Mathilde?' She recognised her from the photograph that Tara had shown her. That seemed like a long time ago now.

'Martha?' Mathilde's voice was much louder and deeper than her petite frame would suggest. 'Is that you?'

'Yes. What are you doing here?'

'You told me to come. In your email.'

'Martha, will you let the poor girl in? She's half-frozen.' This

305

from Robert-Call-Me-Rob on the floor below. From her vantage point, Martha could see the widening circle of the bald patch he hid under various beanies. She looked at Mathilde. 'Press the buzzer, Mathilde. I'm number thirteen.'

'The buzzer's out of whack,' yelled the head of the residents' association, Ben Ryan, on the ground floor. 'I've sent a strongly worded letter to the management company and I . . .' Martha had forgotten about the buzzer.

'I'm coming down,' Martha shouted over him, withdrawing her head from the window. Ben had a tendency to monologue when he got hold of a captive audience. She threw her parka over her T-shirt and knickers, pushed her feet into a pair of runners and ran down the stairs.

Outside, Robert-Call-Me-Rob – his head still sticking out his apartment window – was taking his chances. 'France, I'll wager. Yes? I actually speak a leetle French, as it happens, *zut alors*, heh heh . . .' Mathilde did not laugh. Her expression was one of curiosity, as if she were trying to work out where his Off button was.

'Come inside.' Martha picked up Mathilde's bag. It was light. Inside the apartment, Mathilde looked around, taking everything in, making Martha aware of how messy the place was. She cleared plates and cups from the couch and motioned for Mathilde to sit, which she did, after which she fixed Martha with an expectant look.

'When did you arrive?' Martha managed.

'I came straight from the airport,' Mathilde said. Another expectant look.

'And . . . where are you staying?'

Mathilde looked puzzled. 'With you, of course. You said I should come as soon as possible.'

'Right. You're right. I did say that.'

'Where shall I sleep?' Mathilde asked.

'I have a . . . spare room,' said Martha, picking up Mathilde's bag again. 'I'll just . . . I'll be right back.' She hurried into the spare room and dropped Mathilde's bag on the floor. While she was positive there was a bed in the room, it had been a good six months since Martha had seen it, covered as it was with books, clothes, shoes, printer cartridges that she intending recycling some day, ancient out-of-date technology – there was a Sony Walkman in there somewhere, she was sure – and a box of instruction manuals that she had never read.

She backed towards the wall, leaned against it, closed her eyes. She was not used to houseguests. The door opened and there stood Mathilde, tiny yet somehow larger than life.

'If you give me sheets and a duvet, I will make the bed,' Mathilde said, nodding towards the vague possibility of a bed under the detritus. 'You can make us some peppermint tea.'

'Right. Oh, except I don't have peppermint tea.'

'Really?' Mathilde looked surprised at this statement.

'I have Polo mints. I could infuse them in hot water?'

Mathilde gave this some consideration, then said, 'I will have camomile instead.'

Martha took fresh bed linen out of the hot press then returned to the kitchen, where she found some camomile teabags – left behind by Dan and well past their best-before date.

She threw the last of her Fig Rolls onto a plate and tried not to resent Mathilde when she ate all of them.

'This is a nice apartment,' Mathilde said when she stopped chewing. 'Do you live alone?'

'Yes.'

'Why?'

'I like being alone.'

'Nobody likes being alone.'

Martha opened her mouth to argue, then nodded instead. 'I'm difficult to live with.'

Mathilde nodded. 'Yes, Tara mentioned that.'

The cheek!

'So,' said Martha. 'What's your plan?'

Mathilde straightened. Took out a notebook, opened a page where she had written a list of at least – Martha craned her neck – four bullet points. At the head of the list, in capital letters and underlined – twice – were the words À *Faire* which Martha guessed was the French version of a to-do list. Mathilde was trailing down the list with one of her tiny fingers. When she got to the third bullet point she stopped. Read out loud. 'We go to the hospital where Tara will tell her family about her and I, after which I shall accept her apology and agree to a reconciliation.'

'Right,' said Martha. 'Well, that all sounds very . . . feasible.'

'You are making fun of me?'

'Maybe a little.'

Mathilde nodded her tiny head. 'Tara said you use humour to disguise your insecurities.'

'Jesus, did she say *anything* good about me?'

'She did,' said Mathilde. Martha waited but Mathilde said nothing further on the subject.

'What's the fourth bit of your plan?' Martha couldn't help asking.

Mathilde closed her notebook. 'That is a private matter,' she said.

Martha looked at her watch. 'Visiting hours are nearly over at the—'

'Then we should leave immediately.'

They drove mostly in silence to the hospital. Martha was not especially gifted in the art of small talk and Mathilde, it seemed, only spoke when she had something to say. 'Your car smells of cigarettes.'

'Would you like one?'

'No. Thank you.'

Visiting hours had just finished by the time they parked and made their way into the main foyer of the hospital.

'You can come back tomorrow,' said a woman behind the reception desk, barely glancing at them.

Mathilde shook her head. 'I cannot come back tomorrow. I am returning to London in the morning.' Part of Martha felt relieved at this announcement. She would be alone again, in her apartment, where she could be as difficult to live with as she liked.

'Why are you leaving so soon?' Martha asked her.

Mathilde shook her head. 'I cannot make myself available to Tara indefinitely. She knows how I feel. And now it is time for her to tell me how she feels. To show me. Today.'

The woman behind the desk continued tapping her fingers against a keyboard.

Martha wanted to shake both of them.

'Hello, Martha.' It was Joan, who was on her way out of the hospital. 'You're here late. Everything alright?'

Martha looked at Joan. She didn't want to involve her. The woman had probably just completed a twelve-hour shift. But Mathilde was standing there, her arms tightly crossed, her face impassive, waiting for the clock to strike twelve after which she would flee, like Cinderella, except she would bring both shoes with her. She would leave nothing behind and Tara would be devastated and become more depressed and . . .

'Is there any chance that you could get us in to see Tara?' Martha said. 'The receptionist says visiting hours are over but Mathilde here has come a long way and she—'

Joan shook her head. 'I'm sorry, Martha, they're especially strict about visiting hours in cases like Tara's.'

Martha glanced at Mathilde who remained mutinously mute.

Martha turned back to Joan, tried again. 'It's just . . . I think it might do Tara some good. I really do.'

Joan hesitated, frowned.

'I was speaking to Cillian about it the other day,' Martha continued. 'He thought it might make all the difference to Tara. A visit from Mathilde.'

'I'll make a phone call,' said Joan, sighing. She could never say no where Cillian was concerned.

Martha allowed herself to hope. She smiled at Mathilde, who had uncrossed her arms and was maybe even entertaining hopeful thoughts herself. But Joan, when she returned, shook her head. 'I'm sorry, ladies, I did my best. Mrs Bolton told me that Tara is trying to get some sleep.'

'Did you tell her I was here?' said Mathilde, confusion spreading across her small face.

'I did.' Joan's smile was apologetic. 'Why don't you come back in the morning? When everyone's fresher.'

Back in the car, Mathilde did not cry, or shout, or bang her fist off the dashboard. She was stoic in her acceptance of what she saw as Tara's rejection. 'At least I know now where I stand.'

'You're wrong, Mathilde. Tara loves you. She told me.'

Mathilde shook her head. 'Words are easy to say.'

Still, Martha did not start the car. Perhaps some ancient, superstitious part of her believed that once she drove away that would be it. 'You love her, don't you?'

'I'm here, am I not?' said Mathilde.

'Yes, but you need to give her some more time, you need—'

'No,' said Mathilde, cutting Martha off.

'Maybe tomorrow, we could . . .' Martha began, but Mathilde shook her head again.

'I see now that Tara will not change. She will not accept herself. Maybe she will end up marrying a man who works in a bank and has a pension and a share portfolio and they will have babies and the babies will grow up and the man will get fat and bald and wonder why Tara drinks too much, or takes too many pills, or never closes her eyes when she kisses him. He will never know her because she refuses to know herself. To accept herself. She is ashamed of herself and her shame is contagious and I don't want to catch it. It is like a poison, her shame.'

She looked at Martha, who could think of nothing to say after Mathilde's bleak pronouncements. 'I will return to London tomorrow,' she said, quieter now. 'At first light. Can you give me a lift to the airport?'

'When you say first light, were you talking around ten-ish?'

'I can get a taxi.'

'No. No, it's OK. I'll take you.'

There was nothing more to say so they said nothing, until they reached the outskirts of Swords.

'Can you stop at a pharmacy?' Mathilde asked. 'I need to buy some Rescue Remedy.'

'Rescue Remedy?' said Martha, arching an eyebrow. 'You sure that's wise?'

Mathilde did not appear to notice Martha's sarcasm. She merely nodded and concentrated on the road as if she were driving.

Martha parked at the Pavilions, where there was a late-night pharmacy. 'Will you come in with me?' asked Mathilde, and her voice was small and uncertain and sad. It tugged at Martha, the sadness. Perhaps because she hadn't been able to assuage it. Or perhaps because it echoed her own.

She heard a sound then. The crisp click of the seal breaking when you twist the cap off a bottle of gin. Hendrick's had been her favourite.

'OK,' said Martha quickly, dropping the cigarette she had

begun rolling into the inside pocket of her bag and pulling the key out of the ignition.

'Are you alright?' asked Mathilde, and it reminded Martha of Cillian, who used to ask her the same thing when she was thinking about drinking when she should have been thinking about something else. Anything else.

You alright, Martha?

'I'm fine,' said Martha, opening the door. 'Let's go.'

Looking back, she wondered if she had stayed in the car, might things have been different? It was difficult to know, when you were retracing your steps, where the first misstep had occurred.

They were the only customers in the chemist's, which was overheated with too many fluorescent lights. There was a special deal with the Rescue Remedy: it came in a pretty little wicker basket, with a stress ball and the *Little Book of Calm*.

'I only want the Rescue Remedy,' Mathilde told the shop assistant, lifting the bottle out of the basket.

'But they all come together – it's a promotion.'

Mathilde pushed the basket with the ball and the book towards the woman behind the counter. 'I only want this,' she repeated, holding the Rescue Remedy inches from the assistant's face.

'It's the same price,' insisted the woman. 'The other items are free.'

'I do not want a ball or a basket,' said Mathilde and her voice had a dangerous edge to it now.

The woman pushed the basket back towards Mathilde, although when she spoke again she addressed Martha, in an almost pleading way. 'You see, they all come together, I can't just—'

'I'll take the basket,' said Martha, and when she grabbed it, the ball sailed out and was caught in the hand of a woman who, Martha now noticed, was standing behind them.

'Oh, I caught it! My boyfriend always calls me a butterfingers, *hahaha*.'

She had short brown hair and a northern accent. Donegal, Martha thought. With one hand, the woman gave the ball an experimental squeeze. Her other hand held fast to a pregnancy test.

'Thanks,' said Martha.

'I wonder if they work,' said the woman, handing Martha the ball. 'Not that I'm stressed or anything, thank goodness, *hahaha*.' Her voice had a shrill breathiness to it. The sound of it, with the heat and the harsh lighting and the smell of perfumes jockeying for position, made Martha feel lightheaded and thirsty. She did not reply to the woman, just did her best to smile and nod in her general direction.

She glanced at Mathilde, who was paying by card, and now the sales assistant was rolling her eyes and smiling a smile as bright as the fluorescent lights. 'Oh, the machine is on a go-slow today. Like the rest of us, eh?' and then a tinkling laugh and Martha gripped the *Little Book of Calm* in one hand, the ball in the other, squeezed them both.

Nothing happened.

'You're Martha, aren't you?' the pregnancy-test woman said now, peering into Martha's face. 'Martha Wilder?'

'Eh, yes.' Martha looked urgently at Mathilde but the Frenchwoman had her back to her, while the receipt for her purchase inched out of the machine.

'Oh, yes, I recognise you from when you used to be on the news.' She extended her hand. 'I'm Stella, by the way. Stella Bennett.'

She did not add that she was Cillian's girlfriend. She seemed to know that that particular detail was unnecessary. Martha couldn't believe how small and soft and dark she was, like a chocolate truffle. Nobody had ever likened Martha to confectionery. Nor would they. She knew that for a fact.

Martha's hand was pumped up and down with great enthusiasm. Stella nodded towards the box in her hand. 'I suppose Cillian mentioned our news when you went for coffee the other day?'

'Eh, he . . .' Martha hadn't thought Cillian would have told Stella about being at the Wooden Spoon the other day. But then again, why wouldn't he? Nothing had happened. Of course not. And yet . . . Martha had the feeling that something *had* happened. Nothing she could put her finger on. Just a vague sensation of something shared. Something good.

'Och, he's not saying much but he's excited all the same. Sure, you know Cillian – cards close to his chest, that fella, but soft as butter on the inside.' Stella touched the bridge of her nose with the tip of a small, squat finger. 'Anyway, it's not official yet.' She nodded again towards the pregnancy testing kit. 'But I'm pretty sure what this yoke is going to confirm. You just know, don't you?'

'I am ready,' said Mathilde then and Martha felt almost hysterical with relief and with something else. Something sharp and sore, like an abscess on your tooth you keep probing with your tongue even though it just makes it hurt more.

'Right,' said Martha, and then, 'Lovely to meet you, Stella,' and she gripped Mathilde's skinny little arm and walked out of the shop and out of the centre and kept going until Mathilde finally said, 'You are hurting my arm,' and then she stopped and said, 'Sorry, sorry, I . . . sorry, Mathilde, I just need some fresh air, the shop was . . . I'll take you to my flat now.'

'There will be no further discussion about my plans for tomorrow, Martha. I cannot be persuaded. Yes?'

Martha nodded. 'Yes,' she said. 'I understand.'

Mathilde seemed surprised by Martha's quiet acceptance of her vivid declaration but did not comment further.

Martha sped all the way to her apartment, daring some copper to pull her over. It would have been for the best, she knew, if one had.

Mathilde did not appear to notice the speeding. She drank her Rescue Remedy and closed her eyes, jerking left and right as Martha scorched around corners.

She skidded to a stop outside her building. 'Here's the key of my flat. I'll be back soon.' She tore the key off her keyring, thrust it at Mathilde.

'But . . . where are you going?'

'I have to attend to some business.'

A question flitted across Mathilde's face but she did not ask it. Perhaps the Rescue Remedy had some use after all?

Mathilde nodded, got out of the car. When she closed the door, Martha pulled off, driving now in the direction of Swords village.

She felt relieved. That this battle she was about to lose would soon be over. She was tired of it. The relentless everyday-ness of it. Becoming an alcoholic had taken time. Years. A slow trickle of addiction that you don't notice until your entire house is flooded with it. Sobriety was a more sudden, savage affair. Like hacking off a gangrenous limb.

It wasn't great company, sobriety. Especially when you came to it late. Too late to fix things. To put things back where they were. It felt like everyone was leaving her, all over again: Tara, her father.

And Cillian. The recent realisation that she missed him. Every day. She was tired of missing him. It was like something physical. Like walking up an endless flight of stairs. Over and over. Hauling yourself up.

She was tired.

She parked – illegally – right outside the pub.

The Pound pub.

The door was closed but Martha knew it was only a matter of putting her two hands on it. Pushing lightly.

It would swing open, as it always had, and she would walk in the way she had always walked in, feel at home.

Already, she could hear the low rumble of conversation inside, the snatches of laughter.

And she could see the tumbler of Scotch. How the light would filter through the amber liquid when she held it up, steered it towards her mouth.

She put her hand on the door, felt the grain of the wood against her skin.

She went inside.

She sat on a tall stool, hung the strap of her bag on one of the hooks below the counter.

'Where's Fergal?' she asked a man behind the bar. Fergal had been her barman. Had said, 'The usual?' when she walked in. Had known her. Known what she liked to drink. What pace she was in the mood for. When she wanted to talk. And when she didn't.

'He left a year ago,' the man behind the bar said. Martha looked at him. There was something familiar about his long face, the shine of his pate, the determined set of his mouth.

'What are you havin'?' he asked, his hand resting on a beer tap.

'I know you from somewhere,' she blurted. Which was strange because she hadn't even had a drink yet and she wasn't a blurter, in the main, and she couldn't care less if she recognised this man or where she might have seen him before.

She just wanted a drink.

He looked at her, nodded. 'AA,' he said. 'I've seen you there too. Sitting outside, reading your notebook. I've often wondered when you're going to come inside.' He grinned.

Martha flushed.

'Sorry,' said the barman then. 'I didn't mean to embarrass you.'

'I have my reasons written in that notebook,' Martha said, without realising she was going to say anything at all. 'Six reasons.'

The barman nodded. 'It's good to have them written down. I keep meaning to do that but I'm not much of a writer. More of a talker.' His smile was apologetic.

'Five reasons actually,' Martha went on. She couldn't believe how much she was going on. 'Two of them are the same reason.'

The barman propped his elbows onto the counter, tucked his hand under the awning of his chin. 'Some reasons are like that.' When he spoke it was almost like he was talking to himself. He looked at her. 'Is it a someone? The two reasons?'

Martha nodded. 'He's with someone else now. They might be having a baby.'

'That's hard.'

'It was my own fault.'

'That's even harder.'

'Is it not difficult for you? Working in a pub?'

'It's a deterrent, bein' honest.' He nodded towards the end of the counter where an ancient man with a red face and a few wisps of white hair floating around his head slumped on a stool, watching the froth inside his pint glass slide down the edge.

'I'm Seamus, by the way,' he said then, extending his hand towards her. She shook it, said, 'Martha.'

'How long?' she asked him then.

'Four years, nine months, three weeks and a day.'

'Don't you ever stop counting the days?'

He shook his head. Smiled. 'Every day is an achievement.'

A customer approached the counter, a crisp twenty euro note folded between his fingers. He glanced towards Seamus, cleared his throat.

'I'll be right back to you,' the barman told Martha. 'You sit there and decide what you want.'

Twenty Seven

It was a murder case now. Manslaughter if Roman was lucky.

Cillian sat in his car up the road from Jimmy's house. He'd been keeping tabs on him since they'd taken the drawing from Lenny's place. He might try to run if he thought the guards were on to him. Also, Cillian was worried about Rosa.

He checked his phone again. He was expecting two calls today. The lab should have results for him on the drawing.

And Stella. She had been in bed, asleep, when he got home late last night. In a box, in the middle of the kitchen table, was a pregnancy test, unopened. He lifted it, surprised at how light it was.

He undressed in the dark and got into bed, careful not to wake Stella. He had found it difficult to sleep.

Stella was still asleep this morning when he was leaving the house. He put his hand on her arm. Shook her gently. 'Stella?' She moaned and turned over. 'Stella,' he said again, louder this time.

'What?'

'Why didn't you do the test last night?'

'What?' She opened her eyes, struggled into a sitting position.

'The test. You didn't use it.'

She rubbed her eyes. 'I wanted to wait till you got home.'

'But you knew I'd be late. And I have to leave now. I just . . . I need you to do this, OK? Will you ring me later? Afterwards?'

She punched her pillow, lowered herself back onto the bed and pulled the duvet around her shoulders.

'Stella?'

'Yes, yes, fine, I'll ring you,' she said, turning away from him.

It had been a funny few days. Strange. He tried not to think about Martha, not to attach importance to his name on her list. Twice. He had convinced himself that he was over her. And he was. It was just . . . it had been a strange few days.

His phone rang and Cillian grabbed it, but it was only Tony ringing to see if he could come over to fix the leak in the shower on Saturday while Joan was at her Pilates class.

'Would you not get a plumber?'

'It's just that Joan thinks I can fix it so . . .'

'OK, then, I'll see what I can do.'

'Thanks, Cillian, you're a star. You're also the reason my marriage has lasted this long. And the great thing is, Joan doesn't suspect a thing.'

'That *is* great.'

He said goodbye, hung up, looked at the house again. Jimmy Carty wasn't what you might call house proud. The cobble-locked driveway was overgrown with weeds and three wheelie bins took up most of the sorry patch of grass. The curtains across the front-room window were drawn. They sagged towards the middle, not quite meeting.

Cillian looked at his watch. Rosa hadn't left the house yet, which was strange. He was sure she'd have gone to the hospital by now. He looked for her in his contacts, called the number. Her phone rang out. When he rang the number again, it went straight to message as if it had been turned off.

Cillian got out of the car. Walked towards the house. At the front door, he paused, pressed his ear against the glass. He heard nothing.

He knew they were in there.

He rang the bell. A thud upstairs, like something falling. Cillian put his finger on the bell again, rang it over and over. He took a step backwards, looked up at the bedroom windows. The curtains were drawn there too. He saw one of the curtains move, as if someone had tugged it. He opened the letterbox, pushed his ear against it. From upstairs, he could hear raised voices. A man and a woman. Then, a sound, like something falling. Hitting the floor.

Cillian climbed over the gate, ran down the side passage. The back door was locked but a small window beside the door was ajar. He stood on the windowsill and reached inside, stretched his arm towards the door handle. The tips of his fingers closed around the key in the lock, managed to turn it. He moved silently through the kitchen, into the hall. At the bottom of the stairs, he hesitated, listened.

'I said don't touch me. Get out of my room.' Rosa's voice was an angry shout.

Jimmy laughed. 'This is *my* room, remember. And you're only here because I felt fucken *sorry* for you, remember?' Cillian eased his way up the stairs.

'You're a murderer.'

Jimmy laughed, a short bark of a laugh.

'That's an ugly word for such a pretty lady.'

'You shot Mr Hartmann.'

'Yeah, I shot him. Does that turn you on?'

Cillian was at the top of the stairs now. The door to Rosa's room was ajar and he could see Rosa, breathing hard, pinned against the wardrobe door by her arms, which Jimmy held above her head.

'I will tell police,' Rosa shouted as Jimmy rubbed himself against her.

'Who the fuck is going to believe a scrubber like you?' His breath came and went in short spurts.

Cillian kicked the door wide open. Ran inside.

Jimmy wheeled around. 'What the fuck?'

Cillian grabbed the man, turned him around and slammed him against the wall. 'You're under arrest, Jimmy, for the murder of—'

'You don't have a warrant. And you're trespassing. I'll have your badge for this, Larkin.'

Cillian pulled handcuffs out of his pocket, put them around Jimmy's wrists. He looked at Rosa. 'You OK?'

She nodded, straightening her skirt, her blouse. She stepped towards Jimmy. He flinched. She looked at him. There was a calmness to her now as she raised her hand, slapped him. Hard. Across his face. Jimmy squealed like a pig.

'Did you see that?' Jimmy shouted at Cillian. 'She's after assaultin' me.'

Cillian dragged Jimmy out of the room, down the stairs. He radioed for backup from his car after he pushed Jimmy into the back seat.

'I want my fucken solicitor,' Jimmy shouted. 'This is garda harassment and I want my—'

'Is that the solicitor who signed a statement saying you were in his office at the time of the robbery? You could be in luck – I'd say he'll be at the station shortly,' said Cillian. 'Trying to defend himself against a charge of perverting the course of justice.' He slammed the door, checked his phone. A missed call from the lab. He rang back.

'Any developments on the drawing?'

'Yeah, we got a bullseye.'

'Go ahead.'

'Three sets of prints. Tobias Hartmann, Lenny Henderson and Jimmy Carty.'

Cillian smiled. 'Anything else?'

'A few fibres on the drawing that match the interior of the victim's safe deposit box.'

Two squad cars arrived and Cillian handed Jimmy to them. 'I'll be back at the station soon,' he told his colleagues. 'Just want to check on Rosa, OK?'

Inside the house, Rosa had changed her top. She was in the kitchen, plaiting her hair.

'Are you OK?' Cillian asked.

She nodded. 'I am going to visit Roman now.'

'Did he hurt you? Do you need to see a doctor?'

'No.' She looked worried then. 'I shouldn't have hit him.'

Cillian feigned surprised. 'Did you hit him?'

Rosa smiled a small smile. 'Thank you, Cillian. For everything.'

'Come on, I'll drop you at the hospital. You can tell Roman the good news.'

As he drove away from the hospital, his phone rang. It was Stella. He jabbed at the screen with his finger. 'Hello?'

'Cillian?'

'Yeah.'

'Sorry the line's not great.'

'I can hear you just fine.'

'What?'

'I said . . . never mind. How are you?'

'I have some news,' she said.

Twenty Eight

When Martha woke up the next morning, she was seized by the Fear. The Fear had been a regular visitor before. Waking up, trying to remember what you'd said, who you'd insulted, how you got that bruise on your knee, that rip in your dress. What time you got home. How you got home. Who you brought home.

Her mouth was sticky with dryness and her head ached like there was a war raging inside it. She sat up, slow and careful, looked around. The bedroom seemed . . . not tidy, it was rarely tidy, but undisturbed. There was her handbag, her wallet sticking out of it. There were her boots, sitting neatly together at the door of her wardrobe. Her jacket was draped across the back of the chair where it was supposed to be. The blinds were down, the curtains closed. She was wearing – she lifted the duvet, peered down – a T-shirt and knickers. Her violin was in its case, her manuscript on top of her laptop on the bedside locker, her red pen on top, ready to do its worst.

Everything was where it should be.

The details of the night swam to the surface of her mind, like bubbles of air.

One year, four months, three weeks, five days.

Every day is an achievement.

The barman was right.

Mathilde was already in the kitchen, sitting on a chair. She was dressed, her coat folded across her arm. On the floor beside her, her overnight bag, packed. Her face was paler this morning and there was a pink puffiness around her eyes that her mascara and eyeshadow had failed to conceal.

'I'll be ready in five minutes, OK?' said Martha, putting the kettle on. Mathilde looked unconvinced.

'Do you want tea?'

'No. I think we should—'

'You saw how I drove last night. It'll take me two minutes to get to the airport.'

'Did you attend to your business?' asked Mathilde, her tone chilly. 'Last night, when you practically shoved me out of your car?'

'I'm really sorry, Mathilde, that was so rude. But yes, I . . . I attended to my business.' Martha beamed.

'You seem . . . euphoric,' Mathilde said.

'Well, euphoric might be a little strong,' Martha said, although she was not entirely sure that was the case. This morning, her sobriety felt like something precious, almost reverent. One year, four months, three weeks, five days.

She had not squandered it.

And no, it was true that sobriety couldn't share her bed or read several drafts of the same article without complaint or take the stairs to her apartment three at a time, swinging a bag of Chinese food when Chinese food was *exactly* what she had been thinking about.

Or kiss her like that.

Nobody would ever kiss her like that again.

So no, definitely not euphoric. But still, something. Something good. She tried to put her finger on it. 'Today is not a day for regret,' she said, surprising herself by saying it out loud.

'What is it for?' said Mathilde with no great conviction that it was for anything in particular.

'Today is for living.'

'Have you been reading the *Little Book of Calm?*' Mathilde asked.

'Christ, no,' said Martha. 'I just mean . . . we're taking the bull by the horns today.'

'What bull?'

'I'll explain in the car.'

'On the way to the airport?'

'I have lemons,' declared Martha. Mathilde looked confused.

'I'd say you'd love hot lemon water, wouldn't you?'

'How did you know?'

'Just a hunch.'

It was rush hour. Inside the car, the two women sat in silence as they inched along, Mathilde occasionally sighing and checking her watch, while Martha couldn't help noticing buds swelling at the tips of tree branches. She also neglected to shake her fist or gesticulate with her fingers at drivers whom she considered dangerously stupid. Not because she didn't consider them dangerously stupid – she did – but this morning, she felt disinclined to display her annoyance.

In fact, she didn't feel annoyed. She put it down to the feeling that persisted inside her. The not-quite-euphoric.

At the airport roundabout, Martha turned left instead of right.

'You have turned left instead of right,' said Mathilde, stiffening in her seat.

'This is a shortcut,' said Martha.

'We are going in the opposite direction to the airport.'

'Technically, it's more of a detour than a shortcut.'

With the airport traffic behind them now, Martha accelerated.

'We are driving towards the hospital,' said Mathilde, examining the dashboard as if she were looking for the eject button.

'You have a great sense of direction,' Martha said.

'You are diverting me with compliments.'

'Is it working?'

'Pull over!'

'I will. When we get to the hospital.'

Mathilde leaned back in her seat and closed her eyes. Perhaps Tara had told her about Martha's stubborn streak.

When they arrived at the hospital, Martha parked and turned off the engine. She turned towards Mathilde. 'Listen,' she said. 'I was asked to write an article on regret and I wasn't going to do it but now I am.'

Mathilde shrugged. 'I am going to miss my flight.'

'And the reason I'm going to do it is because I know a lot about it.'

'I will have to buy another ticket at the airport.'

'And if I don't frogmarch you back to the hospital to talk to Tara, I'll regret that too. And so will you.'

'You cannot . . . frogmarch me,' said Mathilde, but doubt flickered in her widening eyes as her pupils dilated. Perhaps Tara had mentioned Martha's unnatural physical strength.

Martha stepped out of the car, closed the door behind her and was on her way around to the passenger side when Mathilde tumbled out of the car, both hands in front of her, in a *halt* action. 'OK,' she said, backing away from Martha. 'OK.'

Martha, glancing behind every now and then to check Mathilde's progress, strode through the main doors of the hospital, past the reception desk, towards the lift, where she slapped the call button with the heel of her hand.

'This will not make any difference,' said Mathilde, perhaps braver now that there were people around.

Martha stepped inside the lift, pulling Mathilde in after her, punched the button for the fourth floor and glared at a doctor in green scrubs who teetered at the doors before stepping back, mumbling something about going down, not up.

Mathilde slumped against the wall of the lift, eyed Martha cautiously. 'What is your plan?' she said.

'I appear to be making it up as I go along.'

They rode the lift to the fourth floor in silence.

The lift doors pinged and Martha stepped into the corridor and said, 'Follow me,' in a low, set voice, like she was a modern-day evangelist on a recruitment offensive.

Mathilde did.

Martha stopped outside the door to Tara's room. Hesitated.

'What are we going to do now?' Mathilde whispered, looking furtive.

'We're going to storm the Bastille,' said Martha. She pulled the door open, rushed into the room, pulling Mathilde behind her.

'What do you think you are—?' Mrs Bolton sat on a chair beside the bed where Tara lay, seemingly asleep, her lank hair draped across the pillow. Mrs Bolton set her knitting on the bedside locker and glared at them.

'Hello, Mrs Bolton,' Martha said, in what she felt was a perfectly reasonable voice. 'We've come to get Tara.'

Katherine, whom Martha saw now on the other side of the room, put herself between Martha and the bed, like a dam. 'Martha, I know this is difficult but the doctor said that Tara needs—'

'What do you mean get me?' Tara looked so frail as she struggled into a sitting position. Martha hardened her resolve, dragged Mathilde out from behind her.

'It's time,' said Martha, eyeballing Tara so that she knew exactly what she meant.

'No!' Tara did her best to shout but the word dribbled out instead, like food from the corner of a baby's mouth. She groped for the oxygen mask on her bedside table, breathed deeply into it and held it there with a white-knuckled hand.

Mrs Bolton rushed to her daughter's side and put a protective arm around her shoulder. 'You have to go,' she said in a high, shrill voice. 'Katherine, escort Martha and . . . whoever that is out, please.'

Tara covered her face with her hands so she could not see Mathilde's face, falling like a brick thrown from a height.

Katherine approached Martha carefully, as if she were a security guard approaching an unattended piece of luggage at the airport.

'We should leave.' Mathilde tugged at Martha's sleeve.

Martha, who still had no plan, sidestepped Katherine and rushed towards the bed. Katherine spun around and Mrs Bolton clutched Tara to her chest as Martha reached for the oxygen mask and reefed it off Tara's face. She grabbed Tara's arm and played a brief game of tug-of-war with Mrs Bolton, who conceded after a few short seconds, allowing Martha to hook her fingers into Tara's armpits and pull. Through the flimsy material of Tara's nightdress, she could feel stubble, which shocked her to the core, but she kept pulling, despite a cacophonous background of screeching (Katherine and Mrs Bolton), wailing (Tara) and crying (Mathilde). Martha propped Tara against a wall, held her there by her shoulders and waited. Tara's cheeks were flushed and her breath was coming fast but not panic-attack fast. Just pulled-out-of-bed-unceremoniously fast.

Martha was breathing fast too. She struggled to control it.

The room was quiet for a moment.

'Tara?' Mrs Bolton whispered, standing up and peering at her daughter. 'Are you OK?'

'She'll be fine,' Martha said, matter-of-fact. 'She just needs to tell you something.'

She looked at Tara. Smiled. 'Don't you?'

Tara looked resigned, possibly sensing that Martha had dragged them all past the point of no return. Way past. Still, she said nothing.

'Do you want me to tell them?' Martha asked.

Tara nodded.

Martha lifted her hands from Tara's shoulders, waited a moment, but Tara showed no signs of falling. Then she turned so she could see the others. Cleared her throat. She wondered how to begin. She thought brevity would be best.

'Tara is gay.' Behind her she could hear Tara hold her breath. 'And she's in love with Mathilde.' Martha gestured towards the Frenchwoman. 'And I'm fairly sure Mathilde is in love with her, which is . . . well, it's lovely, isn't it? I mean, nobody wants to love somebody who doesn't love them back. Do they?'

'What are you *talking* about?' demanded Mrs Bolton.

'And while we're all getting things off our chests, I'd also like to say . . .' Martha took a breath '. . . I am an alcoholic and I went to my first AA meeting last night with Seamus the barman from the Pound.'

She looked from Mrs Bolton to Katherine to Mathilde to Tara and she knew she was smiling because of the ache of the muscles in her face. Nobody said anything. Martha felt she should add something. Some form of conclusion. 'So that's it, really. Just thought it was about time that you knew. About Tara. Being gay, I mean. And me. Although I realise it's not really anything to do with you. I mean, it won't affect you personally. Me being in the AA now. But still, I thought it best to say it out loud so I can't, you know, change my mind when I . . . when things get back to normal. You know?'

Now Mrs Bolton spoke. 'My daughter is most certainly *not* gay. Don't you think a mother would know something like that? She is suffering from post-traumatic—'

'I'm not, Mum.' It was Tara, her voice quiet. 'It's true, I'm in love with Mathilde.' She looked at Mathilde and Martha could see a shine of tears in her eyes. 'I'm so sorry, Mathilde. I've been so . . . pathetic.'

Mathilde smiled through her tears, her mascara forming fine dark lines down her face. 'I was scared too. It was Martha who made me come back,' she managed to say.

'I merely suggested—' began Martha.

'You were right about her,' said Mathilde. 'Everything you said was true.' She stumbled towards Tara, threw herself into her arms and they hugged and it was Tara who put her hands around the small heart of Mathilde's face and kissed her.

'You don't smell great,' Mathilde said when Tara released her.

Mrs Bolton sat on the edge of the bed, clamped the oxygen mask to her face and breathed into it.

Katherine threw her eyes to heaven and began folding Tara's belongings into an overnight bag she slid out from under the bed.

Martha slipped from the room and drove home, still not inclined to shout or gesticulate with her fingers at dangerously stupid drivers. She knew it would return, this inclination. That not all of the days that lay ahead would be like today.

Some days would be like yesterday. When the mistakes you've made are held up to the light so you can see them in all their ragged splendour.

She knew that. How close she had come.

Back in her apartment, Martha made tea and switched on her laptop. She emailed the editor of the *Irish Times* Magazine.

Do you still want me to do that article on regret?

Twenty minutes later. *If you can deliver the copy by close of play today, yes. Otherwise, no.*

Martha sat in front of the blank page for a while. Then she turned the laptop off and went into her bedroom, opened the wardrobe door. On the floor, near the back, was her father's old Remington and, beside it, a box of A4 pages and some carbon paper. She hauled everything out, arranged them on the kitchen table. She fed the paper into her father's typewriter and, with her forefinger, banged out the word *Regret* at the top centre of the page, pressed the carriage return lever twice and began to type.

It was one of those rare pieces of writing that flowed from the start. She was a blur of fingers, pounding on the keys, the carriage shuddering along, left to right, turning letters into words that poured onto the page like they were already written some place inside, and it was just a matter of letting them go.

Twenty Nine

Cillian parked outside his rented house in Mount Charles, sat there for a moment letting the engine idle. It felt strange, being back. The house looked like someone else's house, some place that Cillian was visiting, not returning to.

'There's a job here for you, beanpole,' the Super had said as Cillian cleared out his desk. 'You don't have to go haring back to that culchie-infested outpost you know.'

'Have you ever even *been* to Donegal?'

'Why the fuck would I go there?'

Cillian put his Dalek mug into the box, the framed photograph of Naoise on the climbing frame that he had made for him, the bottle of whiskey the lads had given him as a leaving gift.

'I've stuff to sort out,' Cillian said, closing the box, 'in Donegal.'

'What kind of stuff?'

Cillian shrugged. 'Just . . . you know, personal stuff.'

The Super examined his fingernails, cleared his throat. 'So. I see Jimmy's solicitor is singin' like an *X-Factor* hopeful.'

The Super was a covert *X-Factor* fan, although everybody knew about it.

Cillian nodded. 'He's been a wealth of information alright. And Lenny of course. Once he got a sniff of a deal.'

'How's the boy? Roman?'

'A lot better. Judge Cassidy says she'll hold a restorative hearing when Roman gets out of hospital, which should be in a couple of days. She'll be recommending a caution and a period of supervision but she'll be sending him home.' Cillian picked up the box, moved towards the door. 'I won't say goodbye, boss, I know how emotional you get.'

The Super grunted.

Outside the station, there were still a few journalists, although a lot fewer than before.

'It's a media *frenzy* out there,' Clancy had said when the news first broke about Tobias Hartmann.

Then he darted to the jacks again, to comb his hair with his fingers.

In a way, Cillian thought it was a good thing. That Tobias hadn't lived to see his life splattered across the media the way it had been these past few days. They had camped outside the nursing home where Rosa worked too, desperate for the story of her relationship with the famous artist. Cillian had seen her on the telly, picking her way through them, smiling with her mouth closed, telling them nothing. It didn't stop them telling the story anyway. She was his muse. His lover. Or perhaps she was his daughter. Or his granddaughter.

The speculation was endless.

Cillian lifted his suitcase out of the boot, carried it to the front door and shoved his hand in his jeans pocket, reaching for the key. He unlocked the door, pushed it wide with his foot as he bent to pick up his case.

He stepped inside the house, walked down the hall, opened the door into the sitting room and was nearly blown backwards by a great chorus of 'SURPRISE!'

It took him a moment to focus. There were people in his house. A lot of people. Crammed together like spectators at a match.

Not just people. They were Stella's people. Her parents, her sisters, her sisters' husbands, her sisters' fiancés, her sisters' children. They wore identical T-shirts bearing the words WELCOME HOME CILLIAN with a smiley face beneath.

Stella ran to him, her arms outstretched, wrapped herself around him, whispered, 'I'm so glad you're home,' her mouth wet against his neck.

'Well,' he said, setting his suitcase on the floor and gently extricating himself from her grip. 'This is . . . an unexpected –'

'I knew you'd love a surprise party,' said Stella. 'We're all just so delighted to have you back. We wanted to do something special.' She beamed at him.

'Great . . . good . . . but . . . how did you manage to get in?'

Now it was Stella's turn to look surprised. 'My cousin owns the house, remember?' Stella said. 'I got the key off him. Now come on in. Go and say hello to everyone and I'll dish up. I've made that curry you like. The makhani, remember?'

Makhani? He'd never heard of it.

They bore down on him, all seven of them – Saoirse, Susan, Sarah, Sorcha, Selene, Sadie and . . . he couldn't remember . . . oh, yes, Sam, short for Samantha – taking turns to hug him and shake his hand and pat him on the shoulder.

'This is a double celebration really,' Stella's mother said, her voice quavering with emotion, 'what with young Brendan finally popping the question.' That's what Stella had rung him about, that day, outside Jimmy's house. That had been her news. That the politician had finally popped the question and Sadie had said yes, and the size of the wedding they were planning – huge because Brendan wanted to invite as many of his constituents as Lough Eske Castle could accommodate – and how Stella would have to go home immediately, to help Sadie plan the engagement party and . . .

It had taken Cillian a good while to find a gap in her monologue. 'I thought you might be ringing about the . . . did you do the test yet?'

'The test? Oh, goodness, yes. I mean, no, I didn't. What with all the excitement. And I seem to have come down with one of my kidney infections and they are notorious for interfering with those tests. Sam got a false negative with one last year, when she had the same thing. We're all prone to them, I'm afraid. Bad genes, *hahaha*.'

'So when you do think you might . . . ?'

'Dr Doherty will sort me out with a prescription for antibiotics when I get back home. But, look, don't be worrying, darling. Whatever's for us won't pass us, as Mammy says.'

Cillian bit back his frustration while Stella supplied further details about the upcoming nuptials of Sadie Bennett and the outgoing TD Brendan Doherty.

That was four days ago. Three more days of the antibiotics left to go.

Eventually, Cillian managed to squeeze his way into the kitchen at the back of the house, which was overrun mostly with the husbands and fiancés of the Bennett sisters.

'I'd say you're looking for a beer,' said Mr Bennett, winking at him. 'You've the look of a desperate man about you, am I right?' Mr Bennett struggled through the crowd, opened the back door and dipped his hand inside a bin Cillian had never seen before, filled with ice and beer.

'She thinks of everything, our Stella,' he said, handing a bottle to Cillian. He nudged Cillian's ribs with the hard bone of his elbow, then stretched his neck up, towards Cillian's face, whispered, 'You could do a lot worse.' Another wink and he disappeared, having been pulled by his wife into the sitting room where a singsong was getting up.

An actual singsong.

Cillian leaned against the fridge. Closed his eyes. Tried to block out the din.

His phone rang and he picked it out of his jeans pocket.

'Just checking you arrived in one piece.' It was Joan. She had a thing about journeys. Always wanted to know when they were over.

'Yeah, no worries.'

'What's going on up there? It sounds like an All-Ireland final at Croke Park.'

'What did you say?' Cillian couldn't hear a word. 'Hang on a minute,' he told her, ducking into the utility room where there was – mercifully and possibly only momentarily – nobody. He sat on the floor with his back against the door to ensure against intruders.

'What on earth is happening?' said Joan.

'The Bennetts are happening. They're everywhere.'

'Were you expecting them?'

'No. It's a surprise party.'

'Oh Jesus, you poor thing.'

'They're singing now.'

'Dear God!' said Joan who was – ordinarily – unflappable.

The handle of the door jerked up and down. 'I better go,' said Cillian, holding the door closed with his back as he pushed himself off the floor with his feet.

There was a herd of children on the other side of the door. They wanted to play hide-and-seek and one of the sisters – Selene or it might have been Susan: it was difficult to make out the names amongst the clattering of their voices – had said they must ask Cillian because it was his house and he was in charge.

Cillian found that amusing.

'I'll tell you in the hall,' he told them, taking their hands and using them as a human shield to run the gauntlet of the kitchen, the danger of the sitting room – where . . . it might be Sorcha . . . was on the umpteenth verse of an ancient Irish dirge.

Despite their diminutive size and giddiness, they managed to ferry Cillian to the safety of the hall without attracting many obstructions. There was a smell in the hallway, warm and cloying. A mix of the central heating that was belting full blast and the flowers Stella had arranged on the hall table in a vase he did not recognise.

'Here,' Cillian said, fishing a handful of euro coins from his pocket and dispensing them into their small outstretched hands.

'Is this a reward?' one cherubic boy asked, his blue eyes round and curious.

'Yes,' said Cillian and, without further ado, he grabbed his suitcase and hurried up the stairs.

His bedroom was not the sanctuary he had anticipated.

Stella was there. Sitting on the edge of his bed.

'I hope you don't mind me hiding up here,' she said and her voice was small, a little drained.

'Are you OK?' he asked.

She smiled brightly. 'I'm fine now.' There was an emphasis on the *now*. 'Sometimes I forget how noisy they are when they're in a confined space.'

Cillian opened the wardrobe door. The empty hangers moved against each other in the draught, producing a melancholy sound.

'Do you want a hand unpacking?'

'No. Thank you.'

'Seriously, it's not problem I can   '

'So, how are you feeling? Your infection?'

'Oh, yeah, fine, a little tired maybe.'

'And still no sign of your, eh, visitors?'

'Oh, God, sorry, Cillian. I completely forgot to mention it, with all the organisation for your surprise party.'

'Mention what?'

'My visitors. They arrived yesterday.'

Relief poured through him. And euphoria. Was that too strong? No, no, it wasn't. He sank onto the bed. 'That's . . . that's great news,' he said.

Stella stood up. 'I'll get you some food. You must be famished after the drive home.' She trotted towards the door.

'Stella, wait, we should talk.'

'Oh, but they're all downstairs and you—'

'Stella, listen—'

'We can talk all day tomorrow. And the day after that. And the—'

Honesty is the best policy. That was one of Joan's mantras. Her staff had felt the brunt of her honesty many's the time.

'This isn't working, Stella,' said Cillian.

She stood there for a moment, not saying anything, not moving. Then, 'You wouldn't be saying that if I were pregnant.' She glared at him.

Downstairs, they were starting in on 'The Fields of Athenry'. Cillian shook his head. 'I would. I'm sorry.'

'What, you would have abandoned me and my baby?' Stella put her hands on her hips, glared at him.

'No, of course not, but . . . we want different things,' said Cillian.

'I want you.' She whispered it, began to cry softly. Cillian steeled himself against the sound. 'We can make it work, you and me,' she said.

'No,' he said, gently but firmly. 'We can't. We'd regret it. In the end.'

Stella stopped crying, just like that. Now she was shouting. 'It's because of that bloody article, isn't it?'

'What article?'

'Don't pretend you don't know. Your ex, the alco, that stupid article in the paper today.'

'I don't know anything about it.'

'Liar!'

Stella wrenched open the bedroom door, stormed out. She paused on the landing long enough to shout, 'You're just like Patrick, you selfish prick.' Downstairs, the Bennetts' soaring voices – on the last verse now – dribbled away into silence.

Everybody left pretty soon after that.

When they were gone, the house was quiet. Cillian pulled the silence around him like a blanket, sat in an armchair and luxuriated in it, like it was a warm bath. He should feel worse but, for the moment, relief had the upper hand. He made a banana sandwich, washed it down with a mug of tea, then set about clearing away the debris of the Bennetts, flinging the windows open, sweeping the floors, filling the bins. All the while, he thought about the article. The one Stella had mentioned. The one that Martha had written.

What had Stella said? *It's because of that bloody article, isn't it?* What had she meant?

He went into the sitting room, where his laptop was. It took ages to boot up. Much longer than usual. He drummed his fingers against the keypad. Waited for the green light.

Martha's article was the headline on the cover of the magazine that came with Saturday's edition of the paper.

My name is Martha Wilder and I am an alcoholic.

And then, in smaller print below, *Inside: Martha Wilder writes about regret.*

A photograph of her in the corner of the page, sitting cross legged on the sofa that was too big for her apartment. The one she'd bought anyway. Her hair was caught loosely in a side ponytail that reached almost to her waist. She was nearly smiling – that twitch at the corners of her mouth – and the photographer had captured the sceptical glint in her bright green eyes. She wore skinny grey jeans and a black T-shirt with the words *I don't give a book* printed across the front.

She looked exactly like herself.

She looked beautiful

He began to read.

I don't believe in regret. For starters, it's a terrible waste of time. A non-achiever of an emotion. Redundant. Like men's nipples.

It's like someone saying I told you so when the damage is already done.

Regret is what happens when you realise you've lost something – something you value – and there's no one to blame except yourself, and it's too late to do anything about it.

I learned about regret the other day. Of course, I'd heard of it before, knew the dictionary definition of the word: 'Feel sad, repentant, or disappointed over something that one has done or failed to do.'

But it was only the other day – broad daylight, walking around, minding my own business – that I acknowledged it. People talk about pangs of regret. This felt more like a wallop. A backhand in my face.

I won't bore you with the details. Especially since I don't use words like love of my life if I can help it.

But, yes, I had to admit to feeling sad, repentant and disappointed over something – someone – that I discarded, oh, a long time ago now. Back when I was a working alcoholic, although I did not refer to myself thus, only as someone who had an 'uneasy relationship with alcohol'.

There's nothing like a dose of alcoholism to keep things at bay. Things like regret. Sadness. Disappointment.

In this regard, I cannot recommend it highly enough.

I put my back into it. I was the best alcoholic I could be. An A-plus student. It went really well for a long time. And then came a period I like to refer to as 'a series of unfortunate events'. Highlights included getting fired, marrying in haste, bereavement – the usual.

That period culminated in me pouring an excellent Scotch, a case of a fairly bland Bordeaux and a bottle of Baileys – which was out of date but, let's face it, I would have drank it anyway – down the kitchen sink one glorious summer's evening. Then I went to bed, slept for two days straight, got up, had a shower, drank two cups of tea and proceeded to get on with what my friend Tara menacingly referred to as 'the rest of my life'.

Sobriety – for alcoholics – is like travelling through a foreign land with no currency and little language and negligible social skills. And *just when you think you've got the hang of it – you have acquired a number of pertinent phrases, people you meet assume you are normal and you do not disabuse them of this notion, you even have money, since you stopped drinking twelve-year-old single malts – that's when it happens.*

You meet someone you used to know from that faraway land we call The Past and you realise, all of a sudden, what you had.

You realise what you lost.

That's when regret sidles up to you, taps you on the shoulder and says, I've been expecting you, in a soft, sinister voice, like some James Bond villain.

There was more but that was the bit that Cillian returned to. He read it three times. *The love of my life.* She couldn't be talking about Dan because . . . well, her marriage was listed as one of the 'series of unfortunate events'. She'd had other boyfriends before Cillian, of course she had. But she had referred to them as short-term and non-committal, in the main.

Cillian sat in the armchair in the sitting room for a long time. When he looked up, he was surprised to see that night had fallen. He should do something. Finish unpacking. Turn on the telly. Something.

Instead, he read the article again, all the way through this time, right to the end:

Regret, pointless yet persistent, needs to be spoken to firmly. Needs to be gripped by the arm, persuaded out the door, sent on its way.

Because the past is not for turning. There is no changing it. All we can do is acknowledge it, then step away, move along.

Say, Yes, mistakes were made.

But that was then.

And this is now.

Thirty

It seemed natural that Seamus would become Martha's sponsor. 'I have an informal sponsor but he's quite drinky and he's also my ex,' she told Seamus at her second AA meeting.

Seamus laughed until he noticed Martha wasn't laughing. 'Oh,' he said. 'You're being serious.'

Martha wanted everything to be clear. 'You're not helping me because you want to have sex with me, are you?'

'No.' Seamus was adamant. 'I'm helping you because, five years ago, somebody helped me. And five years from now, maybe you'll help someone else. That's the idea.'

'Five years?' Martha looked dubious. The slope of the mountain she was climbing seemed suddenly steeper.

'One day at a time,' said Seamus.

'Sweet Jesus,' said Martha.

Martha spoke for the first time at her third AA meeting and, while there was no round of applause nor shuffle of approval, she nevertheless felt the support of her fellow-alcos as clearly as if they had put their arms around her.

Afterwards, she decided to visit her mother. It had been a while. On the way, her phone rang. It was Tara.

'How are things?' said Martha.

'A bit better. Mum only cried twice today.'

'Where is she now?'

'At mass.'

'Praying the gay away?'

They laughed and it was such a familiar, good sound that Martha found herself saying, 'I missed you so much. When you were doolally.'

'Christ, you haven't been at the *Little Book of Calm*, have you?'

'I'm sipping lavender milk as we speak.'

'Will you be my Best Woman?'

'I thought I already was.'

'Will you?'

'I will.'

Her mother was in the kitchen when Martha let herself in.

Oh,' her mother said. 'I wasn't expecting you.'

'Is it a bad time?'

'Not at all. I was making tea. Would you like some?'

'Thanks.' Martha sat down. 'Were you at Sunshine House?' she asked.

'Yes. The fundraising committee were dotting the i's for the sponsored cycle.'

'You're great, you know,' Martha said.

Her mother looked surprised. 'What do you mean?'

'Just . . . all the work you do at that place.'

'It's not entirely selfless. I feel close to Amelia when I'm there, you know?'

'I can hardly remember her,' Martha said. She felt bad saying that. Was sure her mother would be hurt by it but she shook her head instead. Said, 'You were only little – how could you remember her?'

Her mother made tea and chicken salad sandwiches, cut into triangles with the crusts off, as if Martha were still a fussy kid.

They were delicious.

'I've decided to get rid of my sofa. Finally,' Martha said when she had finished eating. 'So I can take Dad's chair. Save you having to dump it.'

'But you love that sofa.' Martha wondered how her mother knew that.

'It's too big for my apartment. You said so yourself.'

'Yes, I know. It still fits, though.'

'Look, it's fine if you want to keep the chair. I just thought you were going to throw it out.'

Her mother looked sheepish. 'I don't think I ever really meant it. About throwing it out. This will sound silly but . . . sometimes I sit in it. Swing myself around.'

'Really?' Martha grinned at the image this provoked.

'I told you it was silly. It . . . I suppose it reminds me a bit of your father.'

They smiled at each other, then took to their tea. The silence between them was neither harsh nor awkward. It was simply there.

'I bought the couch with Cillian,' said Martha then. 'I mean, he was with me when I bought it.'

'Did he not tell you it was too big?'

Martha laughed. 'Once I'd bought it, he didn't mention it again.'

'Wise man.'

'It's a bit like Dad's chair, I suppose, the couch. It sort of . . . reminds me of him.'

'Is that a bad thing?'

'Well, it can . . . hurt sometimes.'

Her mother nodded like she understood.

'I read your piece in the *Times* today,' she said.

'I didn't think you read that paper.'

'I don't. But Norma at Sunshine House told me you were on the cover of the magazine so I bought it.'

'What did you think?'

Martha found herself putting a hand behind her back, crossing her fingers. It was a habit that had persisted from childhood.

Her mother leaned towards her, touched her arm, briefly, with her hand. 'Your father would be very proud of you,' she said, and

344

her voice was tight, like she was holding onto it with both hands. She stood up, gathered their plates and cups, carried them to the counter. The clattering of the crockery filled the space between them now.

She raised her voice to be heard over the sound of water filling the sink. 'Would you mind getting my slippers for me, Martha? I think they're under my bed and I'm getting too old for bending.'

Martha had to lie on her stomach on the floor beside her mother's bed and stretch out her arm to its full capacity before she managed to reach the slippers under the bed. Beside them, a wooden box with a leather handle and brass catches. It looked ancient and curious. Martha slid it out, sat up and blew the dust off it. She released the catches, opened the lid. Inside, cuttings. Hundreds of them. Her articles, her stories, her opinion pieces, her columns. Piled one on top of the other. Martha lifted them out. They were in date order. At the very bottom of the pile, her first piece of writing. In pencil, the letters big and crooked and, sometimes, the wrong way round.

My News.

Her mother had kept them. Kept them all. Martha knew it shouldn't matter. She was too old now for things like that to matter.

But it mattered all the same.

In the space provided at the top of the page, Martha had drawn a picture of her family. A matchstick man and woman and, between them, two matchstick boys and one matchstick girl. They were holding matchstick hands. Beside them, a rectangular house with a triangle for a roof and four square windows in each corner, a front door in the middle. There was a matchstick dog that had not yet been put down. A circle for a sun with straight lines poking from it. A cloud with a scalloped edge and, sitting on top of the cloud, barely discernible, a tiny matchstick girl.

She had put Amelia in. She hadn't forgotten her. She'd been there all along.

Thirty One

At midnight, Cillian sat up, pitched his duvet on the floor, jumped out of bed and threw clothes on, without reference to temperature, season or coordination. Just whatever he could find. He couldn't get them on fast enough.

He took nothing other than his phone, his wallet and his keys. He threw them on the passenger seat and turned the key in the ignition. The engine roared to life. It sounded like a cheer from the sidelines.

He drove.

The drive between Donegal and Dublin had sometimes taken him as long as five hours when he had the time. He liked to meander along the back roads, ignoring the motorway that promised a faster, more fuel-efficient turnaround. In this way, he passed through villages and townlands, drove over rivers, through valleys, under the shadow of the cliffs of Magho as he negotiated the twisting edge of Lough Erne, the water gathered around hundreds of tiny islands whose names he always wondered at but never got around to investigating.

Tonight, he drove for just under three hours, arrived at her apartment block at exactly ten past three in the morning.

Some people might call that the middle of the night.

Looking back, he had no real recollection of the journey. He focused on the destination. The mindfulness people would be up in arms. He grinned when he thought that. It was such a *Martha* thought.

He wasn't sure what would happen when he got there. He just knew he would get there. Whatever happened next would happen and he would not stand accused of doing nothing.

He would regret nothing.

The buzzer wasn't working. He hesitated – only momentarily – before heading to the patch of landscaped grass at the front of the building. He scanned the apartments on the third floor. They were all in darkness. Had he been a different kind of person, he might have taken that as a sign.

He wasn't sure which window might be hers but on the third windowsill from the left there was a kitchen roll holder, except instead of a kitchen roll it held a vast array of hair scrunchies in many, many colours apart from red.

Cillian threw a stone at that window.

Nothing happened.

He threw another. Then another.

A window opened. It was not the third one from the left.

While Cillian didn't know this at the time, it was, in fact, Robert-Call-Me-Rob from apartment thirty-seven. 'Not again,' he wailed into the night sky.

Another window opened, this time on the ground floor. 'Is that buzzer *still* on the fritz?'

Cillian ignored them, gathered another handful of pebbles.

A window yanked open. The third window. From the left.

'If that's you again, Mathilde, I swear I'll blacken your eye.'

And there she was. Martha. Martha Wilder. Her red hair stormed around her face like a platoon of angry troops and she wore a faded, threadbare T-shirt with . . .

'Is that my Kurt Cobain T-shirt?'

'Cillian?'

'Yes.'

'What the fuck are you doing here?'

'I read your article today. Well, yesterday, I suppose. I . . .'

347

'It's three o'clock in the morning.'

'It's thirteen minutes past three, actually.'

'I could have rung the talking clock if I needed that kind of detail.'

Cillian took a breath. 'Was that me you were referring to? When you said "love of my life"?'

'I can't believe the editor let that bit go to print.'

'Was it?'

'Why do you want to know?'

'Answer the bloody question.'

'Fine then. Yes, it bloody well was.'

There was a pause while Cillian let that sink in.

'That's handy so.'

'Why?'

'Because you happen to be the love of my life.'

'What?'

'I SAID, YOU'RE THE LOVE OF MY LIFE.' He shouted the words and in the gentle still of the night, lit by a sliver of moon, barely there, the words sounded between them as clear as the ringing of a bell. They reached the dark facade of the building, pushed against the brick and hung in the air, suspended on a thread of night itself, like a messenger, bearing glad tidings.

'For fuck sake.' An apartment dweller on the second floor pushed his head out of his bedroom window.

Cillian said, 'Maybe I should come up,' at the same time as Martha said, 'I'll come down.' They met somewhere in the middle, on the stairwell. She hesitated when she saw him. Cillian, who had run out of lines since the *love of my life* declaration, came up with, 'Is this an inconvenient time?' which made Martha smile.

'Well, it's three o'clock in the morning.'

'Three sixteen actually. But you haven't answered my question.'

She was beside him now. He saw the gap between her front teeth, the fleshy red of her bottom lip. A muscle jumped against the pale skin of her neck.

'What was your question?' she said.

'Is now a good time?' Cillian said again.

She nodded. 'Yes,' she said. 'Yes. Now is a good time.'

Epilogue

There is something in the air.

On a day like today, one wonders if perhaps it is always there and it is we – scurrying about the world like lines of ants – who fail to notice. The something that is in the air.

No matter. We notice it today.

It is difficult to put a name on it, the something that is in the air. To define it in a way that allows us to understand what it is.

Excitement? Anticipation? A sense of possibility? Happiness even?

Whatever it is, it is there and the people who are gathered feel it as surely as a warm breeze against their faces as they look at the sky that is end-of-term blue with occasional wisps of pale cloud, trailing on the breeze like ribbons in a child's hair.

A string quartet begins to play.

Heads turn to look at the musicians. To wonder how the hairs of a bow against a string can produce such a beautiful sound. The music soars and people are reminded of a bird, perhaps, spreading its wings for the first time, teetering on the edge of a branch, high in a tree. The music swells and the bird is airborne, looks down at the ground below, wonders why it ever felt afraid.

Three of the musicians are men, in black tuxedos and crisp white shirts. The violin player is a woman. Her long neck tilts against the mellowing wood of the instrument where cracks are visible. This instrument has been damaged and repaired. The violinist's red hair – drawn across her shoulder – flows like a tide down her body towards her waist, glinting gold in places as if the sun itself has become entangled in its length.

When the music finishes, she stands and the expression in her bright green eyes is one of surprise, as if she has arrived at a destination she never expected to reach.

Perhaps she has.

We are in a garden behind a cottage. A large garden, almost a field. Raised hedgerows mark the boundary. The hedgerows are threaded through with the colours of summer, bursting with ragwort, bluebells, cow parsley, fuchsia, wild garlic, mint.

The flow of water nearby over smooth, flat stones is like another kind of music.

Another kind of something, that is in the air.

In the centre of the garden, rows of chairs have been set, separated in the middle to form a grassy aisle across which crimson rose petals have been scattered. The chairs face a table, covered with a linen cloth. Rose petals are scattered here too and a woman and a boy put the finishing touches on two bouquets of wild flowers that sit in metal watering cans on either end of the table. The boy has the gangly build of a teenager who has recently grown taller than he ever thought he would be.

They are mother and son. There is no way to be certain and yet the people gathered know this to be true. It is perhaps in the way she glances at the boy as if she knows things about him that he does not yet know. Good things. He stands, studies his arrangement and looks at her and there is a question in his look and when she smiles, her dark grey eyes lighten and now we can see a trace of blue in them. We see her beauty there. Her strength.

And now the music begins again and two women appear at the bottom of the grassy aisle, both in dresses that seem to float around them, as if the delicate fabric is melting with the warmth of the sun. They each hold a posy of pink roses and the fingers of their free hands are wrapped loosely around each other's, like a promise made. A promise about to be made.

Everyone in the garden that day smiles when they see the faces of these two women.

Perhaps it is because of the something that is in the air.

They begin to walk. At the top, there is a man with a book, open in the palms of his hands. He would look officious were it not for his attire – a lime-green short-sleeved shirt, patterned with strawberries, the flushed colour of lips that have been kissed at length, a pair of white linen shorts to the knee. Short legs ending in long feet that are accommodated in thick-strapped brown sandals.

'Are you sure you're qualified for this, Dan?' one of the brides – Tara – had enquired at the rehearsal earlier in the week.

'I can assure you that I am a fully approved solemniser,' Dan had said, drawing himself up to his full height, which wasn't very high. 'That's Sol-emn-iser, by the way.' He winked.

'You are the first professional solemniser I've met,' said the other bride, Mathilde.

Dan beamed. 'Nobody's ever accused me of being professional before.'

'Why you do this job?' she asked.

'Well,' said Dan, 'I think, if I am to be thwarted in love, I may as well be instrumental in encouraging the love of others to flourish.'

The mother and son take their leave of the garden. They pile into a van, the sides of which are painted with wild roses that sweep and weave around a single word.

Rosa's.

'Wait.' It is the owner of the cottage that could be described as being in the middle of nowhere, one supposes, but which in fact is halfway between Ashbourne and Finglas.

'Did you get sorted?' he asks. He is a tall man with metal grey hair. Rosa – the owner of the van and indeed the flower shop of the same name – shakes her head. She can't help smiling at the man in an almost-flirtatious manner. When they pull away, her son will tell her of her almost-flirtatious smile and she will deny this. She is not a woman who smiles almost-flirtatiously at anyone. She is a business woman.

Still, she smiles in this uncharacteristic way, albeit unbeknownst to her. It is perhaps his height, the way he must bend at the waist to speak to her. The studious nature of his eyes, the length of his lashes, the softness of his Donegal accent. She knows he is not a classically handsome man. But, she acknowledges, there is something about him. Something that she cannot quite put her finger on.

She tells him she has been paid and she says, yes, she and her son would be delighted to come for dinner next Sunday – so long as Martha is not cooking. She laughs when she says this, so he will know it is her version of a joke, although her observation is a true one. Martha can do many things, Rosa knows. Cooking is not one of them.

'Are you going to the grave?' he asks.

She nods.

She goes every Saturday, after work. She has planted a rose bush there. She needs to spray the leaves – the greenfly are ravenous at this time of the year. She pulls weeds and keeps the moss at bay. Regular visitors sometimes ask her if she is related to Tobias Hartmann.

She always says the same thing.

Mr Hartmann is my friend.

She brings her son, Roman.

Encased in glass and set in the stone of the gravestone is a print of one of Mr Hartmann's earliest drawings. The nurse – always the nurse – washing the filth of war from the face of the young soldier. The boy looks at her. The nurse's face is in shadow but there is tenderness in the length of her fingers.

Always tenderness.

It has no title but, privately, Rosa calls it *Love*.

Rosa believes that Martha Wilder has done him justice. In the second novel she is writing now, which Rosa is reading as Martha is writing. For Mr Hartmann is in it, as surely as he was in the library on Thursday nights, teaching Rosa English. In spite of all the research Martha has done, the facts she has uncovered about Mr Hartmann's life, Rosa feels that the man in the novel is still hers. The one she knew. The one she knows still.

The grave is covered in flowers and coins. Ribbons and balloons are tethered to the rails that skirt the plot. Some people leave their sketches, in plastic folders, as if hoping for a critique from the great man himself. The anonymous artist who has been revealed to the world.

Rosa is certain that Mr Hartmann is unconcerned with these efforts. She hopes he is at peace. She wishes that for him. It is the least she can wish, since he has given that to her. Peace. Given that to her and her son.

While he left most of his vast wealth to Médicins Sans Frontières – perhaps his final tribute to the nurse that Mary Murphy had been – he had left one drawing, *Meeting*, to Rosa. Malachy Hemingway told her it would fetch a princely sum at auction and he was right. Enough to set up the flower shop. Buy the apartment with the balcony with a chair where she sometimes sits, watches the sun set. Her son has his own bedroom. Roman and his friends – Meadhbh and Adam, who remain friends despite their brief dalliance – listen to their music there. It is a gift, Rosa thinks. To give such a space to your son.

The something that is in the air lingers, even when the last of the guests have gone.

Two people remain. They stand near the bottom of the garden, drops of dew trembling along the stalks of the long grasses that brush against their legs, falling to splash on their bare feet. Their feet move in tandem and, looking up, we see that these two people are dancing. Waltzing. In the long grasses, the light of a full moon shimmering against their bodies, making her red hair glisten, making his dark eyes shine. It is one of those moments where happiness rings at your door, calls out, 'I'm Here,' in a brightly coloured, singsong voice, lets itself in, makes itself at home. She feels full with it. Sometimes it worries her, all this happiness. But not tonight. Tonight, she is an alcoholic who hasn't drunk in two years, six months, two weeks, four days.

Seamus, her sponsor, is right. Every day is an achievement.

Tonight, happiness nudges her and, in her head, she moves over. Makes room for it.

She has been doing that a lot. Making room. It is not something that you can take for granted, happiness. She knows that now. You have to allow for it.

She has been allowing for it since that night he arrived at her apartment block, threw stones against her bedroom window.

Now, they look at each other as they dance.

His arm tightens around her waist. He bends, whispers into the soft mesh of her hair.

She stops dancing. 'Don't say that.' Her voice is low. Hesitant. 'Unless you mean it.'

He looks at her and we don't know what he's thinking but we know it's something good because of the way he looks at her. There is a knowledge in his look. Of things to come. Good things.

'I do mean it.'

'Oh.'

'I just thought you should know.'

A pause. Then, her voice again, quieter now. 'Well, I . . .' She stops. Looks at him.

'Go on,' he says.

'Do I have to spell it out?'

'Yes.'

She reaches up, pushes her fingers through his fringe that is already beginning to hang into his eyes, despite the fierce cut she subjected it to the week before. She turns his head and whispers the words into his ear and he takes her face in his hands, catches her mouth with his and they begin to dance again, dance and kiss, the murmur of the river beyond like the soundtrack of the dance. The soundtrack of the kiss.

It goes on and on.

Acknowledgements

This is my sixth novel. When I began writing – a youngster of thirty-four – I thought that writing books would become easier over time, much like assembling flatpack furniture or coaxing a sponge cake to rise. And no, I haven't successfully achieved either of those but I imagine, if you attempt it often enough, it would become second nature and there you'd be, eating wedges of elevated cake, sitting on a stool you've cobbled together using a few bits of wood and a forty-five-page instruction manual. Sadly, this has not been my experience with the writing life and, despite the many, many words I have written, and deleted, and written again, writing remains a challenge; a solitary one-step-forward-two-steps-back maze through which I run, every day, from my inner critic.

BUT I keep doing it. I keep writing. I think it has something to do with passion which is quite the stimulant; it makes me feel alive in a nerve-jangling, blood pounding, slightly alarming way. And I like it. Feeling like that. Actually, I love it. And I'm thankful for it.

Thanks to my family. My children, Sadhbh, Neil and Grace, my husband, Frank, my sister, Niamh, my parents, Breda and Don. Your faithful support and love are things I can count on, every day. I am steeped in great fortune, to have such a tribe.

Thanks also to my extended family, especially my brother-in-law, Neil MacLochlainn, who reads my books and doesn't care who knows it, and to Eamon MacLochlainn, for information on the banking world.

Thanks to my editor, Ciara Doorley, who wields her red pen with great sensitivity and expertise. Thanks also to Emma Dunne, for meticulous copy and line-editing.

Thanks to my agent, Ger Nichol, for her unwavering support of me and my stories.

Thanks to the detectives (they asked not to be named and they may be armed . . .) in a Dublin city garda station who gave me ideas about how my fictional detective, Cillian Larkin, might crack the case in this story, as well as a tour of the station and updating my knowledge of general police-type stuff (my only previous source came from weekly fixes of *Starsky and Hutch*).

Thanks to the readers of various drafts of this novel: Niamh Geraghty, Yvonne Cassidy and Dominic Bennett. Thank you for your time, your insight and your encouragement.

Thanks to Gráinne Folan, Anna Maria Tuckett and Magdalena Bowler for help with Polish matters.

A huge rush of affection and gratitude goes to my readers; you know who you are. It still feels a little surreal, that there are people in the world who read my books, who are not my mother or my sister. Surreal but lovely. Really lovely. Like a turf fire in a stone cottage in Connemara. That kind of lovely. Thank you readers. You make this writer very happy.

8 January 2016
Ciara Geraghty

If you loved *This is Now* and would like to know more about Ciara Geraghty and what she's doing next, here are some easy ways to stay in touch:

Follow @ciarageraghty on Twitter

Like the Facebook page:
www.facebook.com/ciara-geraghtys-books

Visit Ciara's official website to find out more and read her blog: www.ciarageraghty.com

Ciara Geraghty

NOW THAT I'VE FOUND YOU

Vinnie is an ordinary man. Ellen is an ordinary woman.
Ellen is unable to move on after a terrible accident
that left her mentally and physically scarred.

Taxi driver Vinnie is struggling to cope with bringing up two children on his own.

Everyone deserves to find that one person
who's meant for them, don't they?

Fall in love with the story of Vinnie and Ellen.
Because ordinary lives can be extraordinary.

Out now in paperback and ebook

HACHETTE
BOOKS
IRELAND

Ciara Geraghty

LIFESAVING FOR BEGINNERS

Kat Kavanagh is not in love. She has lots of friends, an
ordinary job, and she never ever thinks about her past.
This is Kat's story. None of it is true.

Milo McIntyre loves his mam, the peanut-butter-and-banana muffins
at the Funky Banana café, and the lifesaving class he does after school.
He never thinks about his future, until the day it changes forever.
This is Milo's story. All of it is true.

And then there is the other story. The one with a twist of
fate which somehow brings together a boy from Brighton and a
woman in Dublin, and uncovers the truth once and for all.

This is the story that's just about to begin . . .

Out now in paperback and ebook

HACHETTE
BOOKS
IRELAND

Ciara Geraghty

FINDING MR FLOOD

Dara Flood always says the most interesting thing about her life
happened before she was born. Thirteen days before she came into
the world, her father walked up the road and never came back.

Now in her twenties, she lives a quiet life with her mother
and sister, Angel and works at the local dog pound – she
finds dogs much easier to understand than people.

But when Angel gets sick and neither Dara nor her mother is a match
for the kidney she desperately needs, Dara knows she will do anything
to save Angel – even track down the man who left them behind.

So with the help of a scruffily handsome private investigator
with a few secrets of his own, Dara steps anxiously into the
big wide world with a dream of finding Mr Flood.

But as you know, following your dreams can
lead you to unexpected places . . .

Out now in paperback and ebook

HACHETTE
BOOKS
IRELAND